K. MELDRUM DENHOLM

Yesterday's Song

a novel

Print paperback ISBN: 979-8-9907307-0-0; Ebook ISBN: 979-8-9907307-1-7

Library of Congress Control Number: 2024916288

Credits: Copyeditor: Revision Division; Cover design: Damonza

Publisher: Lake Overlook Press LLC, address above, book printed and distributed by KDP and Ingram Spark.

Note: Suicide ideation referenced. You are never alone. If you are struggling or in crisis, please call or text **988** for help.

Reviews

"Denholm's sweeping novel, steeped in references to the rock music of the era, goes deep inside the minds of the characters to capture the hopes, dreams, and fears of a generation." - *Kirkus Reviews*

"Like a carefully curated mixtape, *Yesterday's Song* weaves together decades of musical references to create a powerful narrative about love and resilience." - Annie Zaleski, music critic and author, *Duran Duran's Rio (a 33 1/3 book); This is Christmas, Song by Song; Pink, Raise Your Glass; Taylor Swift: The Stories Behind the Songs*

"*Yesterday's Song* is for those of us who always hold a song in our heart. Every scene, every character, every moment of our lives should have a soundtrack like the one that carries this story from page to page." – Kristin Nilsen, author, *Worldwide Crush*; Co-host, The Pop Culture Preservation Society podcast

"*Yesterday's Song* is a groovy page-turner best described as: Love, Loss, and What they Listened to. Perfectly attuned to those of us who came of age in the 1970s and '80s, it really rocks. After reading it, I missed the characters, which, to me, is always the mark of a great read." - Rebecca Rego Barry, author, *The Vanishing of Carolyn Wells: Investigations into a Forgotten Mystery Author*

"This One's For You"

For my family with love

'70s Playlist

As you read, enjoy the story's playlist on Spotify: "Yesterday's Song,
a novel by @writerkmd"

Part I: "How Can You Mend a Broken Heart"

1

"Rock and Roll Never Forgets"

Cal, July, 1988

When the phone rang just as he turned on MTV, Cal dropped his fast-food chicken. Mort beelined for the legs and drumsticks, but Cal snatched them away before the basset hound could choke. The dog stared with such forlorn eyes that Cal apologized to him and tossed him a boneless wing as he picked up the phone.

"You the one who sang Girl It's All for You?" a voice said.

"Yeah, is this the producer for the '70s one-hit-wonders segment on *Solid Gold*? Been waiting for your call with the details." Cal set his plate on the TV, too high up for Mort's snout. "I was so shocked when your assistant found me after all these years and asked me to appear next month that I forgot to ask—I don't have to wear hotpants, do I?" He chuckled and patted his paunch.

"Let's spare the country, shall we?" the caller said, his words fast, tone gruff. "Because I know what you did back then."

"Ha! Like the movie? Good one. Is this Sarge? Your disguise is weak, buddy. Hey, sorry I didn't tell you about the TV show, but didn't want to jinx it."

The man exhaled. "Nope, not him."

"The only heavy panting I do anymore is running into 7-Eleven for a doughnut," Cal said.

"I can let the country know. Everyone loves a secret scandal."

"Was I late at Blockbuster Video again? But I rewound…"

"I'll expose you, you cold prick, right before you sing your song on national television."

"What kind of a stupid prank is this?"

"It's far from a joke, *Cal Leonard*. I know what you did. That's what the old song—and I do mean *old*—is about. Song's not so beautiful as people think, huh? Packs a powerful punch, don't it? If I go to the press before the show, everyone will learn what you did, you callous ass."

Whoa. His stomach dropped with what he'd buried in his soul and psyche for years. "Dude, you're blackmailing a nobody. You think I'm rich? Surprise, I got a bum deal on that song. You picked the wrong musician to extort."

"Many witnesses that day."

Sweat beaded on his forehead as the worst day of his life flooded over him. Through the years, he'd replayed the scene like a tape stuck in the VCR. The pink sky lighting the horizon. The car doors slamming. The families bolting out of Saturday mass. The fear entrenched in her baby blues, tears streaming down her red face. Marvin's song in his head.

"Should I take the story to *Inside Edition*?"

Cal's heart sank, but not for himself. "No, please, whoever you are—"

"Wonder if I can get more from you or the tabloids?"

Cal's eyes lowered. "Don't. I beg of you—" He scanned the empty living room for the bottle he'd hidden. Richard Marx taunted "Should've Known Better" on TV.

"I'll be back in touch before we rock and roll."

Cal slammed down the receiver. *No.* If the truth spilled out, millions—okay, the mere thousand who remember the song—would find out what he did. That would destroy this second chance at a career, but for the two people who mattered to find out this way would be unbearable. Cameras thrust into their unsuspecting faces as they'd find out publicly, their private lives splashed on tabloids as entertainment fodder. People who didn't understand would spew their venom, but worse, take them along as collateral damage. Reporters would ask *how it felt* just for a day's buzz. Listeners would mock a genuine song of apology, love, and remorse, with disdain, gossiping like they'd never held regrets in their own hearts. *Did you hear what that old '70s song's really about— what's it called again? By old what's his face?*

Cal found the bottle under the futon by the dog's tennis ball. Mort looked up with a hopeful plea.

On MTV, VJ Nina Blackwood introduced a legend, a *real* artist back on the charts. "Got My Mind Set On You," George Harrison sang from a leather chair.

That was just it. His mind had always been set on this, his deepest regret. Even now. How could he have done that, indeed?

Eighteen years before...

2

"Bridge Over Troubled Water"

Cal, July 3, 1970

When Cal came to, gripping the cot, his eyes darted around the white tent. Throngs of people waltzed past. Chatter. Laughter. Whistles. Electric guitar riff. Is that Gypsy? *Man, they're shredding.*

A white coat loomed over him and blotted his hot forehead with a cool washcloth. He squinted at the nametag. *Great.* His fate landed with a kid named "Bif, Pre-med."

He rubbed his temples as Mama's words returned. When they watched TV in her hospital room just two months ago, she'd said he looked just like that "fine, responsible young man." Cal had frowned at the character's description, a square. *Responsible* is hardly a chick magnet, geez. Though if he was here in a concert medical tent this early in the game, she was right. He sighed. Cal Leonardowski at the Second Atlanta Pop Festival is like Greg Brady at Woodstock.

"What did you take before you fainted?"

"Not enough."

"Only a couple Schlitz in the parking lot," said Cal's buddy, Troy. "We got a six from a gig we played at Bob's Bowling and split it three ways."

Cal patted his pocket that held his late dad's canteen. "And a shot of whiskey. But that's it."

"A few puffs during 'Whipping Post,'" his friend Terry added. "And that brownie."

The volunteer narrowed his eyes. "Any LSD? Quaaludes?"

He scratched his head, tracing his memory bank. "From that dollar dude, maybe?" They'd arrived around noon after driving through the night ten hours from Northern Virginia to this soybean-field-turned-raceway-turned-three-day-rock-concert in Byron, Georgia. They'd guzzled beers in the blazing sun, watching girls skip the fourteen-dollar ticket fee, saying only, "Music is for the people," though he and his buddies paid. They'd raced into the festival when the Allman Brothers opened. After enjoying an incredible set, they spotted a guy holding a sign— "Pills, $1.00"—and used rolls of pennies they'd saved. They waited for the high to kick in. Something, anything? Nothing. Cal tripped playing Frisbee, stood back up, and then passed out. There he lay, by baggies of grass on the grass, hot but out cold.

"It's ninety-seven degrees, and you fainted from heat and dehydration, because we're hearing that buck acid isn't acid," the volunteer said. "Could be saccharin—or birth control pills."

Terry patted Cal's shoulder. "Congrats. Your first trip on your first road trip was a literal trip."

"Those hormones will mess with you," Troy teased. "We'll catch you later. Don't want to miss any more bands and babes."

His buddies dashed out, the gust of air in their wake smelling of funnel cake. "Wait for me..." He stood, but when John Sebastian's voice bellowed "Are You Going to San Francisco?" Cal plopped back down. He could only hear Mama singing it.

He'd borrowed a cassette player from the school library and recorded Mama's favorite songs off the radio, like this one. In her cold, stark hospital room, she had sung along in a weak voice, the IV beeps keeping time like a metronome. Her bony, bruised hand reached for Cal's. "This is lovely, my sweet son," she rasped, looking at the April daffodils he'd brought. "But you should give those to a prom date tonight instead." Who cared about that dumb dance? She'd only told him the day after Christmas about the "pea-sized thingy"—that spread to her bones, liver, kidneys—-that she'd beat because she was only thirty-nine.

She died May 4, the same day as the Kent State students, when news-papers proclaimed innocence was lost—and so was he. He crumbled into a ball, wanting only Mama's hug to comfort him. Her insurance covered a casket, plot next to Daddy's, some cash. When the lawyer read the will, also giving him the furniture in their rented townhouse, Daddy's old Cutlass Supreme, and her wedding ring, he shook Cal's hand. "Son, the good news is, you're eighteen, no foster care. Bad news is, you're eighteen in a godforsaken draft. Get out of Dodge."

But Cal couldn't plan the future. He could only gasp for breaths in the sea of grief, awaking flailing, like he was drowning in the deafening quiet. Sunrises once bristled with clanking dishes, bacon and eggs sizzling, Mama singing "Suspicious Minds" with Elvis on the dial. Now it was only the thump of the *Washington Post* thrown at the door.

As this latest grief wave ripped through, the student handed him a salt pill and water and said to rest. "Thanks," Cal said. "It's actually miraculous I'm still here."

A month ago, he'd almost ended it all. After his graduation, when parents cheered their kids crossing the stage, he'd heard only *orphan, orphan, orphan* looping in his head and pity-clapping when the principal called his name. His parents would've cheered and jockeyed for pictures; the loss felt most raw and fierce then. That night, he eyed Mama's left-over painkillers from "Your *Family* Pharmacy." Even the label taunted him—everyone had a *family*—and he shook the bottle. Enough to end this misery for good. *What's there to live for? To get called to Vietnam?* Just then, a lone voice from the kitchen radio spoke. "The second Atlanta

International Pop Festival promises three days of peace, love, and music. Jimi Hendrix Experience, Allman Brothers, Grand Funk Railroad, BB King," the DJ said.

"That'd be cool," he'd said. He wasn't one-millionth of the guitarist Hendrix was. *Jimi riffed with his teeth*! Mama had said he was too young for Woodstock last summer, but now, no one said no. As the news had droned on of the Cambodian campaign and inquiries into the Kent State and Jackson State shootings, Cal had set down the pills, walked to the record player, picked up the Rolling Stones' *Let It Bleed* album, pulled out the sleek vinyl from the dust jacket, and perfectly placed the needle on the groove. Soon the bass reached inside, the vibration soothing him. He picked up his acoustic guitar—a tenth-birthday gift from his parents—and jammed along.

Maybe Atlanta could be my first—and last—taste of sex, drugs and rock and roll.

He had strummed for a while, with practical questions— *how to pick up a chick? Is a nickel bag a nickel?* — before he called his buddies Troy and Terry, his last place bandmates in the Battle of the Bands. "Let's cruise in my Mustang to that Southern Woodstock thing? We can load up coolers, pitch a tent..."

Yeah, he had decided, this concert would be a life raft in the waves of grief, a rock and roll respite, before he blew this popsicle stand.

Yet here he sat, sidelined in the tent, mopping his sweaty forehead with his dark blue T-shirt, when commotion interrupted. His eyes froze, mouth agape.

"I've had chills since the sun began to set!" a topless long-haired redhead said with a lilted accent, crossing her chest, hugging herself. She sported hot pink shoulders and face—which made her deep-set aqua eyes pop— and paced in only short-shorts and one flip-flop. "I'm shivering!"

Cal's heart raced off like he'd looked at *Playboy,* as the student bounded away, shined his flashlight on her chest but diagnosed first-degree sunburn on the shoulders, and left for supplies.

The siren sat down a mere two cots away, arms still locked covering herself. "I'm an *eejit.* What does an Irish gal know about the sun?"

He chuckled. He wanted to play it cool, like Miss Julys always talked to him, so he tossed her the hospital blanket for the chills. *Wait, bonehead, that obstructs your own view. Dang nice guy Brady trait strikes again. But chicks dig bad boys, don't they? Should grab that blanket back for myself and ignore her!*

It was too late. She nodded her thanks and wrapped it around herself like a towel.

He cleared his throat. "Lost your flip-flop too, huh?"

"That's another thing! Kicked them off to be footloose, but now I can only find one bloody sandal!"

"Oh well. Shows off that tattoo on your ankle."

"Isn't it grand?" She extended her leg, and Cal was perfectly fine with that. "Got it when I stepped off the plane. Saw the tattoo parlor and thought, *why not?* My adventure begins! So, what are ye in here for?"

He looked away, towards the distant stage, trying to conjure up a rocking story.

Her eyes widened. "Is it bad? You all right, lad?"

But Cal frowned, grappling with telling the cold hard truth.

"What is it?"

Oh, for crying out loud...

"What?"

"Frisbee accident."

"Ah. Those come at ye fast," she said with a straight face.

"But I caught it. Or so I hear." He cleared his throat again. "Hi, I'm Cal, from Virginia."

"*Dia duit.* Nainsi. County Dublin."

He looked a second longer at her striking blue eyes, which held a green tint, like Grace Slick's. "What brings you here? I mean, why are you in the States?" He hoped "states" would make him sound well-traveled. Or, traveled.

"I'm a nanny for an Atlanta family. For now." Her eyes traveled to Mr. Pre-Med, who returned with a bigger bath towel than the washcloth he gave Cal, and enough calamine lotion and hydrocortisone cream for an Army squadron, plus a beer with two aspirin. "*Míle buíochas,*" she said. She gulped the beer and pills then slathered on cream with a wince. "I'm so stupid taking off my top straightaway after going on the sesh."

"I don't know what a sesh is, but I hope more chicks do it," he said.

She laughed, and her eyes moved to Cal.

"If it makes you feel better," Cal said, "I faint from heat and birth control pills."

"Fancy we're festival rejects?"

"Maybe a 'D' in Rock Partying 101—but time left in the semester."

"My friends and I had a few pints and said it was a new decade and we knew no one here anyway, and we whipped off our bikini tops for women's liberation. But now here I am burnt. Dumb."

"Sorry." But he was not sorry, the view was like a toke from the rock gods. Still, he pulled off his damp T-shirt and gave that to her for the chills, too. "You don't have to wear this shirt though. I'm fully in favor of women's liberation."

She smiled and turned her back on him, dropped the blanket, and wriggled into his shirt with another wince. It draped over her like a dress. "You think I'm going to hell for taking off my top here?"

"Definitely not. And sweaty navy blue appears to be your color."

She turned back around and shivered. "If my devout family and priest heard I was walking around half *nocht,* they'd be reciting the rosary and lighting candles."

Cal raised his eyebrows. "Candles? Funny, my band is called the Ex-Candles."

"Why?" She scooted forward, sipping the beer—seeming ready for a good story.

"Oh, it's..." He hesitated, the truth a bummer.

The music slowed, and as they listened, a breeze drifted through. She asked again, her eyebrows crinkling and compassion shining from her eyes.

He took a breath, and soon he shared the story, how his father died when he was ten, and he'd asked Mama if Daddy would see his baseball games from heaven. She lit a candle at the solemn dinner table—the only sounds fork scrapes, Sinatra, and the timer's ding at the frozen pizza—and buried her head into her hands. "We might only go to church twice a year, my sweet boy, but I pray for us with this candle every day. Pray hard when you look at the flame. It helps." He stared at the candle in earnest that night, praying for the pain to go away, but his heart still felt ablaze, like he had touched the stove with it, so he woke her with, "It doesn't work. My heart is burning." She said heartburn was from the pizza and keep trying, but he collapsed in Mama's arms, crying about missing Daddy, her softly saying, "My sweet boy, I'm sorry. It's not fair, your daddy loved you..."

Eight years later, when she died too, he whipped her latest candle, rocketing his grief into the wall.

Her voice lowered. "I'm sorry."

"Praying to candles never worked. So, 'Ex-Candles,'" he said. "What will be—"

Nainsi's eyes glistened. "The Beatles say Let It Be...but it's impossible."

"Warned you story's a downer."

Her gaze shifted to the horizon. "How are you doing with it all? Because I know...I lost me Ma too. A year ago."

"Really? Man, I'm sorry." A loud guy staggered into the tent, and Cal shot him a look, annoyed for the interruption. "It feels too early for them—and for us. But hey, we don't have to talk about it if you don't want. Revisiting it is like reliving it, and who wants that?"

"But you're an orphan, that's worse. I'm so sorry. I'll ask my family to add you to mass intentions. But beware, when everyone starts talking at the pub, they'll add to the story. After you threw that lit candle, you narrowly escaped a fire, then your band trashed a hotel room and ended up in a drunken brawl."

"Was I jailed?"

"Until your manager put up bail, but now you owe him a rare old whiskey."

He smiled just as the band Mountain erupted in a phenomenal jam. "Let's check it out?"

"My mates are probably looking for me."

"I'll help you find yours if you help me find mine."

"Sure." She swooped up the beer, blanket, towel, and stuffed the lotion and more aspirin into her pocket. They waved thanks to the kid doc treating a dude seeing Puff the Magic Dragon. Cal offered her his sandals, but she shook her head— "I'm all right barefoot"— and carried the lone flip-flop.

As dusk turned dark and they weaved through thousands of people, they chatted easily for hours. She told him about the day after she passed her secondary school exam —when Cal was weighing his very life—as when she boarded a plane from Dublin to JFK Airport, then flew on to Atlanta where the uppity Mr. and Mrs. Sarlington picked her up. She watched their four rambunctious kiddos in exchange for room, board, and stipend. "I'm only working here for a year while I decide which college music program. I want a major in music promotion, management, or journalism, not sure where, but I'll visit all the music hubs like LA, New York, Nashville, Chicago, and New Orleans."

"Dig it. Music's my thing too. We're starting to get gigs."

Cal told her more of his band. She asked questions, laughed at stories and jokes and told some of her own. He talked of how he'd wished he'd seen Creedence, Janis Joplin, and Led Zeppelin at this festival last summer. He cited sacred verses from the prophets Robert Plant and Jimmy Page. She quoted her favorite singer-songwriters, guys like James Taylor and Van Morrison, but a spark lit her voice when she talked about her beloved, The Beatles, shared how she cried for weeks over their break-up, teardrops dripping on the Abbey Road album. They made up a game—start the lyrics, the other finishes. They got them all.

"I've met my match," Cal said.

She flashed a smile. "Maybe you can work for me someday?"

They skirted around the masses through another set, and Cal blocked a few people from running into her.

"Nice to have a tall, cute guy pave the way," she said. This time, Cal smiled—and soared.

A drum solo sounded as they came to a fence decorated with peace flags and protest signs. Lights illuminated smoke billowing over the crowd. Tents, pick-up trucks, and El Caminos lined the gates. The lure of roasted pecans floated through. She set down the blanket. "Let's sit for a wee bit?"

"Sure. Good time for a breather." But his breathing was just fine. With each breath tonight, he'd forgotten grief. He'd been numb since May, but now with the smell of fried foods, sound of guitars, and sight of this cover girl—albeit a sunburn prevention magazine—he buoyed back to life.

"Then we'll find our mates," she said.

The starry night carried a soundtrack of crickets and clamor, Cal slapping mosquitos feasting on his bare chest, her scratching her ankles. They talked until they dozed off. When they blinked their eyes open, it wasn't from the dawn. It was the light of a photographer.

"Sorry to wake you folks. *Atlanta Journal-Constitution*." A man flashed a press badge, asking names and hometowns, vanishing as swiftly as a waft of charcoal.

"Mmm, someone's frying bacon. I'm starving!" Nainsi scrambled up, slathering on lotion, pulling out a comb from her back pocket and fixing her hair. "Lad, don't say 'top of the mornin' to ya.'"

"I won't—" Cal finger-combed his clumpy hair, striving for cool cat Jim Morrison look, but his wavy hair was too short. "—if you don't say lad. I'm eighteen like you. Sunburn better?"

"Stings, but shivers gone. But gosh, my bloody feet look cut up! I'll feel better when I hunt down food and find my pals."

Cal's smile fell and he unbuckled his sandals. "Here, a parting gift."

"Oh, no, I couldn't."

"What if you step on a needle?"

"All right. Nice of you." She slid into them and buckled, her small feet swimming in his size thirteens. "*Go raibh maith agat.* Thank you. For helping me through last night, too, Callum."

"It's—" No point in telling her it was Calvin. He'd never see her again.

"What?"

"Just—bye."

"Glad I met you. *Slán!*" She galumphed off, disappearing into the hordes.

"Nice knowing you," he said, though a blast of a sound check drowned out his farewell.

3

"Saturday in the Park"

Nainsi, July 4, 1970

Nainsi charged into a parking area searching for her friend's Chevelle, singing along with John Lennon and the Plastic Ono Band's "Give Peace a Chance" blaring from a van.

In Nainsi's family, saying John Lennon's name in the same sentence as Jesus Christ was punishable by hellfire. When Aunt Mary Louise, Ma's sister, drove her to Dublin Airport, praying the rosary for safe travel and tucking a St. Christopher prayer card into her hands, Nainsi had damned herself forevermore. "They're working on a musical called Jesus Christ Superstar," she'd said. "They want John Lennon to play Jesus."

Auntie had swerved the station wagon, and her voice shot up an octave. "Blasphemy! He said the Beatles were bigger than Jesus!"

She should've known better; Auntie named her sons Matthew, Mark, Luke, and John. "He apologized. He meant the Beatles had gotten so popular," she'd explained.

Auntie said, "You shouldn't lust, nor have idols."

"Lusting after idols is doubly sinful, then?"

But Nainsi's humor didn't help, her aunt rattling like a drum groove, pounding beats of disdain, lashing cymbals about this generation's self-ishness and missed holy day obligations, ending with, "Make ye saintly

Ma proud in America." She hugged her goodbye, her four brothers plastering their faces onto the window tracking the 707s at Aer Lingus terminal. Her big ol' Irish family exit. Few noticed if you left. Only if you died.

"Hey, Irish lass!" a blond Beach Boy-looking lad called standing atop the Chevy van, even holding a beach ball. "Remember me?" He leapt off, hitting the ball to other girls, and stumbled over to her. "It's me, the student doctor. Well, college junior. How's your sunburn?"

His eyes landed on her chest, and her face flushed. "Better. Thanks for the stuff."

"Right on. Hey, nice sandals. Good night, eh?"

She pursed her lips.

"What happens here, stays here," he said. "I take my oath seriously."

"You have a medical oath in pre-med?"

"My fraternity oath." He chuckled and she rolled her eyes. "Been volunteering all night. Snoozing in the van soon. Keep me company, hot stuff?"

Hot stuff? She tensed. She was not here to rock a van; she was here *for the music.* On the way to *university and a career.* "No. Looking for my friends. They're au pairs from other countries too."

"Bring all pairs, heh. We'll have a Hendrix party later. Dave, gimme more breakfast for my lassie here."

She shook her head at the misogynistic imbecile, but her eyes spotted a paper plate loaded with bacon, sausage, and eggs. A griddle of hash-browns smoked nearby, and her stomach growled. "Well, I am hungry—"

"Sure, sweetheart," he said and handed her a full plate.

She devoured the food as the windbag talked about himself non-stop. "May I have another plate?"

His bloodshot eyes leered at her while piling high the food fresh off the grill. "Dig a chick with a juicy appetite."

"You know what? My friends need to meet you. I'll be right back."

"Hurry. Napping soon."

She thanked him and dashed away, searching the grounds like a waitress with a hot order. When she spotted the good-looking, sun-bronzed dark-haired guy listening in rapt attention to a band, his lean body parked exactly where they'd slept, she ambled over. "*Dia dhuit!*"

"Hey," Cal said, eyebrows raising over his dreamy chocolate eyes. "For me?"

"Already scarfed down my breakfast."

"A woman after my own heart."

But it was her heart that fluttered. Talking to the nincompoop to get this plate was well worth seeing Cal's dynamite smile again and glint of cheer in his brooding browns, a depth she never saw in lads their age. Certainly not in guys that acted like BMOCs, Big Men On Campus, ogling girls from atop their love machine. She wondered if Cal's soulful tenderness was because he suffered a permanent hole drilled into the heart too.

Three hundred sixty-eight days ago, she and her brothers bolted off the school bus to find Da home from his maintenance job at the National Stadium. Eyes bleary, work shirt half-tucked, he blurted it out in the kitchen.

"Ma died," he said as he snuffed out his cigarette, a swirl of thick smoke hanging over his balding head. An ectopic pregnancy—in her tubes—had burst.

Nainsi's heart exploded, too. Her breath caught, insides reeling, and she fell to the cold olive linoleum. Da said, "Get up, she'd want you to be strong!"

Her three brothers ran to their two bedrooms. Nainsi picked herself up without a hug, helped her four-year-old brother Liam to his room, then escaped into the twin bed in her stuffy attic room, the Beatles posters watching her cry.

Father Gallagher visited, saying to rejoice, Ma's in heaven. She seethed. *Be happy?* She was *bereft*, the loss of Ma searing, the tears soaking her pillow! Only tunes comforted her sobs now. *God, why'd you take a good soul like Ma, instead of a murderer or something?*

Her brothers hid tissues in their fists by day, sniffling at night. "Big girls don't cry," said Auntie, who visited Sundays armed with shepherd pies and casseroles. "We must help the men."

"Geez, this is great, thanks again," Cal said, crunching bacon.

Her eyes dropped from his masculine jawbone to his wide shoulders and strapping chest, like he'd regularly lifted weights. Heat warmed her face. Was this from her sunburn?

"This plate's so full it's like Thanksgiving."

"What's Thanksgiving?" she asked, just to see his hunky smile again. "Well, I couldn't find my friends."

He shrugged. "Me either."

"And I had to bring your ugly sandals back."

"We'll find your flip-flop, Cinderella. If it's the last thing we do."

Inside she was amused, but she chastised herself. *No,* she was only here because this handsome, good guy was hungry, and she was only doing what Ma taught her. "Do you know you look like that oldest son on TV, the one that sings with his family?"

"That Brady nerd? Great. Not the sexy image I need."

She grinned. "Aw, I like him, but not him. There's a new show coming. I saw the commercial. *The Partridge Family?* You look like David Cassidy. With wavier hair. And taller."

"Is he a heartthrob?"

"Makes girls scream."

"That's me, then."

His deadpan was solid game for a Yank—but she bit back an appreciating smile. "My girlfriends must be worried, so I should go." *Or were they?* She'd only met them at the playground two weeks ago with their charges.

He patted the blanket she'd taken from the tent. "Patience. You'll find 'em. Hang out for a while? I mean, who doesn't want to rest again on a blanket as thin as paper?"

She grinned. "Maybe for a wee bit." She unbuckled his clunky sandals, welcoming the dew on her swollen feet, scratching a bug bite with red painted toenails, before she sat down and they talked. And talked. And talked some more.

The sun beat on them throughout the day with scorching hundred-degree temperatures. She bought him a new t-shirt, though she hadn't minded the view of his chiseled chest; he bought her a hat and fashioned a sun tent with the towel. They gulped jugs of ice water from trash cans as the fire department sprayed the growing crowd. As they lathered up with more lotion, they analyzed the Beatles break-up—"Can I ask you something, Callum? Why do guys always blame the woman? Why are they wary of Yoko the artist?" she asked—and all day they talked and danced and joked and played in the crowd of what felt like half a million people.

When the sun began to set and a summer wind blew, they followed folks to a pond where dozens of bodies skinny-dipped, and they waded in.

"Want to?" Cal said.

"Want to what?" She splashed him. He splashed her back.

But then, the first notes rang out.

"Him!" Cal yelled with the fervor of hallelujahs at a revival, grabbing her hand, pulling her out of the tepid, knee-deep water, toward the shrill of electric guitar. She tried to keep up, but his long legs raced faster than hers.

"Are you a basketball player?"

"Is every tall guy from America a basketball player? Are you a dancer, gal from Ireland? Faster, it's the holy grail." Cal sprinted a football field away to Jimi Hendrix Experience's eleven songs, saying they "pulsed with perfection at every lick."

She drank in the incredible talent too, and as Cal's eyes danced at Jimi's Star-Spangled Banner, she grew mesmerized by the purple haze, sparklers, and lighters like sparks of magic under the stars. "Y'all know how to party here."

"Little thing called Independence Day," Cal teased, reveling in the finale.

"It's like the Man Upstairs reaches down and plucks his guitar."

Cal nodded, his eyes studying it all. "The white Fender Stratocaster tonight."

The crowd roared, and thunderous applause shook the site. Soft-spoken Hendrix seemed grateful. Love flowed as a verb from audience to artist and back. She saw camaraderie waving through the crowd like a Dublin parade. It affirmed her career choice, wanting to make enchantment like this happen.

As a boom, ripple, and pop shot up into the night, and fireworks kissed the sky, Nainsi exhaled. After thirty-six hours of peace, from pot or play, love or lust, Jimi or Cal, she even felt Ma's death lift off her burnt shoulders. For the first time since that fateful day, Nainsi's frantic bustle slowed, and relaxation swept over her. She wasn't thinking anymore. She was soaking in moments of peace with a kindred spirit. Goosebumps crawled on her arms, and her fingers grazed Cal's hand. "Who needs acid to trip?" she said.

"I've transcended too." Cal looped his arm around her. A couple with flower power shirts twirled nearby.

Nainsi leaned her head on Cal's shoulder and breathed in deeply. His chest and biceps tightened, and she snuggled into his solid warmth. A current of electricity charged through her, though she attributed her heart pounding to the fireworks. She gave herself a warning. *My mission is college and career! Right, Ma?*

He pulled her closer. "Wish I could bottle this night and store it, like in my dad's old liquor cabinet."

"Me too," she said, nestling into his embrace, cherishing his light stroke on her back. A safety lived here, like she could share about the achy loss trapped deep inside, how she could still see Ma in the kitchen when she came home from school, stirring beef stew, swaying to the music in her head. *Why didn't I ever ask what's playing on your tape, Ma?*

Cal turned and faced her, nestling his hands on the small of her back.

Maybe she could just enjoy this moment? That was all. She traced his lips with her forefinger. "Your smile is out of sight."

A blush deepened his tanned face, and his head tilted to the side. He touched her chin and nudged her face up to meet his gaze. He closed his eyes and leaned down to kiss her. She shut her eyes just as quick, escaping into the intensity of his lips, taking in their chapped, rough warmth. With sound still buzzing in her ears, she drank in his firm kiss longer, sinking into this heat now melting her insides, the charge begging to last through the hot summer night. *More, please. Oh, my gosh, more.*

Though she'd never had a kiss this delicious that seared through her—certainly not like the clumsy make-out with Sean Collins—she pulled away. "You know I'm not looking for anything, right?"

"Geez. Neither am I," Cal said. "Peace, love, and music for a weekend. Then I'm out of here."

"Canada?"

He said nothing. Just kissed her again, her feeling his warmth fervently, him pressing into her lips, welcoming his strength. Tingles swept through her, leaving tranquility in its wake.

"You smell good. Sun lotion agrees with you. Try it next time," he said.

She smiled. "Cute. But maybe you smell the Chanel Number Five. My last present from Ma." She pointed up.

"Your Ma was on Apollo 11?"

She gave him a playful shove. "It was for my last birthday before she died. We'd had a perfect day on a trip."

He looked at her, clasping her hands, and she read what seemed like genuine interest in his eyes. "Where'd you go?"

"London for a relative's wedding. When Da and my brothers were at the hotel watching a football game, Ma and I walked through the fashion district window-shopping. When we turned on to Savile Row, bracing ourselves in the blustery January wind, these vocals from above greeted us, like from heaven. Would you believe the Beatles played from a rooftop? We screamed and danced. Bliss."

His eyebrows raised. "Seriously? Far out."

Her eyes looked away, towards the crowd dispersing, and then to her ankle. "That's the tattoo I got, so I can keep the best ever memory close. See 'Ma' written in the building? See the roof? Ma said in my birthday card the next week to remember surprise joy happens like that day. Not so easy, though. After this year, I feel like the other shoe always drops. But that miraculous day showed me what I wanted."

"Amazing," he said, and with a caring look she'd never seen before from any guy, asked, "How did that day show you what you wanted out of life?"

"I'd blasted my albums, loved my part-time job at a record store. But that time with Ma? I knew then, Callum. I wanted a career that rocked, to work in the music business. A career like Ma never got. I mean, my senior paper was 'The State of Women's Rights in Ireland,' like illegal contraceptives, unequal pay, lack of restraining orders against abusive husbands. We have so far to go! At home, the good womanhood path is work until you marry, bear babies, arrange sacraments.

"But I don't want that. When I got my first D, I cried to the guidance counselor, 'What if Ma wanted a career?' I said I didn't want to marry and mother by twenty, nor be a nurse, teacher, or a nun like the other girls. Ma gave up everything for us, and what did she get? Death! I never even got to ask her anything!" She swallowed hard, looking out at the crowd breaking up. "So I chose to study the music industry, live and work in a music city, and somehow be part of making that same live music happen that Ma and I knew that day."

"A career that breathes and rocks out. Totally get that. Go for it."

"To think those people on the rooftop or stages are getting paid."

"Right? But how did you end up in the U.S.?"

"When the counselor slipped a flyer into my hands for American Au Pairs, I swear "California Dreamin'" popped into my head. I thought of the Beatles at Candlestick and all my other favorites at the Monterey Festival. I thought of all the labels in L.A., and the singer-songwriters I love at the Troubadour. I thought I could work here for a year, while I figure out what music biz program. I put 'California family' on the application, so I could explore UCLA or the peace, love, and music of Berkeley. I'll be a woman of the seventies."

"Digging your hope. You got something to live for."

A breeze tussled her hair, and she swept strands off her face. "When Da crawled into his recliner that evening, I sprung the idea of working here." She could still see how he dropped the *Catholic Register*, eyes on Ma's picture on the mantel above the crackling fire. "He said, 'Your Ma always wanted to go o'er there.' I was shocked. Why had she never said? What *did* she want? Da pointed out the protests and civil strife here, and I said it's in Ireland, too. Cal, y'all think the Vietnam War is the only thing going on, but last August the Troubles began with three days of riots in Northern Ireland, when Catholics and Irish nationalists clashed with Protestant British. Eight killed, hundreds injured, homes and businesses destroyed, most Catholics. Da called it a pogrom, said they were being targeted, though Auntie said it was just up North, and we were safe in County Dublin near the sheltering Wicklow Mountains."

Her gaze shifted to the now empty stage. "Anyway, Da smoked his cigarette and said, 'Don't roam wild with wanderlust o'er there. Sex, drugs, and rock and roll is evil incarnate. People died at that concert in California. Our ancestors didn't survive a famine for hooligans. Hurry back.' I jumped up and down in glee and promised I'd make him and Ma proud of me."

"I have a feeling you will. You landed in Atlanta, though?"

"I got assigned a family here instead of California. But I'll visit every-where." She shrugged. "Meanwhile my brothers said Ma's rolling over in the grave, her girl's falling into women's lib nonsense. But no, no, she is not. If I close my eyes, I can still see Ma dancing to the Beatles playing 'Don't Let Me Down' that day. So, I promise her I won't let her down..." Her voice trailed off and she paused. "Do you ever talk to your mother up there?"

"No. She doesn't talk back."

"I know." She gave an empathetic smile, yet when Nainsi talked with Ma each night and played "Let It Be," sometimes she heard her mother whisper it was okay to go for what she wanted. She wrestled with guilt, though. When Father Gallagher said, "Did Jesus roam America making *himself* happy?' her heart had pinged. *Ma, is it wrong I want college and career? Did you? Oh, why'd you die before I could ask you?*

She had even started to postpone her dream, for her family's sake. Da had never cleaned. Her brothers couldn't even fry hamburgers. Fragile little Liam needed help. Yet she boarded that plane. Now was her only chance.

She spotted a vacated space near the stage and they moved to claim it. "I'm bleedin' tired. Isn't this a grand place to catch a wink before the Sunday concerts and finding our friends?" She set down the blanket there, next to a bedspread blob that was moving and grooving, and they laughed sheepishly. Cal stretched out prone, and she rested her head on his chest, her new bucket hat a pillow. They zoned out looking at the stars for a long while. "Thanks," she said. "I've never had anyone listen to me like this."

"Did you say something?" he said.

She laughed, and they laid without speaking for a few more minutes. Until she said, "Do you think we'll always miss our moms this much?"

"Yeah. But let's not think about it now. Like that new song, 'All Right Now.' It's all right now, this weekend, being here with you. Or with Jimi. Whoever."

"You got an easy vibe."

He thumbed her peeling pink shoulder. "You're cool yourself."

"Sunburn doesn't sting anymore."

"Good, then this will feel okay." He kissed it gently, moving up to nuzzle her neck, behind her ears, and landed on her lips for another glorious minute.

She stroked the rough stubble on his cheek and gazed into his deep eyes. An exhilarating rush shot up before she chased it away. *No. Guys are distractions!*

But something whispered back as she let her crisp skin be caressed, messy hair spill down, and summer breeze blow beneath the twinkling starlight. *But they're mighty fine distractions on a hot summer's night, when the music is rocking, the crowd feels like neighbors at a potluck, and his warmth sends bolts through your being.*

"You're right. Now is all we got," she said. "Should we ban thinking this weekend?"

His answer was muffled into one last goodnight kiss, before her breathing slowed. In the wee small hours, they lapsed into a slumber with his arm wrapped snugly around her, until a rooster crowed them awake, and they drank in Sunday's pink-streaked sunrise together.

4

"An Old-Fashioned Love Song"

Cal, July 5-6, 1970

Come Sunday's nightfall, as the allure of fried dough wafted through the air, things changed.

"Callum," Nainsi announced in the same tone as the bartender's last call for alcohol at a dive his band had played. He loved how she rolled her *l*'s, so he still hadn't corrected her it was Calvin. "I want you to know—"

He cringed. He could tell what lay ahead in how she lowered her voice. They'd danced under a cobalt sky to a fantastical Grand Funk Railroad set, air-guitared with B.B. King, and soaked up the Bob Seger System like there were no tomorrows, but now finality oozed from her tone. "I'll always remember this, but—"

"Yeah, yeah, yeah." His heart began its descent.

"I've had a whale of a time with you. And to think we found my other flip-flop—but not our friends." Her gaze followed people with peace signs. One said, *Does God kill or does man?*

"What are you thinking, Nainsi?"

"That though we had a hot dog lunch and two drafts from that guy with a keg, I'm hungry again."

Cal smiled. He meant the philosophical question, but true, *no think-ing this weekend*. His stomach growled, too, and he pulled out the whites of his pockets. "I know a cheap place for food, let's go." He took her hand, leading them toward an exit. For a mile, he rambled about his baby before he pointed to it. "Ta-da! My surprise joy—from my mom."

For his eighteenth birthday in January, Mama had sent him outside. Parked in the townhouse lot was a 1970 grabber-yellow, six-cylinder Mustang hardtop with a hot 8-track tape deck. It was the best surprise ever, he exclaimed as he hugged her. She said she'd put $750 down, and her life insurance would cover the remaining $2100.

"Stop. You're fine, Mama!" he said as he jumped into the bucket seat, her calling shotgun and sliding in her Beatles tape. She turned up "Two of Us," the two of them screaming up Route 234 boulevard singing.

As Nainsi's fingerprints streaked through the pollen, she seemed to study what she called his bittersweet look more than the car. "That was so amazing of her. What a beautiful gift of love."

They peered into the back seat and cheered for finding a few eats left in the cooler. They climbed in the back bench seat, rolled down the windows, and put the cooler up front. "A thousand degrees," he said, fanning them with his band's flyers, as he folded his six-foot-one frame next to Nainsi's petite size. They inhaled the last soggy PBJs, peaches, and sodas.

"That was good," Nainsi said.

"If you think that's decent, you should see my bologna sandwiches."

Her smile was radiant, her luminous look glowing just like the dash-board lights, campfires, fireflies, lit cigarettes, and faraway footlights that dotted the night.

"Just thought of how we could say goodbye."

Her sunburn brightened. "Hmm. How?"

Cal leaned over and kissed her, fifteen—or fifty—minutes. The make-out was three parts fierce, sensual, and passionate, maybe only one part fumbling. "Man," he said, "you need to be a yoga master to maneuver in here."

Her grin seemed forgiving as she chuckled, unadorned lips looking like they belonged in an ad for the natural look. "Where's the how-to *Cosmo* article for cars when you need it?"

A distant melody drifted into the car, and frogs and owls lent the backing chorus. "You're even more gorgeous when you laugh, you know that?"

Her face flushed. "Go away with that talk."

"Have you taken a compliment all weekend?"

Her aqua sea eyes settled back on his. "I was thinking..." She paused. "Oh Callum, it's been the most perfect weekend mucking around with you. What about our own finale?"

He coughed. *What, what, what?* His first time getting lucky? Or maybe she meant something else. Was this free love? Maybe not. She was a good Catholic. And he was a fair Presbyterian. Or wait, was he Lutheran? Methodist? Some kind of Protestant, definitely. One in which the Ten Commandments didn't *specifically* mention Southern Woodstock. "Really? What about—"

"We're fine. I just finished my—never mind, that's unromantic," she whispered. "I'm here to live and learn in America. Life begins now, and there's no better moment and place and person for our first times. Remember we said, let's live for now?"

"Yeah, but what about—"

Even the crickets chirped, as if to urge him, *c'mon, man, the first base coach is waving you home.*

"It's nineteen seventy, women's liberation, we can say what we want—equal voices, right? —and I want us to be together. I'm crazy about you."

"I feel the same about you." He paused before he gave a sly grin. "And again, who am I to mess with women's liberation?"

She threw her head back and cracked up, running her fingers through his hair.

Thump went his heart.

What happened next, below the plume of smoke hovering over the lot, Cal would remember on the drive back home in flashes. It was the sound of Zeppelin's riff in "Whole Lotta Love." The whiffs of Chanel and coconut suntan lotion and charcoal and s'mores. The feel of a warm touch in swelter and the slide of sweat on a sticky vinyl seat the size of a two-by-four.

Cal even planned another trip to Atlanta as he whispered sweet nothings into her ear, and soon they who had been in sync all weekend, who did not miss one beat together, fell asleep wrapped in each other's arms.

Waking Monday to legs cramping, songbirds chirping, and the fieriest sunrise yet, they found their way to each other again. As Richie Havens strummed more rapidly than the speed of sound, playing the most incredible cover he'd ever heard of "Here Comes the Sun," Cal's heart beat with a newfangled feeling—hope.

She cupped his jaw. "Beard will be a good look for your next concert."

"Concert is a stretch. We play dances. Come up for one?"

She paused. "This will always be a bloody great memory. But I must crack on."

A stanza of silence rocked the car, and Cal's soaring heart plummeted. A couple danced, shedding clothes onto his hood.

"Want to dance?" he asked.

She nodded, and they dressed and climbed out of the car and pressed their bodies together to sway in one last slow dance.

"I'll miss you," he whispered. It was okay. He wasn't planning a future like she was. And despite what his parents' generation said, the sexual revolution was like a gift from above to a hurting soul below. She was dynamite for his first—and last.

The grounds emptied. Folks packed up; roadies broke down. Someone yelled the dope was gone. Exhaust fumes blasted the lot where overflowing garbage cans stank, and swarms of flies buzzed over the trash. Holding hands, the bedraggled, sun-kissed twosome finally found her friend's car.

"*Go raibh maith agat.* Or as you say, thank you. May you have goodness." She kissed him, a hint of peaches lingering in his mouth.

"Bye, Nainsi Mary Rose Murphy of County Dublin," he said. Two months ago today, the universe abandoned him. Now, a three-day high seeped in and stirred his heart.

"Good luck, Callum Frank Leonardowski of Manassas, Virginia." She blew a kiss. "May laughter and music always lighten your load."

Cal waved goodbye, watching his T-shirt leave him too. He walked to his beloved Mustang through pecan trees, scratching the stubble covering a pimple. Next week, his buddies will move in. On the drive down, he'd asked them to, for noise in the townhouse. They'll work as construction apprentices by day, play gigs at night. Then, after they settled, he'll leave a note, giving the guys his guitar, the Mustang, and his old man's Cutlass as thanks for their friendship, which brought him their band and this unforgettable festival. Then he'll polish off that pill bottle and float like this forever.

For now, though, the world hugged him like he wasn't forgotten. If only for one weekend in Atlanta, peace, love, and music reigned, via a sweetheart from Ireland. For now, he forgot the pain.

5

"The Night the Lights Went Out in Georgia"

Nainsi, July-August 1970

As they sped past cows grazing in farmlands and wound their way into the Sarlingtons' development, the young women deconstructed their rocking weekends, giggling like girls sharing secrets at a slumber party.

"He's *deadly*," Nainsi said.

The other nannies claimed she was beaming. "Love or lust?" they asked.

She didn't know, only that his dark eyes and soulful musician spirit shot right through her heart, shook her, and his essence dwelled in her mind. "We, like, *totally* understand each other."

He was cute, easygoing, and encouraged her dreams. She didn't have to explain how grief pangs rolled over her from a song or a memory so vivid that it cut you then and there. He got it. How could harmony happen this fast? So, when Cal had ducked into the jacks, she rooted through his glove compartment, foraging for a pen, and scrawled the Sarlingtons' phone number on his trifold map. Maybe long-distance beaus could be an exception to her rule prohibiting boyfriends, because he lived too far away to make demands on her plans.

She thanked them as they pulled into the driveway. "See you tomorrow at the playground!" She slammed the car door, reminding herself she was a '70s woman now, on her own in exciting, hip America. She could go for college and career in the music biz first—only occasional, exhilarating visits with Callum. Full steam ahead. *Live like Ma never got to!* She skipped into the house. *It's not Berkeley, but this could be a summer of love!*

Come Monday night, the kids had sucked up her high, and she fought off a disappointed ping when the guest bedroom phone did not ring. Nor the next night.

The third night, her hope plummeted. Father Gallagher's homily flashed through her mind, condemning heathens to dwell in flames of fire, to not pass go, go directly to hell, as the shame of a thousand nuns taunted her. She could still feel the sharp sting of Sister Ruth's, who intercepted a note she'd passed in a boring eleventh grade church class, to her friend, admitting making out with Sean on the fourth date. The teacher read it aloud. Sean turned red as a beet across the table; Connor patted him on the back. Her friends muffled sympathetic giggles, but Nainsi's face flushed like it did when she had scarlet fever, and she laughed with embarrassment. That irked the good sister, who whipped her knuckles three times with a ruler.

"Ow, oh my God!" Nainsi blurted out, rubbing her fingers.

"Don't say that, mouthy *Miss* Murphy!" Sister Ruth then whacked her mouth with the ruler, and Nainsi's bottom lip bled, cheek stung, and the humiliation as ablaze as the welts. When Ma arrived, Sister Ruth informed her as Ma cupped the mark on Nainsi's cheek. "You are never, *ever* to touch my girl again, or we will leave this parish!" Then, Ma whispered to Nainsi, "Don't worry, I won't tell Da."

Nainsi glanced at a quiet phone. *Ma, I never thanked you for standing up for me,* she thought as she played "Let It Be," reminding herself of the silent vow she'd create her own life, make her own choices, like Ma never got. She climbed into bed grimacing because the first time actually hurt—*leefs!*—and begrudgingly decided to let go of Cal. Time to focus on her future, not what the newness of *heat* felt like. "But," she asked the Fab Four as the record finished, "why don't they shame the men in summers of love?"

The next night, after a fourteen-hour day of taking the kids to vacation Bible school, then the zoo, swimming, laundry, and making dinner while refereeing sibling battles, she tucked the kids into bed with a story. She tiptoed to her room, closed the white lace curtains, and collapsed under the flowered bedspread.

The phone woke her.

"Nainsi?" said the low, throaty voice barely over the air conditioner's hum. "Sorry I didn't call earlier. Was busy getting my roommates moved in this week, and then today I waited until after eleven o'clock to call. When rates go down."

Her heart skipped a beat. "Did anyone ever tell you that you have a great voice?"

Just like that, nightly pillow talk became her highlight. For a month, they swapped stories instead of spit, talking about their parents, countries, debating Beatles vs. Stones vs. Zeppelin, sharing facts like how Cal loved veal parmesan and Nainsi refused lamb chops, or how the bowling alley manager unplugged their amp, claiming the pins shook. Their talks grew more intimate each day as they revealed grief and fears.

On the final night, when Cal played her "Rainy Night in Georgia," his lower register carried the melody right to her heart. The way he sang, his gritty, masculine sound, she may have swooned. "Make a record someday, Callum."

"You're crazy."

"Now who won't take a compliment?" She cradled the phone, yearning to slowly dance with him again. They fell asleep mumbling, phone dangling from the bed. Nainsi jolted up at 4 a.m. "Wake up Cal! The long-distance bill!"

"Oh no."

"Before you hang up—"

"Yeah, babe?"

"I'm touring NYU next month," she said, picturing gallivanting around the Big Apple together, catching a show at a coffeehouse and nightclub in Greenwich Village she'd read about in *Rolling Stone.* "Want to go?"

"I'll try to get off work. Call me tomorrow."

"Good night." She hung up at 4:07 a.m., the time bright on the new alarm-clock-radio-cassette player. The kids would be up in three hours. Her mind raced, so to drift off, she scribbled a postcard to her family in the moonlight's glow.

> *Dia Dhuit! Sorry I left, but if I hadn't taken this grand adventure now, I never would've. Planning to see NYU soon. The kids are a handful, but they're easier than the parents. It's not California, but it's a fun, sunny metropolis. Went to my first rock festival. No one died. Met a groovy guy. Lost his Ma, too. Pray for him? xoxo, Nainsi.*

She dotted her *i*'s with hearts, then closed her eyes, dreaming of exploring NYU by day—and each other by night. Her heart fluttered. Her stomach somersaulted. Ten minutes later, her boxed tuna casserole dinner churned.

By 4:35 a.m., she knelt over the yellow guest room toilet, clutching the matching shag toilet cover, retching, praying to the patron saint of flu to avoid vomiting on the new bathroom carpet. But she threw up again, muttering, "Fine, I'll go to confession!" She pressed her warm face against the cool toilet base.

"Sick, dear?" Mrs. Sarlington said with not a hint of genuine maternal care. How she missed Ma, who'd even pull her hair back. "Can you still take Johnny and Timmy to golf and Lexie and Deborah to tennis, eight sharp?"

Nainsi nodded into the washcloth, but as her boss turned, she hurled.

"Aw. Bless your heart. Feel better soon. Would you launder that separate from ours? Toodles."

She clicked off the hall light to leave Nainsi gagging in the dark. She was still battling by dawn's early light.

6

"Stumblin' In"

Cal, August 10, 1970

One hot August night, Cal's life changed again.

Cal lifted the living room windows higher as a DC-area weather-caster giddily chatted about skyrocketing heat indexes. In this steaming five-room townhouse—a living-dining room, eat-in kitchen, one bathroom and bedroom downstairs, and Cal's bedroom upstairs—the guys jockeyed for the fan, slammed cold beers from another Bob's Bowling gig, and scarfed down hot dogs and chips.

"Before rehearsal, let's talk cash," Cal said.

Life had catapulted him into adulthood. He fretted about rent, utilities, food, gas, and car insurance, and lived a crash course in balancing a checkbook with construction work and bookings. "We need more gigs."

Troy picked up his drumsticks atop the newspaper pile. "Screw more gigs. We need better-paying ones."

Terry plugged in his keyboard. "Be more selective. Strategy. Raises our mystique."

"Feck that," Cal said. "We need two things—cold, hard cash, and to stay out of Vietnam."

"Feck?" Troy said. "One weekend in Atlanta and you're a leprechaun?"

"Shut up." Cal smirked, but the new hole in his heart ached. She'd stopped taking his calls. *What did I do wrong?*

"You haven't said her name lately," Terry said. "Haven't heard you on the phone either. Sorry, dude."

He was sorry, too. Sorry for playing the fool. Hell, he'd stayed *alive* by hearing Nainsi's voice, though he never told her that. In hindsight, probably just her gift of gab, but her electricity, laughter, and warmth made him think they'd had something. She'd even invited him to New York. Thus, the push for more gigs.

But a week ago, he called at the usual eleven o'clock. She didn't answer. The next night, he let it ring twelve times. Same the next evening. He wrote a letter, but without an address, he crumbled it up and tried the phone again. "Stop calling here!" her boss snipped. "Or my husband will call the police." The phone line went dead. So did he. Nainsi hadn't had the courage to break up with him herself.

He'd worn his heart on his sleeve and lost his first girlfriend. What a *gobshite*! Cal had whipped the receiver into the drywall and dented it. Weird how Cal's grief for his parents crashed heavier after she disappeared. He only got out of bed to work and cold call for gigs to help his roommates. The painkiller plan popped into his head again.

"Not worth it for a chick," Troy said when he patched the wall. "Save your energy for figuring out how to flee to Canada."

Cal lifted his blonde jumbo guitar and strummed with Troy drumming and Terry ticking the keyboards. They played it twice before a rap at the door interrupted.

"Fellas, turn it down, for heavens' sake," called the elderly next-door neighbor Mrs. Henderson. "The sound is coming through the walls."

They yelled apologies, unplugged the amp, but with the swelter, didn't close the window. They ran through it again before another loud knock.

"Where can we practice?" Terry sighed.

Cal marched to the door with another stock "sorry." But when he swung it open, relief washed over him.

Nainsi, dressed in his navy-blue T-shirt, stood before him, carrying a backpack, a gentle smile on her face. Her fair skin was pale, her long, lustrous hair pulled back, and her eyes red and puffy and streaked with mascara. A taxicab pulled away with a honk, leaving a suitcase. Cal pulled her close, breathing in Chanel, and she hugged him back tight.

"*Dia dhuit.*"

"Did you take the train? I could've picked you up from the depot. On the way to New York?"

She tucked her hair behind her ears. "Can we talk?"

His stomach dropped. *Can we talk* were the three worst words in the English language. Was it ever good news? Like when his mom said, "Can we talk? There's a spot..." He frowned and left her luggage outside.

"Guess practice is over," Terry said and turned on the Orioles-Yankees doubleheader on the Magnavox.

Cal sighed and took Nainsi upstairs, apologizing for the tools and socks on the landing. "We're going to clean tomorrow. Vacuum if I buy bags."

In his room, her eyes scanned posters of Willie Mays, Roberto Clemente, and Raquel Welch, moving to baseball trophies on the dust-laden dresser, before landing on his turntable and mega speakers under the window.

He tugged the ceiling fan cord. The oven-like heat barely moved. "Not the Ritz here." He patted the baseball bedspread draped over the double bed and steeled himself for rejection.

"You know I'm crazy about you," she said, staring outside as she sat down. "We got on." Her eyes shifted to him.

"Got someone else?"

"That's not it." She fell backward onto the bed and rolled over. She buried her face into his baseball pillowcase, but then she lifted her head and stared at it.

"Yeah, time for grown-up sheets. Guess I don't shop white sales like my mom did." He dodged a grief strike by walking downstairs to the bathroom and back up. He handed her three squares of toilet paper. It was their last roll.

"Never expected to meet anyone at the festival," she said.

"Right. Because there were only a zillion people."

"We had the time of our lives."

He sat down on the bed. "That's what you came here for, to say it was fun? Yeah, far out. I don't remember driving home. Troy and Terry said I was head over heels."

"Really?"

He had said too much. He shouldn't give away his feelings to someone who's about to pounce on them. She'd strung him along daily for four weeks of talking and longing, then not a single word. "Go ahead, say it. 'You're a nice guy, but...'"

She stared at the woven oval bedroom rug.

He glanced at the white briefs and t-shirts heaped in a pile. Mama said his room would embarrass him one day. "What blarney do they say in Ireland?"

"I'm pregnant."

He laughed, tossing the strewn clothes in a hamper. "That's what they say?" He turned to face her.

Her eyebrows raised, eyes intent on him.

He froze. His three-hot-dog-dinner dropped in his gut.

"I'd thought we'd be okay because I'd just had my—uh, monthly visitor, but..."

Cal studied those arresting aqua eyes. "What?"

"And even sloppy sex can—"

His mouth dropped open. "You're really pregnant? Wait, back up. Sloppy sex?"

"Oh, I mean, no, it was wonderful, but—"

"Are you sure?"

"It was. Oh! You mean, about the pregnancy? Ha, I'm sure. I was sick every morning and went to Mrs. Sarlington's doctor."

Cal slapped his knee. "Knew I should've carried rubbers."

"Should've worn a chastity belt like *me oul fella* said!" she said. "I've cried every night. What about college? Everything is ruined. That's why I didn't call you. I had to figure this out on my own, but I can't. I could've told Ma, but Da and Auntie will freak and Father Gallagher will send me away to nuns who run a laundry."

"Huh? A laundry?"

She sat up in his bed, and they sat shoulder to shoulder, staring ahead at the dirty clothes hamper. "There are sisters who send away unwed pregnant women to work at the Magdalene Laundries. Their babies are put into orphanages and sold. Some girls disappear, silenced, punished, invisible for this 'deviance in morality.' Told their souls are hell-bound unless, you know, they pay penance. Single moms don't hide away here?"

"I don't know, but it's, like, 1970. Isn't it the sexual revolution or something? Can't you do whatever? What do I know? But surely you can tell your family. They'll understand we're human. Mama would've."

Cal stroked her hair as she leaned her head against him and wiped her tears. Maybe they should marry, make it acceptable for her?

She got up and walked to his window, her back to him. "I can't be a mother now, and I can't tell me family. Promised I'd make them proud. Da will go ballistic. And poor little Liam, he needs help. I'm a mess! I can't return now, without school—and with a baby! Out of wedlock! With a *Protestant!*"

He raised his eyebrows. "That's a thing? Look, I don't want you to go back now either. But it's not like we're criminals, like Charles Manson or something. C'mon."

She walked back to the bed, waving her arms. "I'd be a disgrace. And if I do what Sally Seffenauer did, well you don't even want to know the burning condemnation—besides, I don't even know where to go here. Some back-alley doctor with a coat hanger? Geez, no!" Her words flew fast, choked out by rapid breaths. "So I thought about having the baby while working in Atlanta and told Mrs. Sarlington. She went crazy. Berserk. She'd been thick with me anyway once she found out I went to the festival, but now..."

Cal pushed dirty socks off his bed and reached out. "How'd she know?"

She sat back next to him. "Our picture showed up in the paper."

"Really?"

"She called me a *hoor*. Called it 'abhorrent, sinful behavior of the flesh.' Said I was a bad example for the kids, and she fired me. Said to get out, she wasn't a halfway house."

He exhaled. "Oh, Nainsi, I'm sorry." He pulled her close. "We're a guy and girl who dug each other. It's natural. But a baby, whoa. Wasn't ready for that news. Guess that birth control pill I took didn't work?"

She didn't laugh. "Oh, Callum, I don't know what to do."

"Let me get this straight," he said. "We may rot in hell for being together. You can't tell them back home or the nuns will sentence you to do laundry or clean or something? Oh, and you lost your job and have nowhere to live."

She blew her nose into the crumbly tissue.

"So, we take it as we go." He stood and paced, each step creaking. "Move in here. Yeah, it's a two-bedroom townhouse. But it worked for my family of three. At least it's not the gates of hell. Baby's room can be my parents' old room, now Terry and Troy's room. They'll have to move out eventually, and we'll both take care of our baby."

"I don't know." Tears trickled down her face, and she cried on his shoulder for a while. He held her, rubbing her back for another hour, before she said, "You think I could get a job straightaway?"

"Lots of help wanted signs around."

"And we don't have to marry, right? We just won't tell my family. And I can still look for schools after I have the baby..."

"Don't tell them now. You don't have to give up your dreams. We're in this together. I'll work overtime at the construction site and look for more gigs to afford this kid. Don't give up your goals...just postpone...we'll work it out. Patience."

"You have way more than I do." She took a breath. "You really think we can do this?"

"Mama was young too. Wasn't yours? So what if we don't have a piece of paper? Who freaking cares?"

"Maybe I'll find something that pays decent—didn't the ERA pass here? —and I can help you find gigs as your manager. I don't have to give up my life, right? We'll just keep the pregnancy a secret from back home."

"For now." Cal was hopeful. "So...you, me, and baby make three?" They'd make this living together thing *work!*

She reached for him. "If it's a boy, Callum can be the middle name."

"Oh. That. Name's Calvin. But call me whatever, Cal, Callum, California."

She smiled as they hugged, and she pulled back to meet his gaze. "I didn't want to say it on the phone, but...do you know I love you?"

"Yeah?" With the passion of a teen in a back seat or a young man in the throes of a first love, Cal kissed her deeply. Terror shot through him. He knew nothing about babies. But a whole life lay ahead of him now—his nights entangled under the covers! —with her nestled in his arms. Soon they'd have a child to love. Cal was alone no longer. *A family!*

"I love you too, babe."

From his transistor radio, the perfect big intro began, horns and guitar and piano blaring, static crackling through the sound. He kissed her again. Why had he never noticed the bridge in Elvis' "Wonder of You" before? The King's vocals were hopeful. The song took him higher this time; its heights echoed inside. They made more sloppy sex, lying under the hum of the ceiling fan, holding each other for a while before they dressed and broke it to his roommates she was moving in. The guys could stay until April. They were having *a baby!*

Troy's and Terry's faces lost color. They stewed for a while before saying, "Okay, Irish lass from Atlanta. Just don't mess up our band like Yoko."

7

"Smoke From a Distant Fire"

Nainsi, 1970 - 1971

October 5, 1970, Postcard, Battle of Manassas/Bull Run

Dear family, I miss you!

Visiting my new boyfriend Cal in Virginia. He lives near this U.S. Civil War site. He's teaching me how to drive from the wrong side of the road. Haven't decided on college yet because I've been busy. Pray you're well!

Xoxoxo, Nainsi.

Dec. 25, 1970, Christmas Card, Nativity Scene

Merry Christmas! Chatting with you on telephone today made me homesick! Glad to hear Auntie made the big traditional meal and Ma's soda bread cookies after Midnight Mass. Did you ever get the presents I sent? Your gift may have gotten lost here in Atlanta mail. Missing Ma and you all, especially at Christmas. Xoxoxo, Nainsi.

February 10, 1971

Nainsi rubbed her ballooning tummy and trudged through the door after working a ten-hour shift at the diner. She spied an envelope forwarded from Mrs. Sarlington and breathed relief at the mail with her last paycheck—*finally!*—but inside she unfolded a telegram.

Sis. Can't reach you. Da walking near a hotel downtown when Wolf Tone statue exploded. Force threw him to cement, windows blown out & glass rained on him. He cracked his head, cuts over face, neck, blood from ears. Acoustic trauma, partial hearing loss. Call home. Michael.

Nainsi dialed with trembling fingers. A bomb in Dublin? The violence was in Northern Ireland, so this made no sense. This happened a week ago! What kind of daughter was she, gallivanting with her boyfriend now? Da had been through so much agony when Ma died. She wanted to be there, to crack jokes to cheer him, bake Ma's recipes for her brothers, and help Liam. How could she show up now, though, as her belly bulged? How would she explain? She'd bring shame to the family.

When no one answered, she hung up and put on Carole King's *Tapestry* album and scrubbed last night's dishes to avoid losing her mind. The guys would be home soon, tired from their construction jobs, before they headed to the Elks lodge to play a fiftieth birthday gig. Things had been good, but the other shoe always drops. With Da laid up in a hospital, who would help them? As the only daughter, was Nainsi being selfish being here? *Ma, we need you.*

"So far away…" Carole sang. Her vocal reached into Nainsi's soul and shook it. For the first time since the hot August night where she'd found a safe harbor in Cal's arms, tears fell.

8

"Danny's Song"

Cal, March 18, 1971

That morning, as bare tree branches scraped their window, Cal played "Here Comes the Sun"—Richie Havens' cover in Atlanta was their story now—while Nainsi tossed in bed wearing one of his extra-large T-shirts. "What's up?"

"Nothing," she said.

The first two trimesters, days sped by at work, evenings at gigs, and nights wrapped in each other's arms. Their new life together felt like that surprise joy their moms had spoken of. They had all the fun and laughs and coziness and loud music and wild nights and cheap dates to the drive-in he could've wanted, scenes that made him grin when he was driving to work.

Yet whenever Nainsi spoke of living *in the now*, deep in his heart's recesses, Cal feared they were just playing house as nineteen-year-olds.

They never made the fall trips like she wanted—and he felt bad about that—but money talked. So, the weekend they were supposed to visit New York City, she had cheered on the Ex-Candles playing at a barn at the Prince William County Fair. With manure smells wafting, kids jumping off haystacks, grandparents and young couples alike dancing to their covers, the band rocked, earned fifty bucks for the gig, got their name out—and Cal sucked in each intoxicating moment with the beers afterwards.

"You sure you're okay?" Cal got up to change albums. Increasingly, her moods in the last trimester swung, coupled with worry over her father's injuries, and her mind often split to a place faraway. She wanted to call every day, but the international costs would be brutal, so they settled on once a week, and she asked her brother to call mid-week with updates. She loudly spoke to her father, who struggled with partial hearing loss they hoped would be temporary. His bloody head had needed dozens of stitches where shards of glass had gashed his face and slashed his neck, barely missing his carotid artery. His right arm was broken in three places and his left shoulder needed surgery and rehabilitation. Michael said he acted differently too. Depression and anger crept in. Head trauma caused strange things, the doctors warned.

"I'm fine," she said, irritation in her voice.

"Fine is like chick code for not fine."

She struggled to roll over while he put the needle on the new Doors' album, reading the song list and every credit on the back cover. She grew pensive with the song "LA Woman." When she finally spoke, she said, "I always thought it'd be cool to work at the Capitol Records building that is shaped like a stack of records. The Beach Boys used the echo chamber there for Good Vibrations."

"Don't worry, we'll get to LA someday to see it all, babe. Maybe baby's first vacation? We'll try to save a few more dollars each week."

She rubbed her eyes. "It may take us a while to earn enough."

Cal sighed, as the band had only made about twenty bucks each last night. Last night's gig was the Ex-Candles' first Saint Patrick's Day show at a pub, complete with green beer and tissue shamrocks, but they butchered "The Unicorn." "What kind of Irish band doesn't have a fiddle player?" heckled a drunk. "We never billed ourselves as Celtic,"

Cal shot back. "And our Irish manager is fine with it—" He pointed to Nainsi's table—empty.

In the next song, she walked back from the restroom. She slumped in her seat drinking a Fresca, coughing in the cigarette haze, eyeing the clock. "My first St. Patrick's Day in America stunk," she'd said on the way home.

"How rare we're both off work today," Cal said now as the record played until the needle clicked at the end. Cal never wasted time on the dead wax of the void. At the run-out, he shuffled to the stereo, filling the silence like a DJ, finding Led Zeppelin's newest album, an irresistible purchase. "Props to Page for the guitar, but I don't like this balladry 'Stairway to Heaven'. It's not them. What do you think?"

"They'll have a megahit," Nainsi said. "And props for playing Belfast and Dublin. *Me oul fella* could've gotten me tickets at the National Boxing Stadium..." Her voice trailed off. "What hell he's going through. I didn't think through the decision to leave home. Just jumped. Maybe I should've stayed there. Oh, Cal, baby just kicked hard!"

He placed his hand over hers. "Hi there, little one. Are you going to be a punter or do you not like Zeppelin? Unforgivable. Nainsi, go easy on yourself. Hang in there. Your aunt and brothers can help your dad while you're becoming a mom—and baby's kicking that you'll be a great one."

Cal slid back into bed, bringing her hands up to his lips to kiss, but Nainsi's gaze fell. He tried to read her distance, like lyrics to decode. "I know you miss everyone. When you call them, I'm quiet, but...maybe level with them now? Then we can visit soon."

"No."

"Well then don't worry. With all the wars and tragedy, the Pope is too busy to put a hex on you," Cal said. He looked out his window at the neighborhood swing set, wondering if their toddler would play there like he did. "We got each other now. You've helped me see that, feel hope again. I want you to feel better, too. We'll save for trips. I'll ban myself from buying albums."

She messed his hair. "Will you survive that?" She reached for him. "Thanks for reassuring me it'll be okay."

He wrapped his arms around her and kissed her, but the doorbell broke the tenderness. Cal growled, ambled down the stairs, and opened the door to see elderly Mrs. Henderson. She was holding a box almost as big as she was. Cal took it and sneezed.

"Brought you some hand-me-downs, kids." Her hands reached for her back. "My babies' old clothes."

"Oh, wow." Cal brushed off the box's dust, much like the cupboards they didn't clean. If her kids are in their sixties, Cal calculated, the box must pre-date World War I.

"Very thoughtful of you," he said as he set it on the table, moving things around to make room. The table's memories of death—his dad, his mom's melancholy dinners and cancer medicines—now touted the artifacts of life. Cloth diapers. Waitress paystubs. *Life* covers with Muhammad Ali and Frazier.

Nainsi padded downstairs. "Please stay, Mrs. H. Would you like tea?" Nainsi had been talking to her for advice and loneliness. Mrs. H declined, stating she was working on their baby present, but shared the story behind each outfit—the shirt Billy wore to church, the dress Susie wore to the circus.

When she left, Nainsi pulled out a few items, the sunlight highlighting the dust flying into the air. She popped an RC Cola tab instead of making tea and dug through the box, finding old books written by Irish writers Yeats and Joyce. She coughed at the must, skimming pages of prose, while Cal strummed the guitar to JT's "Fire and Rain." "You know, Cal, the best songs are stories. You should write. You're a singer-songwriter at heart."

"No, I'm not. Ex-Candles play covers for cash, fun, free beer."

"Let's try a lullaby?" She grabbed the electric bill while he played chords, threw together melodies, and she jotted phrases on the envelope.

By the time the guys got up at noon, they laughed at their prize line, "Oh baby, please don't fuss/Sorry, baby, you're stuck with us."

"You got a way to go." Troy teased them as he poured a coffee. "Can we talk?"

Cal flinched. Nainsi looked up.

"We got news," Terry said. "Since you wanted us out by April."

"This bloke is heading to Canada," Troy said.

"What?" Cal's insides clenched at the loss of his friend first, band second. "What do your parents say?" Mr. and Mrs. Woodley were godsends when Cal's mom died. They'd helped him at the funeral home.

"They're going, too," he said.

Terry wrung his hands. "And I've enlisted. What with you lovebirds having a baby, it's a sign. Leaving for basic April first."

"Is this April Fool's?" Cal asked. "You guys have been like brothers to me..."

"Me too," Nainsi said, her eyes watering. "I wish you lads wouldn't go. It's been grand."

"Good day," Paul Harvey said from the kitchen radio.

9

"Silly Love Songs"

Nainsi, April 25, 1971

Hair-raising. Bloodcurdling. Ear-piercing. The baby's screams continued to rip through the still night, and Nainsi groaned. She threw off the covers and glared at Cal blissfully slumbering. "I've had a whopping one-and-a-half hours of sleep. Glad you're getting eight."

He didn't move.

"Fine!" This was her last attempt at consoling the new *Guinness Book of World Records* holder for Strongest Lungs Ever. Teetering on collapse after ten days of crying—newborn's and mom's—Nainsi reached for writhing Rhiannon in the rummage sale bassinet. "Sweet pea, I just fed you."

She shuffled to the rickety changing table someone in their townhouse row had thrown out and tossed Rhee's wet nappy into the diaper pail. The tiny hands clenched as she screamed and kicked while Nainsi fastened the pins on a fresh cloth diaper. She washed her hands with her daughter slung on her chest and patted her back. The cries turned more urgent.

"Shh, Daddy's working tomorrow morning. You're stuck with me for another week." She was an hourly employee plus tips who could only take off two weeks.

Nainsi wrapped her in the striped hospital blanket, carried her to the kitchen for water, and turned on the radio. Half a million protesters marched on Washington yesterday, and Vietnam Veterans Against the War threw their service medals.

"They need to stop this unjust war. Violence is never the answer." She shuffled to the living room, turned on a *Mary Tyler Moore Show* rerun, and plopped on the couch. "I wish I were you, Mary Richards."

She hiked up Cal's comfy blue T-shirt, now with milk stains, and directed her engorged breast into her baby's mouth. Rhiannon refused. Nainsi tried the other side. Rhiannon turned her head.

"Why don't you like me?" She tried again, but she wouldn't latch. "I don't blame you. They're like rocks." Sometimes, nursing miraculously worked—but when it didn't, she fed her formula.

Ma, if it's natural, why can't I do it? Her mom had breastfed. Five times. In these moments, Nainsi missed her most and wanted to ring her. *Shouldn't I know what to do? Why can't I calm her? I'm a failure at motherhood.*

These days had taken a sharp one-eighty from the euphoria immediately after birth. After twenty hours of excruciating cramps with only ice chips for sustenance, she forgot the labor pain the moment Rhiannon barreled out. Instant joy swelled in her and warmed her whole body. The nurse whisked the baby away and reported six pounds, two ounces.

Ma, see this angel?

Later, when she put her into Cal's arms, he cuddled her as if she'd break. They marveled at her tiny perfection, caressing her angelic smooth skin like a porcelain doll, and stroked a swath of peach hair atop her soft spot. Did she have Cal's Mama's smile and Ma's sapphire eyes?

She and Cal sang her part of the lullaby they'd written and hadn't finished.

We'll be there, like you can plan
on/ We'll be your feet to stand
on/ We'll always love you, little...

What word to finish the rhyme? Nainsi blurted, "Rhiannon." The Celtic name came from a myth she'd heard or a novel, but it felt like home. Nainsi gave her the middle name of her late mom, Mary Rose, and Cal added a middle name, his late mom's, Elizabeth. Four names that signified loving, brave women, an original name for a classic girl. When they sang the only verse, she even grasped Nainsi's pinky. A fierce, immense love flooded her as Cal beamed and said they were a family now.

But reality set in at home. Rhiannon screamed all hours. Nainsi called the doctor one night when the baby arched her back. She feared the wrath of disease. How she wished she could ask Ma. The doctor minimized her fears on the phone and patronized her as a "frantic new mother."

Cal called the next time. The doc arrived with a stethoscope and scale. He listened to her heartbeat and lungs and proclaimed them normal and clear, the baby healthy and growing. He couldn't advise on breastfeeding but affirmed the bottle was fine. In a tone that called her a little woman, he spoke to Cal. "It's like that sweet Mustang in your driveway. Just learn maintenance here, young man."

The next night, Rhiannon refused to eat at her 2 a.m. feeding. Nainsi rocked her, tried to read her Yeats poetry from Mrs. H's book. In these early hours she cried that despite having had a mother who did this young too, despite being a big sister and working two months as a nanny, Nainsi was an inept disaster. She loved to cuddle her little baby by day, but these nights were brutal.

The next night, Nainsi shook Cal from his slumber.

"Hold her!" She handed over flailing Rhee. "I'll ask Mrs. Henderson." She marched away, stomping down the stairs and slamming the front door.

"Colic," said Mrs. H at her door. "Swaddle, white noise, and dab whiskey on her gums."

But when Nainsi returned ready to try it all, Rhiannon had already settled. Cal was strumming the guitar, playing Crosby, Stills, Nash & Young's "Our House." Rhiannon lay calmly on the bed. Cal stopped playing— the cries revved up—and asked what she said.

"Vacuum and whiskey?" Nainsi said.

"Okay," Cal said, bypassing the vacuum cleaner and heading to his father's ancient stash above the refrigerator. He returned with two shots.

"*Sláinte*," Nainsi said, and they clinked glasses. The whiskey never made it to Rhee's gums that night, but the crying became bearable. They took turns feeding her a bottle, and played their game of play a verse, name that song.

Tonight, after Rhiannon sucked down formula and burped while TV credits rolled, Nainsi climbed the stairs to their room and set her in the bassinet with a pacifier. Then she crawled back under Cal's dreadful baseball bedspread. Just as she dozed, Rhiannon wailed. "You're not crying again, I'm crying!" Nainsi stumbled out of bed and set down the needle on *Déjà Vu*. When she quieted, Nainsi jumped back under the covers. Ten whole seconds later, the next wail was sharp.

Cal startled and shot up. "What? Huh? Oh... I got her." He shuffled over, scooped her up, kissed her forehead, danced with her, and sang along with "Our House." Soon Rhee settled.

They swayed through two more songs, and Nainsi lay there watching in awe. The moonbeams peeked in, silhouetting their dance. She stepped over and wrapped her arms around them, letting the harmony pour over, joining the family slow dance.

"I've never loved you more," she whispered to Cal.

10

"Sweet Life"

Cal, July 6, 1971

When Cal turned on the AM car radio after work, he pounded the steering wheel at the news jazz legend Louis Armstrong had died. Then he thought to himself of a wonderful world.

Cal was five. It was late. He padded downstairs to tell Mama his tummy ached, and as Cal stepped to the bottom stair, Sinatra's baritone filled his ears. The song skipped, which his old man fixed by putting the needle ahead, and the voice carried through the room again. Cal watched him twirl, then dip Mama. She touched her beehive, giggling. "Harry, you old romantic you. You're smooth on your feet, darling."

After they kissed, his old man walked to the cupboard and fixed their drinks. "A nightcap," he said, as they toasted and dragged from their cigarettes, snuffing them out in the ashtray stand. The next record in the stack dropped, and Louis Armstrong's voice now soothed everyone. "One more dance?" his father said to Mama's smile. Interwoven in each other's arms, they danced through the swirling smoke to "A Kiss to Build a Dream On." Cal was safe and sound.

After Cal parked, he sat there, stunned at the news. Armstrong's death was the fourth death of a legend after an ominous trifecta of twenty-seven-year-olds. Hendrix in September, ten weeks after Atlanta. Janis Joplin in October. Doors' Jim Morrison three days ago shook and rattled him like they were old friends.

He shut off the radio and headed into the music store to find a present for Nainsi for their one-year anniversary. Brushing off the sawdust from his jeans and digging into his pockets, he found a measuring tape from work in one but five dollars in the other. Enough to buy her the newest Allman Brothers album, *Live at Fillmore East*. Maybe it would make her eyes light up again, remembering Atlanta. Maybe Rhiannon would like it, too.

By the time Cal pulled into their townhouse parking lot, he pictured how Rhiannon smiled and slept more. Nainsi, however, remained withdrawn. He chalked it up to exhaustion. They worked opposite hours, so someone would always be with Rhee. Mrs. Henderson must've deduced it wasn't easy, because she gave them the name of an acquaintance who was always volunteering for things, a church lady an hour away who might babysit for free if they both had to work. They never tried her, as she lived too far away.

The radio news spoke about the Pentagon Papers, bombs in Ireland, and a brutal living room massacre in June of eight African-Americans in Detroit, and his heart plunged again. "Judas! What kind of world is this?" He shut off the radio and parked. When he opened the front door, Rhiannon was crying in the playpen. She spotted him, kicked harder and wailed.

"Hi Rhee!" He wedged off his scuffed work boots, scooped her up and kissed her head. Her onesie was soaked. "Where's Mommy? Be right back, okay?" He put her down and gave her the pacifier. She spit it out with shrieks.

He climbed the stairs two at once and swung open the door. Nainsi had bunched the covers over her head. He set down the music store bag and gently nudged her.

"Thanks for changing her, Mrs. H. Sorry to see you go," she mumbled.

"Nainsi, it's me. Sorry to wake you, but she's wet and crying. I'll change her, but should I feed her now? I'm dirty from work, I wanted to get a shower first—"

She pulled down the covers. "What do you want, a medal?"

Cal ignored the barb. He'd only asked if he should feed her now because Nainsi liked a schedule with their crazy hours. "How about spaghetti and salad for our anniversary?"

She looked at the clock with bleary eyes. "Does that say six o'clock?"

"Yeah, babe. When'd you fall asleep?"

She looked annoyed at the question. "Why?"

"When was her last bottle?"

"I don't know. Noonish?"

He bolted back to the door. "She's gotta be starving. Let me—"

"Did you hear the news?"

"The War, the Troubles, or Louis Armstrong's death? It's like pick your tragedy anymore."

She sat up. "Louis Armstrong died?"

"I know, right? Look, let me get to Rhee. Come down, we'll celebrate."

Cal ran down the stairs and changed her, dressed her in another sleeper, and then heated formula, which she sucked down. He burped her and set her in the playpen with Mama's baking cups. He planned his shower for later, hoping maybe she'd join him when they laid Rhee down. Cal boiled water, tossed in noodles, heated Ragu, slid frozen garlic bread in the oven, and lit a lilac candle Mrs. Henderson had given along with a casserole when they came home from the hospital. He hoped the smell of the sauce would beckon her downstairs, but when that failed, he called upstairs. Several times.

But he ate dinner alone, pitching the sauce jar into the trash with a clash. After he sifted through records, finding his parents' Armstrong

LP, he danced with Rhee. "We're having a memorial concert tonight, sweetie."

Fifteen minutes later, Nainsi shuffled down the stairs as she pulled her hair into a ponytail, flip flops snapping, and wearing the same short shorts as when they met, with her favorite thrift store top she'd called "bohemian peasant." She blew her ruddy nose into crumbled toilet paper. "Hi."

"Dinner's cold," said Cal, swaying with Rhee. "For what it's worth, happy anniversary."

Rhee cooed and waved her arms, but Nainsi looked at the candle flickering on the table. "I didn't feel like eating, sorry."

"What the heck blowing off our anniversary dinner?" Cal said, a thought flashing through his mind why all the tears, moodiness, sleep. *Was she pregnant again?* Two kids by the age of twenty? He stopped. "Do you feel okay?"

"The news is—" Her eyes lifted slowly. "Mrs. Henderson left."

"Oh, phew!" Cal exhaled. "I mean, she left?"

"Her son Bill came." She picked up a blanket. "Saw him loading his car with boxes, so I asked if they were traveling. He said he'd retired, and since she's eighty-one, he wants her to live with them in St. Louis."

"Good she'll be with her family—but I'm sad for you. You were becoming friends."

"She's all I had for motherly and grandmotherly advice. Look at what she gave us." Nainsi unfolded a huge pink and blue baby quilt. "She worked on it for months. Said she wouldn't move until she finished. Isn't it beautiful? She hugged me and said to say goodbye to you."

Cal touched the center square image of a guitar, warmed by their only maternal gift, a personalized one. "So nice."

Nainsi wrapped it around her and shuffled to the couch without looking at Rhiannon. "I don't have anybody here."

Cal, swaying with their baby, held out his hand. "Malarkey. You have us. Dance?"

"I can't even take you two home. And I'm no good at taking care of a baby who doesn't want her mother. If I were her, I wouldn't either. She deserves way better."

He looked at Rhee, then to Nainsi. "This too shall pass, my mom used to say."

"Walter Cronkite said the violence is escalating in Ireland. My brothers talk mad after the bombing that hurt Da. I should be there."

Cal dipped Rhee back into the playpen and put on a James Taylor record. "Yes there's violence in the world everywhere, but we're safe here. One day at a time."

"Sadness is crushing me," she said. "It's weighing on me. I was so selfish to come over to America to find myself, to see what music major and career I wanted. Wasn't that ridiculous? Such grand dreams of working for a musician or promoting a festival or a label. Silly girl. Instead, I'm homesick, worried, and yet still want college and career and to make Ma proud. I love our baby, but maybe the writing's on the Dublin Wall."

"When my mom died, I felt hopeless. Like I wanted to die, but then I met you and we had Rhee. Y'all saved my life. Let us save yours."

Her look seemed blank.

"Look, we should visit," he said, though a flinch of panic seized him about missing work. He was hourly. "We'll break the news together. Your family and priest can curse me, whatever. Let them see how much I love you both."

When she shook her head, shutting her puffy eyes, Cal noticed the dark circles underneath. "By next year then, and maybe then I'll be on salary with vacation time," he said. "I'll continue working weekends to save money, and I'll find another band, and if you can find a nicer restaurant—"

She stood, bypassed Rhee, and walked to the window. She took a deep breath. "I should go back now."

"Yeah."

"Not a visit. Move back."

The blood drained from his face, and his gut tumbled. "What? You can't take Rhee and go. You two are my world. I just said y'all saved my life."

"I'm cursed. I can't even comfort my own screaming child. And we don't have anyone to help. I can't do these monster shifts anymore, scheduling them around your work. It's impossible. Neither of us has a mother or a grandmother at our side now. We have no one. *No. Fecking. One.*" She faced him. "And how do I ever work towards my dreams now? I can't have it all after all. Mary Tyler Moore had a career and an apartment, but she didn't have a baby."

"Stop. You only had a baby three months ago. We can get you pills or something. Let's toast to something good. Us." He strode into the kitchen to pour whiskeys, fixing two tallboys in McDonald's Peanuts glasses.

The twilight skies darkened, and the streetlights clicked on. Distant thunder rumbled. The fan hummed with only quick hits of relief.

"It'll all be okay." He lifted the glass. "To one crazy but awesome year. Babe, I love you. I love your laugh, zest, spirit, how we understand each other, your insight in what you hear. I love how you mumble advice to Rhee when you play Carole King. We're better because of you. I even 'recycle' now. Sometimes." He cracked a smile.

She stepped back. "I love you too. And I love Rhee." Without a sip, Nainsi set down the glass on the windowsill. "But I'm going to the airport now."

Cal's eyes widened. "No. It's no life without you and Rhee."

"Are you still not getting it?" she said, tucking the quilt under her arms and walking to the hall closet. "You're going to take our baby." She pulled out her backpack and dragged out her suitcase. "She adores you most. She cries when I hold her. She stops when you do. I read her poetry and play her music, and she sobs. You read her album notes, and she's entranced."

"She just doesn't like Zeppelin. Really, any heavy metal, but I've told her it's an acquired taste. Give her time."

She lifted the suitcase without a smile. "Raise her. Keep her safe, and maybe in turn she'll keep you safe too. Pre-med guy said dads don't get called over to Vietnam."

"Oh, Bif the genius, right. Nope, the family exemption was cancelled long ago." Cal looked at Rhee, and back at Nainsi. "You're not actually considering—"

She stepped toward the door, averting her eyes, and he moved to block her way.

"You and Rhee will be all right, Cal." She stopped, turning back and finally gazing at Rhee. She put down her luggage. She walked to the playpen as she watched Rhee mouthing her fist. She took a deep breath and then the tears came. She leaned down and grabbed her daughter's waving hands. "Oh, my angel, I can't believe I'm doing this, please know I love you to no end, forever," she whispered, kissing her hands and cheeks as Rhee babbled. "If you hear 'Our House,' I'm sending love. Feel my hug wrapped around you, our precious."

Anger flew over Cal, beads of sweat dampening his shirt, and he clenched his fists. "This is crazy. She needs a mother. A song's not going to cut it."

She wiped her face and turned and lifted the suitcase and struggled to the door. "It was a shock for me too. But I need to figure this out on my own first. I need time, space, and to see my family now."

"We're your family," he shot back.

A sob escaped from her throat, and she looked away. "And if I took her back home now, it'd be a scandal of shame."

He studied her eyes, rolling his. "You're exaggerating."

"Am I? You don't believe me some single mothers aren't heard from again?" She looked only at the cracked door. "Tell her I loved her, *le do thoil*. In the meantime, don't find me. Don't call me. Don't sway me with that voice of yours. Respect my decision."

He pounded his fist into the air. "This is your child!"

"You don't think this is the hardest choice ever? Grant me this space and time for now and tell her of my love, and then maybe someday, when my family's stronger—and they do away with calling women 'fallen' and children 'bastards' and being condemned at church—or I'm just much stronger—I'll find a solution. Maybe someday, I'll write to you, saying I've made the worst mistake ever and can't live without you both, but for now—for now—"

"Wait." This "for now" bullshit grated on his nerves. He cursed that he ever mentioned his "All Right Now" motto for climbing out of grief with baby steps. He bounded up to their room and back with the record store bag and a small silver box. "An anniversary present."

"No. Don't make this worse." Then, she took a breath, and she walked out.

He trailed outside and glared in disbelief. "For real?"

"I'm driving up to New York for a flight home."

"Don't. Give us time and patience to figure this out!"

A lady walking a dog across the street looked over, and little girls playing hopscotch stopped and stared.

Nainsi's voice softened. "I'll miss you, Cal and Rhee. Know deep in my heart will always be love for you both. Don't let her think it's her—it's me. But—I must go now before I change my mind. And I must beat the storm coming. Goodbye. May you have goodness."

May you have goodness? What she'd said the last Atlanta morning one year ago wasn't so charming anymore.

"No," he shouted, but she loaded the trunk, got in, and fired up the ignition.

She wouldn't look, her puffy turquoise eyes fixed at the rear-view mirror.

"Ahem!" Cal said, anger ripping through his voice. This was all wrong. Not how he wanted to do it, but it was his last chance. He dropped to one knee on the sidewalk. When he opened the box, Mama's silver and diamond ring sparkling, he said, "Will you marry me?"

Her hands flew to her mouth, but after a pause she dropped her head. "I'm so, so, sorry, Cal. I can't. Know I'll always love you both, I mean it." Her eyes moved to the mirror as she shifted the transmission. "*Slan.*" She backed out of the parking space.

Rage heated his face and gripped his hands and with the grief of an orphan, the passion of a musician, and the rage of a jilted lover, Cal whipped the box at the trunk as she drove away. It ricocheted off into the front yard. "This ring was a true mother's! How could you leave your only child!"

He chucked a handful of stones and doubled over at the curb.

A minute or five may have passed before Cal went inside. Rhee was fine, rocking side to side in the playpen trying to roll over. He pulled the new Allman Brothers' album and flicked it against the wall like a Frisbee. Next, he picked up the yellow vase Nainsi painted with a lyric from "Our House" and whipped it upstairs at their bedroom door, and it shattered.

Rhee startled, clutched her Raggedy Ann doll, and cried, and he picked her up and cuddled her. "Welp. Got a game for you. It's called, 'Let's Find Your Grandma's Ring.'"

Searching through the scorched grass and dandelions on the dry little lawn he hadn't cut in a month, he found the box. He sat with it at the table of the dinner for one, site of his dad's last breath and sad candlelit dinners with Mama. He blew out Mrs. H's candle, the sweet scent lingering. "Once again, candles don't work." He drained both whiskeys. "We'll forget she ever walked the Earth."

He poured another swig. That was when it hit him. The final blow. She took the Mustang.

11

"Born to Run"

Nainsi, July 6, 1971

Don't think. Go. Nainsi sped east on I-66, the thumps of her racing heart drowned out by Joni Mitchell's *Blue* 8-track. But when she neared the Capital Beltway, traffic crawled to a halt. Local newscasters spoke of jams every day. Letters to the editor filled the *Post* ever since it was built in '64, Cal had said.

"C'mon people!" she yelled. The quicker she arrived at JFK Airport and bought a plane ticket to Dublin with Cal's credit card, the less chance she'd second guess this idea she'd hatched today.

She pulled out the Northeastern map from the glove box. Of course, she hadn't studied the route. Who was she kidding? She didn't study things ever. Jumped in pools cannonball.

A drizzle began, and brake lights illuminated the creeping darkness. She clicked on the overhead light to see the map, daunted at the freakish number of interstate highways, state and local routes, loops, ramps, and merges. Bloody hell. She squinted at the lines that looked like an Etch-a-Sketch. Turns from the wrong side of the road. She couldn't even turn right right.

Lightning flashed and a crack of thunder made her jump. She eject-ed Joni and turned up the DJ on 100.3 FM, who confirmed isolated thunderstorms were rolling through the area. A car honked. She wasn't inching fast enough, apparently. "Hold your britches, bloke!" Raindrops fell harder, and she flicked on the fastest wiper speed. *Dublin's calling.*

Nainsi couldn't wait to get home and sleep for entire stretches, clear her head and think. She wanted to hug and help her Da and see Michael, Ian, Vincent, and Liam, even if they'd only fight over the TV. It felt like a dream to lie in her own bed as Auntie's savory corned beef aroma wafted through. *What did I just do, Ma?*

"Temperature at Dulles, eighty, folks, and storms will be cooling off this humidity," said a jovial radio voice.

Dulles! The international airport between Loudoun and Fairfax counties must fly to Ireland. Easier than driving to New York City, *duh!* She'd only thought of JFK because of her trip that had stopped there before Atlanta. She exited at the Vienna ramp and pulled into a gas station.

Though he was creepy, the attendant's directions to the airport were stellar, and ten minutes after she was back on the road, golden arches, office buildings, and yellow ribbons tied around old oak trees lined the landscape. The rain turned into a downpour, water dumping like in a torrent. Her hands shook on the wheel when she could see only five feet ahead. A light was out at an intersection. Rumbles roared overhead. She breathed relief from the harrowing drive when terminal signs and gateways to all over the world appeared.

She'd probably scared the ticket agent with her frazzled ponytail strands askew, teary raccoon eyes from cheap mascara, but the prim woman said, "Certainly, miss. I'll check flights for you." She took what felt like an eternity—or the eight minutes and thirty-seven seconds of "American Pie"—but found a direct flight. In two days. For five hundred seventy-five dollars.

Her gut dropped like it had with morning sickness.

"Excuse me." She turned away. The charge would kill Cal and Rhee financially. He'd already be upset about the car, but she'd planned to send him a note of where she parked it. He could keep her last diner paycheck, but all she had was one good tipper's chunk of cash.

Plus, she couldn't wait two days. In that time, she'd fall into Cal's strong arms and beg forgiveness for her rash decision. Frazzled, her muscles aching like at her mother's wake, she lost her adrenaline and collapsed in a waiting area to catch her breath. Ten minutes later, she trudged to a phone booth and dialed collect.

"Michael, it's me."

"Sis? It's like five a.m. here."

"Oh, right. Sorry. Tired. How are you?"

"Fine. Da's doing better each day. Has his moments, but docs say he's improving. Liam's seeing a new doctor. Um, is everything all right there?"

Her heart felt so heavy that her voice came out weak. "Thinking about...coming home?"

She could hear Michael's famous loud yawn. "Soon?"

"But it costs a lot—"

"Not like we got it, sis! Hey, ye may be safer there anyway. Dubliners may be hit next in a takeover. Two men just been killed by the British army up north, in Londonderry. Troops opened fire on a crowd with rubber bullets and gas. They were innocents...telling ya, we're next."

Her insides twisted, but she wasn't sure if she was feeling doubt, homesickness, or a sickening disgust for what she'd just done.

"Call back later when we get up? We'll pass the phone around."

"Sorry to wake you. Maybe I just need sleep, too." She hadn't slept one full night since April. That was what she craved most. Just one uninterrupted eight-hour sleep, and she'd see more clearly about how to get a ticket home. She was so spent she wasn't sure what date it was, nor could she string together a coherent sentence. Couldn't. Even.

She hung up and walked into the rain, her faded flip-flops wading in puddles. She must've dragged her heavy suitcase and backpack a mile searching for the Mustang, and her shoulders throbbed. When she finally found it ten aisles away, she was drenched. She shook her body and climbed into the cramped back seat, drying off with Mrs. H's huge baby quilt. But when she closed her eyes, heartache shot through her, and her breasts swelled.

She could feel Rhee tug at her hair, wrapping her little fingers around a long strand. She could see her gummy smile, hear her squeak and coo and laugh when she blew raspberries on her soft tummy. What was wrong with her?

Ma, not only did I fail at being a saint like you, but I crashed and burned at motherhood—and I'll never have college and a career either. Your hopeless daughter is a failed feminist who misses her baby.

Sleep came after the sobs. A decent rest, even, and she awoke to roaring planes at sunrise. When she climbed out of the car to stretch, she saw vans, taxis, and shuttles drop off briefcase-toting men in suits. Families with strollers unloaded, and couples kissed in passionate embraces. People with purpose walked toward destinations, living out their dreams. She slid back in and turned the ignition. Cat Stevens' "Wild World" blared. Her depression even lifted a bit.

"Mr. Stevens, ye get it." She took a deep breath. No matter how stupid she was to leave her loves while she figured it out, maybe the idea for time and space *was* worth a shot. And if she didn't have the money for the trip home, and her family didn't expect her yet, and if she could extend her visa, could this be a chance to try again?

Cal was good for Rhee. He was a great father, patient and loving, but she was a restless young woman with stars in her eyes and a dash of wanderlust, still wanting an education and career. Now was the last chance to find out what she could do, what she wanted, what Ma never got, like her plan before it went to pot. Was it okay to pick her own dreams first?

No. She'd be tarred and feathered in the church. Da and Auntie would disown her. But what if someday *soon* she could send loads of money back to the two families on Battle Drive and Clare Street? How good would that feel? She'd be a breadwinner. All she needed was time to figure it out, learn how to do it all. She didn't have to abandon herself yet for changing nappies and round-the-clock feedings, and never sleeping again. Men never did. Wasn't this women's liberation?

Oh, but my precious lovie Rhee. Pain shot through her heart. *Cal, don't forget, she likes Goodnight Moon.*

She swallowed hard. Wiping the humidity from her brow, Nainsi drove out of the airport lot, squinting at the glare. Helen Reddy's voice filled her ears with "I Am Woman." "Sing it, sister," she said, rummaging through the glove compartment and pulling out Cal's mom's sunglasses. She'd definitely need to mail these back to him. She took a deep breath.

It was all her call. She wasn't owned as a girlfriend or fiancée, ineffective mother, sub-par daughter, absent sister anymore. She could choose life on her own terms. For now, anyway.

Ma, am I making a terrible mistake?

12

"She's Gone"

Cal, August 7, 1971

Instead of playing the usual "Here Comes the Sun" in the morning, Cal played "One Less Bell to Answer" as he fed Rhiannon a bottle of formula. After half a bottle last night—his, not Rhiannon's—his head pounded. He can't remember what they told him last night when he called JFK airport parking asking them to search for his car, but it involved laughter. Theirs.

"Your mommy is a different breed from your grandma, who would've never pulled a stunt like this," he said. "Why *did* she throw us away?"

He burped her, placed her in the playpen, and made coffee. He gulped it down with aspirin and circled yesterday's newspaper want ads. Without a babysitter, he'd lost his full-time construction job. The band's demise hurt too. With absolutely no cash, he filed for unemployment. Planned a garage sale. The dark cloud of grief returned and pulled up a chair.

The kitchen radio announced Paul McCartney's forming of Wings and how George Harrison's Concert for Bangladesh in New York City rocked, and Rhee gurgled.

"You remember dancing to 'Long and Winding Road' with us huh?" His last slow dance tiptoed through his mind as he stepped onto the stoop and picked up the newspaper. Then, his stomach dropped. **"LOCAL MAN KILLED IN PLANE CRASH UPON DESCENT IN VIETNAM,"** the headline read.

> Terry Blenkovich, 19, of Manassas, was killed upon arrival
> in Saigon, when the plane...

What? Cal reread as his stomach tumbled. His friend, roommate, bandmate Terry—who'd just enlisted, who'd just given Rhiannon a parting gift of Raggedy Ann—*dead*? After basic training, he'd left for Vietnam. He hadn't even survived the plane ride.

"No!" He threw the newspaper at the wall, and inserts scattered. "No!"

Rhiannon jarred and he leaned down to the playpen and gave her a pacifier. As he paced, wanting to call Troy but not having a number, she fussed again and lifted her arms, and Cal picked her up and pulled her close.

"You would've called him your Uncle Terry," Cal said, strapping her in a bouncy chair. Out of the corner of his eye he saw his own bottle, still on the counter from last night. "Daddy definitely needs some juice today," he said and sucked down a shot.

She kicked and waved her arms and spit her binky out of her mouth.

"You still hungry, baby girl?"

The Saturday mail flew in through the door slot. On top, a postcard carried the USAF logo, a message jotted from high school classmate Lou DiPitro. *Sorry about your mom. Here's my address at Da Nang Air Base. Write.*

"Good luck buddy," he said with an exhale and a prayer.

He dumped canned green beans into the blender to puree. He wasn't sure what Mrs. H or Nainsi's Dr. Spock book—or even *Marcus Welby, MD* on TV—advised about solid food for baby, but she seemed hungry for something more than her bottle half the time. He'd tried instant potatoes and oatmeal, thanks to a church's food pantry a couple days ago. He hit the button for the blender, and Rhiannon startled at the sound.

"How could Terry be dead already?" he said, dumping the mush into a bowl and feeding her a spoonful. She turned her head. He tried the choo-choo trick with the runny beans. Another spoonful made her spray the concoction in a six-foot radius.

"Judas," he muttered. Mama had told him as a kid never use God's name in vain, and instead to use the traitor's name, which he still did. "I know. The world sucks, baby girl. But eat anyway, you'll need your energy."

He gave her a bottle of juice instead and sifted through the bills looking for his first unemployment check. He stopped and froze at the last envelope. His blood turned cold.

Selective Service System.

No! Yep. He'd gotten sauced watching the lottery on TV the other night when his draft number was called, ninety-five. Year of birth, 1952. This meant he could get drafted anytime. He broke into a cold sweat then, pacing drunk. By two in the morning, he was peering into his old man's liquor cabinet for more. There wasn't enough numbing in all the world. "Not old enough to have a shot, but old enough to be shot," he said as he drank two more shots of vodka and downed two of Mama's painkillers. His last thought before crashing was, *if the war is winding down, won't it take a while to find me?*

But now the letter found my sorry self. Maybe he wasn't supposed to live at all.

He opened the letter.

You are hereby directed to present yourself for Armed Forces Physical Examination and report to the Federal Building.

"Like hell I am! Terry died fresh out of basic, assholes."

He thought of deferments, but he wasn't a student or disabled, and marriage and family deferment were things of the past. In the mid-sixties, couples married and conceived in droves before the deferment expired by LBJ's executive order.

No more. They needed bodies. The category of fathers was up to the local draft board, desperate for young, able-bodied men. He could only imagine men like Old Man Potter, from the movie he and Nainsi loved, *A Wonderful Life*, as head of the draft board, stamping "denied" on his form.

Cal scanned the fine print for single dad information. None. Of course, he'd plead for deference, but without the connections of "Fortunate Sons," it was up to the benevolence of a bureaucrat, and bodies were the game. Construction work kept him in good shape, so it was unlikely he'd fail the physical exam. Should he shoot himself in the foot like Greg Allman? Cal only had a nail gun.

Rhiannon rubbed puree over her face. "I was orphaned at eighteen years, but you're eighteen *weeks!*"

She stared at him.

"Your mommy said not to find her, but these are extenuating circumstances." Cal wiped her face, picked up the phone, dialed 0, and asked for a Dublin, Ireland, operator. Once connected, he asked for a phone number to the Murphys.

The laughter was snide. "I have eighty-nine, sir."

"It's an emergency. Please."

The operator sighed, then fast and furiously, gave him the numbers, men's names as head of the households. His hand throbbed writing them down. The calls would spiral up his phone bill, but what did it matter? He'd be dead before the bill arrived.

Ten calls later, he did a shot. Another ten calls, another shot. Busy tones. Hang-ups. One lady yelled, "Creeper, don't call here again!" He popped a painkiller of Mama's and tried to brainstorm, but his brain would not storm.

"We could make a run for it like Troy," he told Rhee. "Bet Montreal is nice. I could get us to *la salle de bain* or *boulangerie* with my high school French." When she gurgled, he said, "Okay, Niagara Falls, Ontario, then? Your granddad once said someday we'd take a vacation there and ride the Maid of the Mist, see the waterfalls lit up at night. I studied all the province capitals and collected Canadian quarters. Someday never came."

He thought of his father, a man who jumped out of planes in Normandy, freeing the world being his noble legacy, yet he never spoke of fighting the axis of evil. His father's only advice on war came after Cal turned ten in 1962, after President Kennedy gave a State of the Union address. His dad said Viet Cong had attacked South Vietnamese troops, who'd asked for more military aid from the Administration. American helicopter units were helping their troops prevent a communist takeover.

His father had lit a cigarette, tossed ice into his drink and said, "Son, the Leonardowskis are good men of responsibility. That means when your country calls you to duty, you go. Even if you must down a bottle of whiskey beforehand, you serve, young man, to save the next man. If you don't go, someone else takes your place. The crybabies who run and hide, who don't help their fellow man because they care only about their damn selves, are weak. A brave, honorable, patriotic man takes care of God and country and serves others."

When Mama put Cal to bed later, she said how brave Daddy had helped liberate a concentration camp. *Daddy saved people!*

Cal's childhood was destroyed not long after that. Right at this very table. The memory washes over him quickly, and he can't stop it. It's like he's there again.

Cal was ten. He'd walked in from playing outside and saw his father, wearing a work shirt with Battlefield Auto Body Manager nametag, slumped over at the table. Sometimes his dad went out with his coworkers for "a shot and a beer," but today, Mama, sporting a royal blue apron, fixing meat loaf, baked potato, and yucky green bean casserole, spoke with a raised voice that got higher, shriller. With no response, she slapped Daddy across the cheek, a red welt emblazoned on his face.

"Dammit, Harry, wake up! For the love of God!"

His old man didn't flinch.

Cal's eyes widened, and he froze.

His mother wiped Daddy's forehead with ice. "For Pete's sake, you're a D-Day hero who braved machinegun strafing from the Germans, who saw your buddies blown to smithereens, who survived unimaginable violence, and you're passed out now?"

His belly did not rise or fall.

"Don't cry, Mama. He'll wake up," Cal said when he ran to hug her.

She squeezed him tight. "Of course, he will, my sweet boy. He needs some help, though. I'm going down the street to that neighbor in the green house. His Oldsmobile's there. Eye doctors go to medical school, don't they? They must. I can't move your father, so I'll ask him to help us. Why don't you hold your dad's hand and tell him I'll be right back? Be a brave boy. Can you do that?"

He promised, and whispered to Daddy it would be okay, as Mama raced outside. A spring breeze whistled through the kitchen window.

"Crying" by Roy Orbison played on the kitchen radio. He turned the knob full blast to wake Daddy. He won't cry. He knelt next to him, clutching his leg, praying all he knew, "Our Father."

Dr. Samuel, who'd just pronounced Cal with 20/20 vision last summer, rushed in with Mama. He peered into Daddy's eyes with a flashlight and checked his pulse. The two of them—Dr. Samuel looking the grimmest—loaded him into his Olds, and they raced to the hospital where another doctor spoke to them. He told of his "cardiac arrest" matter-of-factly. "He's gone," he said, like he'd been traded from the Senators to the Orioles.

There was silence all the way home until Mama said, "Your father was a brave man, and you're a brave boy. You've helped so much today."

Cal snapped out of the memory when Rhee cooed. "My old man was a hero, and I never told him that. I was a kid when he died. What if we let had Hitler rule the world? The world's a better place because of your grandfather and his generation."

Terry was brave enough to serve. Lou DiPitro serves. Am I brave?

Cal looked out the window. Mrs. Henderson's flag flapped in the wind next to the "For Rent" sign. His eyes traveled to a newspaper clipping still on the refrigerator. Cal had written a seventh grade essay, and Mama had sent it to the letters to the editor.

> The flag heralds the US as a free people, east and west, north and south, black and white. Freedom isn't free. It comes with sacrifice. Like my dad's. Here in Manassas, the monuments and cemeteries are reminders of the brutal Civil War, but what if the Union Army had never fought to save enslaved people?

Cal said, "Could I save people, Rhee? The draft dodgers—yes, Troy—and those whose privilege fixed it, let others go to war in their places. Which one am I?"

Be a brave boy for Mama, would you, my sweet boy?

"And your brave grandma showed courage, too, battling grief, raising me alone, fighting cancer. Wish she was here now. How she would've loved you."

Perspiration trickled down Cal's forehead. He could honor both of his parents by being brave. He never got to tell them, but the chance to show them, to save people, held meaning now. But this chance to be somebody meant he'd die doing so. Images of Dan Rather's reporting by the body bags haunted him. Everyone he'd loved had left him. The universe had readied him to die.

Serving would be his last chance to make Mama and Daddy proud. They never got to see him as a man. *That's our brave boy serving,* they'd nod. A scrappy fighter born on a battlefield would die on a faraway battlefield. Better to be killed this way, fighting to save others' lives under the blazing sun.

Rhee babbled, and her darling look turned his insides to mush.

"But I can't orphan you like I was." He had no one as a young man. *She'll have no one as a toddler, girl, teen.* This precious girl deserved permanency, stability, safety. Someone with regular paychecks, a house, home-cooked meals, siblings, and cousins. A family she wouldn't lose.

His dad's voice echoed. *Even if you need whiskey to answer the call, you serve.*

The shots and painkiller had helped settle his nerves, but a day this devastating called for a drastic solution—the old man's bottle of single-malt whiskey? Not every day a guy both lost a friend in war and got called up. That 1960s bottle on the top shelf held his name. It might taste like moonshine rotgut, but it'd clear his mind.

He left his fingerprints on the dusty bottle when he poured a glass of what looked like watery-brown Tang. He slugged it back, and it burned down to his gut.

He gagged—and poured more. Soon thinking grew muddled, but peace descended like pot at Atlanta. He called more Murphys of County

Dublin. No luck. He bargained. If he called the rest without success, he'd let it be. Nainsi made that much clear, asking for time and space to think. Please. As if he didn't need it.

Hours later, as Rhee napped in the playpen, after another 7 & 7, he made his last call which rang twenty-five times.

He had a solution, now he just needed to act on it. Prayers to candles for miracles failed. But what if Rhee never knew of him? He was going to die, but a baby wouldn't feel the searing loss like he did as a teenager.

He paged through the phone book until C, Catholic Church. Even found an Irish one, St. Ronan's, about forty-five minutes northwest. A nod to Rhee's mom, perhaps born of guilt, because in his furor, he'd torn up Nainsi's Yeats book and Kodachromes of their life together, and Rhee wouldn't even have a trace of her. She would've wanted Rhee raised Catholic, even if she didn't go to mass or confession anymore, he supposed. The church was a trek, almost to Maryland, but it ensured he'd be anonymous. He checked today's mass times. Saturday at five, six thirty. He could do right by their child. No one was going to say no to a beautiful baby there. He prayed for a sign.

Notepaper by the phone caught his eye. Mrs. H had once left a first name and number of an old church friend, for babysitting, if they were desperate. They'd ruled it out, as she lived a distance south of Washington, but maybe she'd know a good family. He shakily dialed the number and stammered about St. Ronan's.

Her animated voice contrasted with his weariness. "Why, St. Ronan must be paging me. I won his prayer card at Bingo two weeks ago! However, I don't understand. How can I help you? You sound distressed. One moment." She turned off the blare of the *Lawrence Welk Show*. "I suppose I could travel to mass there today. It's far. Heavens to Betsy, not even in my diocese. But far be it for me to turn down St. Ronan! Perhaps it's the reason I snagged a mighty fine deal on green beans today! I suppose I could take them to their food pantry..."

"It's a sign. I just gave her green beans," he said.

She chatted for ten more minutes—it involved a comparison of every store's prices on beans—and he hung up. She sounded loopy, but who was he to speak? He was soused.

"This lady's heart oozes service. She'll find a nice big Irish family to care for you. But I can't tell her my name. You can't know of me. The loss won't hurt that way. Better me hurt now than you. Because I ain't never coming back alive."

He kissed Rhee's forehead and crammed her diaper bag with outfits, bottles, diapers, and threw in a guitar pick as a good luck charm. He changed her from her spit-up-and-bean-stained outfit to her soft blue butterfly sleeper and laid her on his bed. Her crystal-blue eyes twinkled.

He swallowed hard and reminded himself nothing lasted forever. Even this horrid feeling would leave. He learned as much from his old man, Mama, and Nainsi. "You won't be alone," he said. "You'll have a family."

His mind shifted to practicalities. He'd sell everything in the house and send the money anonymously to the family, care of that church. But for now, he needed cash.

Rhee moved her arms and kicked on the bed.

He grabbed his guitar and strummed. He sang "Long and Winding Road" and "Sweet Baby James" and "Our House." Her eyes widened from the first chord, and she quieted.

His heart throbbing, stomach clenching, and throat swelling, Cal kissed his daughter's head on the soft spot, and then he said goodbye to the guitar face too.

What the hell was he doing?

No, he must sever ties immediately, like a doctor who tells a kid their father is gone. Rhee wouldn't know he existed.

Tears clouded Cal's eyes as he buckled her into her baby seat in Daddy's old Cutlass Supreme. He drove on a wing and a prayer—swerving twice, straddling a curb thrice—to a pawnshop on Route 234. Earning two twenties for the guitar, plus a twenty for the albums, he stashed the cash in the diaper bag.

The smell of a fast-food burger joint beckoned. He devoured a meal, which helped his dizziness, and fed her a bottle along with her first spoonful of a chocolate shake. She loved that, smacking her lips and taking more, and she was one happy baby. He shook his head as they got back into the car, and he went north on a thoroughfare a good way until he spotted the church across from a pub.

The lump in his throat returned when he turned up the song on the radio.

"Don't Worry Baby..."

13

"Hey Nineteen"

Nainsi, August 7, 1971

Nainsi walked into the admissions department of university, picking lint off her stupid housekeeper uniform with its' sewed-on apron. "I'm here for my appointment."

The student-typist glanced at Nainsi's uniform with a snide look and straightened her shoulders. "Just a minute."

The wall clock behind her showed twenty-five minutes left on her lunch hour from The Groove Inn Motel & Groove-y Lounge. Nainsi had walked into the ramshackle motel when she'd spotted the neon "Help Wanted" sign mega miles off-off-Sunset Boulevard.

As a room air conditioner blew on a fake fern, the owner Ricky had stood at the orange laminate desk and informed her the job was housekeeper and other duties as assigned. "We're a sought-out vacation location," he said as he stared at her legs. He claimed high standards—no rentals by the hour, pool at your own risk, nightstands stacked with a Bible and phone book. "Minimum wage went up to a buck sixty an hour in February, that's all I can do, sweetheart. Plus tips," he said, counting cash. She must've looked ambivalent, because he offered free boarding if she could be "on call." He threw in a parking space for "that hot Mustang from your sugar daddy."

A month in, alleged tips for cleaning customers' gross messes never materialized. Six days a week, Nainsi donned gloves and stripped sheets from beds and stuffed them into washers. She swished toilets with blue cleaners and sprayed diluted fluid around baths and sinks. She emptied ashtrays and trash with syringes, maxi pads, and other biohazards. She cleaned windows with views of six plastic lawn chairs around the tiny pool in the parking lot and the liquor store with bars on the windows. A billboard high over gas pumps across the street changed often, which proved to be her only Hollywood entertainment. Unless she could count when a mouse ran over her feet and Ricky handed her a trap. "When ya see the dead bastard, throw him out."

Yet, like when Ma died, keeping busy aided the new horrific hole in her heart.

After all, the magnitude of walking away from Cal and Rhee had proved too much to bear on the three-day trip here. She'd only fitfully slept in the car at rest stops, and mostly wept constantly as she drove long stretches. Somewhere passing corn fields in the hinterlands, if she wanted to emotionally survive, she buried the memory. It simply hurt too much. She wouldn't call either, because she'd feel tempted to run back, and it was too soon; she'd give up her dreams forever. Her one chance was now or never.

Yet each day in her new crappy life, a different, quiet grief plagued Nainsi. A fierce longing shot through her, an aching so great she feared she was having a heart attack. It sprouted up at odd times. Her bedroom view of the pool— "Can you lifeguard, sweetheart? And clean it, too?"—made her picture Rhee in the cute baby sunhat she'd found at a garage sale. A sign for Disneyland reminded her of the trip Cal and she wanted with their girl someday. At a drugstore, she remembered how a pink antibiotic cured Rhee's first earache. Even an ad for new disposable diapers blew her mind.

A sharp-dressed man snuffed out a cigarette in the ashtray on the receptionist's desk. "Nainsi Murphy? Come with me."

"Thank ye for seeing me," she said as they walked back to his office. The space was not much bigger than the supply closet at work, only lined with mahogany bookshelves she could scan all day. Her eyes dropped to the framed picture of a toddler behind him, and she felt her heart squeeze.

"You're from Dublin? Wonderful city. Been to a conference at Trinity College, saw the Book of Kells. Amazing, eh? So, what are you interested in here?"

"Do you have a degree in music entertainment, like promotions, management, or journalism?"

"You're the next Ben Fong Torres at Rolling Stone?"

"Loved his profile on Ike and Tina Turner."

He handed her pamphlets and highlighted a chart for full tuition, room, and board. "We have outstanding classes here."

Nainsi's eyes widened. "Does that say—twelve hundred dollars?"

"Oh, well, not the first year—"

"Phew."

"Because there's also the registration fee of three hundred dollars, and an educational fee of a hundred fifty a year. You're looking at sixteen hundred plus."

She inhaled sharply. "It's not free here in California?"

He chuckled, sat back, and steepled his hands. "You're a nonresident, an international student, correct?"

Her stomach sank as he explained costs, residency, requirements, state funding, and name-dropped prominent alumni. She couldn't swing the cost by cleaning rooms.

Out the open window, a guy on the quad threw a Frisbee as "Riders On the Storm" blared. She thought of Cal and their meeting after his "Frisbee accident." She half-smiled until her throat closed.

A terrible idea popped up and the thought plunged her to a new low. Still, she said, "Would twenty-five hundred cover almost two years of tuition, room, and board, and I could start this term?"

"More or less," he said.

"Can I call you tomorrow?"

***

After work, she dashed to the motel parking lot, planning to drive the Mustang to a car dealer to see what they'd offer on this mint condition vehicle with an 8-track deck. She bet he missed the car bad, but Cal once said if they were dead broke— as in, an emergency—the car would fetch $2500. If she could sell it to fund her education, why, she'd be closer to making solid career paychecks, and sending good, breadwinning money for Rhee. Would Cal forgive her for this then?

But Nainsi scoured that little lot forever. She checked outside every room, even though she knew she parked it close to the pool, right near the cracked concrete where everyone tripped.

The Mustang was gone.

14

"American Pie"

Cal, August 7, 1971

He'd been the only guy at Finnegan's nursing a whiskey and rye—while bouncing a baby. After the last nip of numbness, he slung a packed diaper bag over his shoulder and staggered across the street, holding his fifteen-pound baby in her blue-flowered romper.

He stopped for a breather, picking up her Raggedy Ann doll, swaying, staring at the gigantic brick building with elaborate stained-glass windows. "St. Ronan must've been something."

She gazed up at him with her baby blues and gurgled. Good churchgoers booked out of five o'clock mass, bolting to the parking lot.

He gathered composure on the steps, tucking in his t-shirt, as a scowling woman sniffed. "Eau de Jameson," he muttered.

Rhee pulled at a fistful of his medium-length, scraggly hair—finally like Morrison's—which would be shaved soon enough. He climbed the brick stairs against the crowd scurrying out. Another lady frowned, likely at his dishevelment, his T-shirt soaked with perspiration and baby drool.

When they entered through the double glass doors, a wave of incense greeted them. Rhee sneezed and he wiped her nose with his shirt as he approached the font, scooping the holy water and sprinkling her forehead. "You're either just baptized or been cooled off."

Cal slid into the back pew and knelt as he cradled her. "Forgive me," Cal prayed to whoever. God. Rhee. Nainsi. His parents.

"How about a song?" he said as she snuggled against his heartbeat and baritone's vibrations. Dozing, his beautiful baby looked peaceful as he stroked her gentle cheek.

He took a breath, stood, and swayed, heading out the doors to the grand steps. He pictured brides and grooms dashing out here, dodging rice. Nainsi never gave him the chance. "You deserve better than us," he said as he faced the four-lane street, the cars pouring out of the lot. Was the lady coming?

Rhee awoke from a five-minute nap, sucking her fingers. His entire body trembled as he patted her back. He'd lost control of his very *limbs!*

An older, matronly lady shuffled out of a Pinto that she double-parked. With a slight limp, she scurried toward the church hall with a grocery bag. The woman, early sixties, with a short, salt and pepper-colored curly perm, looked dowdy in a long frock, a navy cotton dress. She wore round bifocals like John Denver's and her stance held the capable, authoritative air his school lunch lady held. He could still hear it: *Scoop, slop, 'Move along, son.'*

Cal noticed the woman's bag overflowed with green beans. *Her?* The woman had talked his ears off about making bean soup, comparing prices of green beans, lima beans, kidney beans, navy beans. "Gertrude?"

She turned without a recoil at his alcohol stink, though her chestnut eyes narrowed, and she gently touched Rhee. "Yes, I'm Gert. Are you the young man who telephoned me? I investigated it for you, and they're having a parish dinner tonight, not that I can stay, but you and your baby can. I could introduce you to people right now. The sisters will feed you both in a heartbeat and direct you to any—help—you may need. Stay for apple pie. An apple a day keeps dentists at bay!"

Rhee was chowing down on her fist. Parents rushed past, reprimanding kids for dallying. Car doors slammed. A van honked at a back-up in the jammed lot.

"My, she looks hungry. Or is she teething? Do you know what's good for teething, my friend used to say? Whiskey on those gums."

"For her or me?" He smiled. "Can I carry that bag for you, and you can hold her?"

"I have it, sir. Thank you, though." A horn beeped at her car blocking a lane, and she yelled, "For Saint Pete's sake, go around! My flashers are on! Mercy! So, you folks go here?"

Shaking his head, he noticed the jewelry pinned at her collar. "Is that a medal from the armed services?"

"Goodness, few notice this." She shared about the distinguished service cross for her husband, killed at the Battle of the Bulge in World War II. She'd taken it to a jeweler, who made it into a brooch. "Bertram was brave," she said, her eyes moving to the clouds.

Brave, just like my old man in World War II.

It was his sign, really. She was a brave widow like Mama, someone who loved and lost—and still got up the next day. A strong, loving woman must be able to find a strong, loving family for his precious girl, wouldn't she?

Cal's throat tightened. "Sorry for your loss, ma'am. He's a hero."

Rip off the bandage—the quicker, the better. Like when they lowered Mama into her burial spot next to Daddy, Cal left fast. When he didn't have anyone at his graduation, he bolted afterwards. When Nainsi split, he moved on. No babbling, questioning, or prolonging agony.

Cal took a breath. "So..." He shifted his weight and shook his head. *He cannot do this. No, no, he can't.*

Rhee smiled at him.

Stop that cuteness, Rhee!

She waved her arms.

You're so adorable, baby girl.

"So, uh…" He looked away, his heart sinking to his stomach. Then, ever so slowly, Cal placed the sweetest love of his life into the lady's flabby arms, stringing the diaper bag on her shoulder. "Take her, please." He stroked Rhee's soft skin on her cheek—she dropped her green beans bag—and kissed Rhee atop her strawberry strands. "Name's Rhiannon—we call her Rhee. Born April fifteenth, almost four months old, smiling now. Well, sometimes. Starting to teethe. Curious. And she just rolled over for the first time. Loves the guitar. Even before she was born. Maybe because—well, whatever. Tell her we love her so much. That we're sorry." He paused a few more beats. "On second thought, don't, it's best she knows nothing of us. Don't tell her we blew raspberries on her face and she giggled. She won't feel loss if she doesn't know, you know?"

"Sir?"

His eyes cast down. "It's just…" He stepped back. "Ain't never coming back alive."

"Afraid I don't understand? Why, hello there, Rhee."

This woman had to be a grandma. This sturdy, salt-of-the earth type, who could probably whip up eggs for twenty in five minutes flat, scrunched her forehead, a deep wrinkle crinkling between her eyes. "Sir, you needed babysitting, right? Can you grant me a few minutes to get you help? Come in—"

But Cal turned, his stomach somersaulting, lungs squeezing shut, and slunk away.

"Sir! We'll get you help in a jiffy!"

He shouldn't have glanced back. They made eye contact. Rhee began to scream.

It'll be okay, baby girl.

But he wasn't so sure. Her look of despair gutted him; her cries at her daddy walking away cut him deep inside his heart. She wailed with her arms out and writhed to escape the lady's hold.

"But I don't have a soul in this world for you, angel," he said softly. *Hold on for now, baby girl. She's your life jacket. She'll look for a good family!*

"When will you be back, sir? An hour or two?" she shouted above Rhee's cries. "Aw, there, there, your daddy will be right back. Sir! I'm due to help with Bingo at my parish tonight, over an hour away!"

Tears welled in Cal's eyes and the lump stayed lodged in his throat. He wouldn't turn back to face her again. It'd kill him. He'll die anyway, but she'll live.

Halfway down the road, he stumbled on a sidewalk crack and broke his fall with his hands and blood filled the scrapes. As he sat on the cement to let the dizziness pass, he saw four lanes of cars come to a screeching halt for geese waddling across the busy road. He looked up at an intense pink six o'clock sky. Mama used to say, "Pink sky at night, sailor's delight." Now the fair skies offered no beauty, only the promise of a dark tomorrow.

Sweat poured from his skin, the mugginess—or this cockamamie idea—drenching his T-shirt. Heaviness perched on his gut.

Forgot to tell the lady she likes "Sweet Baby James."

Cal's insides churned, plunging to new lows. He gagged with the aftertaste of the whiskey, and of the chocolate shake he'd just let Rhee try, and the greasy burger he'd shoved in his mouth.

Cal Leonardowski felt deserving of whatever lay ahead, every bullet fired at him, every land mine exploding, every enemy torturing his shell of a being. He'd learned one thing. Nothing lasted forever. Love splits. Life gives you only a couple people—and then robs you of them. Daddy, Mama, and Nainsi had left. Now it was he who abandoned someone who needed him, but it didn't feel any easier. Thank God she was too young for this memory. She'd be spared grief. She could go to safety and life as he went to peril and death. He only prayed this widow would find her a nice home with a big, boisterous family, so that she'd never be alone, even if she wanted to be.

Please, God, get her to a good family. Put St. Ronan on the case. If only I knew who he was.

"For a better life, Rhee. It's all for you." His lungs tightened, perhaps hyperventilating. He longed for a breeze, a forgiving "Summer Wind" like his middle namesake Frank crooned. Only Sinatra could bellow this ache. How long he sat on the sidewalk in the stifling air was any fine churchgoer's guess. At some point, he heard the new Marvin Gaye song, "What's Going On," in his head. The melody felt like a salve to the burn.

Can't answer your question, Marvin. Can't answer anyone. If only someone was asking.

Part II: "Who Are You?"

15

"Fire and Rain"

Nainsi, February 2, 1972

Despite what her mother once told her, Nainsi wasn't a rock after all. Did a rock get called "a hot mess" by a leering boss rock? "Whatever, Ricky," she said as he walked away. Her miserable cleaning job was clearly penance for leaving, borrowing Cal's beloved car, considering selling it, *and* getting it stolen. Served her right.

"Happy twentieth birthday to me." She grabbed a stale pretzel rod and sipped a flat soda in the empty lounge that held six tables, bar, and a fridge behind the counter. A plug-in blinking sign and posters of scantily clad women decorated the fake, paper-thin wood panels, underneath windows looking at a gas station across the street. Their trash overflowed. Bars covered their windows. Under a sign advertising malt liquor, teenagers smoked by a gas pump.

Earlier, memories had bombarded her of Ma's chocolate cake and Cal's mix tape he made for her last birthday. She'd longed to hear Rhee say "Ma-ma," though undoubtedly her first word would be "Da-da." Where were they living? The box of his mother's sunglasses and tapes she'd mailed was returned months ago, unopened, marked "Return to Sender." Of course, she had no right to a forwarding address. The gnawing feeling bubbled up. Walking away from her loves to try life on her own terms, to start a career for what she wanted, was wrong. She'd finish a few more months here just to send money to them.

"Flames erupted at the British Embassy in Merrion Square in Dublin, Ireland, tonight, amid massive crowds protesting Bloody Sunday in Northern Ireland," said a newscaster from the TV on the bar. She gasped at the fire footage. Three days ago, there'd been a civil rights march in Derry, Londonderry, North Ireland, protesting British rule, turning violent. The British Army responded to peaceful marchers and taunts of rocks with rubber bullets, tear gas, water cannons, and unloaded a hundred rounds of military ammo. Twenty-eight unarmed civilians were shot and thirteen people killed, including a seventeen-year-old. When she called home, Da called it a massacre.

"Oh!" Nainsi dropped her glass, and it shattered.

A voice from a customer parked at a corner table stood up.

"I'm okay, just—" she said, grabbing a broom from a closet, "—me brothers were there, marching in the protest today. Hope they're all right. Looks like mayhem!" *They better not have taken little Liam! He could get trampled.* She said a silent prayer to Ma. *What was she doing here, working sixty to eighty hours a week, while applying to office jobs at record companies and studios on her lunch hour, enrolling in one class a semester?*

"Be careful, there," the man said, coming towards her and taking the broom and dustpan from her hands. Tall, and broad shoulders like Cal, with short, neatly combed, auburn hair, dark eyes and a dark five o'clock shadow, the cute guy swept up the shards and emptied the pan into the trash, then slid into a bar seat near her. "So you're from Ireland too?"

Her mouth dropped open. "County Dublin. Nainsi."

"*Dia dhuit.* Killian O'Brien. I have family and customers in County Limerick, though I've lived here for twenty of my thirty years."

"Wow," she said. "Then you get my worry." She turned back to the TV, her ears affixed to the dizzying talk of British and Irish governments,

Catholics and Protestants, IRA and Ulster factions, and days of protests throughout Northern Ireland and the Republic against Bloody Sunday, solidarity from Shannon to Waterford to Galway.

"Fire probably started with Molotov cocktails," he said. "IRA boys in that crowd."

They watched the report. All of Dublin seemed there. Coffins draped in black with "13" painted on them passed through the crowd. Gardai charged crowds with batons, pushing people back from the embassy, but it was futile. Petrol bombs were thrown, and by seven, the eighteenth-century Georgian building was engulfed and ablaze. The fire brigade couldn't get through the cheering crowd. Ireland's national day of mourning for Bloody Sunday had turned into fiery fury.

"Burn, baby, burn," said Killian, his hands in fists and voice lowered. "For the rage of the people." His eyes danced at the chaos. He seemed to revel in it, like he was cheering a football game.

Nainsi worried about her family. It'd be too late to call. The TV news now talked of the upcoming Olympics in Japan.

Killian touched her elbow. "Can I buy you a pint?"

"Oh, uh, no, can't." The handsome chap had the build of a firefighter, but her same rule applied. She wouldn't get distracted from her future for a second time. She'd never be swayed by good looks, kind conversation, and a sexy smile again, even if he's Irish too. "Bartender's only here Friday and Saturday nights. Ricky's too cheap. Our lounge says open, but it means 'the maid-slash-other-duties-as-assigned will fetch you a beer.' Plus, I can't accept on duty."

"When are you off duty?"

"Never. I live here."

"Is that legal to make you work all the time? Even today, practically a US holiday, Groundhog Day?"

She smiled. "Ha! And me birthday." Nainsi pointed to drug dealers and prostitutes loitering outside their chain-link fence, near the parking lot pool. "Does it look like Ricky's worried about me? Say, would you like a pint?" She scrounged for a can of beer for him and gave him one.

He lifted it. "*Slainte*. To your birthday...and Ireland."

"To peace everywhere," she said. As he sipped his beer, she told him he was the second Irishman she'd met in LA in six months. When she filled out a grand larceny police report, the cop shook his head because she hadn't locked it. He'd asked pointed questions when she couldn't produce a deed, registration, or monthly payment book either. A priest in the precinct overheard her and said, "Irish? *An bhfuil tu ceart go leor?*" She answered yes, she was fine. He'd handed her a card on her way out: *Father McKenzie. Retired Priest & Police Chaplain. Free "Poems, Prayers and Promises."*

When she looked at it, she said, "Father McKenzie? Been wanting to meet you all my life. Loved the Beatles."

"Why do ye think I keep my name?" he said with a wink.

When she asked if he knew *Poems, Prayers, and Promises* was an album by John Denver, he'd laughed. "Perhaps he got the idea from me?" He explained how he gave people a poem, prayer or promise at each meeting. He'd gone to seminary across the pond but had worked here his career, most recently as a police chaplain. He warned her off certain streets for drugs, gangs, or recruiters for Moonies, People's Temple, Children of God, then invited her to visit anytime, a tiny chapel nestled in dilapidated buildings in the neighborhood behind the motel.

Killian cleared his throat. "Thank you for the beer, Miss Bartender Housekeeper Lifeguard Maid."

"At least not washing machine repairwoman. Yet."

"Paging Nainsi." On cue, her boss stood at the door and spoke into a play microphone a kid left behind, which now doubled as his microphone. "Would your big strong friend walk with you out to the lot—and walk around it twice—for security tonight?"

"If we had real security, the car wouldn't have been stolen, Ricky," she said.

Killian smiled as they talked more. He downed half the can, and then opened his wallet and left cash on the bar. After a brisk walk around, he waved goodbye. When she walked into the lounge to turn off the lights and deadbolt the doors, a cocktail napkin note caught her eye. *Your first tip. Happy birthday! Good luck—Killian.* A crisp fifty-dollar bill lay below.

Alone, she did a little jig, but then thought she shouldn't take pity money. Yet, it would sure help her empty bank account. She pocketed the lone gift on this lonely birthday.

When she lay down that night, her hair wet from the lukewarm shower, her mind was not on the cash or the good-looking customer. She could see only the blackened and crumbled building with flames shooting out, Dublin's umbrellas bobbing under sheets of rain, smoke and soot raining on the crowd as they passed a coffin around. She could only imagine Da's scars on his neck, where the shards just missed slicing his carotid, the cuts now pulsing with rage.

What had she complained about as a tired new mom watching the Supremes on the *Tonight Show*, begging Rhee to eat? She wasn't a young widow nor a grieving parent of the Troubles or the Vietnam War. She pounded the pillow. All she wanted was to pull Cal close. She wanted to whisper she needed him, that the world in 1972 was looking scarier instead of better, that there had been senseless shootings up North on Sunday and she watched the British Embassy burn down in retaliation, and she feared for her brothers in all that bedlam. She wanted to feel Cal's arms wrap around her, and hear him say it was all right now, babe...

She picked up the phone to call the operator. Maybe he bought a house with a yard for Rhee. He'd answer the phone with that hunky voice, say happy birthday, and she'd blurt it was all a huge mistake. She'd spit out how life gets ugly and bursts into flames, your world gets destroyed, changed in just one moment, right before your eyes. She wanted to squeeze their baby girl tight with these empty arms and kiss her soft little baby face again.

Mommy's still here, she'd tell her. *She's just lost between two countries' shores, stuck at the intersection of hope and despair.*

16

"War"

Cal, March 30, 1972

About twelve miles from Saigon, Cal wiped the sweat from his brow as he ate at the massive, sprawling Long Binh post. He was holding a cold soda can to his forehead with one hand and scarfing down ham and salami with the other when Pvt. Herb Lemows, eating a slimy-looking fish sandwich, reminded him of the Good Friday fast from meat.

"Nah, I'm Lutheran. I can eat meat," Cal said. "Or wait, I'm Methodist. Or maybe Episcopalian? We can eat whatever whenever. I think."

But the thought of Easter sent a dagger through Cal. *Rhee.* When wasn't he aching at what he did? He choked up last in the barracks picturing her getting an Easter basket—and smashing her little hands into a first birthday cake in two weeks. Cal barely survived her first Christmas. It was only thanks to a USO show with comedian Bob Hope that he stayed afloat. The rum and Cokes at the nightclub afterward helped.

He'd been here for over four months. With the US relying on air power, it left only 133,000 US servicemembers in South Vietnam to fight and train their army, the ARVN, against the communist North Vietnamese Army and Viet Cong.

Cal had wanted to save people, so he'd trained as a flight medic. After eight weeks of basic at Fort Dix, New Jersey, Cal took two more months of specialized training at Ft. Sam Houston, Texas. On Veteran's Day, 1971, he reported to the medical brigade, the US Army Health Services Group, Long Binh. He worked onboard a helicopter with two pilots and a crewman. They flew to the front lines to evacuate the wounded—soldiers trapped, pinned under mortar or small arms fire, bleeding from bullet holes or limbs blown off from grenades. Treating them on the way to the 91st or 43rd, Cal cleaned wounds, fashioned tourniquets, shot morphine. He still felt helpless.

He knew he wouldn't survive his tour. They'd dodged hails of gunfire, landmines, and harrowing descents into enemy jungles of heavy brush, carrying first-aid supplies, water, and body bags. Despite getting soldiers into the more capable care of outstanding nurses and docs at the evac hospitals, whenever he closed his eyes to sleep, he still heard the day's men yelling for help with bullets lodged in their guts. They evacuated all but couldn't save all. Cal figured if their luck was up, so was his. There's no earthly reason he was still here.

"I'm spent and it's still morning," Cal said with a gulp of cola. On high alert daily, junked up on caffeine and adrenalin, he replayed trauma at night. Yesterday, a soldier's gaping hole in his throat needed an emergency tracheotomy. The young man—in his pocket, a picture of his prom date—didn't survive the flight. Cal heaved upon landing—and thought of it all night. Last night, Cal also remembered what someone's skull looked like, because half his face had blown off. He bandaged his head, the blood soaking through the gauze in one second. The man grabbed Cal's hand and barely uttered, "Two are gathered, pray for me." Cal nodded, but his urgent prayer sounded measly. Worse was when he said, "Hang in there, man!" when he fell unconscious.

"Some Easter weekend," said Lemows.

Cal told him of a Catholic friend he'd made, an ARVN he'd met training two months ago at the landing zone, swapping stories. "My buddy, Giuse," Cal said, "his wife's due this weekend." At twenty-one, Giuse's wife was carrying twins; grandparents on full alert. Envy flashed over Cal, then anger for his situation. A family destroyed.

"Giuse is a saint name—Joseph," said Lemows. "But watch yourself with him, Leonardowski, you know some are spies for the NVA or setting up guerilla ops for the VC."

"Not him, he's cool." Giuse had earned Cal's trust by bartering. Every day, Giuse gave him a sixer of beer for his crew, in exchange for any MREs, CRAT pouch rations, or candy from the mess hall. The beer satisfied way more than the food. Cal grabbed two, passed three out to his crew members, and saved the last one for the next rescued soldier.

A siren blared and conversations in the mess hall ceased. The radio halted midway through Harry Nilsson's "Without You." They jumped up and ran to duty.

When they landed—by 1200 hours, 20,000 NVA troops had crossed the DMZ and forced South Vietnamese units into a retreat— and he wiped the dust from his eyes, he scanned the battlefield. Outnumbered, outgunned, caught in crossfire, soldiers lay moaning. "Hell on earth," Cal yelled as the stench of death and a rotten fish stink flooded over him. He turned one way, stepped in a pile of vomit and feces and blood, and retched. The Easter Offensive was an onslaught.

Cal and Pvt. Jeremy Sandoze raced to the groans of the first wounded soldier. He lay in the brush, throwing up blood, with a hand missing. Cal wrapped his arm in a tight tourniquet, and they pulled him onto a stretcher. By the time he ran back to help more men, the NVA advanced again and pinned them under gunfire. The crunch of shell cases under his boot, Cal gripped his .45 caliber 1911 semiautomatic pistol and fired back. An explosion sounded five hundred feet away. The ground shook and tossed them around. He sensed other men hid in trenches, and they crouched and zigzagged away from each other to look for them. Cal lost sight of him as he maneuvered around terrain of heavy clay, sinkholes, and planted punji sticks and sharpened bamboo shafts in holes, camouflaged in tall grass, to slice through soldiers' feet. When Cal darted another ten yards to help the next man, he wedged in the muck. With twenty pounds of equipment, he sank in the foot-high mud just as a burst of rapid gunfire erupted.

It's over, Rhee.

He froze for a minute. Or more. Did it matter?

Like I predicted, Rhee. You are better off now. I love you.

He closed his eyes, immobilized with incoming fear of capture, torture, an agonizing death. Yet what he heard now in the soundtrack of battle laid a more powerful cacophony of sound. His parents' voices on a Sunday drive singing "Come Fly with Me." The hushed graduation audience's pity claps. The bowling pin crashes at the Ex-Candles' first gig. Hendrix's live electric sound in Atlanta. The Mustang's ignition. Nainsi's blast of Van Morrison's "Into the Mystic." Rhee's sweet coo and laugh. *If he could just hold her again!*

In the blaze of a thousand suns, in quicksand like what he'd only seen on *Lost in Space,* he stood stuck for who knows how long. Like a hunkered statue—a literal stick in the mud—his gut clenched and his nerves raced, prepped for the shrapnel and bullets that would riddle him. *May this firing squad be quick like death row.*

But *kill or be killed* pierced through his head instead as a survival mantra. *Kill or be killed,* it spoke until fear morphed to fury, like it was rising through the Earth, coursing through his legs and arms, shooting straight up to his head. His blood now boiled with rage. No, he'd at least die fighting for every life cut short. For every love ripped from him. For every life he couldn't hold on to. He would shoot the bastards for killing his brothers in arms, fire for Terry's plane going down. Cal would go out thrashing, fighting back for the kid who died holding a prom picture with *Love, Ellen* written with a heart.

He used all his might to extract himself from the mud and reload. *Fuck this shit!*

How long he'd been shooting back was unknown when Sandoze grabbed him from behind and pulled him over to the helicopter. "We got everyone, they're onboard! Move it, go, go, go!" Men were crammed in, injured bodies jammed in every nook, and he was shoved on. In seconds they hovered and climbed higher into the unfriendly skies.

That was when he saw Giuse on the ground. His hands reached up. Alone.

"No! We've got to go back to save him, Sandoze!"

"The Arvin will get him. We're full!"

"His twins are due!"

"It's on the radio. They'll get 'em!"

"But—"

"*We're out, man! We're fucking full!*"

The helicopter jerked and whisked them away, the deafening echo pounding into his body. Muck and blood covering his fatigues, he trembled with the last image of his friend. *Why the hell wasn't it him instead?*

✳✳✳

After a copper-colored shower, sleep lasted two hours. He dreamt of Giuse, Nainsi, and Rhiannon, who floated above him, unreachable, as "Stairway to Heaven" played. Rhee was crying unconsolably. He awoke with a soaked pillow like when Daddy and Mama died. Like when Nainsi left. Like when he left Rhee.

"Write what you feel," Nainsi urged him after a gig once, as they lay in bed after making love, the radio playing Elton John's "Your Song." "Who knows, your thoughts, your song."

He took her into his arms and laughed. "Me? Can't even write a lullaby."

Cal tore down his in-country countdown calendar taped up in the barracks. He scribbled some words on the back, writing an apology to Giuse, then to his parents for not saving them, either. Maybe if he'd learned how to do CPR instead of holding his dad's hand, he wouldn't have died...or if he'd found a better doctor for his mom...or if he'd been a better man, he'd still have a family. But the mourning morphed into a heartfelt apology for his little girl. "You were stuck with us," he wrote, the throwaway line from their unfinished lullaby.

Was this a letter, journal, or poem? Didn't matter, because where would it go? Not one person cared about his ramblings. He stuck it in the pocket where he carried Mama's ring. Maybe when he actually died next time, Rhiannon could read this writing in war archives someday and realize this lousy piece of paper was for her. Then she'd know he was only trying to spare her pain, and give her a better life, a real family, instead. If nothing else, someone somewhere would know he lived and loved on this ugly Earth. Once.

17

"O-o-h Child"

April 15, 1972

Dear Cal,

Bought this yellow submarine toy and Big Bird birthday card for Rhee's first birthday, but don't know if it'll reach you two. Tried to return your mama's sunglasses and Beatles tape but they came back, "Return to Sender." Praying it was just a mail glitch before. I have something to tell you, too, once we are ready to talk again. I miss you both so much! My arms ache to hold her, kiss her rosy cheeks, and sing Happy Birthday with you. This is harder than I'd ever imagined. I'm a mess. How do I make this all right? Please give me a wee bit more time? Love, Nainsi.

18

"Do You Know Where You're Going To"

Cal, November 1972

When the jet full of troops cleared Saigon's airspace headed to Okinawa before Hawaii, and soldiers erupted with cheers and applause, Cal could only think, "Why am I here?"

Palpable elation pulsed through the cabin. Hearty laughter bounced around. Stewardesses poured bubbly and toasted to surviving a year in-country. Nixon had promised the end of the war and won re-election. The Long Binh base was being handed over to the Army of the Republic of Vietnam on November 11. Men passed around pictures of girlfriends, wives, kids. Lemows spoke of meeting his four-month-old, Jessica.

Same age as Rhiannon when I left her. Cal stared out the window as the cabin broke into a rousing "Here Comes the Sun." It only reminded Cal of Richie Havens' version in Atlanta—and his lost family.

While Cal's mental state changed quickly—moods volatile, jumpy, sad, or once, hallucinogenic—this moment carried exhaustion instead of glee. A doc had told him living with interrupted four hours of sleep, surrounded by trauma, running on adrenaline in a heightened state of alert, would mess with anyone's psyche. He'd feel better when he got home, he said. "I don't have a home," he shot back. Not one letter at mail call.

The trip was long and excruciating, and sleep was scattered. When Cal came off the plane in San Francisco, he saw dozens of reunions. Soldiers raced into the waiting arms of families. Women screamed and smothered them with kisses. Hugs with kids lasted for minutes, and tears and teddy bears abounded. *Rhee.*

Outside, a chilly gust blew, bringing damp mist to his face and cool relief to his body. It'd been ninety-three in Saigon. Here, fifty—and no landmines, bullets, and beef-in-a-can. He'd take it. "All I want is a prime rib and a peek at the Golden Gate Bridge," he said to someone's waiting limo driver. The guy offered him a cigarette, which he took, since he'd taken up the habit over there.

He smoked a long drag by a stop sign, grateful for the nicotine lull, when two girls in a Beetle with painted peace signs came to a stop sign and hurled trash. "Baby killer!" they called as the car backfired when it zoomed away. Cal hit the asphalt at the sound and lay on his stomach for seconds, wondering what just happened.

"Looking for your smoke?" said a guy with a bandana around his long, stringy hair.

Cal held out his hand. "Thanks, man." He thought the dude was helping him up.

The guy refused his hand, taunting him with his burning cigarette, while his buddy laughed.

"Whatever," Cal scrambled up.

They circled him. "We got a gift for you, son of a bitch." The first guy cleared his throat. "This is for every defenseless soul you killed." Then, they coughed in unison—and spit at him.

The phlegm hit both sides of his face. Heat shot to his clenched jaw. Cal charged at them, and they sprinted away. "Fuck off!" he yelled and stopped when a kid with a balloon and his mom stared. He wiped his face with his shirt. "And how dare you, my mother was the best mom around!" Those pigs were a-holes whose parents got them out of service, and they spat at him? For what, serving his country?

On the leg to Atlanta, he shut his eyes, but only ugly scenes replayed again. He asked a flight attendant for paper, scribbling as a purge like he did after the Easter Offensive. But his writing held no panacea; he couldn't make sense of war and being spared. He'd learned to take baby steps, like for his other losses: Get through each hour. Follow the military schedule. Do what he's told. That gave little leeway to think, as empty hours depressed him. But now, he wrote how he didn't understand—he'd tried to help his fellow Americans, yet he was in the good ol' US of A for two hours before mucus nailed him. *I've been spit on for opening a government letter and saving some wounded.* He unloaded this stream of consciousness on the paper like a madman's rant in a horror story.

A *ding* sounded. The seat belt lights lit. "Beginning our descent to Atlanta," the captain said.

He slipped the ramblings into his pocket and stared out the window. Instead of the sun and purple lights for Hendrix, he saw rainy skies and sprawling malls in Atlanta. Peace, love, and music, gone. When he landed, he dashed to the airport bar first.

Hopping a Greyhound to Raleigh, he thumbed for five miles for a ride to the base in Fayetteville, North Carolina, where he would work for the next eight months. That didn't faze him. He wasn't traipsing through mud, ducking bullets, wrapping a skull, loading a brother into a Chinook anymore.

A teenager picked him up, blurting out that his older brother was killed in Nam Penh. "Buried at Arlington, best big brother ever," he said. "Beat up Johnny Delvecchio when he stole my lunch money."

"I'm sorry, man," Cal said, staring at dense woods they passed. *Why couldn't it have been me instead?*

Cal tried to give him a few bucks, but he asked if he'd just pay his respects at Arlington Cemetery someday instead. "Absolutely," Cal answered, jotting down his name and saluting before he did an about-face to the new base. Except for the pilot's handshake and flight attendants' winks, he hadn't heard "welcome home" on the thirty-one-hour trip. He lugged his duffel bag through the gates—the souvenir Browning M1911 on the way via US mail. He clutched his dog tags and patted the pocket that held Mama's ring, the good luck charm that must've kept him alive. It was all he had for a new life.

19

"She Works Hard for the Money"

Nainsi, November 7, 1972

When Nainsi called from her motel room one morning before work, her aunt said, "Your inkling was right—the Holy Spirit's talking to ye—new doctor thinks Liam's waddling gait and trouble falling and running aren't normal. May be a form of muscular dystrophy! They worry about heart complications and—"

Nainsi's heart sank, her aunt's voice fading like the adults on a Charlie Brown special she'd watched with Rhee. _Wa-wa-wa-wa-wa-wa_. Her mind traveled to a Jerry Lewis Labor Day telethon on TV in the States. Kids in wheelchairs. Adults who couldn't eat. No, no, no. She wanted to hug Liam, who was probably sitting on their burnt-orange-and-avocado plaid couch watching cartoons, Ma's Mother Mary statue guarding him atop the fireplace mantel. Her little brother didn't deserve this. This sweet boy's life would be too hard. _We lost Ma! Da's injury! Why?_

But _why not you?_ took root. Was it a curse for leaving both families, wanting Cal to raise Rhee while she started her own future? _This was a mighty punishment!_

"More tests are needed. Pray." Auntie's tea kettle whistled. *The Today Show* blared a reminder to vote in the presidential race of Nixon versus Senator McGovern. "And pray for me. I can't do it all, between raising Matthew, Mark, Luke, and John alone with Paddy gone—God rest his soul—and cooking and cleaning for our two houses of seven teenage boys and poor little Liam. Your father can't do anything for himself. I've worn out my rosary beads!"

"Can you give them hugs for me, please? I'm saving for a ticket...miss you all..." She hung up and released a torrent of tears. It was too much. Her eyes fell on Father McKenzie's card. She had one half-hour before work.

***

The chapel was jammed, turned into a polling place. "Vote," a woman said, handing her a leaflet. "Nixon promises to end this war and bring our boys home."

The woman's button, a picture of her son, saddened Nainsi. "Hope he comes home soon."

A guy asked for money, and she reached into her apron pocket for the vending machine granola bar for breakfast and handed it to him. She'd eat apples from the front desk bowl. If she'd remembered to buy them.

"This all ya got?" the man yelled just as the smell of a sausage and peppers food stand floated through. It made her stomach growl too, and reminded her of the Atlanta festival to boot.

"If it ain't Miss Nainsi of Dublin by way of the Groove Motel," said Father McKenzie, standing on the sidewalk in a small crowd who dispersed, handing the man a ticket with, "For your next meal."

"Father, you remember me?" Nainsi asked.

"Of course," he said. "Though you have a nametag."

"Oh, duh." She tapped her forehead. "Even had it on during my music theory class last night."

"Here, sit. A rock-solid cement bench because we priests like to make it as uncomfortable as possible to ease your burdens."

She sat down, bracing her hands at her sides. "I only have a few minutes."

"As I remember, you're taking one class a semester? How did the music appreciation class go?"

"Good. But at this rate, it'll take forever to earn a degree. Will be in my thirties."

"Downright a dinosaur. But you're going to be in your thirties anyway. Why not thirty with your goals fulfilled? And you're as young as you feel. I'm sixty-four years old. Only feel sixty-three."

She smiled. "Of course Father McKenzie is *sixty-four*." Cars blew by and voters clutching pamphlets bounded through. A school bus slowed and braked. "So, I just start—here? Weird. Okay. Bless me, Father, for I have sinned. It's been two years since my last confession."

"Confession? Is that what we're doing?"

"And I can't give to the church now and—"

He winked. "My ears are free. Someday when you're able, a few bucks for the community plate inside helps. I'm just here to meet people where they are. My mission is to help people find peace, one person at a time."

"Tall order."

"But be it disasters, tragedy, grief, crime, violence, conflict—big and small—everybody hurts, it's human. Nothing to be ashamed of."

Nainsi looked away, watching someone walking past with their dog. "What if we caused our own pain?"

"Like life as a punishment or reckoning for a sin? You see God as a vengeful deity? No. We all suffer and need to know we're not alone. If someone's seen violence, gotten cancer, been drafted into a ferocious war, or they've had a fight with a boss or mother-in-law or a car died, no matter what it is, we can hear each other, offer peace to another soul.

Everyone's pain is real to them. That third grader waiting for the bus could be distraught over his test today or a bully. It's an elephant."

She nodded, her eyes casting down. "Da got hurt from a bomb. My brother might have a muscle disease. And I left people I loved behind...for a career that may never happen. Oh, and I can't seem to make enough and send money to everyone—well, it's all awful."

"Sounds terribly difficult. You're worried."

"I am. It hurts. I screwed up badly and my family's been so angry for Da's injury. They were in that crowd at the embassy fire. And poor Liam, he needs a mother. It's unfair."

"I'm sorry. I'll add you and your loved ones to my prayers. Where's your mother?"

"Ma died from an ectopic pregnancy. Child six."

"Tell me about her?"

The kind question brought a lump to her throat. No one except Cal and Mrs. H had asked what she was like. *She used to dance in the kitchen, waving a spatula like a maestro! Oh, Ma, it's wrong your life was cut short!* "We don't have time."

"You're wondering if you should go back to help your brother, be like the mother you all don't have anymore?"

"Never thought of it like that." A garbage truck drowned out her wavering voice. "But...it's not that simple."

"Never is, I'm afraid."

She looked at his watch and kicked pebbles. "I...can't be...a mother...but I still want to be there for him. Yet I also need to be somewhere else first if—well. Another heavy grief sits on me, but one I chose. I wake up unable to breathe, even cry at a sign for Disneyland. I'm here only to work at a bloody awful job—not even in music, which is why I'm here, for the classes I'll never finish. Oh, what a mess." The garbage men threw trash into the truck, and a wave of stink floated through. "And I tried to send a letter, twice, but it came back 'Return to Sender.'"

"To?"

Her breath caught and she stood. "I'm late. What do I do for absolution? Our Father and Hail Mary?"

"Whatever you want. How about visiting each week? Between eight and nine is good, then?"

"Way too much confession for me."

"Come just to talk. And pick one—a poem, prayer, or promise today."

"A promise?"

"All right," he said. "How about 'Peace and love are eternal'?"

"From Jesus or the Pope?"

"John Lennon."

20

"Drift Away"

Cal, November 1973

A commanding officer had sent Cal to an Army shrink. Seemed he couldn't get his act together, "volatile," "erratic," "alcohol abuse" noted on the order. *So, he snuck a beer or three into a file cabinet? Whatever. The flask in the desk drawer? Big whoop. Settled the soul. Sgt. Smith was smoking marijuana in the john!*

Cal had numbed the trauma, swimming in a heavy dose of survivor's guilt, the doc had said. Yeah, he answered, he felt like shit every effing day. *Sir.* He had brief bouts of sleep punctuated with heart-racing nightmares and sleepwalked with his gun sometimes. Once they found him armed in the parking lot, peering into an empty Mustang.

The psychologist wrote in his file and said, "Depression. LAJ: Lay off alcohol. Amp up exercise. Join something."

He wanted to say, *holy smokes, Batman, you got a degree for that?* Did you see a battlefield or a college quad at nineteen? Evac a kid bleeding out? Were you ever orphaned? Did your girlfriend split? Are your friends dead or in Canada? Ever get sloshed and *hand your baby to a stranger?*

But he didn't say that. He rolled his eyes at the feeble advice and did the opposite of LAJ.

Life had changed too much. In Vietnam, danger reigned, adrenaline coursing through his veins. In the desk job at Fort Bragg, the constant state of alert was a hard habit to break, even zoned out as a procurement clerk handling medical supply acquisitions, crunching numbers, shuffling paper. By day, next to phone numbers for chain of command, he kept three numbers by his desk: 58,000 (dead), 150,000 (wounded), 1,000 MIA. He dedicated his work to them. Even after the Paris Peace Accords were signed, causing 591 POWs to be released and the last US combat troops to leave South Vietnam, Cal felt numb. How would he ever not feel this hopeless and lost? Even in the idle night, he soothed the trauma by drinking, because that was when they announced, "We're here!"

Cal earned a nickname at his new base, The Pitcher. After consuming pitchers of draft beer, he pitched things. Pilsner glasses, saltshakers, didn't matter. If something ticked him off, his anger spewed into an object, like when he flung Mama's ring at the car. Once he whipped a soap bar into his reflection in a bathroom mirror, and it shattered. His pay got docked for restitution. Sgt. Winslow added, "You ain't no Tom Seaver."

Last month, stumbling home from the bar after work, he walked past a storefront with TV consoles in the window. On one, Greg and Marcia Brady battled for class president. He rolled his eyes. That chipper dude sure as shit didn't fire an M16 in a real battle. His eyes darted to another screen. Even though few soldiers remained in Vietnam—Marines protecting installations—news footage showed people burning a uniform with a flag patch. Suddenly he was outside the airport again, where he could see the stones thrown from the backfire, feel the ground at his stomach, wipe the sting in the spit on his face. He took off his boot and pitched it at the plate-glass window. *You crouch behind a fucking plant under rapid fire.* The shoe bounced back.

Cal wandered into Sam's Tattoo Parlor, rolled up his left sleeve, and handed the guy a twenty. "Burn me, make it scald," he said, unrolling a sketch he'd drawn, and wincing as he did just that. The sunrise burned into his bicep forevermore was gorgeous. One word centered in the sun—Rhiannon. The I was dotted with a musical note.

When his eight months were up, he filled out the DD-214 discharge paperwork. Sgt. Winslow said, "Pitcher, there's no place like home, huh?"

But Cal didn't have one anymore, nor did he have any purposeful destination when he bummed a ride west from another soldier, Isaiah, who chain-smoked Pall Malls with him. He was traveling home to his close-knit family in Nashville and an offer of a reporter job. Cal's jealousy turned to sympathy when he said his mother had been beaten in civil rights protests years ago, and that's why he wanted to report—to show how racism still existed. "It's like the media has forgotten the movement, but we still have far to go, you know? Like we're still separate." Just then, a car passed with a Confederate flag bumper sticker, and sorrow flickered in Isaiah's eyes.

Cal nodded, emerging from his own pain to see his friend's, but like when that one guy asked him to pray as he was dying, he struggled with what to say, feeling his words too weak to comfort anyone.

Just then, Al Green's smooth vocals glided out from the radio, and they both reached to turn up "Let's Stay Together." The hopeful horns filled the cab, soothing the layers of pain left unsaid.

When the song ended, Cal said, "Man, if only I would've had this song in my back pocket to slow dance with Nainsi, she wouldn't have left."

"Dude, you really think a song could save your sorry butt?" Isaiah said with a grin.

They joked and talked for miles. When the landscape gave way to the rolling hills and steep peaks of the Blue Ridge Mountains, it felt sturdy, sheltering. At a gas station in Asheville, Cal decided this place would be as good as any. He'd seen help wanted signs posted. The Biltmore and mountains drew tourism, hotels, bars, which brought the three *w*'s. Work, whiskey, women. Only the first two he could count on.

Cal grabbed his backpack and camo jacket from the '67 pickup. A plume of smoke escaped when he opened the door and breathed in the chilly mountain air. "Thanks for the lift. Good luck, brother. Bet I'll see your byline on the front page someday."

An eighteen-wheeler rolled into the gas station, blocking a station wagon. "Moron!" yelled a dad at the trucker, and they both stuck out their middle fingers.

"Good luck to you too. So long, brother," Isaiah said with a wave before he sped off. As only a man with a job, mission, and family could.

21

"When Will I See You Again"

Nainsi, January 31, 1973

Transcript

Father: The bombings in Dublin, three killed and one hundred eighty-five people injured since November. You must be worried.

Nainsi: So much. It shook my family.

Father: I'm sorry.

Nainsi: I should be there.

Father: But what would you do?

Nainsi: Help somehow.

Father: Shield them from the mighty Troubles? An unrealistic goal for a human, don't ye think? Though, have you thought of moving your family here to the City of Angels?

Nainsi: They won't. And I can't find them...

Father: Who?

Nainsi: I...can't...say. I can't even admit it to myself.

Father: All right. So, how are you otherwise? Last time you told me about work, school, and the second job at the record store, but how's that good tipper who comes into the pub Fridays and asks you out and you turn down the poor lad?

Nainsi: Killian, who drinks Guinness?

Father: Aye. Could use a pint of black and tan myself.

Nainsi: Come in on my twenty-first birthday next week, and one's on the house for you. I've called more beer distributors to stock us and created a drinks-around-the-world menu. Our receipts have tripled.

Father: Excellent!

Nainsi: But we have a way to go. Inspectors from the city, county, state would see the books are a mess. I'm helping Ricky work on this. Anyway, you asked about the handsome and spiffy Killian, Mr. Easy on the Eye. He's kind of mysterious. Do you think that's because he's almost ten years older than me? Forgive me for a few lustful thoughts, but he's a good guy. Darn near devout with daily mass. He's asked me out four times. The last time to a movie, *The Way We Were*. But I had to study for my music education class.

Father: Even if Robert Redford is stunningly handsome, like me?

Nainsi: [chuckle] Hadn't planned to date anyone until... well, I screwed that up before. But Friday night, he came into the bar after work and--

Father: What does he do?

Nainsi: He's an exporter. Holy statues, knickknacks, trinkets bound for Catholic gift shops, you should like that, eh? Like I said, he's mysterious and cagey about his work though. It's odd he doesn't talk about it, even though he has customers back in Ireland. Anyway, Friday he asked me out "one last time." And I caved.

Father: Really?

Nainsi: He pulled out two tickets to see Bruce Springsteen next month at the Troubadour! Van Morrison and Pointer Sisters will play there soon. Elton John's played there. Billy Joel played there last year, and the year before that, Carly Simon opened for Cat Stevens. It's where she met her husband, James Taylor. I used to play his albums when—well, never mind. So, this time I said yes, practically skipped back to my room. For two minutes, I was happy. I should've known, because mail had been slipped under my door. Just like my family says, the other shoe *always* drops. My letter was returned from the people I left behind, "No known address" scrawled over it. My heart ripped open, like I was back there again, pulling away.

Father: That sounds painful.

Nainsi: I've made the biggest mistake ever.

Father: Would you like a poem, prayer, or promise today?

Nainsi: A poem. The prayers aren't working. The Troubles are worse. I need money. I miss Ma so much. Liam's muscle weakness. Da's slow recovery. And I'm devastated I don't know where—they—are. And I've even had his Mustang stolen! Everything's my fault. My heart's so heavy, it hurts all the time.

Father: A poem you say? Written by a Protestant chap, an Irish nationalist who lived on Dublin's Merrion Square. "September 1913," by W. B. Yeats. [Reads all stanzas, ending with] *For men were born to pray and save/ Romantic Ireland's dead and gone/ It's with O'Leary in the grave...*

Nainsi: I read that one the book Mrs. H. gave me. You know I love anything lyrical. I like the balladry, the alliteration, the enjambment in this poem...but how is this bitter grieving of what Yeats saw of Ireland then give me advice now?

Father: Yeats didn't want piety. He was mourning what he saw as the end of idealism, frustrated with people not working for a cause or the greater good. What if our deepest pain can inspire us to act to help another? What can we do with our anguish?

Nainsi: I don't have any idea, but if you're asking me to volunteer, I don't have time. I'm broke. I'm sorry. Please just tell me what to do for absolution?

Father: You're forgiven. Pray how you'd like.

Nainsi: You're different from Father Gallagher.

Father: Well, like another poet by the name of Morrison sang... [clears throat, sings] People Are Strange...

22

"Changes"

Cal, September 1974

At nine o'clock on a Saturday morning, Cal stood in his kitchen, popped open a Pabst from the fridge, and downed two aspirin as "Nothing from Nothing" played on the radio. He jammed dirty clothes into a garbage bag of his $125 a month one-bedroom apartment.

By day, he'd been working construction for nine dollars an hour, and, with his first paycheck, he bought a second-hand bed and stereo. At Salvation Army, he found this kitchen radio like Mama's for fifty cents. Paychecks went to a used motorcycle, rent, food, definitely beverages, and an occasional album, like the Stones' newest bought yesterday. At night, he drank and passed out, weapon tucked under his bed.

"Had a bad night last night," he said to Billy Preston's voice. "Why is my gun here on the kitchen table? Judas." He scratched his head and took his firearm back to its mattress home before he trudged to the laundromat early for the empty washers.

"Ahhh." He inhaled the calming, sudsy scent, infinitely better than his bag's odor of tube socks and what Nainsi called "skivvies." He dumped laundry into a machine and inserted a quarter, cramming in his four towels last.

"You have a good voice," said a soft-spoken woman sitting in the corner, twirling her blonde hair as long as Cher's.

Cal turned. "Me?"

"Um, no one else is here?" Her smile revealed straight, unstained teeth highlighted by a porcelain complexion untarnished by make-up or blemishes. She had to be a model for Ivory, pretty in a wholesome, sparkling-clean way.

"Wow, thanks," he said. He couldn't remember anyone but Nainsi complimenting his scratchy voice, unless you counted the eighth-grade girls shrieking when the Ex-Candles played dances. "Do you sing?"

She loaded her clothes into a machine. "No." Her eyes shifted back to her laundry.

"So, what do you do?"

"I'm a secretary. Weltz and Sons."

"Great." He had no idea what a Weltz or Son did. "Cool." He weathered the hum and drum of the machines for one long minute before he tried, "Say, is that 'You're Having My Baby'?" Cal motioned toward ceiling speakers. "Such a cheesy song."

"I like it."

"Oh. Sorry." Cal tapped his toes. Maybe to backpedal.

"Though, *his* baby?"

He shrugged. "Paul Anka wrote it for his wife, and he also wrote the Sinatra song, 'My Way.'"

"See, *My. Way.* Male superiority."

Calvin Frank chuckled—it seemed like something Nainsi would've said—but *thou shalt not diss Frank* was his personal eleventh commandment, handed down from his old man. "A woman could've sung 'My Way' and it would've meant the same." After all, Nainsi and he would dissect any lyrics, word for word, for hours.

She set a bar of Fels-Naptha soap in her basket. "Well, I don't listen to much music, so granted my music analysis is off. Usually I'm glued to news like Watergate and Nixon's resignation."

"Ah, you need music in your life for a break then. Course, I'm biased. Played guitar in a band with two buddies."

"What kind of music?"

"Rock. Troy was drums, Terry keyboards, but..." His voice trailed off.

"Vietnam?" Her eyes softened into a light sheen when Cal nodded. "I'm sorry. It's so wrong." She pulled out a quarter from her bell-bottomed jeans, walked to the vending machine, and selected crackers. "What do you do?"

"Work at that new doctor's office building."

She raised her eyebrows. "Are you a doctor?"

"Uh, no. I mean building the building. Construction."

"Oh."

Another minute ticked by, and he couldn't think of anything to say. Should he sit here tumbling in spin cycles, her wiping crumbs into the trash can, or order a beer and beef brisket at the place next door? His stomach growled, but he was drawn to her cute dimples, honest smile, and normalcy. Like the girl next to him in calculus who'd tell him when homework was due.

The laundromat soundtrack switched to Gordon Lightfoot's "If You Could Read My Mind," and Cal said, "Depressing song, huh?"

"I like it," she said.

"It's easy to read their minds. It says their time is up."

His buzzer sounded, and they laughed at the synchronicity. He threw his clothes into a giant pile back in the bag, and the boxers and socks fell onto the floor. She picked them all up and gave them to him.

"Thanks," he said, shoulders sinking, as two items had holes.

When her buzzer sounded, she jumped up and folded her clothes into perfect stacks of equilateral squares, sorting by color and item. He was awed by her precise folding of a fitted bed sheet, a trade secret that evaded him, his mom taking it to the grave.

"That's impressive," Cal said. "My corporal would've adored you."

"You were military?"

"Drafted. Vietnam."

"Some hard stuff you've seen." Hers was the first kind gaze he'd found lately. She walked to her last load, a fresh linen scent floating through with her.

"Smells like when my mom used to bring in our clothes from the clothesline."

"Wasn't that the best smell?" She came alive telling him about home, Oklahoma City, an only child of a working-class dad and a homemaker mom.

"Me too," he said, appreciative they'd finally found common ground after two whole cycles of suds. "Only I'm from Manassas, Virginia."

"Anywhere around Alexandria, near DC? A co-worker told me of well-paying jobs there at our association."

"Not far at all," he said. "Grew up in Prince William County before I was drafted to Vietnam and things went into the crapper."

"If you'd ever like to talk..." she said, a seemingly sincere look in her eyes. "It's something we advocate at work. Mr. Weltz himself says processing helps us with what we see and deal with every day. Maybe why their family business is successful. Talkers, too much actually, every one of them."

"Oh. Thanks." But he wasn't into chatting about the war, much less the year before life went to hell. He conversed plenty with Mr. Bud Weiser. "Forgive me, but who's Weltz and Sons? Lawyers?"

"Undertakers. We're the funeral home on Sixth Street. Here, take my Bold detergent, that's the scent you like. I've more back at my place." She pointed across the street.

"Oh. Thanks. You live there too? I'm Cal, by the way. Guess I'll see ya around, neighbor. Rather see you there than your place of business."

A brief smile flashed with those perfect teeth. "Stop by my apartment for piping hot brownies anytime, Cal. I make them every Saturday like my mom."

He tasted his mom's fudge brownies in that moment. "Aw, thanks...nice to meet you."

She walked to the door. "Bet you were good in that band. A friend said they have an open mic thing at Duncan's every week. They pass around the hat. Winner gets the cash. You'd win."

"Might be fun for a happy hour. Maybe I'll try sometime."

She waved goodbye, flipping her waist-long hair behind her shoulders, her gleaming white sneakers making barely a sound.

Though the allure of warm brownies was promising, avoiding deep talk with small talk with a nice girl seemed laborious. Talking to her meant discussing death, in her job and in his life. No thanks. *Anyway,* he thought as he pulled out of the dryer one lone sock without a match, *I've forgotten to ask her name or apartment number. It wasn't meant to be.*

23

"Honesty"

Nainsi, November 1974

Transcript

Nainsi: Did you hear about bombs in Dublin at rush hour and a fourth in Monaghan ninety minutes later? Hundreds injured! Thirty-three people killed, a full-term baby died, nothing makes sense anymore!

Father: Aye. A constant cycle of retaliatory violence. Awful. I pray for healing, reconciliation, and peace.

Nainsi: When Auntie took Liam to the car after the doctor's, he yelled, "Look under it!" I should go back home. Why am I still here in the States?

Father: What is your heart telling you to do?

Nainsi: It always gets me into trouble.

Father: Be still and listen.

Nainsi: Too busy to be still.

Father: Shall we give a little think about that?

Nainsi: I don't know.

Father: All right then. What's the craic? How's the bloke you're dating?

Nainsi: Can you believe we've been dating for a year? When I'm not working or studying—which is always—we catch a movie, walk on the beach, make dinner together, cruise the Ventura Highway. We bought one of those maps and drove past stars' homes. Cheap dates are much-needed fun. The best part, since I don't want a relationship now, is we take it slow—though he pushes the envelope. Guess what he did? He called my family to introduce himself. He even sent Liam trinkets from his business. It was sweet, but—

Father: What did he send?

Nainsi: A little Mary statue since Liam started collecting them in memory of Ma. She loved hers.

Father: Very kind.

Nainsi: But I did something wrong. Again. For some reason he tells me to not to look in his business boxes he ships out from his apartment. One day, the curiosity was too much. So I--

Father: You don't trust him?

Nainsi: He says strange things, sometimes. Like, he's evasive about simple things about work. Anyway. It *was* all in my head. It was holy statues, like he said. But I goofed. Mentioned to Killian that I peeked and had loved the Infant of Prague statue, even if it was a little dusty. Anger flashed in his eyes. "You looked? Touched?" He got irate, squeezed my arm hard—left only a little bruise—and pushed me. Yelled I should trust him. He's right. I apologized.

Father: He shoved you? Left a *bruise*? Dear, don't you know it's good to question? It's how you can build faith. Doubting Thomas was still loved! Skepticism is healthy. Legitimate beliefs hold up to scrutiny. Beware of those people— groups, cults, religions and governments— who condemn you just for questioning. And if he touched you in anger--

Nainsi: Oh, he didn't hurt me. It wasn't a big deal. It's my fault.

Father: It's not okay.

Nainsi: Anyway, I wanted to talk about yesterday, at my second job at the record store. I heard "Cat's in the Cradle," and broke down. Have you heard it?

Father: How does it go?

Nainsi: I can't. I'll lose it right here.

Father: It's okay. Why did you cry?

Nainsi: I haven't been able to tell you...I left people I love behind... I trust Cal, but...

Father: [pause] If you're not going to tell me, do you want a poem, prayer, or promise today?

Nainsi: Let's try promise this time?

Father: [He bows his head and prays.] Okay. There are two types of people in this world. The Irish and those who wish they were. [chuckle] Okay, another. You're not alone.

24

"You and Me Against the World"

Rhiannon, October, 1975

About forty miles south of DC, in a little pink house on Baker Street in Virginia, in a row of Cape Cods built in the forties for returning GIs—except for Gert's GI, who did not return—four-year-old Rhiannon danced around, oblivious to the nun leaving with a bag and catalogue.

"Bye, Sister. Thanks for the purchases!" Gert called. "Hope that hoodwinker Sister Mary Margaret doesn't abscond with one of your ten bottles of Skin-So-Smooth! She can buy her own from me!"

Rhiannon turned up the volume on the six TV siblings singing as The Silver Platters on *The Brady Bunch*.

Gert chuckled, shutting the door. "See, a frog jumped on our porch yesterday, Rhee! It was good luck."

Rhiannon rolled the *TV Guide* into a microphone and pretended she was Marcia, though she was smaller than the youngest, Cindy, but wore pigtails, too. "Do I have any brothers and sisters, Miss Gert?"

Gert shuffled to the worn brown davenport and sat. The tabby cat, Ezekiel, leapt and curled up on her lap and purred. "Perhaps you do, dear."

"Where are they?"

Bobbing the tea bag she'd reused all day, she said, "Sweet honestly, Rhee, you're so glued to those musical families on TV, perhaps you're one of them. Let's write and ask if they're missing anybody."

"OK! The Bradys have two parents, six kids, Alice the housekeeper, Cousin Oliver, and Tiger the dog."

"Mercy, Alice is the rock of that family, I tell you."

"Remember when she went to Hawaii with them?"

"And rightfully so."

"Can we go on vacation?"

"Why, we just went to New Jersey to see that lovely Mother Mary shrine."

"Why can't I call you Mommy?"

Gert's smile dropped. Even the cat leapt away.

"Why?" She acted like one, just older. She'd even just got her a grown-up bed from a truck marked "Catholic Charities."

Her eyes fell. "Because I'm just your silly old foster-mother-guardian-babysitter, dear-heartie! Would that be fair to your poor mother if I stole her name? If the Lord had wanted me to be a mommy, why, he would've given me a baby with my dear, departed Bertram."

Just then, a boom shook the house and ground, and they both startled. It always felt like an earthquake when it happened. Gert often said not to be scared "of the big guns firing at Quantico base," but she held a faraway look in her eyes and talked of missing Bert. What would he have been like as her daddy?

"Bert and Gert, sitting in a tree, K-I-S-S-I-N-G!" She giggled. "But who are my mom and dad?"

The color drained in Gert's ruddy, round face. Her delicate eyes softened as she stared out the window, beyond the saint statues lined up on the windowsill like chess pieces. The gravel crunched from Mr. Miller's car next door, rolling into the carport at dusk. Like always, the six o'clock news would be on next, Gert saying "Glory Be" that the war was over. Then they'd eat spaghetti slathered in sauce-in-a-jar.

"Dear girl." Gert patted Rhiannon's back, her gaze landing on the Mary statue on the coffee table. "It's time to tell you, sweet Rhee." She drew a breath. "They left you, swaddled in a bassinet on the church steps, with a note inside the diaper bag with your name and birthday."

The way Gert's body tensed up and face wrinkled, this couldn't be good. "Who left me?"

"I ripped open the diaper bag looking for their names. Nearly sent it off to the FBI for fingerprints!"

Her heart pinged. Why didn't her parents want her? Was something wrong with her, and they were trying to return her to God at church, like when Miss Gert goes back to the grocery store if the bananas are brown?

"Who?" she asked again. The show's theme song ended, the big family smiling from nine squares. "Why?"

Did her parents forget to pick her up, like when Miss Gert leaves her glasses somewhere? Maybe they should go to the zoo to ask the storks. Maybe she was from another planet—a Jetson! Or, maybe her parents divorced, like Sonny and Cher on TV who still sang together and held their child's hand, and they just forgot whose turn it was to get her. "What if my parents are waiting at lost and found? Remember when we found my Raggedy Ann there?"

Miss Gert looked off, her shoulders dropped, and her face began to look sad, and all she knew was she didn't want to hurt her feelings. She loved Gert fiercely, this lady who played her mom but who looked like the grandmas on TV. She read to her every night and let her roll up pennies to take to the bank. Should she not ask anymore?

Gert stroked her pigtails and cupped her face. "Don't worry, Rhee. I'm taking care of you. I have marching orders from St. Ronan himself! Heaven knows why me that day, but who am I to say no to St. Ronan? I'm just a batty World War Two widow and of the Lord's volunteers," she said, looking like she was having trouble swallowing. "Why, I was like a cat in a dog factory. Went to a church an hour away to donate a ten-pound bag of green beans-- and came home with fifteen pounds of peach fuzz!"

"Did they die?"

Now, tears glistened down Gert's face, and she wiped the fleshy waddle jiggling below her chin. "If they've passed away, they've found Bert in heaven and they're all taking care of us from above."

Rhiannon patted Gert's flappy skin on her arm. She knew just the trick to help her feel better. "There, there, Miss Gert. 'Have You Never Been Mellow?' Just 'Lean On Me!'"

Like magic, Gert laughed and gave her a big ole hug. "What a unique gift you have of remembering songs, dear-heartie! Heavens to Betsy, perhaps you are from the Bradys or Partridges, indeed!"

Rhiannon smiled, her eyes traveling back to the TV, her brain still searching for answers. It was good Gert's tears had stopped— yet hers lie trapped inside.

25

"Don't It Make My Brown Eyes Blue"

Cal, February 1976

Cal was downing his fourth beer at Duncan's when he first heard the song that felt like a taunt by the universe.

"Rhiannon," sang Fleetwood Mac.

Entranced by Stevie's vocals, Christine's keyboards, Lindsey's and John's guitars, Mick's drums, the melody battered his heart. With each note of the refrain, he ached and traveled faraway. His mind fled to his girl's twinkly eyes and grin, and the way she turned her head to him when he strummed. Like that last day.

Memories turned on him like that in seconds. That was trauma, the Army shrink had explained of war, when your mind replayed the reels, trying to make sense of the nonsensical, normalizing the abnormal. Blah, blah, all Cal knew was as the song played, he tasted the whiskey and rye from that fateful day. He heard himself say, "Ain't never coming back alive." He felt his arms put her in a stranger's. He saw his baby cry with outstretched arms, begging for her daddy to come back.

"Rhiannon," Stevie Nicks echoed, and he set down his juicy, half-pound burger. "Bartender, turn it off."

A woman two seats down, tossed her long red hair—Nainsi's exact shade—and said, "She's not worth it."

Why was anyone talking to his scraggly self? After work at the construction site, he meant to go home, shower, and change, but a cold one—or five—was calling, so he had only splashed himself in the restroom to clean up. He touched his beard, ran his fingers through his swamp of dark hair, waves hitting his shoulders again. Thanks to beers here on Tuesdays (open mic night), Thursdays (half-price night), and Fridays (ladies' night—he was no dummy), he'd gained twenty pounds on his lanky frame.

The "Rhiannon" refrain ended. "No, she was worth it. But the song—"

"Is fantastic." She swirled the sizzle stick and sipped on an amber cocktail.

"Never want to hear it again." He ordered his fifth beer, or ninth, from this bar the laundromat girl recommended. He'd become a regular here.

"Care to talk about it?" Her brown eyes looked gentle, her tone kind. But what surprised Cal more was how she hopped over to the stool next to him, smiling wide with fire-engine-red lipstick. Like Nainsi's, too. *Danger, Will Robinson.*

"No. What are you drinking? Can I buy you a round?"

"A Slow Comfortable Screw, and sure."

He smirked. "Southern Comfort, bourbon, OJ, and sloe gin?"

"A man who knows his drinks."

The conversation flowed, as she could talk about any band or musician. Cal didn't even have to conjure up witty repartee. He'd had some dates, flings, and a few short relationships, but this time, he sensed a connection. They did kamikaze shots before wobbling down into a sunken conversation pit, talking by a lava lamp. When she laid her manicured hand on his forearm, he asked if she wanted to go out sometime.

"Oh, Hal...sorry, you misunderstood."

"It's Cal." He frowned. "Did I miss something?"

"My boyfriend's over there. But you've been so fun to talk to. Happy to make a friend tonight. You're so nice." She pecked his cheek and clunked off in her clogs.

A burly guy, gripping a pool stick, shot a menacing look his way. "Leave my lady alone."

"Shut up," Cal said.

As fast as a pro rugby player, the brute charged him, slamming Cal against a wall. Cal shoved him back and tried to throw a punch when Duncan's owner, Mac, restrained him. The bartender grabbed the bozo and pushed him out the door.

"Hey! Guy's a jerk. Let it go, buddy. I'm not letting him in anymore. Started fights before." Mac led Cal to the kitchen for an ice pack.

"Whatever, thanks." Cal ducked out, staggering home on a mile walk icing the back of his head while pissed off he'd never find what he had with Nainsi. He was long over her, yet three years of meaningless dates and relationships felt unfulfilling. Why couldn't they be in bed right now, Rhee babbling in the next room? Was he meant to be alone? His last thought before passing out was his daughter was probably singing the ABC song by now.

In the morning, his head pounded, and the bedroom spun. The kitchen radio—which he played 24/7—drifted in with Elton John's "Sorry Seems To Be the Hardest Word."

Sure is. Nainsi never said it. Could he? He'd tried to forget, but maybe these memories kept coming back because he owed their baby an apology. What if Rhee's life wasn't as good as he hoped? Should he find her now? He was still a motley mess.

As he slid on jeans, a news break spoke of Ford's pardon of Nixon. "Cripes," he said, grousing often at everyone in the effing government, all who'd decided life and death for the little people, drafting them to fight their godforsaken wars. How many kids lost a father? He'd never pick duty to the country over his child again. No siree. Cal would flee.

A DJ said Natalie Cole won Best New Artist, the first African American to win that Grammy. Joni Mitchell's "Free Man in Paris" began. *If only I could free my mind.*

He'd purged his mind a little after the Easter Offensive. Writing had helped release his burdens. Now, an urge to write something lasting rolled over him, less stream of consciousness, more tribute for a special someone who needed to know of his remorse, but mostly, explain how he'd only wanted what was best for her. He flipped to P in the phone book, found "pawn shop."

By dinnertime—a frozen Salisbury steak dinner and beer on a TV tray—he'd taken the ramblings he'd written in the war and on the plane and rewrote as he strummed melodies on a beat-up jumbo maple-faced acoustic guitar he named The Hendrix. Soon his measly lyrics, chords, and changes emerged as two songs.

Looking at the yellow pad, he shook his head. He was no Fleetwood Mac. No Jim Croce. Certainly no James Taylor or Billy Joel or Neil Diamond. He was just Cal Leonardowski. But the most special song, "Girl It's All for You," was borne of his deepest torment. He stared at the words. The end rhyme was juvenile. Yet, wasn't that the point?

At its core, it was a song of unconditional love, for the one and only Rhiannon. He owed her the fiercest, heartfelt apology. Where was his three-year-old? Watching *Sesame Street* with her siblings, curled up in footie pajamas, and munching snacks, he hoped, but gosh, he didn't know. That killed him. Her life was better without him, but maybe someday, when he got his shit together, he'll look for her. Until then, the ballad for his little girl, which he vowed would never see the light of day—it would make Dylan vomit —purged what was left of his cold, dead heart.

26

"Use Ta Be My Girl"

Nainsi, February 1976

Transcript

Nainsi: Why is it for women to succeed we must prove ourselves by "working our way up," but men don't? Why do we have to fetch coffee? And not just get it, but buy and make it for all...and then run and get more? *Why* am I in charge of Ricky's *coffee*? But worse: why do we have to put up with lewd comments to climb the ladder of success? Why do we have to work extra hard just to be taken seriously, whereas a man walks in the place, and he's respected? We're equal.

Father: 'Tis a shame. You're working doubly hard. I hear frustration in your voice. Sorry it's not going well.

Nainsi: But it is, actually. I'm doing everything Ricky wants and more. Well, not *everything*, you know, but with the shows I've added, I've quadrupled the bar's receipts. Profits are soaring. Convinced Ricky to put cash into renovation—new flooring, painting, upgrading bathrooms, adding a jukebox, and now I'm overseeing all the bids and contractors. Since I've made myself the lounge manager, and showed Ricky what a cash cow the bar is, he finally hired someone else to clean. That's the best news yet. He needed a vision that included live music. His vision was only x-ray.

Father: Congratulations! Your career goals are just beginning, and while you're in school, to boot. Cause for celebration, yet... I'm detecting sadness in your voice. Take a deep breath, my dear. Breathe in four, out for eight...there you go...do this whenever you face troubling comments. Think of something else—one of my poems, prayers, or promises, perhaps?—and let feelings to react in anger pass. You have control over your thoughts and actions, more than you know. Therein lies your power.

Nainsi: I tend to spout off in the moment. I'm impatient.

Father: [chuckle] Ye think?

Nainsi: [pause]: I needed to see you today.

Father: How can I help?

Nainsi: Heard a new Fleetwood Mac song. "Rhiannon."

Father: A sad song?

Nainsi: Only to me. Like a sword had pierced my heart.

Father: You knew someone named Rhiannon?

Nainsi: There's something I haven't told you. Why I cry every day, even four years later. [long pause] I lived with my boyfriend, Cal. I know, the Church thinks I'm going to hell. And I can't even admit this without aches shaking my whole being— but we had a child. Rhiannon. A beautiful baby with a swath of peach hair atop her head. A radiant smile that lit up our little place. But I walked away, leaving her with only her father. I've kept this a secret because of everyone's condemnation of a mother leaving her child to her father. And maybe because deep down I know I've made a big mistake. Oh, how I miss her like mad.

Father: No eternal damnation here. No one is going to hell for having a baby. Call me a radical reformer, or a second opinion to your parish priest, but no.

Nainsi: I wasn't ready to be a mother like Ma. I wanted college and career. And I'd promised Ma and Da and Auntie I'd make them proud—not ashamed of me. I grew depressed after she was born, grieved Ma more than before, wanting her advice. It was the perfect storm. Oh Father, I was a coward and left the loves of my life. I'll never forgive myself for choosing my dreams, the money I wanted for them. I left her motherless, with only her father.

Father: Like you're motherless, with only a father?

Nainsi: [long pause] Never thought of that. But it wasn't Ma's fault, like it was mine. I make abrupt decisions...turning every which way in the wind.

Father: You brought a baby into the world, gave your child a better life with her father, until you can be ready to be a mother. No fire and brimstone here, but you're wrestling with your decision?

Nainsi: I feel a punch at the word "mother." How could I walk away? The song brought the pain back in the moment, with a vengeance. Her absence is unbearable. I'm always thinking of her. I tried to write—but now I can't find them. The door's slammed shut. They don't want to hear from me. No forwarding address, like I did. I deserve the shame and scorn.

Father: You're not being punished. Have faith you'll find answers. What else is there if we don't hope?

Nainsi: You're more understanding than Killian. I finally told him. His look wasn't compassionate like yours. More like disdain. We argued. He said, 'What kind of mother keeps a child a secret?' Like he can't believe a father should raise a child. He wants a houseful of kids someday. I said I just want her. He called me a waste of time and walked out.

Father: Don't ever confuse someone else's deep-seated issues with your sense of self-worth.

Nainsi: His eyes bore into me with a glare. Cold as ice.

Father: It hurts to lose a close relationship.

Nainsi: I threw myself into my work even more. Remember last year, when men ambushed Miami Showband members on the A1 in

Northern Ireland going back to Dublin? My heart broke for those poor men—who were trying to unify people through music. Life is short and bloody awful, and now I think it's more important than ever to bring live music to people.

Father: That was an awful incident, taken off their bus, a bomb planted. Always praying for peace o'er there.

Nainsi: Can't get it out of my head. Anyway, two weeks after our break-up, Killian waltzed into the record store with flowers. He looked so sharp in his light gray Italian suit and this peach pocket scarf. He apologized for calling me names, said my "shameful secret" made him reassess his mistakes. Ready for this? He got down on one knee and asked me to marry him!

Father: What a turn of events, whoa. I trust you reflected on a man who belittled your pain, then?

Nainsi: His temper got the best of him. He's sorry.

Father: Oh, dear. I'd suggest a premarital class.

Nainsi: Forgive my answer, Father, but I said, 'Let's live together. I need more time to decide.' He blew a gasket again because I didn't say yes to his public proposal in the store. He stormed home but cooled off by the time I talked to him later. Am I making the same mistake living with someone? But then again, a church wedding would make my father and aunt so happy, and I might have a chance to see Rhee again if I'm more stable. Do I deserve a second chance? Should I bring my daughter to the new union? Should I walk back into her life? And how do you know if someone is right?

Father: Dear Nainsi, think and pray, and if you're still, you'll hear answers. Otherwise, you'll hear noise.

Nainsi: If I move in with him, at least I won't have to dwell in a motel room anymore. And maybe he'll help me be a better person?

27

"Best Thing That Ever Happened To Me"

Cal, January 31, 1977

As the TV blared ELO playing at the American Music Awards, Cal yelled into the phone, "What?"

For over two years, Cal had slogged along with a routine: awake hungover, down two aspirins with a beer, work construction nine to five, suffer excruciating headaches, take more aspirin, bake a frozen dinner, strum guitar at home or go to Duncan's, slam two shots like medicine to sleep. Rinse, repeat. The twenty-five-year-old veteran felt forty-five.

Open mic nights at the bar had buoyed him. Though he was only a mediocre singer in Asheville's thriving arts community populated with musicians galore, he had fun crooning covers. It was a blast playing rock and roll favorites but also the new number one, "Baby Come Back"—though that too shot through his heart. Oh, if his baby would just come back.

One night after a handful of beers, he played his own heartfelt song for Rhiannon, "Girl, It's All For You," and his voice cracked. It felt natural to release the song on his heart just to folks he saw every week. The crowd cheered like he'd never heard. Familiarity and safety, he guessed, so he played the other song he wrote too, about the homecoming spit that stung his face. He screwed up a couple times, playing an E chord instead of a C chord at the intro and refrain. Stumbled over a few lyrics. Yet they went nuts again, clapping, people even sending over drafts. A few women with black and purple urban cowgirl boots made eyes, but their judgment was surely impaired. Margarita pitchers littered their table.

Not much later, as Cal was slugging his next beer, he was stunned when the Duncan's owner, Mac, ambled to the stage. "Leonardowski won tonight's pot of gold," he said.

The crowd whooped and hollered, pounded on tables, and Cal scratched his head. He won for the first time ever—with his *own songs*? It was far from perfect, yet people seemed to like the sentimental stuff born of his pain, sung with his gravelly voice, played with errors from a callused hand. Was it the melody, words, or he'd shown up enough here, and he was just familiar to them now? He bought everyone a drink with the cash prize. Nainsi had taught him the fine art of Irish rounds.

"You should record those songs," Mac said at the last call for alcohol.

"Right," Cal said, tone dripping with sarcasm.

Through the fall, he played it every week. It even became the song Duncan's patrons asked for. They didn't know it was about his deepest regret. If they knew it was about his abandonment of his baby, they sure wouldn't applaud. When the bartender asked if he wrote it for the one who got away, he said, "Sort of."

Christmas Eve, he opened a card from his employer, the construction company, which had won another contract thanks to the newly completed office building, to find a bonus of *five hundred dollars.*

"Hell, yeah!" He jumped on his motorcycle and sped to the bar.

"You can record those songs with that dough," Mac urged like a broken record. Turned out he was part owner of a studio renting at two hundred dollars an hour. They'd even send the demo to a co-owner's brother's friend's sister's husband, an agent and producer in New York City.

What do I have to lose? If only Rhiannon could one day hear this secret apology song...

He booked the studio on a day between a lonely Christmas and New Year's. He recorded two songs in two hours, and Mac sent it through the chain to the "sharp Evan Gilotti."

Two weeks later, Mac asked Cal to sing the songs at Duncan's that night.

He lifted his cold draft beer. "But it's not an open-mic night. It's half-price night."

"Just do it," Mac said.

Cal shrugged and strolled up to the mic. "Sorry, folks. I'm only here because Mac will give me free booze if I sing this."

Afterward, the applause was hearty. A short man in his thirties, with slicked-back hair and an immaculate three-piece suit with open collar revealing a gold chain over his thick chest hair, approached. "Evan Gilotti," the agent-producer said, with a firm handshake and a fast patter, like one run-on sentence. "Got your tape—could use some work, but your songs seem genuine—there's a hunger in your voice, can't put my finger on it—you got this melancholy but strong vibe shakin'—like who, Stevens, Chapin, Croce, Fogelberg?—no, not Neil, not Billy, not lyrical like Barry, hell no—dunno, but the singer-songwriter era captures your longing, for what, who knows, pal, but you got something now. I'm all for us making some money together. Let's cut a better demo in the Big Apple. You in?"

Nothing good and lasting ever happened to Cal, so he tensed at the fast-talker. Yet another feeling also came over him. In his dreams, Rhee could hear the song someday. She could know of his sorrow-- but also love. "Sure. I'm in."

When word got around a hometown boy done good, Mac passed the hat again. Patrons coughed up enough for one night's hotel in New York. Cal was so overwhelmed by the generosity and he didn't want to tear up, so he slipped out the back door to record a demo with Evan.

"Will let ya know if I get any traction," said Evan after their session. Cal knew it wouldn't get anywhere.

Until this phone call tonight.

"Come again?" Cal said, bolting up from his beat-up couch, holding the phone that never rang, stretching the long, curly cord to turn down the TV as Olivia Newton-John won an award.

"Hold on to your hat," said Evan. "One of my small labels liked our demo and wants to release 'Girl, It's All for You' as a single— 'Spit' as B side."

Cal's mouth dropped open. "Are you kidding?"

"Told ya—you got this genuine quality—plays to people in the heartland and crap," Evan said. "The execs said you breathed some kind of brooding, longing vibe into your record, and I said, 'He's like *real*, man.'"

Cal exhaled, his head in his hands.

"So, you'll sign this contract pronto," Evan said. "You're going places, baby."

"Unbelievable," was all Cal could say, shaking his head.

"Once we ink the deal, we'll work on a promotions plan—dude, you have *no* image—we gotta create a persona around you—listen, I told the label 'Cal Leonard' sounds good."

"But my name's Leonardowski. My grandparents emigrated from Poland, and my entire family is gone, so I'm the only one left—"

"Too ethnic," he said. "Anyway, we need to work up lots of stuff—them's the ropes—congrats, man."

Cal stared at the tube in shock. The audience applauded Elton John on TV. How was Cal Leonard/owski getting signed?

ELO's "Strange Magic," played. Cal had no luck, but Rhee did. Her enchanting smile could soothe two scared nineteen-year-olds in a townhouse. He lifted a shot. "Here's to magical, musical you, Rhee. And here's to the Hendrix, Mac at Duncan's, and my new smart friend Evan. And here's to a New York Blizzard of '77 snowball chance in hell the 45 makes the radio. *Slainte.*"

The liquor warmed his throat, but deep in his gut a lonely pang burned. It was no fun celebrating alone. He flung open the door.

28

"Take the Money and Run"

Nainsi, February 1, 1977

Transcript

Father: Catching your impersonators' show Friday night. Got a kick out of the ad—Ol' Blue Eyes, Diana Rossi, Babs, Aretha Frank-lynn, Spinnerz! Proud of you.

Nainsi: Thank you! So busy working sixteen-hour days. The addition of a dance floor was instrumental. Saturdays I turn the lounge into a disco, Club Dancing Queens, Sunday nights I book up-and-coming singer-songwriters. Thursdays it becomes an Irish pub, half-price Guinness, singalongs, and open mic Limerick Night. It's taken off. Ricky had to hire a bouncer and more bartenders. Though, funny how they don't fetch his coffee, but I still do.

Father: Congratulations on turning that place around!

Nainsi: I've got much more exciting news. You know how I've applied to work at every musical show, venue, and record company for years now?

Father: You got a call?

Nainsi: Not to work for a TV show, but to play a game show called *Name That Tune*, where they play notes, give a clue, and you identify the song. It's like my superpower at the record store. A customer says, 'What's that song? I forget the name,' and sings a lyric. I usually know the song. Actually, Cal and I invented it! Ha! Anyway. So, I filled out a questionnaire, they auditioned me, and I became a contestant! We taped a show.

Father: No kidding!

Nainsi: I'll let you know when it airs, but confidentially, I almost won the pot of gold. Made it to the final golden medley—one note and clue. Unfortunately, it was a forties song, so I lost.

Father: Aw! Sorry.

Nainsi: Don't be. The runner-up got twenty-five hundred dollars and a car! I cruised home in a new Chevy! With the cash, I bought two tickets to Ireland, and I plan to give them some help toward medical bills. Then I banked money for Rhee and registered for my next class. I've a donation for your plate, too.

Father: Whoa! That's incredible! What did Killian say?

Nainsi: That's the bad part...we quarreled about what to do with the money. He yelled at me so loud the neighbor knocked and asked if I was safe.

Father: Were you?

Nainsi: Of course. He just gets carried away, and I deserved his ire. He brought me tulips later at work. The card said, "Hope is blooming. Forgive me?" I should forgive, right?

Father: [long pause] Aye, but it's not so simple.

Nainsi: "Not so simple." Funny, that's what I told Cal when I left. [Silence]. True, Cal never would've yelled at me, but Killian's a devout man--he sees my mistakes and helps me do better. He's good for me.

Father: Oh dear. A poem, prayer, and a promise today...

29

"Give Me Love (Give Me Peace on Earth)"

Cal, 1977

At nine o'clock on a Saturday morning, Cal's alarm rang. He downed his aspirin, took a two-minute shower, threw on jeans and a t-shirt, brushed his teeth, combed his shoulder-length Morrison hair, and trudged across the street to the laundromat. An organized woman who sorted and color-coded her laundry would be routine and punctual. This was his last shot. He'd already looked for her by parking in a lobby chair to watch people amble to the elevator. He only met the lady at the front desk, Mabel, who chatted incessantly about her ten grandchildren.

Cal shuffled over to the vending machine for a soda and sat next to a dryer. Then he hit his forehead with his palm. He'd forgotten his laundry.

The doorbells chimed and she stepped in with her basket. "We meet again, Cal," she said as she loaded two pre-sorted piles, darks and lights, into different washers.

How would he explain not having any laundry here? "Fancy seeing you here."

"I'm same time, same place each week."

"Not me. I only do laundry when I run out of underwear."

Her dimples danced in her smile.

"How's the death business?"

"Steady," she said. "So, how much longer are you waiting on yours?"

"My death? I don't know, another forty years?" He patted his belly. "Though my burger and beer diet says maybe ten…"

The next smile was gentle. "How much longer on your laundry?"

"Put it in a second ago."

"Keep me company?" She crossed her legs, jeans embroidered with daisies at the flare, her pedicured feet peeking out in Dr. Scholl's.

"I never got your name." He offered a handshake, her perfect pink manicured hand soft in his rough hand.

"Judith."

"Judy? Like 'Suite: Judy Blue Eyes,' the Stephen Stills song for Judy Collins?"

"Well, not Judy. Judith."

"Sorry. Never could find you, you know. Even sniffed the halls for brownies one night."

"Oh?" Her eyebrows raised. "Wish you would've."

"Got your hair cut like that Olympic skater."

She patted her short hair. "Yes, the Dorothy Hamill cut. More feathered on the sides, though."

He nodded, hiding his disappointment. Water poured and pumped, rotors chugged along, and Barbra Streisand belted "Evergreen" from the speakers. He asked about her childhood, and that seemed to get her talking.

She chatted about family in Oklahoma, her mom as a homemaker and Girl Scout leader, and her dad as a truck driver who smoked two packs a day yet jogged ten miles a week. Cal said he was going to quit, talked a bit about his family and his childhood dog, Hoovie, and how he wants a dog someday. She'd gotten a bird, a yellow and gray cockatiel, a year ago. The buzzer sounded, and she sorted her laundry and folded perfect squares. "Yours is taking a while. Guess this is goodbye until next year?"

She was sweet, cute, together, even remembered his name. Someone who made him feel like things were okay. Dare he say normal? "I wanted to thank you."

"Me? Why?"

Cal stuffed his hands in his pockets. "That open mic night you suggested was a miracle."

She turned to face him, her forehead crinkling.

"Long story short, it led to a record deal. A song of mine is on the radio, well, on a few stations, anyway. Crazy exciting, but more importantly, it could help me with something important...Anyway, if it weren't for you, that wouldn't have happened. Thanks."

"Really?" Her hazel eyes widened, her lips parting to reveal the pearly whites. "I'm happy for you. You know, as a secretary, it means the world when someone says I made a difference. I rarely hear that. Thank you. And you're welcome."

"I guess you can't hear that from the customers," he said.

The door jingled and loud voices bounded in. "It's time you learn how to do laundry. You're going to college," said a mother to a teenager rolling his eyes.

Cal's mom taught him too, when she was sick. He shook away the memory and pointed to Judith's laundry. "Can I carry that for you back to our building?"

"Don't you have your laundry, too?"

"Oh, that. Well—"

"You don't have it, do you?"

"Guilty. I, uh, had hoped to ask you out."

"Are you still?"

He paused, unable to read her. "How about where it began, Duncan's? They have a good menu. For bar food. They usually ask me to sing my song. You can hear it."

"Can I pass on the noisy bar?" she said. "Was so busy all week at work, just wanted a quiet weekend reading and knitting."

"But I'm fresh out of yarn, and don't have a library card." He smiled, deflection his go-to, and waited thirty seconds before he tried again. "How about a jazz place, then?"

Her eyes seemed to calculate the pros and cons of a date with him, in the same way he evaluated his paycheck: How much of my soul to hand over this week?

"If it's not too smoky and loud. Want me to bring brownies?"

"Only if they got hashish," he said. "Kidding. Haven't had those brownies since a rock festival."

"I won't even put formaldehyde in there," she said.

He did a double take. She winked. He smiled.

They exited, and Cal darted across the four-lane street like the experienced jaywalker he was. She waited at the crosswalk a hundred feet away, so he had to wait for her to walk to the apartment together.

When she opened her door, pink greeted him, splashed on walls, curtains, couch pillows. Ivy in a macrame planter hung from the corner. A vase of tulips and a pastel peace sign candleholder stood on the white stacking coffee table. A large photograph of a pink bird hung above the couch upholstered in pink roses.

"Wow. You have a very pink place."

"Thanks. A blush pink, primrose pastel."

"Never seen a bird like that picture. Only plastic pink flamingos in my neck of the woods."

"That's the Pine Grosbeak. Part of the true finch family. Found in northern Eurasia and North America."

He nodded, knowing he couldn't keep a bird conversation humming. He was a fowl fraud.

A whistle cut through the silence.

"You got a roommate?"

"Ready to meet Pauly?"

"Sure."

"He's like a parrot. Only he whistles." She walked over to the corner and pulled off a matching floral towel over its cage. "Time to say hi, Pauly." The bird hopped onto her index finger, and she stroked him softly. He stared at Cal and bobbed.

Cal waved his forefinger and pinky, calling "Freebird." The bird whistled back.

Judith walked to her bedroom and the bird walked around the fresh towels in the laundry basket. There were whistles when drawers opened and closed. She said goodbye to Pauly, turned down his motorcycle offer, and they left in her '74 Plymouth Valiant.

At Ella's, as a piano man played under an Armstrong picture on the wall, they shared a bottle of merlot at a prime corner table warmed by a roaring fire. The table was a perk from the hostess who complimented Cal for his music at Duncan's, and he thanked her. As they listened to Nat King Cole, Miles Davis, and John Coltrane standards, and ate Judith's tasty, unlaced brownies, he talked of the single and the "up and comers tour," Memorial Day to Labor Day, touring his music with other unknown debut artists.

"Lots of publicity and image strategy sessions Evan and the label concocted for me," said Cal. He shared how Evan wanted him to say in press interviews that the new single was for "a special woman, the one who got away," the one crying at the church with outstretched hands. Allude to a busted engagement at the altar.

"Really?" Judith said, but she didn't ask exactly who the song was for.

Cal breathed a sigh of relief. He could omit the full truth. When Cal had only told Evan the real story over a pitcher of Manhattans, Evan said it was "no biggie," and the baby was better off. Cal winced when Evan said his "career would've been saddled with a kid."

Cal shared more about Evan's design to tell the media Cal was a bachelor looking for an amazing woman to love, to mend his heart and build a life with, after recovering from the lost love in the song. This would build ticket sales by those who felt compassion "knowing" this soulful songwriter.

"The label doesn't love the song 'Spit' quite as much. It's the B side," Cal said. They'd warned pensive solo numbers stemming from the Vietnam conflict might fail, drowned out by disco, punk, and heavy metal music arriving in clubs. "People want to forget the war," they said. Fine. He wanted to erase those memories too.

"Your songs sound like they have depth," she said. "And I detest disco, hard rock, punk, and bubble-gum pop anyway. I can tolerate soft jazz, like this, or classical is nice." She listened to NPR, read news magazines, watched CBS, but liked silence much of the time, she said.

They talked a little about the news and Carter Administration pardoning draft evaders, and he told her of Troy. She didn't ask more about life as a soldier, which was fine with him. Answering calls from grief-stricken families, greeting them in their darkest hours, showing catalogues of caskets to families meeting with undertakers, and writing obituaries weighed on her heavily, she said in a factual tone. Seemed she kept trauma at a distance too. Six words summed up her life philosophy: Move ahead. Focus on the future.

She was attractive, considerate, and razor smart, and he deemed the date pleasant when he took the check and she reached for her wallet. "No, it's my thank you, remember?" he said. "After all, I have a royalty payment coming, thanks to you." She smiled an acceptance, and he saw a humble, practical person. Mama would've liked her steadiness.

"I liked talking to you," she said when he walked her to her door.

"You too." A bird whistled. "Wanna go out for a movie tomorrow?"

"I don't usually on a work night, but..." She opened the door. "I'm home, Pauly!" She giggled, admitting two glasses made her loopy, and swayed to the neat galley kitchen. She returned with her phone and apartment number on violet-scented notepaper.

The next night, they saw *Airport '77* and went out for a double-cheese, pepperoni pizza. It was such an easy time that twice a week—then upped it to four times a week—they went to movies and tried every pizza or hamburger place in Asheville. They saw *Annie Hall, Smokey and the Bandit, The Spy Who Loved Me, Close Encounters of the Third Kind, Oh God, Goodbye Girl, The Deep, Saturday Night Fever*, and *Star Wars*.

By April, three months of dating nearly every night (except for Duncan's open mic night), he'd found a girlfriend who kept him warm, safe, dry. The comfort eased his spirits and kept loneliness at bay, though he'd gained ten more pounds, because they found the best pizza, Frank's Pizza, and of course the buttered popcorn at the movies. "I'm going to buy a new track suit to jog and lift weights while on tour," he said.

But more surprising than a new relationship, his single started to get more radio play locally, thanks to a swarm of Duncan's patrons and the guys at work who requested it—and bought all the copies in town. The suits used that success to market elsewhere, and soon Evan reported "Girl It's All for You" generated airplay in the rust belt cities of Cleveland, Akron-Canton, Youngstown, Pittsburgh, and Detroit-Windsor's CKLW. With a Bob Seger-heartland rock sound, he resonated in the Midwest, just as Evan had predicted and packaged, and Cal's little song entered Billboard Hot 200. He jumped up and down in his apartment before Mabel at the front desk called that people below complained.

But the next shock was not long after. New York City radio picked up his song, and he'd rocketed up to number ninety-eight. A music magazine interviewed Cal, who repeated what Evan told him to say about his songs. The media attention helped. A few weeks later, the song crested at number fifty, and he was speechless. Literally. In his new suede fringe jacket, a gift from the label for photos, he bought another round for the Duncan's crowd as thanks.

Then, Dick Clark mentioned the song on American Bandstand on Saturday. "Get out," he yelled as goose bumps crawled up his arms. Come Monday, he was hammering a nail into a two-by-four when he heard a DJ from the supervisor's transistor radio say, "This song is a newcomer to the top forty. Look for it to stay."

Cal's jaw dropped.

"Leonardowski actually made the *top forty*, holy shit!" the guys yelled and banged hammers. Evan sent over a bottle of champagne with "WE HIT #39!" on the card. His song. *Her song!* The magic of his baby. He dreamed Rhee would hear it, learn his love for her was unconditional, his apology true. They'd go from there. After work, he called Judith.

"Congratulations," she said, inviting him over for a celebratory "salmon croquettes with creole aioli and roasted parmesan potatoes." At dinner, she articulated the recipe in detail as well as the one for the savory chocolate mousse dessert. All he could say was "Thank you. This is so delicious." After dinner, they moved to the couch to relax for a while, before they headed to bed with the bottle of champagne.

"To you and the future," she said and toasted his success. "I love you, Cal."

"I love you too." They kissed again. "Cheers. To good times and hope!"

In the soft linens of her bed, Cal woke up the next morning to the bird whistle. It all seemed oddly normal. Was his trauma losing its foothold because of a steady, peaceful, loving girlfriend and an actual hit? He hadn't had a nightmare in months. Cal floated through new days, lifted by the sweet surprises of the popular song. Maybe when this whirlwind settled down, after the summer tour, he'd look for Rhee and tell her *that song on the* radio *is* for you, my little girl. He wanted, *no, needed,* to know she was okay. *She was six!*

As Cal soared at number thirty-nine for one glorious week, the phone that never rang, rang. Casey Kasem's producers called. Merv Griffin's producers called Evan back, who dangled Johnny Carson's and Glen Campbell's shows too. They were in talks with *Midnight Special.* Evan said these appearances would guarantee gold. The label execs pushed him to do an album, starting production immediately after the tour. They strategized over audience demographics with other singer-songwriters. They held meetings over genre and packaging. A pop storyteller with heart? A southern rocker? Folk artist with a rock sound? One LA radio exec even declared his sound Irish folk. Meanwhile, the suits pushed the romantic, mysterious, solitary balladeer image, "a guy with a broken heart, open to a new love" to drive women wild. They would buy in droves.

Evan reported tour sales brisk. The label had placed him and three other up-and-coming acts into a package tour, pitched as "an exclusive acoustic evening with four hot new singer-songwriters," singing a handful of songs each. They billed it the "Nearly Famous" tour, booked in intimate venues like dinner theatres and fifteen-hundred-seat auditoriums, aimed to connect his vulnerability, depth, lone voice, and bare-bones acoustic guitar with the audience. "That brooding vibe," one suit said. It was authentic because he'd never forgiven himself, he wanted to say, but he did not. He lost everyone he ever loved!

In May, after a full day photo shoot, belly stuffed from Judith's amazing coq au vin dinner, he decided the time was right. A month ago, when she had peeled off his shirt on the couch for a back rub, she'd traced the Rhiannon tattoo and stiffened. "Who's this?" If he told Evan the song's origins, shouldn't he trust her, too?

He stammered then. But on the evening before he left for tour, when she lit a candle, he took the hand of his sweet girlfriend of four months and led her to the couch with a bottle of wine. He put his arm around her. She curled up next to him and he swigged the merlot. "Last month was my daughter's birthday."

"Your daughter?" She turned and raised her eyebrows, an I-didn't-hear-this-right look on her face. "You're telling me now?"

He took another sip. "It's my deepest regret. I gave her to a stranger when I was drafted, convinced I wasn't coming back alive. Hell, my roommate-bandmate died just landing over there. And with my parents' deaths, no relatives, and Rhiannon's mother leaving us in the dust, I had no one for her. I felt profoundly alone. Reeling. If I died, I couldn't bear her being alone again. Knowing the loss I knew—"

"People place their children for adoption all the time." Her tone was kind yet factual, like a doctor's. "It's the most loving, selfless, trusting gift someone could give."

"Adoption is great. This wasn't that. Unplanned. No agency. No lawyer. No social worker. Got my draft notice, got sauced, asked a *stranger* to find her a family. So drunk I didn't even hear where the church lady said she would take her. Inside to the nuns? To an orphanage? To the police? *Sold* on the baby market? On good days, I pray an agency matched her with a big, loving family like I wanted. But in low times, I fear she bounced through the foster system or in a crazy, ill, abusive, neglectful home or a hellhole—God, what if she landed in some cult? I'm an asshole." A tear rolled down his cheek, and she wiped it away. "I can't even hear that song by Fleetwood Mac."

"Who?"

"Never mind." He should be teaching Rhee how to play the guitar now. He wanted to save the bulk of the tour paycheck—fifteen thousand dollars—for her or donate it to St. Ronan's with a note. Cal shared how leaving her haunted his dreams, and he may have talked about Nainsi for too long.

Judith's brow furrowed and her gaze fell. "I've never been the love of someone's life."

"The song's for my baby girl. Not her. *She left us.* In shambles. It's not like how Evan promoted, that the song is for a woman I've never forgotten, that I'm looking for a new love on tour. He's painting a different picture, making me sound like whatever spells sales. But the truth is it's an apology song for the child I never knew. I want to know her now. What I did is the biggest regret of my life."

"Mmm. Sorry I've been busy and haven't heard it yet. I should. Sing it to me?" When he did, her eyes widened, her frosted blue eye shadow glistening, her voice lowering. "That's pretty. You loved them so much."

"I'm sorry I didn't tell you earlier." He touched her chin and brought her face to his and kissed her softly. She returned it as gently as soap lather.

"It's okay. It's in the past now. Wow, you smell good," she said, sniffing his neck splashed only with Old Spice. "You know I'll miss you on tour, right?"

She blew out the candle, leading him to her bedroom. With her light touch, and a whiff of Prell from her hair, calm overtook him, and his tired soul was soothed. If being with Nainsi had been a red-hot, passionate love, lovemaking with Judith felt like a place to fall. Her arms held a delicate reassurance, a safe harbor.

He slept soundly and awoke needing only one aspirin. When they kissed goodbye, Judith cried and said she was afraid of losing him to the road. She'd read about rock stars trashing hotels.

"I'm not exactly Joe Walsh," he said.

"Who?"

"Never mind. I'll call you."

"I'll be waiting," she said.

The "Nearly Famous" summer tour, with Cal Leonard and three other singers with only singles and covers, kicked off in Topeka. Despite opening-night nerves, he trembled at first but soon soared with energy, the hearty crowd, demonstrative in applause and affection, easing his jitters. Rapid City, Dubuque, St. Louis and Indianapolis were next. They gathered steam with each show, through Dayton, Canton, Cleveland, Youngstown, Pittsburgh, Erie, Buffalo, Syracuse, and Albany. Eventually, thirty cities in ninety days.

Though surprised at the long days—rehearsals, sound checks, technical troubleshooting, promotional events, meet and greets, meetings about lights, equipment, coordination, hotel check-ins, and administrative items that left no time for the gym—the tour was a rush. He loved every fast minute. Thanks to intimate venues, it sold out, filled with attractive women who asked for autographs and Polaroids. One woman tossed him her hotel key, and he thought it was an accident and handed it back with, "You dropped something, miss." Surreal, but in the back of his mind, he knew good times wouldn't last. The other shoe would drop. But it was all right now, he was thankful for the ride because he'd gained new energy from singing live, and the applause affirmed his musicianship. What a kick. The four singers became friends, too, sharing meals, booze, cigarettes, and grass on the bus. After shows and drinking at after-parties, he calmed down from the high by calling Judith, hearing her tranquil voice.

When he spotted a short August break on the calendar, he said, "I miss you. Fly out?"

"Come home," she said.

Home.

He rented a car. When she opened her door, he stood with a birdhouse with feeder he'd bought for Pauly in Topeka.

"It's like a charming dollhouse!" she exclaimed as she thanked him, covering him with kisses and setting it on the coffee table by a vase of white hydrangeas, atop her copy of *All The President's Men.* They tried to entice Pauly into the birdhouse to no avail, before they collapsed onto her cozy bed, burying themselves under her fluffy comforter.

After sixty days apart, the lovemaking was gentler than the fireworks he'd imagined, and she fell asleep quickly in his arms while he stared at the ceiling. It was okay. He'd had a fiery passion with Nainsi and look how that turned out. Maybe wild, hungry sex, a blazing fire, was only once in a lifetime? It was more crucial to trust a lover wouldn't abandon you, their calm giving you strength to survive. Judith was as solid as a rock, someone serene who loved and needed him, who he loved and needed. They were building a love now, taking it slow, and that suited him fine. This low-key love was probably how it was supposed to be. A burning love didn't keep Nainsi around. Devoted love didn't keep his parents alive. A higher love couldn't keep good guys like Terry and Giuse alive. Unconditional love didn't keep Rhee from his recklessness.

He got up, careful not to wake her, and scrounged around in her fridge for some beer so he could wind down. None. He dressed, left her a note, and headed to his apartment for one. He pounded four while zoning out to the TV glow and buzz of *Midnight Special*, his mind drifting to wondering what "in love" meant.

A nice, safe love is what love is, *isn't it?* It stays gentle, solid, and trustworthy. *Let this soap commercial girl erase my dirt. Maybe I don't need passionate love, roaring laughs, wild fun. It's nice to have stability and normalcy to grieve the losses of the past, calm loneliness, and balance the lows of war, with highs, like this hit record whirlwind.*

"You're helping me be a better man," he whispered as he slid back into her bed at 3 a.m. after the fifth one.

***

The last night before he rejoined the tour, after his sluggishness had abated, aided by a savory Beef Wellington dinner and talk of birdwatching, they moved to the couch like usual.

"Can we talk?" she said.

"Ugh." He reached for his cigarettes and flicked his lighter and lit one. He inhaled and blew out the smoke and sat back. "No, I'm not sleeping with any groupies. Should I ever get any."

"I'm pregnant, Cal." She spoke in a factual tone, her eyes firm, jaw set. "I'm keeping the baby."

He coughed. "What? You can't be. We've only—"

She smiled, yet he still couldn't read her eyes. "It was before the tour. Guess I'm fertile Myrtle."

"Oh, wow, wow, wow." He looked at her for ten seconds. He took an even longer smoke and blew it out. "Didn't see that one coming."

He wasn't ready to digest the news during his tour and more promotion ahead. Then again, he wasn't ready with Nainsi either. He sure didn't feel the same for her as he had with Nainsi, but he'd learned his lesson from her—you couldn't fully trust someone wouldn't split—but he should've been a better partner. Took care of Rhee more, or whatever Nainsi needed. He couldn't mess this up again. He drained a glass of red he poured for himself and gave her a berry-tasting kiss. "This is great news."

"You mean it? Because I think so, too. It's amazing, Cal, isn't it? We were meant to be parents together."

He wrapped his arms around her. "I'm thrilled." He snuffed out his cigarette in her new purple ashtray she'd gotten for him and led her to her bed. "Let's celebrate."

After they made love and she planned the baby's future, or at least the first year, while he calculated the costs, they fell asleep. In the morning, he awoke sweating. It was the first nightmare he'd had this year, about machineguns firing on him. He shot up. His heart raced and nerves pulsed like he'd guzzled an espresso. Rain pounded her window. The air conditioning unit hummed in her closed-up apartment. *It's an oven in here!*

The bedside clock clicked over to 6:00. The bird whistled from his towel-covered cage. *Am I supposed to feed him?*

Cal pulled on his shorts, shuffled to her peach kitchen—*coral*, she once specified— said hello to the bird but didn't take the towel off the cage, and took the eggs from the fridge. This gentle, normal love has just given him another chance to have a family, another baby to strum to sleep. He could be a dad again, giving her the four kids she wanted, and Rhiannon would join them one day. A family of *seven*.

He turned on the kitchen radio.

"We're talking about the terrible news yesterday," an NPR voice said, "that Elvis Presley, forty-two, died of heart failure at Graceland in Memphis..."

"What?" He recoiled like he'd been sucker-punched with a left hook out of nowhere. *Not the King!* He cracked three eggs into a bowl with a ferocity, whisking in shock as the reporter spoke about drugs and alcohol. *No!*

Cal's mind traveled to "The Wonder of You." He and Nainsi loved the song, lay in bed dissecting how the chorus, melody, and bridge worked together to build hope. "The wonder of you," he said after she craved ice cream at 1 a.m. He could only find a freezer at a twenty-four seven gas station. Biting into a cone with a wide smile, she said the wonder was the surprise joy of unexpectedly loving someone so fiercely. She patted her tummy; he put his hand on hers. Rhee kicked from the sugar rush.

When he poured the eggs into the sizzling pan, he sang. Judith appeared in his t-shirt, rubbing her eyes. "Is that one of your songs?"

"No, it's Elvis. Awful news. He just died."

"Oh, no, that's too bad." She looked at the plate. "I could've made those for you. Here, why don't we add some Gruyère?"

Cal gazed outside for a good long while as the steady downpour belted the window. Minutes later, he cleared his throat. "In Kentucky Rain, he's searching, an urgency in his voice. I guess I've been searching, too...for someone permanent. Since Nainsi and Rhee, I can't bear to think of a future without love."

Then, maybe for the first time ever in Judith's kitchen, the scrambled eggs burned. As the announcer reported grief-stricken fans nationwide, Cal dropped to bended knee.

"Will you marry me?" He reached in his shorts pocket and pulled out his late mother's silver ring, the one that never made it to Nainsi's finger.

"Yes!" said Judith, wrapping her arms around him and kissing him.

The ring didn't fit. She moved it to her index finger. Her mouth twisted and lips pursed, and she forged a polite smile. The diamond heirloom didn't provoke the same reaction as the birdhouse. "We fit together as opposites, don't you think, Cal?"

They kissed again. To Cal, the moment felt orderly. Transactional. Like getting a paycheck.

At breakfast, she spoke of china patterns. At lunch of turkey and brie croissants, she planned the ceremony for Church of Our Savior they could book by a donation. She buzzed with details for "a simple, small wedding." Her parents and a handful of undertakers.

When he remembered what Evan had said, "Don't let the press know you're dating someone-and don't get married- you're a mysterious bachelor looking for someone special, an intriguing, solitary, sexy, songwriter," Cal said, "A low-key wedding is fine."

By the time they ate a succulent chicken parmesan dinner, she'd chosen a wedding date in one month, September, so she didn't show, and a lunch reception of thirty people. She wanted rich fall hues, sunflowers, mums, and a pumpkin at each table. "Let's get a flutist?"

"You don't want me to sing or play guitar for a song or two?" he said.

"You don't have to work."

"It's not work."

"No, it's okay," she said.

He fixed a Manhattan; she declined one. "Sure, Judith." Time to be a grown-up. "Sure."

30
"Everlasting Love"

Nainsi, August 1977

Transcript

Nainsi: It's a miracle! When I was working at the record store, the manager played a new 45, "Girl, It's All for You." I almost fainted. It's by my old boyfriend, Cal! They changed his name to Cal Leonard. It's beautiful, a wee bit brooding like only Cal can. For me, it felt like decoding Yeats. What did it mean? It's a regretful song. Not any scene I remember. But the record was the sign I needed. See? Now I have an address to write to them! The label can forward it to his management or whatever! So, I wrote again, apologizing for the worst mistake ever, and asked to visit. I finally have hope to see our baby again.

Father McKenzie: Wonderful.

Nainsi: And, if Cal writes back, then I'll have my answer about a future with Killian. It's just, since Miami Showband and Elvis—I've been thinking about how short life is. I must see her.

Father McKenzie: Poem, prayer, or promise today?

Nainsi: Can you pray Cal responds? I *must* see her. Rhee's *six!*

31

"Witchy Woman"

Rhiannon, September 7, 1977

"Kids, simmer down," said Sister Mary Anne as Rhiannon walked to the front of her first-grade class. "It's her turn for the family tree project."

Rhiannon inhaled the smell of freshly mimeographed dittoes in the air to stop the jitters. It didn't work. She hid by clutching her posterboard over her face, but her trembling fingers made it shake. She hoped they'd admire her artwork. Gert raved about how tall and thick she'd drawn a tree trunk and colored the leaves with every green in the sixty-four-crayon box. Nestled in the tree, she'd pasted a picture of Gert, who'd copied her old black and white yearbook picture at the church, and she'd drawn a picture of the cat. "This is my tree—Miss Gert, Ezzy, and me."

"That's so tiny!" gross Billy Buvorga teased. Kids chattered. Some tapped pencils. A kid burped. One yawned.

Sara Smythe, a girl who lived on their dead-end road, said, "Where are your branches? It took me *forever* to do mine with all the uncles and aunts and cousins and grandparents and great grandparents."

Rhiannon had seen a bazillion kids and a pony there last year. "Why didn't I get invited?" she'd asked Gert, who answered, "You did. I declined because I didn't have money for a party dress and present. But I got you this for your birthday next week, dear-heartie." She handed

Rhiannon an envelope. It was a renewal notice for *Catholic Digest*. She cried.

Jimmy yelled, "Who's the lady? Your grandma?"

"Miss Gert's my guardian. She's nice. Packs my Bee Gees lunchbox every day and leaves a note from BG—Big Gert! Get it, Bee Gee? She works as a Savon Lady and she also goes to a shelter to feed people even though her hip hurts. But it can tell her the weather. She's a church volunteer everywhere, and that's how she found me alone. At St. Ronan's, like an hour away. Cost her only gas money she said."

The class hushed. Sister Mary Anne cleared her throat.

"Well, duh." said Billy. "Ask her who your parents and grandparents are. That's a family tree, stupid!"

"Enough, Billy," snapped the teacher, waving a ruler. "Rhiannon, I love how you chose the granny apple color mixed with the goldenrod hues."

Beverly raised her hand. "There's a song called 'Rhiannon.' Maybe they're your family?"

Rhiannon gasped. "Really? Gert only listens to the AM dial. Is it on there?"

"Beverly's dumb," said Billy. "My dad said it was about a witch. Maybe you're from the Wicked Witch family!"

As the class snickered, her insides twisted. She looked at her scrawny tree of three, feeling different from the other kids. Even though Gert said they must've died, she longed to know who her parents were, where she was born, what land her grandparents came from, and above all, why they all left her. Was something wrong with her? She vowed to ask the Dream Weaver tonight in her prayers. *Tell me where I come from*!

"Billy, put your head down." Sister Mary Anne's voice carried exasperation. "Rhiannon, your homework is to listen to the song with your name. Then tell me what you think it means."

"Thank you, Sister Golden Hair," she said, handing in the poster. The class laughed. The teacher did not. She did not hang up her project with the other trees.

32

"Come Monday"

Nainsi, October 15, 1977

Dear Fr. McKenzie,

Having a wonderful visit home in Ireland. Cooking, talking with my family, listening to music with Liam. He's in leg braces now. I went to Ma's grave and planted tulip bulbs and talked to her. Da wept when I gave him a check toward medical bills.

But I wish I could see Rhee, and I never heard from Cal. Clearly his love song must be for someone else, but it's terrible he couldn't even bother to answer my apology nor invitation. But I've another chance to see her, right after we get back to LA. The Merv Griffin talk show announced upcoming guest Cal Leonard, and I got a ticket for the studio audience. Planning to show up backstage and demand to see Rhee. It could happen soon.

I've said yes to Killian but asked for a long engagement. No date set. But the news made Da so happy—he was worried I was an old maid at twenty-five. Killian was charming, asking my brothers to be ushers and Liam to be ringbearer.

Miss your poems, prayers and promises!

Xoxo, Nainsi.

33

"Please Come to Boston"

Cal, October 15, 1977

At the Charlotte Airport counter before boarding a plane to LAX for *The Merv Griffin Show*, Cal trembled while his eyes scanned for a bar. His nerves were already shot. He'd rehearsed both the song and the Merv patter with Evan, but he still couldn't relax. *National television*! The ticket agent confirmed his name and then handed him a yellow message with "Call wife at home ASAP," scrawled on it, as she tossed his luggage onto a conveyor belt. "Five minutes until boarding."

Wife. He wasn't used to the word yet, but it sounded nice, the permanent kind of love. They'd married a month ago on a Saturday on a crisp September morn, a week after the tour wrapped. It was as pleasant as Judith planned. She looked elegant wearing a three-quarter length pale pink dress and pumps. She walked down the aisle to the traditional Wedding March, escorted by her cordial parents, Albert and Susan, who politely welcomed him to the family as if he were the new mailman. A solemn minister led the service, and her coworkers, Mr. Wertz himself, tour musicians, Max from Duncan's as best man, and his agent Evan, filled four pews at church and long tables draped in linen tablecloths at the reception. Centerpieces were decorated with mums, sunflowers, and plastic birds, and Judith chose a lunch of salmon salad and lemon kale salad. After they cut the "one-tier amaretto and almond wedding cake with rust-colored fresh-cut blooms on top" he'd heard about for weeks, a tranquil flute played Earth, Wind, and Fire's "September." They gently fed each other cake, per her wishes, so it didn't mess her lipstick. When the flutist played "We've Only Just Begun," for their only dance, Judith whispered, "I'm so happy. Everything's perfect." Cal's stomach growled, and he asked if they could get a quarter-pounder with cheese after the shindig.

Her brow wrinkled. "But we just had lunch, darling?"

Cal whispered, "Does kale satisfy you?" She giggled, but later he devoured a chunk of cake outside.

That was where Evan sidled up to Cal with a Cuban cigar. "For you, friend, and don't forget, don't divulge this shackling to the press yet, definitely not at Merv." He took a long drag before he suggested when the album released, they'd leak staged photos of *a secret wedding to a fan.*

Cal scratched his head, but what did he know? He'd leave it to the experts. Publicity was forgotten by the time they'd hugged everyone goodbye. Unexpectedly, a grief wave had rolled over him.

"I missed my parents at the wedding," he'd told Judith. "They would've waltzed the afternoon away, even to flute. Terry and Troy would've been best men. Rhee would've been our flower girl."

Judith smoothed her dress. "I know, darling, but we'll have our own soon."

She kissed her parents goodbye, who were patting Cal on the back. Cal noticed Evan leaving with a bottle of Dom Perignon and the "hot chick" server he'd flirted with. Judith and Cal climbed into the back of Mac's car, the "Just Married" sign and beer cans trailing from the trunk, and the newest Mr. and Mrs. zoomed off to their serene honeymoon with sweeping vista views at Smoky Mountain National Park—instead of where Cal wanted, Thunder Island, off the coast. There, she phoned her doctor twice to ask if he was *sure* sex was okay in pregnancy-- and called the bird-sitter thrice to check on Pauly. She also planned the logistics of Cal's move to her place and sold his new waterbed with, "Trust me, you won't be able give it away years from now."

Cal's thoughts traveled back to the upcoming TV appearance, another chance for the song to reach Rhee somehow. As Cal walked quickly to a phone booth, he could only think of *The Merv Griffin Show*. If only Mama and his old man could see him now!

In line for a phone, Cal grappled with *Cal Leonard* as a flash-in-the-pan imposter. After all, the top forty disappeared. This show would keep him relevant after the tour, Evan had said, buoyant over the booking for his budding career. "This TV buzz will do everything, man—your album will go gold, baby—and we'll get crackin' on the LP."

Cal had written zero songs for the new album, so he planned to write at the hotel and on the plane. The tour paycheck had arrived. He paid for the honeymoon and had planned to send half of the money to St. Ronan's, anonymously, marked for Rhiannon. But Judith had urged them to save it for down payments on a house and a big Lincoln Continental Town Car for their soon-to-be family, and to sell the motorcycle too. With her Plymouth, they'd be a safe and sound two-car family.

Cal inserted a dime in the phone near his gate and dialed Judith. "Hi, I only got a minute before they board, but you okay?"

"I just went to the doctor," she said.

"Oh, forgot. Everything good?"

"No." She sniffled. "He said the heartbeat was faint."

"It's early, sweetheart."

"He said to take it easy, take off work, stay off my feet, and we'll check next week. He said not to worry, that stress affects the baby."

People milled about the gate, and Cal shifted his weight. "Sounds like a plan. When I get home, I'll take care of you."

"Please be with me."

"I will," he said as he tapped his foot. "After the show tomorrow, I'll fly home right away."

She lowered her voice. "What if I lose this baby?"

"You won't. Please come to LA. We'll extend our honeymoon. Get your mind off the fears."

"Flying is dangerous in pregnancy."

"You're healthy. After sleeping eight hours a night, you do fifty jumping jacks and eat healthy bran cereal. I drink like a fish, smoke like a chimney, skip veggies, grab a doughnut for breakfast, and I've avoided calisthenics since the Army. You're going to be fine."

A boarding announcement crackled with static. Passengers lined up.

"Please, darling."

"Judith," he said. "It's *Merv*! Promise I'll take the red-eye home right after."

"Postpone it. You'll get another chance. He'll be on the air forever."

"They're calling my flight. I'll be home soon, and it'll all be fine."

She broke into sobs.

"Judith, my luggage is already gone, c'mon, don't—"

"Am I having our baby *alone?*" Her tone fell flat. "If so, I'll go and raise this child by myself."

He threw back his head and exhaled. "Don't do this." Could he lose her—and the chance to be a dad again? Finally, hopeful feelings had arisen. Soon they would be ready to find Rhee. A happy family of four was in his reach.

"Think carefully."

"Dammit, Judith, it's *Merv!*" he yelled in the phone booth as he slammed the receiver down, and the people in the line gawked. He shoved open the door and marched to the gate, ticket in hand.

Hollywood, his biggest shot. Rhiannon might hear it, his heart said.

But he should be there for his wife and their new baby, his brain said.

What if she split? What if I lose two families?

He walked back to the phone booth.

He called Evan and asked to reschedule Merv for a family emergency. What followed were expletives so raw, Cal was convinced Evan invented new ones.

***

Instead of watching monitors in the green room at Merv, the newlyweds spent Wednesday watching Pauly the bird nibble, squawk, and hop.

She read under the dangling macrame planter and later crocheted an olive baby throw. He flipped through *Rolling Stone* under the pendant lamp. At four o'clock, they watched Merv chat with Zsa Zsa Gabor at the Hollywood Palace Theater.

Five minutes later, Judith excused herself to the bathroom. Thirty seconds later, a shriek.

"Cal! I'm bleeding!" she screamed. "A lot!"

On the way home from the doctor's office in her car, he switched off "You Light Up My Life," from the radio. He wanted to say the miscarriage hurt him, too, that he *was* excited about the baby, but the right comforting words eluded him. "I'm sorry Judith. It's a terrible loss for us." He reached for her hand.

She squeezed back, blaming her stress on work and the wedding, making love on the honeymoon, and his summer tour with "psychedelic drugs and pot and alcohol and whores around."

"No, maybe it's because I'm bad luck. I'm like the secretary of death, not you," he said. "Let's grab a drink."

"Wonder if the baby formed wrong because of your hungover, nicotine-laden sperm?"

He sighed, turning into the apartment parking lot. "That's a stretch."

"I've been thinking," she said, as they walked toward the lobby, her fists clenched in her zippered windbreaker, even though the air held seventy perfect degrees. "I sent my resume to an office manager job at a funeral association near Arlington, Virginia, close to DC. They called me for an interview. The salary is excellent, and since your pay is unstable—"

Mabel at the front desk nodded hello.

"A funeral association? What's that, selling the latest and greatest in death gear?"

"The important thing is, Mr. Wertz says he'll recommend me—reluctantly, of course, since they don't want to lose me. I wouldn't be in a funeral home anymore, I'd be away from families' grief and working on the phone with our members."

"I don't know…"

"Nothing's tying you to Asheville."

True. He'd already said goodbye to his work buddies when he resigned due to the tour. He'd miss the Duncan's crowd, of course. But, Arlington was only an hour from St. Ronan's in Virginia. He'd have more chances to find Rhee. He supposed he could write this album there and record it by hopping on the train to New York. "If that's what you really want, Judith, sure. We'll go, and when you're ready, we'll have another baby." *And find Rhee.*

"That thrills me, thank you." There was a long pause, and then quietly she said, "But should we raise our children with a rock star father?"

"What do you mean?"

"When you make the album, you'll have to tour again."

Cal punched the elevator button. "Not this again. I had no groupies. Well, one woman winked at me. But she had a stye."

"You had fan mail forwarded here today."

"Seriously? Cool."

"I've set it aside for now. It's intrusive."

"Look. I get your concerns about tours, women, privacy, but I'm not exactly a sex-drugs-rock-and-roll star—yet." He winked. "And I'm hardly wrecking hotel rooms. Had to beg housekeeping just for toilet paper once. Left a decent tip."

"Elvis died because of drugs."

"I'm hardly Elvis."

Mabel chuckled. The elevator dinged.

Judith folded her arms. "Drinking is a gateway to drugs. Our children need a stable dad. Your music shelf-life will expire. Walk out on top. On a high note."

His face grew hot as he held the elevator door open for her. "You know what?" He waited for the doors to close. "I had a ball on the tour. It was awesome, a total blast. People liked my music. It was freakin' fun. Tiring, but it didn't feel like work. The song is for *Rhee*. You know that, and you know how important that is to me. You want me to apologize for my apology song? Yeah, I know the high of this sweet success will pass, but I just want to ride it, because I know how short life is, and I want to see if the song finds her, okay? Judas."

Her eyes stared at the elevator buttons. "Let's start as newlyweds again. Music will always be here. I might not."

"What are you saying?"

"It's your music—or a long, stable career. But if you choose music, I'll go to Virginia alone."

"Are you serious?" His mouth dropped open, incredulous at the ultimatum. *An album and career—or a new family?*

She folded her arms. The doors opened on their floor, and she walked ahead. "Our first fight."

"No, it isn't." She forgot the tiff she won about taking the tour paycheck. He'd sacrificed the entire first month of their marriage. *Screw this!* Cal hit the lobby button. "See ya."

He tore out of there like a bat out of hell, towards the nature trail behind the apartment. He stepped onto the path of bright orange and golden trees, hearing the crunch of leaves under his feet, but barely looked at the trees in their peak of glory. He walked for an hour, mind swimming in thoughts, only stopping when a huge spider crawled on a web across a path. A crimson leaf floated in front of him, caught in a gentle wind. He breathed in the musky autumn smell.

What was Calvin Frank Leonardowski, whose one hit had only made it to number thirty-nine before petering out to "Disco Duck," supposed to do? He'd been beaten by a quack. What to write about for his new album, a discoing kangaroo hopping around Studio 54? With no job security, pay, or benefits, his mind devoid of words and melodies, his music could be an epic failure. Lose a new family for a pipe dream of another hit?

They hadn't even had time yet to drive down the majestic Blue Ridge Parkway and hike the Appalachian Trail, enjoying the sweeping summit views from Max Patch Mountain. He felt the spring in his step most in fall, loved watching football and building campfires like he had with his old man. One day Judith would make a pumpkin pie while he would rake leaves with their kids—and Rhee would be first to jump in the piles. They'd stuff a scarecrow, carve a pumpkin, trick-or-treat. He'd steal Reese's from the kids' Halloween stash, like Daddy had.

Cal walked into the apartment where Judith zested a lemon in the galley kitchen. He dialed Evan's number. "I'm sorry, but I'm postponing everything," he said. "Call Johnny Carson and Glen Campbell. I can't do their shows either. Taking a hiatus."

"Like hell you are—notfuckingnow—you hear me?" Evan screamed as Cal pulled the phone away from his ear. "You already skipped out on Merv! *No one* does that! Merv and Johnny and Glen wait for no one! *No-fucking-one*! It's just a miscarriage! You didn't need a baby now anyway!"

Judith sobbed. The shot stung Cal just as much. He will *not* lose another family. This decision was *brave*. "A man puts his family first, Evan."

"There's no hiatus in this biz!" Evan yelled. "I put my stellar reputation on the line for your album—which you're fucking contractually obligated for—so you'll pay *me,* or we'll sue your sorry ass!"

As Evan's tirade unleashed a slew of more profanity, Cal kissed Judith, the receiver dangling and the grater dropping.

Okay, I'll go back to Virginia, hang up my guitar strap for a bit, be a good husband and dad, find my girl, fight for her. We'll become one big, happy family soon. Music can wait.

34

"Go Away Little Girl"

Rhiannon, April 15, 1978

Clad in itchy tights, a faded yellow dress from the Salvation Army, and a red party hat, Rhiannon colored a placemat, waiting for her mystery birthday guest at an Arlington diner. Gert gazed out the window at a colossal raven-hued cloud parked above the four-lane Columbia Pike, cars and trucks barreling past mom and pop stores. Would the guest bring a present for her seventh birthday? She wanted Malibu Barbie. Fourth row, K-Mart. A dollar off if you bought it when the blue light flashed.

"This may be the best birthday surprise ever. Someone *important* is coming for you," said Gert, patting her perm, glancing at her Timex. She rubbed her hip. "The rain will be a doozy. My, is he late. Well, traffic's busy as a beekeeper here near DC."

"Who is it, the president?"

"Not that kind of important, silly." Gert drank tea and rattled about the cost of gas as she stuffed five sugar packets and napkins into her handbag. "Free blessings are all around!"

After Rhiannon devoured silver-dollar pancakes, she ran over to the jukebox, shouting that Donny Osmond was in there.

"Let him out then," Gert chuckled, shuffling over with a limp and a quarter. Gert glanced at her watch. Again. "Lord have mercy, he's standing her up," she said.

"Who?" Rhiannon twirled back to her seat, swinging her pigtails adorned in gift-wrap ribbon, with Gert following her. *Why doesn't my only party guest want to come?*

"You don't know him." She placed the used teabag in a pillbox in her handbag. "Let's skedaddle, dear-heartie."

"Will he still get me a present?"

She picked up the check. "I don't know. The invitation wasn't returned to me, so he got it. But he makes his own bed, so now he'll have to stand up in it."

With party hats still on, the two careened in the brown Pinto to the I-95 sign, but Gert made a sudden left onto a side street. Horns and brake squeals abounded. "Didn't they see my bumper sticker, 'I brake for yard sales'?" She double-parked near a split-level.

Rhiannon looked at a table of books that held *The Shining* and a mood ring. Gert beelined for knickknacks, greeting saint figurines like neighbors. "Why, hello, Saint Joseph! Sell any houses today? Saint Anthony, thank you for finding my necklace. I said, 'Tony, Tony, look around, something's lost that must be found,' and there it was." Suddenly, she saw a three-foot statue cloaked in red, shrieked as if the Pope himself had appeared, and crossed herself. "Rhee! It's the Infant of Prague! Boy Child Jesus! I'm atingle. Blessed be, only three dollars."

"Closing up shop, ladies. Can I make you a deal?" said the homeowner.

Rhiannon's eyes darted to a stereo marked with a 5. "Five dollars?"

"It's a beauty, dig it."

Rhiannon bounced up and down. "Please, Miss Gert?"

"But I only have five dollars. We can't afford that and the Infant. Hmm. Suppose I could put him back. You'd pick music instead of miracles and protection for your present?"

"Yeah! Easy peasy!"

"No need," said the man. "Take the record player and statue, five dollars total. The missus and I just bought an enormous eight-track stereo console. It's the future."

Rhiannon's smile almost leapt off her face. She only had one 45, "Rhiannon," but had to play it on Sara Smythe's stereo. Now she could play it often.

"Sir, you've saved the day. Today's her seventh birthday, and I'm afraid it hasn't been what I prayed for. But she loves today's music. Thank you."

He bent down. "Well, then, today's your lucky day, kid. You're ready." He motioned to a box of records, marked fifty cents each. "Albums are all from the seventies," he said, flipping through them, his voice accelerating telling of harmonies and guitars on Fleetwood Mac's *Rumours*, Billy Joel's songwriting on *The Stranger*, and vocals of Journey's Steve Perry, Foreigner's Lou Gramm, Styx's Dennis DeYoung. "Let their voices bellow into your soul, man."

"Sir, we can't afford all those."

"Free. Just passin' the torch."

She'd never gotten this many presents. Sure beat last year's gift, *Children's Bible Stories*.

Gert pulled out her pocketbook. "Just don't play the records backward. You could unwittingly bring on the devil. And no safety pins on your lip!"

Rhiannon crossed her heart, hoped to die, stick a needle in her eye.

"Keep the collection alphabetized. See, kid? Oh, here's one for your grandma."

Gert frowned, but when he handed her Tennessee Ernie Ford's *Hymns*, saying it was his mother's, she chuckled and said, "Alrighty, I'll take Ford in the Ford."

Under the overcast sky blanketing the highway, they rocketed home on the half-hour trek south, well past the outer reaches of the Beltway. Gert thanked the huge statue, buckled in the back seat, for blessings. "Birthday salvaged. A penny saved is a penny *learned*! I'm tickled *pink-y* at our gifts."

Heavy rain pounded the car like a drum, and the wipers kept time. When Paul Harvey stated "good day" on the AM radio, Rhiannon got an idea. What if she took that orange college-lined notebook Gert bought her for cursive practice and created a music diary? Each day she'd write a song she heard, and something that happened. After all, when Marcia Brady kept a diary, Desi Arnaz Jr. showed up. "Maybe then someone *important* will show up for me too," Rhiannon said.

That was when Gert cried. Buckets. It looked like the gushing water on the Niagara Falls postcard from her church friend. "Heavens to Betsy," she said, wiping her wrinkles with her brown-spotted hand. "Sometimes my waterworks come out of nowhere!"

"'Da Do Run Run,'" Rhiannon said.

R'S MUSIC DIARY: DON'T OPEN!

Page 1, Bday #7, 4/15/78. I GOT A STARE-E-O & 70s ALBUMS AT YARD SALE!!! Today, I played A–G: ABBA, Beatles, Bee Gees, Billy Joel, Carly Simon, Carole King, Cars, Chicago, Commodores, Doors, Eagles, Earth Wind + Fire, ELO, Fleetwood Mac, Foreigner, Genesis* (Gert says from Bible), Al Green. 2-morrow, the rest!

35

"All Those Years Ago"

Nainsi, December 9, 1980

Transcript

Nainsi: I'm devastated about John Lennon murdered! I haven't slept since!

Father: So tragic and senseless to lose a gifted artist who's an instrument of peace. People are united in this grief.

Nainsi: Only forty. Two kids. Life cut short, like Ma!

Father: Aye, life is so precious and short. We must live every second intentionally, giving love, peace, comfort. That's why we're here. It's why I do what I do, to "Give Peace A Chance."

Nainsi: It's made me see. Next week, Yoko will have a vigil for him in Central Park. I'm going. Since the bar business is booming, and motel is booked solid every night, Ricky finally gave me a bonus.

Father: Congratulations. Well-deserved!

Nainsi: I came up with an idea. What still haunts me is I must find them. She's always on my mind. I can't just give up after Cal wasn't at Merv Griffin. I called his label and asked if he'd play at the Groove-y Lounge. He's too big for our little bar, but thought I'd try. But they said he's no longer with the label, and they didn't have contact info. [sigh] I can't win! So, after New York, I'm taking Amtrak down to DC, and I'll poke around back at our old haunts in Manassas, to see if anyone—an old construction boss or anyone at his old gigs or the leasing office—has an address. I've *got* to see my daughter.

Father: Sounds like a plan. Be careful, my dear.

Nainsi: Then, Killian and I can set a date. I'm in a better place now at work and school, and if I'm married, I'll have a better shot at visitation and partial custody.

Father: *Go gcuire Dia an t-adh ort.* May God put luck on you.

36

"Imagine"

Cal, December 16, 1980

Fresh pine scent filled the living room, the Christmas tree lights twinkled, and a roaring fire crackled in the fireplace, but Cal couldn't catch the holiday spirit.

Ten days ago, a madman gunned down John Lennon.

Tonight, Cal guzzled beers in his blue suede recliner and watched the news footage of thousands at a Central Park vigil, near where Lennon lived in the Dakota. But when the TV flashed on a somber redhead, her pale face drawn, holding a candle, he choked, and beer spurted out of his nose. *Nainsi?* If only they'd invent a way to back-up and freeze a picture, because his mind played tricks sometimes. Once he caught the closing credits on *Name That Tune* and swore he saw her. He wondered about her life in Ireland. Was she married? How the hell could she discard them? His throat caught as he realized: the same way he did it. He slugged another beer, blaming his own rash, drunken decision. He lit another cigarette. *Rhee is nine.*

"I wish you'd stop smoking. It's bad for you—and it stinks up our house," Judith said with a frown.

The past two years had brought changes to Cal's life yet again. Without an album and appearances, Cal had been "one and done" and "nailed shut the coffin" like Evan warned. Cal had honored his promise to Judith to build their family first. Using a down payment of his tour paycheck, they'd moved and closed on a quaint 1947 three-bedroom brick bungalow between Route 50 and Columbia Pike in Arlington, with a cracked driveway and a yard of weeds and dandelions. Judith had fallen in love with the dining room's archways, hardwood floors, and built-in bookshelves, but the old charmer needed TLC. They'd splurged on carpeting, paint, and appliances, but he'd have work to do, finish the basement, add a bathroom, build a deck, and so on.

Judith busied herself with decorating, choosing gray wing-tip chairs and velvet drapes, a blue plaid French country sofa, and for him, a La-Z-Boy recliner. She also bought a crib and Care Bear sheets for the second bedroom, along with an oak rocking chair where she draped her new crocheted baby blanket, and new Strawberry Shortcake and Smurf dolls. She planned bunk beds in the two bedrooms for the four kids she wanted. But after almost two years of trying, she also stacked up books by the bedside, like *How To Get Pregnant Now*! Cal whispered he knew how.

"I can't wait until little ones fill the house," she said with frustrated hope, he guessed, thumbing through Sears catalog toy pages. "Hearing them say mommy and daddy in little voices, won't that be something?"

His heart twinged. Cal never got to hear Rhee call, "Daddy!" A lump lodged in his throat. *Soon, my girl...*

"Cal? Yoo-hoo? You're far away."

He turned to face her. "What if we paint that third bedroom pink—for Rhee?"

She looked up from the catalogue. "It's not time to find her yet. Wait until things settle down. Marriage, moving, working new jobs, and building a family are the biggest stressors of all time."

No. Grief is.

"How is work going, darling?"

"You should join us after work sometime," Cal said. He'd taken a stable job like she wanted. A medic again, thanks to visiting the neighborhood bar Quincy's when they moved in. He'd wandered into a happy hour and ended up drinking all night with patrolmen, a sergeant, firefighters, and medics after their shifts. He bought a round, listened and joked, and the sergeant urged him to apply for jobs. "Grueling hours, intense," one medic warned, "but you've seen it all in 'Nam. You got this. And hell, we have a good time after work." In the end, like in war, it was a job that could help people. Save a life instead of losing one. *Brave.*

The background application was troublesome. Children? *How does he say?* Have you ever committed a crime? The shame came barreling back as he'd stared at the application. *Drunk driving that awful day. And do you call leaving a baby to a stranger reckless endangerment or an illegal adoption?*

Finding her was never off his mind. Recently, he'd called St. Ronan's, but he hung up when Judith asked what if they'd prosecute him for child abandonment.

He also skipped writing "music career" for his background. No one would figure out Cal Leonardowski was the former one-week-on-Top-Forty Cal Leonard, anyway. Not like he was ever on TV.

They approved his medic application and interview. He took the job, lured by the security, benefits, and pension. He threw himself into EMT training, though he'd already had the skills, just needed updates. He helped other trainees learn about basic life support, medical assistance, first aid, CPR, defibrillators. He studied for exams and received EMT certifications. Soon it was like the music thing had never happened.

But daily ambulance scenes rooted him in trauma again. With calls on everything from falls, burns, overdoses and wounds, to injuries from gruesome traffic accidents, heart attacks, strokes, the fears and flashbacks besieged him. Nightmares began again, but the happy hours with other first responders helped greatly to blow off steam and calm adrenaline, and they bonded into a brotherhood. Then, at the bar one night, a supervisor asked him to be a medic for the PD's elite SWAT and hostage rescue team, and he said all right. It felt good to help others to safety, and be needed and respected.

Now, more evil and violent scenes were thrown at him, helping victims of attacks, robberies, domestic incidents, sexual assaults, and child abuse. The nightmares grew relentless, and he awoke with night sweats sometimes. All he could do to numb and bury scenes was to drink in the evening and work out and lift weights the next morning, which was growing harder with a hangover and a pack-a-day habit. At least he'd dropped his twenty-pound tour beer belly.

With all the baby-making, he thought Judith would rave about his lean and mean physique. "No comments on my new buff bod?" She barely smiled, but the cute bleach-blonde Quincy's bartender, Heather, complimented. He thanked her—and made love to his wife that night. She was ovulating.

"Work's going fine," Cal answered Judith, but he didn't enjoy talking about—reliving--the harrowing calls.

"Maybe I will show up at happy hour someday," she said. He sensed it'd be from jealousy.

"That'd be nice." He watched for Nainsi's lookalike on TV. "Man, Lennon had so much music and life ahead. The world's loss. Yoko's loss. Julian and Sean's loss. Paul, George, Ringo's loss. Billy Preston's loss. George Martin's loss."

"You focus on loss too much." She closed the catalogue and stood.

"Says the woman who works at death's door." He winked and held out his hand. "Say, let's put on his new album. Dance with me to "(Just Like) Starting Over'?"

"Sorry. Starting dinner, but you go ahead and listen. On low?"

Cal frowned. She had the same reaction when, a few months back, he wanted to play Led Zeppelin, troubled by the news drummer John Bonham died. Forty shots of vodka, unbelievable, he thought as he drained his last gulp of beer, remembering how Rhiannon cried through the Zeppelin albums. His mind traveled to when he, Nainsi, and Rhee, slowly danced through their short time together as a family.

"I want to go to St. Ronan's," he said.

The refrigerator door closed. "What if the police charge you? No, let's wait, stick to our plan. Save for a lawyer."

Could they charge him? He stared at a teddy bear ornament Judith had placed on the tree. Yeah, the county had prosecuted people for child abandonment, endangerment, DUI, though he didn't know the statute of limitations. Is *inebriation upon a draft notice and no family* a defense? A lawyer would know. Meanwhile, the label had threatened a lawsuit for failing to do an album. He needed a two-for-one legal special.

A frying pan clanked onto the stove and a sizzle sounded. "Give our family time to grow first, Cal."

That was how it was decided, over a pan-seared steak with garlic butter, with Lennon's music too low, they'd award the third bedroom to the bird, who whistled through dinner. Cal rather liked Pauly now. He was a hint of color in these gray days and an entertaining pal.

37

"You Decorated My Life"

Rhiannon, November 1981

This was a good idea to get off the bus here!

Face plastered on the cold record store window, the breath of ten-and-a-half-year-old Rhiannon fogged up the glass. Stacks of albums and cassettes wrapped in tall plastic lined the aisles. Above the register hung a poster of Human League. Didn't they sing that catchy "Don't You Want Me?" It was Casey Kasem's number one, she thought as John Lennon's album played loud. She could see albums by Journey, Styx, REO, Kool & The Gang, the Police, Stevie Wonder, names recognized from her '70s album collection. The wind kicked up, and she zipped her coat. She counted the quarters from her lunchbox. Thanks to skipping buying school milk each day for six weeks, she'd saved six whole dollars for Stevie Nicks' new album. She opened the door, and it jingled.

A car pulled up and honked the horn, and Rhiannon jumped. "I knew it!" Gert called from the rattling Pinto, her glasses down on her nose, held by a new chain. "When you didn't get off the bus at 3:47, I was a scaredy dog! Dear-heartie, you're going to give me a heart attackaroo, so hop in like a kangaroo."

WWSD--what would Stevie do? Go her own way?

"I'm flummoxed! Why waste good money when you can borrow albums at the library for free? Hurry, I won't waste change on a meter, and it looks like it's about to rain."

She rolled her eyes and huffed as she climbed in, remembering when Gert brought her home from Sara's house when her parents caught them watching the R-rated *Star is Born* on their new cable TV. "Foiled again. Another brick in the wall."

"Dear-heartie, wait to Christmas to ask Santa for any wants. Jesus for any needs."

"Will Santa Jesus bring me Olivia's "Let's Get Physical"?

"No."

"Why? It's about exercise. I saw the video over Sara's house."

***

Once at home, Rhiannon kicked off her Buster Brown saddle shoes—from the hand-me-down pile in the church school office—and slid on the yellow vinyl floor in her knee socks under her grey pleated uniform skirt.

Gert pushed aside her sales ledgers on the Formica kitchen dinette, the three-foot statue of child Jesus perched as the centerpiece and opened Rhiannon's backpack. "Mail call! Let's see. A permission slip for next week's free American History Museum field trip in DC? Wonderful. But ten dollars for lunch at the Old Post Office? No, take your lunch."

Rhiannon flicked on the light switch, and the fluorescence illuminated the small kitchen.

"Please turn it back off. Our electric bill."

Rhiannon turned it off, and they sat in storm cloud darkness with the afterschool snack of raisins on top of peanut butter smoothed on celery Gert called "spiders on a frog."

"You've circled four books and a *Tiger Beat* subscription on this order form. Please get them at the library instead."

Rhiannon frowned. The library wouldn't have the must-have, untold, unauthorized stories of Journey, and she couldn't cut out pictures of Rick Springfield.

"What's this?" Gert unrolled a crumpled paper. The flyer had sliced through Rhiannon's heart an hour ago, stirring the hopeless ache in the hollow space where *family* should live, replacing it with *we're different*. "The Mother-Daughter Tea," Gert read Rhiannon's RSVP out loud, "'Not coming. This is stupid.'"

"You wouldn't want to go anyway," she said to Gert's misty eyes. "They have this dumb talk afterward about periods. I already learned everything from *Are You There God? It's Me, Margaret.*"

Gert shuddered. "Golly Dolly, we just survived Grandparents Day at school, and another event comes calling. When's the birds and bees talk?"

"Fifth grade health gets the talk on gross *inner-course*. Five kids fainted. It must be awful. Hope I don't faint."

"You may." Gert shuffled over to Ezzy prancing on the counter. She scooped up the cat and sat down at the table again. "Would you like to talk to someone from church when you have questions? There's an amiable doctor at the nine a.m. mass every day. She's a good customer. Buys perfume pins for her daughter. Sometimes, she orders at passing of the peace, like 'Psst, order us the special on page thirty-nine?' As if I remember what's on page thirty-nine!"

"No! I would *die* talking to someone about sex!"

Gert covered the Infant statue's ears at the word. "Good thing marital relations are at least twenty years away. Phew, dodged another bullet-proof."

"Another Judy Blume book got passed around school, *Forever,* about teenagers doing it."

"Oh, my word. Tell me you didn't read it."

"Maybe that's what happened with my parents? They fainted and died after they had me. It must hurt so bad it could kill you! Making babies sounds terrible."

Gert laughed, a jiggle passing through her whole plump body. "Why do you think Bertram and I never had children?" Her laughter settled. "He was a real charmer, Rhee. You wait for a gentleman. Our last dance, he sang 'I'll Be Seeing You,' into my ear in this very room. Sent to the war two days later." She cleared her throat.

"Then thirty years later, you find a kid."

"The whole kit and caboodle was a miracle, I tell you. Jesus turned water into wine!"

"Me lying there abandoned is a miracle?"

Gert put one hand on her chest. "First, I spotted the sale on fresh greens. I mean, for pennies! Then when I donated them, I returned with a baby." She threw up her arms. "Marched right home and asked the Lord if he was sure. I must've looked like a raccoon in headlights. What an immaculate interception!"

"You went straight home? Why didn't you take me inside the church or to the police or an adoption agency? Katherine Mellinger was adopted from an agency."

Gert shuffled over to the refrigerator and took out ground beef from the freezer. "My, your questions are getting harder. Well, because I figured we must learn from the lesson of St. Ronan."

"Which is?"

"I don't know, but I'm sure it involves sacrifice! He was a saint, wasn't he?"

38

"It Don't Come Easy"

Cal, September 17, 1982

Hungover, Cal padded down the basement stairs at noon to hatch his anniversary plan.

Last night, for the forty-eighth month since they'd been trying to conceive, Judith got her period. As she always did, she locked herself in the pastel green bedroom she called "seafoam" and cried for two hours. As Cal always did, he dozed in his recliner with cigarette burning, unwinding to MTV and a whiskey and water, after a few pops at happy hour with his work buddies. He wanted to comfort her, but she wouldn't let him in anyway.

"Who would've thought baby-making was hard?" he said to the Marks—Makers Mark and VJ Mark Goodman—as an idea came to him.

"Tomorrow," he said, when she had unlocked the door and he staggered into bed, "for our fifth anniversary, I was thinking—"

She rolled away. "You stink."

He got up, brushed his teeth, swirled with peppermint mouthwash, and snuggled back under the covers. "Why don't we invite the neighbors over for dinner for a five-year anniversary celebration?"

"The couple always having garage sales?" she said. "We don't know them well enough to invite them over."

"That's why you have them over," he said to her nightgown, "to make friends."

"You're right," she said. "We've lived here five years. I know my co-workers...and you know your co-workers, but we don't have any couple friends."

If only he'd made more friends eleven years ago. A good one could've taken care of Rhee when he was drafted. Maybe then...

She stared at the ceiling. "What would we have? A lamb filet with fig sauce? Soy-lemon flank steak with arugula? Seared ahi tuna with chimichurri sauce?"

He chuckled. "Or I could make it easy for you—I'd grill us porterhouse steaks?"

"Or I could try a flambe recipe," she said, eyes affixed on Julia Child's book on her nightstand.

Today, as he descended the basement steps, he planned to rehearse to serenade her at their dinner party. He'd try to bring back those new, fresh feelings of when they met, at the laundromat. Yes, he'd sing Gordon Lightfoot's "If You Could Read My Mind," playing that day. Sure it was a sad song, it would be far better than the other one playing that day, "You're Having My Baby."

The floor in the unfinished cinderblock basement chilled his bare feet. Pulling the string for the light, he thought of how he'd planned to turn this into a rec room someday for the kids, to include eleven-year-old Rhee. For now, though, it held a mini fridge stocked with beer, stereo on an end table, and a secondhand chair and TV tray from his bachelor days. A small bar sported shot glasses below a Duncan's sign and a menu. Next to a space heater sat a crate of albums—a few thanks to neighbor Steve's garage sales—and his old guitar and sheet music. He'd even framed his 45 and a Billboard chart of his week at number thirty-nine. He had some good newspaper reviews of the tour, too, but for now, they laid in a box, a joyous memory—and a painful reminder of what could have been.

The man cave let him escape to a drink, a smoke, and a cranked tune. Judith's oasis was the main floor, though she had now closed the doors to the empty nursery and third bedroom. She'd seen a specialist—had a myriad of appointments--and became obsessed with the first "test-tube baby" born in England. Since she'd turned thirty-one, she scaled back her dream to two kids, who could each have their own room now.

And Rhee. The third bedroom belonged to her, he'd said.

"It's not time to find her yet," she still said. "All this stress."

He walked to the basement corner where the ol' six-string leaned. He hadn't touched it since he walked away from the music scene. He opened the dusty black case and strummed, fiddling with The Hendrix's tuning. His hands found the frets, playing—badly— "Wonderful Tonight." It helped him forget this rotten week. It might go over well, too.

Cal closed his eyes. "Ain't never coming back alive," he sang next, the chord progression echoing off the cinderblock. "Girl, it's all for you…" The bare intro, a slow adagio, sounded decent with simple acoustics. As he strummed, he analyzed why he fell off the charts. Maybe his lone songs about a father at war would've been better positioned in the early seventies, because by the late seventies, people wanted to forget those years. After all, the decade started with the CSNY song "Ohio" penned for four students killed but ended in December 1979 with a literal "Escape (The Piña Colada Song)" as number one. He wished his song had stayed on the charts longer, because it was a fun run, but mostly, more chances for Rhee to hear it.

"Too late now." Besides, the stuffy parts of the biz, like the meetings with the suits telling him who to be, were worth forgetting. The era of the single had given way to the album, and Cal had none. One exec told him real dynamos delivered *entire* hit albums, like the Brothers Gibb, insinuating he didn't have half the talent. True, as he was just being himself, a remorseful dad, singing an apology, and a disco era had danced in—Donna Summer, KC and the Sunshine Band, Chic—and

The Hustle and funk topped the charts. TV showed people grooving, sticking spoons up their noses at swanky clubs. New wave, like Blondie's top tens and punk like Iggy Pop, Ramones, MC5, Patti Smith, The Clash swept through. Metal and hard rock from Van Halen, Scorpions, Rush, and Motorhead claimed heavy audiences too. Was Cal a forgotten AM guy lost on the FM?

"What does it matter now?" He set down his guitar, popped open a Bud, smoked a cig, drank the beer, and reached for the sheet music. He'd surprise his wife with this song tonight, though sung more up-tempo. They'd bond with the new neighbors, helped by the nostalgic music settling in the bones. Cal fiddled with the guitar, practicing chord changes, and downed more beers. He ran through the Lightfoot catalogue before he popped open the fifth beer and guzzled, the cold fizz sliding down his throat.

When numbness began to wash over him, he played Buffett's "Boat Drinks," and when it was over, he cranked Van Morrison for a break. Turning up "Into the Mystic," he couldn't help his mind wandering back to how Nainsi loved the *Astral Weeks* and *Moondance* albums.

Glancing at the *Brahm's Lullaby* sheet music that he saved for Judith's pregnancy, he shook his head, burying the agony of infertility, like much of his other pain, including some rough days at work. He wanted to forget Monday's incident. The hostage team had a carjacking call on Clarendon Boulevard in rush hour. The driver got shoved out. When the PD blockaded, swarming the car speeding toward the 66 ramp, the perp held up a 9mm to a little tyke in the back seat. Cal watched in horror, thinking, *It's not fucking happening. No kid dies today!* When negotiations broke down, the commander allowed the sniper's shot, which killed the suspect instantly. Cal sprinted to the crying toddler, scooping him in his arms, saying, "You're okay little man," and checked him, then gave him a Happy Meal toy he'd kept in the ambulance, just to give kids.

But this week, his mind replayed it in a loop. What if it turned out differently? "Those are normal thoughts in trauma," his cop buddy Sarge reminded him. The supervisor gave him a day off with "But Leonardowski, the boy didn't have a scratch."

He will. Cal poured himself a shot and smoked another cigarette. The cool liquor slid down easily, numbing the edge from the hellish week, old war scenes, and memories of Rhee. *How could he have done that?*

"Darling?" Judith called. "Can you help me bring in groceries? Bought so much food for tonight. We're having a feast!"

Cal stood but swayed. He sat back down, the floor unsteady. He should be in better shape. More jumping jacks. *Jack! Daniels! Good idea*! He slammed another one. He belched and headed up the stairs, but he missed one, tumbled, and landed in a heap.

Judith peered down. "What the—"

"Wanted to surprise you," he said with a slur and a hiccup as Van Morrison sang "Come Running."

She jogged down the stairs, waving her arms at all the smoke. "What kind of surprise is this?" Eyes narrowing at the empty cans and shot glass, she folded her arms.

"Happy anniversary, Judith!" He opened his arms wide which made the basement spin. "Kiss?"

"You've had a rough week, but this isn't how to deal. You already had a party." She stiffened. "How could you, today of all days? I hate you getting wasted all the time." She stomped up the stairs without offering a hand. "Sleep, shower, mouthwash. Be ready at six."

"How am I supposed to shower in an unfinished basement?"

"Your problem," she called down from the top of the stairs. "You were going to add a bathroom there."

The frigid floor welcomed his body. "I will. Soon."

A click locked him in the basement. A phone rang and dishes clanked before he faded.

Voices woke him three hours later. Dizzy still, he slapped his cheeks. He combed his tousled hair with his fingers and listened. *What? No music? Travesty. Even funerals have music. No,* he'll play DJ and save this party now. He scaled the steps and banged on the door, shouting, "I've been working on a song for you!" Under his breath, he added, "The only one you know."

Judith opened the door, patting her blonde curly permanent and sporting a matted-on smile, straightening her fuchsia top, smoothing her denim prairie skirt, and tapping her high-heeled brown boot. The neighbors sipped martinis with olives, dipping cocktail rye bread into a bubbling cheese fondue. Cal staggered toward the appetizer, shoving two in his mouth, a string of cheese dripping down his chin.

"Good to see you guys," he said, wiping his face with his hand and tucking in his shirt, as the neighbors nodded, managing polite smiles.

"Darling, are you okay? Let me get you a washcloth," Judith said, running cold water. "I've told our sweet neighbors how you weren't feeling well. Who can blame you between the rough week at work and—gosh, you still have that cherub nose from your cold."

"Like I said, I've been practicing singing you a special song for our anniversary." Tiddles of his spit flew into her face, and she frowned. "That Lightfoot song—yes it's his divorce song, but it was playing in the laundromat when we met. Remember?"

"Go upstairs and lie down," Judith said through gritted teeth, command in her voice, and blotted his forehead. "Get some sleep. I'm sorry, everyone."

"But let me play this for you—"

She shushed him, and the neighbors helped him to the bedroom. As he crashed on the ugly paisley duvet, Steve said, "He needs to sing her Chicago's 'Hard to Say I'm Sorry' instead."

Isabelle laughed, turned out the light, and kissed her husband.

The next morning, Judith didn't speak to him. Later, he hung her birdhouse on the lush maple tree outside the baby's room window. From the rocking chair, nursing, she could bird-watch.

"Hard to say I'm sorry," Cal said.

"If you could read my mind," Judith said.

39

"It Never Rains in Southern California"

Nainsi, December 1982

At their meeting spot just after the two-hour stadium graduation, Nainsi waved her cap when she spotted Father McKenzie. "You came! It's nice to have someone here for me. Thank you." They hugged just as a huge family next to them screamed and high-fived.

"I'm so proud of you. Doubly proud because you worked so hard for ten years."

She sighed.

"Be proud of yourself! You worked full time, created and managed entertainment, worked part time at the music store, all while studying for a bachelor's degree. That would've taken me forty years and a nervous breakdown."

"But I've applied everywhere here so far, for years, and none of the labels, artists, or venues here have called me. You have to know someone in LA."

"Enjoy your accomplishment. Stop being hard on yourself. Where's Killian?"

Nainsi looked away. "Work. Shipping holy statue orders in time for Christmas. It's fine, really, it's a busy time of year. Want to walk to that deli over there for lunch? I must tell you something."

As they darted around thousands of graduates, families, and friends mugging for pictures, her walking more swiftly than Father McKenzie's slow, intentional gait, she said, "Remember how I couldn't find anyone Cal kept in touch with in Virginia? Knocked on so many doors when I was back east. So, I tried calling Cal's label again. I must find Rhiannon, that's all. This time, they gave me a listing for his old agent. I called him. He said Cal walked away from music, moved to Arlington, Virginia. 'Family man,' he said with disgust. I knew they'd be in Virginia. I just want to see my daughter, start with visits..."

They arrived at a crosswalk. A police officer directed traffic at the intersection, and Father McKenzie waved. "What happened?"

"I dialed the operator. If it worked for Jim Croce, right? I mean, clearly, he recovered, thanks to her! I took a deep breath and called the only listing for Leonardowski. A woman answered. I trembled and asked, 'May I speak to Cal, please?'" She paused. For forever. 'Who's calling? Is this the station? An emergency?' I wondered, a radio station? What emergency would they have? I said, 'No emergency, but I'm...he will know me...' Silence. I listened for my girl in the background. All I could hear was this woman running water. 'Is that an Irish accent?' she said in such a curt manner. The water shut off. A bell dinged. 'Don't. Call. Here,' she said. I begged, 'It's okay if Cal doesn't want to talk to me. But please, can I just *speak* with Rhee? Please, I beg you, mother to mother?' She's caring for my girl, after all. Suddenly it seemed like she hurled a dish, because it shattered. Then, a pot clanked, like it was thrown into the sink. 'You have some nerve,' she said in a clipped voice. 'Do you know how many women want to cradle and love a baby? No. You *left her*. Cal doesn't want to talk to you, nor do I. *Ever*. Now, if you excuse me, we're about to have a dinner party.' The line went dead. And so did I, Father."

A car honked. The officer waved them across the street.

"I'm sorry. How rough. They won't let you talk to her?"

They walked to the deli line the size of the football field. "I talked to a regular at the lounge. A lawyer. He said I'd never win if I tried for custody because I abandoned them. A legal battle would be difficult, as they've been parenting her, giving her a good, loving home. It would be costly. What should I do? Should I start a battle in her life? Does she even want to hear from me? I want to be part of her life somehow...but maybe, not right now?"

"Perhaps consult with another attorney and a family therapist?"

A couple in line in front of them passionately embraced. Nainsi turned around to face Father McKenzie.

"What if her stepmother is right? I'm wrong to intrude now. Reappearing on the scene would be selfish, wreck Rhee as a pre-teen. I'd never want to cause her that strife. She has a stable home with her father and stepmother. Cal undoubtedly says horrible things about me, but maybe I should give my daughter what I wanted, space and time, the gift to grow up in peace and harmony, until she seeks me?"

"Sounds like a selfless choice, that it's about her well-being."

"But that kills me." Her throat swelled. "And what if she doesn't want to find me *ever*?" Despite her accomplishment today, the congratulatory spirit in the air, warm greetings flying around in the deli line, a stab seared her heart. She usually distracted herself with work to avoid this pain and took a deep breath. "Now for the other news. Thanks to my work transforming the Groove-y Lounge, and a rec from the department chair, I got an amazing job offer. They lured me in with good money and live music daily. I'll be able to send home more checks to Ireland and save money for Rhee. But I'll have to leave here. A big move."

"Oh?" Father McKenzie's wrinkly eyes shifted into the distance, past people still pouring out of the stadium. "I'm sad. I'll miss you. You're like the daughter I never had."

"I'll miss you, too. We'll stay in touch. And Father McKenzie, let me know when you finish that sermon."

He smiled, humming "Eleanor Rigby," as the PDA couple in front of them came up for a breather and spouted pet names.

Nainsi rolled her eyes at them as they inched ahead. "Haven't told Killian yet, but the job is like my dream of a live music career coming true, helping people escape— 'come together' in music."

"You're already doing that, bringing people peace through music. Your Ma's already proud."

A lump came to her throat and grief waved through her body. She only wanted to hug Ma and Rhee right now.

"Poem, prayer, or promise today?"

"Pray Killian doesn't hit the roof about this job. He scares me sometimes, some things he says."

"Like?"

"Just stuff."

"Talk to me."

"Not now."

"A prayer for your new adventure then. A classic. May God hold you in the palm of his hand, and the wind be at your back." They shuffled forward in line. "But if I may? Advice about your mysterious man not here today. As my fed friends say, 'Trust, but verify.'"

40

"You Light Up My Life"

Rhiannon, April 2, 1984

The news out of LA sent Rhiannon to her room reeling, like when Karen Carpenter died of anorexia last year. The incomparable Marvin Gaye, whose '71 album *What's Going On* about a returning soldier seeing hate, injustice, and poverty, and that had lodged in her heart long ago, had been shot to death by his father. She put on Marvin's album, and her mind traveled to her own father. Where had he lived? When he was a kid, did he play ball or music?

She picked up the invitation to all eighth-grade girls. *Spring Fa-ther-Daughter Dance with sundae bar & karaoke contest!*

"Ugh." She crumpled it up and pitched it at the wall and flopped onto her bed.

What would it be like to go to an event the other girls took for granted, goofing off with your dad, complaining he's embarrassing? What would it be like for your dad to teach you to drive, see your school play, warn you about boys? What about when he's so proud at your graduation, he cries into his hanky? What's it like when he walks you down the aisle at your wedding, whispering you'll still be daddy's little girl? A lump rose in her throat. She tore the fancy schmancy invitation into a million pieces.

"Whatever." She played Barbra Streisand next, and as her perfect pitch relayed longing and loss, she got out her journal. *Memories, ha! If only I had some,* she wrote. *Barbra didn't know her father either. He died, but at least her mom told her who he was.*

She put down her pen and changed albums to rock, letting Foreigner lead singer Lou Gramm's passionate rock voice belt out an angry edge instead, and then she filled her ears with the solid and gritty voice of Bob Seger. She sang along, writing "Against the Wind" in her music notebook when a knock rapped.

"Open up, it's locked."

Rhiannon lowered the volume and swung open the door.

Gert held a high school registration form. "Had an idea for you, dear-heartie."

"How about no?" Gert's ideas usually involved chores, homework, Savon orders, or church volunteerism.

"You'll like this idea. You'd have to do the work, though."

Please don't make me mow the lawn! She saw the forms Gert held showing a blank "Family Medical History." Gert had crossed it out and wrote in big letters, "UNKNOWN. STOP ASKING!"

Gert's gaze traveled to the crumpled invitation on the bed. "Let's go to the county animal shelter and give an abandoned dog a home?"

Rhiannon gasped. "You mean it? I've always wanted a dog I'd name Boo, like that old song, 'Me and You and A Dog Named Boo'!"

"Boo who?" Gert chuckled. "Okay, Boo it is. Mercy, hope he won't scare the scaredy-cat."

"This is the best surprise ever! What made you—"

"I just didn't want to hear any more of these songs you blast. Earlier, it sounded like someone was singing 'Sexual Healing!' Heavens!"

41

"You'll Never Find Another Love Like Mine"

Nainsi, January, 1985

As manager of a new theatre in Branson, Missouri, Nainsi tugged at her navy Casual Corner blazer and smoothed her pencil skirt, as she waded into the next crowd. Today's 2 p.m. show was sold out. In the three years since she'd opened it, they'd heavily advertised and target-marketed, bringing in audiences with good prices and promotions. The town was building as a family entertainment destination. The Presleys and Roy Clark owned theatres here; rumors flew Dolly Parton might build here.

As folks stepped off a bus marked SENIOR DAY TRIPS asking for wheelchairs, a frail elderly woman using a walker shuffled past Nainsi. Her voice was unmistakable, and Nainsi turned at the woman in her nineties, tapped her three-inch pumps, and followed her into the lobby and aroma of hot buttered popcorn. "Mrs. Henderson?"

"Yes?" Recognition flew over her wrinkled face, and she brightened as her voice shot up. "Oh, my word! I'll be! What a small world. Bill, you remember my old neighbor, Nainsi?"

Nainsi hugged her warmly for maybe a whole minute, but it backed up the line and grumbles spread, so she led them to velvet lobby chairs.

Mrs. H fiddled with her hearing aid. "There we go. How's Cal, dear? You two lovebirds were adorable, if a little loud, though."

Nainsi's face flushed, unsure if Mrs. H meant noise from music, sex, or the baby. Her *baby.* What was so bad about life then? Why hadn't she found a college in Virginia?

"How's Rhiannon? A high schooler now?"

How could I say? Mrs. H's quilt still lay on her bed, and she still cuddled it, missing her. "Did you know Cal and I broke up? It was the day you left..."

"Oh, no! I'm very sorry! He was a nice young man. But if you visit, I'll set you up with my grandnephew." She took a breath. "He's fifty. Is that too old for you?"

"I'm married. Almost four years. Killian is a wonderful man." She wouldn't say how Killian didn't want to move here—and as the jealous sort, he also didn't want her to move there alone. She went, though, and now he quizzed her often, called constantly, asked about her male coworkers. He disliked she worked with so many men who could hit on her—as if he hadn't been one once. She tried to tell him how she loved managing a fifteen-million-dollar facility and supervising a staff of thirty and overseeing the artists and contracts for shows that played six nights a week, two a day. It was a chance to shape this theatre from the ground up, she said.

Nainsi asked him repeatedly to move with her— "Our money goes farther than in LA"—but Killian fumed. A torrid fight had ensued in their last visit, involving a shove against the wall, and one little one just onto the bed, but then Killian's apologetic make-up. He said he had trusted her to go to Branson alone—*if* they married. She could make everyone happy, including her family back home.

Stomach knotted, she walked down the aisle at a gorgeous wedding mass, Father Gallagher officiating, Da ecstatic. Her dashing brothers in tuxes beamed smiles of glee, especially Liam, who walked well in braces.

After a honeymoon of incredible Broadway shows in New York City, she flew to Missouri. "I love it here. The green hills remind me of back home, and the job is music, like I always wanted," she said to Killian, "so won't you think more about moving here?" A month later, he drove her *Name That Tune* car to Branson, checked out her luxury apartment with sweeping views of the Ozarks, toured White Water and Silver Dollar City, took in a show he called "upscale hillbilly." After a long kiss at the gate, his hot breath in her ear, he whispered, "No. Way. In. Hell," and jetted back to LAX.

Mrs. H cleared her throat. "I said, does Rhee have a brother or sister now?"

Nainsi glanced at her watch. "The show's starting soon, so I won't keep you by blabbing. Let's catch up over lunch. Are you still in St. Louis?"

"Yes, but hurry. Who knows how much time I have left." She chuckled. The lights flickered, and a bell sounded for ten minutes until curtain. Nainsi grabbed a brochure, scrawled her number, and hugged her goodbye. Then she directed an usher to give her the best seat she saved for special guests, and off she went to the wheelchair accessible front row.

Halfway to her office, she thought about the call from the public relations exec yesterday. The woman had designs on Nainsi's job, but she had a friend who had a contact who had a boss who knew Bob Geldof, a singer-songwriter of the Irish rock band Boomtown Rats. He and Midge Ure had just composed a number one song by Irish and British artists, "Do They Know It's Christmas?" Geldof and Ure envisioned massive concerts of dozens of acts for African famine relief called "Live Aid." Was she interested in working for them? It meant a move, but for her passion of promoting pop-rock. Despite her family's reservations, she adored the UK. After all, it was the site of the most joyful surprise ever with Ma. *London's calling!*

When she told Killian last night on the phone, he'd said, "No, baby, no. I've *let* you go to Missouri for three long years. It's time to settle down here and have a family." He threatened a divorce, complete with visa scrutiny from authorities.

A lawyer once said she'd likely never win joint custody with Cal. But as a single mom who had split? Fat chance. "We have a family," she had said. "Us and everyone back home...and someday Rhiannon."

"Your daughter doesn't want to see you," he said. "She hates you."

42

"Philadelphia Freedom"

Rhiannon, July 1, 1985

Outside the thrift store in a blighted parking lot off Route 1, with Rhiannon holding a maroon chiffon Gunne Sax prom dress she didn't want because the prom was three years away—but Gert insisted as it was only seven dollars, an argument reached new decibel levels.

"I want to go to Live Aid or I'm going to *die*!" Rhiannon yelled. "Everyone's playing!"

"Two teenagers alone, going three hours away to Philadelphia, in a hundred thousand people? The most preposterous idea I've ever heard! You're most definitely not going. That concert will be pandemonium, I tell you! Befuddled you'd even think of it."

"It's no big deal!" But she knew darn well it was a big deal. A historic concert of epic proportions, tons of rock acts would play for a sixteen-hour day in the US and London, simulcast in dozens of countries. "It's for famine relief. A *good cause.*"

"Nice try. Girlie, you give me a heart attack just asking. Drugs and alcohol and kidnappers and creeps abound. Stranger danger lurking! You and Sara gallivanting around at fourteen? No, no, no! Certainly not!"

She slammed the door of Gert's Pinto. This would not be over.

"And hang up that dress when we get home!"

"I don't want it," she yelled, and Gert's hand flew to her bosom and her eyes looked hurt.

Rhiannon begged all week as she morphed into Angel Teen. She vacuumed, swept, dusted each saint figurine, changed Ezzy's litter box, walked Boo and picked up his poop, cleaned Gert's inventory closet, and delivered her catalogues. She even promised perfect grades and gifted her first-born child Olivia to her. When Gert didn't budge, she had no choice. It was time to call in the Big Man.

Kneeling in a pew, bargaining for intercession with St. Jude of desperate causes, as stained-glass saints peered down at her, a plan emerged. Maybe it was ordained? She came home and prayed to Gert's Infant statue too. *Yes.* With saved babysitting money, she would buy two tickets to paradise from Ticketron. Friday night, she'd sleep over Sara's, who'd saved enough for train tickets. They'd get up before anyone awoke and bike three miles to the train station at Quantico. Then, they'd hop a train bound to Union Station, then to Philadelphia. Sara wanted to see Sting, Run DMC, and Duran Duran, but for Rhiannon, the seventies' legends were the prize, artists singing old songs that held a mysterious call to her heart, like Crosby, Stills, Nash & Young. Her favorite song of theirs was "Our House" for some reason. Give her a gentle harmony sung by singer-songwriters playing acoustic guitar any day.

The plan was fail-proof. She and Sara will rock out at Live Aid tomorrow. Like, totally rad.

43

"Bluer Than Blue"

Cal, July 12-13, 1985

The fertility specialist's office had cranked the air conditioning, and Judith shivered with clasped hands. Cal looked at the hundreds of babies' pictures on the wall behind the doctor's desk.

"At least you're going to someone successful," he said.

The doctor entered and closed her office door with a perfunctory greeting. She sat down and opened their file. "How are you two doing?" she said, but her eyes studied papers.

"We're fine," said Judith with a cool tone.

"Waiting on answers and hope, Doc," Cal said.

After almost eight heartbreaking years, charting menstrual cycles for "optimal ovulation times" and "timing intercourse" every month, taking medication, vitamins, hormones, doing procedures and tests, that approach failed. Next, complete workups, tests for everything from diabetes to autoimmune disorders, gynecological surgeries, and testing for Cal failed to pinpoint the problem. Then, her doctor recommended this specialist in Fairfax. With her, they'd spent $25,000 trying three times "in-vitro fertilization," all failed. She cried for days as she declined friends' baby showers and Cal felt so helpless that happy hours after work stretched longer, followed by drinks in the recliner.

"As you know, even though your initial diagnostic surgery showed some endometriosis, and your husband's work-up showed a lower-than-normal sperm count, we hoped to fertilize outside the womb."

Judith nodded slowly as Cal scoffed. His sperm were just fine, thank you.

"The embryos had implanted successfully, but they did not produce a live pregnancy."

"We know," Cal said.

"I understand your frustration, but remember IVF is still in its infancy. The data isn't there nationwide yet, but I believe more success will be in the years to come. Technology is promising."

"And...?" Judith said.

"But reviewing your records, we've now exhausted all options. It's unlikely you'll conceive. I wouldn't advise continuing with more taxing medical intervention. I must look out for my patient's health first. I don't recommend repeating these medications for the long-term. And it's uncovered by insurance, as you know."

Cal's heart sank. Judith dropped her head. Cal reached for her hand, trying to be brave for her. "You're a fertility clinic. You charge us a bazillion dollars and then say this is it?"

A jackhammer drilled in the distance. The doctor waited for it to pass before speaking in a monotone. "There were no guarantees, as you know. Again, the procedure is in its early stages."

"Eight years of hell," Cal said.

Judith's eyes bore into the doctor's. "Why is this happening?"

"Some couples fall into an unexplained category. Sometimes it's a combination of factors. Forty percent of couples find infertility factors on both sides. The good news is there are other paths to parenthood, but medical intervention is not the one for you now."

Judith's eyes cast down. "I can't do this anymore."

"I'm done, too." He studied the doctor's diploma on the wall. "We can't go through these cycles of hope and crash and burn each time. But like she said, the science is new, so maybe one day..."

"But the risks after thirty-five are much higher at that advanced geriatric age," the doctor said.

"Geriatric? Judas Priest, we're thirty-three. Though sometimes I feel eighty-three."

"We're never going to be parents, are we?" Her bottom lip quivered. She looked at Cal, then at the specialist. "It's all I've ever wanted."

"We will adopt," he said. And we already have a child!

"Any further questions?" the doctor asked, closing the file--and this dream.

"No," Cal said.

"Thank you," Judith said in a hollow tone. They exited and walked down the hall to the elevator, but a mother waited, navigating two babies in a double stroller by a pediatrician's office. Judith hastened toward the stairs.

When they stepped into the sunlight and a heat wave, humidity soaked his shirt by the time he unlocked their four-door family sedan. They drove almost without a word ten more minutes, and somewhere on a jammed four-lane Route 50, after stopping for lights every five hundred feet, parents turning their minivans into Babies R Us and soccer fields and kids' music lessons, Judith's tears fell.

"About adoption," Cal offered. "You once said it's the most loving thing someone could do." His gut dropped thinking of Rhee, how he'd just drunkenly entrusted her to a stranger to find a family. It was time to find her. *What was she like as a fourteen-year-old?*

"How much will adoption cost, and how many years on a waiting list for a baby? Or how long until a girl "chooses" us? Our best years are behind us."

"It's never too late," he said.

Then, much like that day he was about to swallow his mom's painkillers, a radio voice granted Cal a reprieve. "Philadelphia is getting ready for the massive all-day Live Aid concert tomorrow…"

"Judith? Let's forget it all for a bit. Come with me to that all-day concert in Philly." He'd already bought tickets and hoped to persuade her. Either way, he'd planned to rise early and drive three hours to JFK Stadium. Over eighty-thousand people would see everyone from Jagger, Tina Turner, Beach Boys, Kenny Loggins, REO Speedwagon, to the Cars, Four Tops, Santana, Clapton, Petty. Simulcast, London's Wembley Stadium would hold seventy-five thousand fans who would see Queen, U2, Elton John, Paul McCartney, among others. It sold Cal when he heard reunion groups Led Zeppelin—with Phil Collins on drums, playing both shows thanks to the Concorde—and CSNY would play. Worth the thirty-five-dollar ticket on the charge card.

"It'll be hot and crowded and loud and the parking nightmarish," she said. "Why go? It'll be televised."

"Nothing like live music in summer." His mind harkened back to life-saving Atlanta. He wondered if Nainsi would venture to London for this show. She must like her hometown band U2. "I miss the escape. Haven't gone to a concert since my own. My music's a thing of the past, as you know…" He regretted his resentment had tumbled out now, but in his way, he was offering a bandage. "Another Woodstock, once-in-a-lifetime event, and you want to miss it?"

"Had no problem missing Woodstock—or Atlanta," she snapped. "Just watch it on TV."

"Live a little."

"I tried to live— and give. By now, I was supposed to be going to Little League and Girl Scouts." They pulled onto their neighborhood street. Boys played football in the front yard of a rambler. Girls drew with sidewalk chalk. A toddler in a diaper ran through a sprinkler and laughed.

Cal's heart broke. "I'm sorry." He turned into their driveway. "It's devastating news."

She fished house keys from her purse when the car stopped. "Did you ever think, if only you would've stopped drinking and smoking any time in our eight years, then maybe you wouldn't have a low sperm count?"

The shot stung and he shook his head. "C'mon. You heard the doc. Maybe it's both of us. Maybe it's Agent Orange. Doc said depression could contribute. Maybe you need a bit of joy."

"Going to a stadium isn't joy for me." She slammed the car door and marched to the door.

John Mellencamp's "Lonely Ol' Night" came on. Why stick around tonight? Might as well leave for the weekend alone rather than be miserable together. He'd shoot up I-95 to Philadelphia, park, and sleep in this boat big enough for a family of six. He peeled away from the driveway, headed to his first rock festival in fifteen years.

He honked his goodbye, sticking his hand out the window with a wave. *Gimme sun, beer, tunes, and escape.*

44

"Woodstock"

Rhiannon, July 13, 1985

Music blasted in the stadium as sunshine lit the massive audience, most of whom pumped fists into the heat waves.

"Looks like we made it!" Rhiannon threw her hands in the air, her side ponytail, doused with Sun-In to catch blonde streaks, bouncing. "Gosh, it's hot." She untucked her sweaty, oversized t-shirt to blouse it over her neon pink skorts. They climbed on their seats in upper right field to see if they could touch the lights. *Almost!*

"We're sitting in another area code, closer to the Great Ball of Fire." Sara gulped a brew, gripping the can with her lacy Madonna gloves. By 10 a.m., they'd snagged their first beers, thanks to a scuzzy vendor.

"This is grody." Rhiannon made a face as she sipped the beer. "Gag me with a spoon."

"To the max. Heard it gets less narly the more you drink. Wine coolers next?"

"For sure."

"Kids of the eighties, this is your Woodstock!" Joan Baez said. Rhiannon screamed. Live music, not from shoddy speakers. *How lucky are we?* She thanked St. Jude and the Infant statue as they danced through the Hooters and sang with the Four Tops and Billy Ocean. It was in this early buzz, after Ozzy's reunion with Black Sabbath, when a page blared from the loudspeaker.

"Sara Smythe, please report to the information desk."

Rhiannon's stomach dropped. "Did you hear that?"

"No." Sara shrugged. "Lots of Sara Smythes."

Rhiannon ignored the inkling. After all, they were now jamming to Rick Springfield! They'd drooled over his album at Sara's house, hot Dr. Noah Drake on *General Hospital*. He looked fine in his black muscle shirt singing "Human Touch." He strutted off stage to shrieks.

"Sara Celeste Smythe and Rhiannon Cecilia Jaymes of Baker Street in Virginia, age fourteen, report to the information desk at level four immediately."

"Bogus!" Sara yelled.

"We just got here!" Rhiannon cried.

They stormed away from their seats, tossed the last of their first beers in an overflowing trash can, and flagged down an usher who directed them. They walked over a mile and lost the new buzz before they found the info desk.

Sara held the phone out from her ear, mouthing it was her dad. "...DROVE THREE DAMN HOURS... TWENTY DOLLARS to park in this mess...where the EAGLES play of all places! March to gate A!"

"You're *here*? Dad, no! It just started! Bryan Adams and Simple Minds are both coming up!"

"*Now*!"

"Can't we just stay for Madonna? Please?"

Rhiannon overheard a string of words she'd need to look up in the dictionary.

"When we peeked in your room this morning and you two weren't there, we called Gert. She suspected this," Sara's mom yelled. "At this rate, you're headed for a life on the run. So run *now* to Gate A!"

They exchanged aghast looks. The intricate plan borne of fervent holy prayer, foiled. They'd miss twelve more hours of acts. *Tina Turner!*

Sara slammed down the phone. "We're busted. Totally."

"We're going to miss Kenny Loggins, Santana, and CSN," Rhiannon said.

"And there goes the Bartles and Jaymes," Sara said.

The girls trudged and dawdled to the exit. Worse, when they spotted them outside Gate A, it wasn't just furious Mr. and Mrs. Smythe. Gert stood in a floral peasant housecoat dress, sneakers planted wide apart, hands firmly planted on her hips.

"Rhiannon Cecilia Jaymes! You're going to give me a heart attack!" She flung her arms around Rhee with a hug. "You are fine china in a bull shop!"

Rhiannon rolled her eyes. "A bull in a china shop."

"You call this wild rock concert fine china? The lady who sings 'Like a Virgin' is here! Oh, my word!" Gert closed her ears like Rhee used to when she was four. "Heavens to Betsy, what if someone had slipped drugs in your lemonade? What if you breathed in all this mysterious smoke here that smells like fall? What if the heat made you faint like you do sometimes?"

"So what!"

"You snuck out!" She put her hand on her chest. "You gave me a load of bullhorn!"

"But it was all *my* babysitting money."

"You hit the nail on the headache. Your hard earnings went to *this*!" Gert caught her breath. "You're grounded until graduation!"

"That's four years away!"

"So be it," she said. "Into every sandstorm a rainstorm must fall."

They traipsed through mile-long aisles, all perspiring, Gert barely able to keep up. When they opened the doors of the Smythes' Yugo, the three-foot statue greeted them from the back seat, as stoic as ever. Yep,

Gert had called in the big guns. "The Infant of Prague found you," Gert said. "A miracle!"

No one spoke on the way home. They angled for AC vents in the rattling car. Except somewhere around Baltimore, Gert added, "And you will go to confession every week forevermore! No more skipping."

"Call me Sister Christian," Rhiannon said. Only Sara laughed.

45

"I Can't Tell You Why"

Cal, July 13, 1985

A tractor-trailer had overturned on the Beltway, forcing two lanes to a dead stop and the third to a crawl. An hour—and then two— trapped in the traffic jam caused Cal to reassess. Guilt gnawed for leaving Judith alone this weekend after the terrible news that caused a gorge in his heart too. He wanted a baby, too, _and_ his Rhee. Couldn't she see that? _Our family's still in our reach, Judith,_ he wanted to say.

He sighed. Live Aid was on TV like she said, and who knew what monumental sum they were charging for food, beverages, parking? The Buds would be cheaper and colder at home. Eating the ticket cost pissed him off, though, but Cal ached more for their fruitless journey.

Cal inched off at an exit, turned around, and drove back.

When Judith opened the door, he swept her into his arms, and they cried together. "I'm sorry again about the news," he said.

She said she'd sell her '74 Plymouth to help pay the bills, though this would only take care of seven hundred fifty of their twenty-five-thousand-dollar debt. As a one-car family now, she said, they'd save money on car insurance and gas.

"I'll quit smoking like you want," he offered, as they changed for bed. "The money we'll save on cartons can go to the bills."

Over her Quiche Lorraine breakfast and his MTV, he fixed a Bloody Mary, extra tabasco, and double part vodka. Judith threw in a celery stick. He switched to beer later in the afternoon when the savory aroma of prime rib filled the bungalow. "Ain't so bad staying home," Cal said as he watched eighty-nine thousand people rocking on their feet. He briefly feared a repeat of the 1979 Who concert in Cincinnati where people were crushed to death. He watched how every act played a few songs with no encores. He turned it up when Zep—Plant, Page, and Jones, and Phil Collins who made it from London—played "Whole Lotta Love," and "Stairway to Heaven" but fell disappointed after the hype. Plant seemed off. Not Page's best day. Collins didn't fit in. The only solution—Crosby, Stills, Nash & Young. His eyes misted at "Teach Your Children." Unless that was from the beers he'd guzzled while Judith cut up carrots, broccoli, peppers, and mixed in sprouted seeds, nuts, and rice. For Pauly.

"Will Marv Albert be playing the trumpet?" Judith called from the kitchen.

Cal chuckled. "Marv Albert is a sportscaster, so, no. You mean Herb Alpert. Don't think he's there, though everyone else is."

Everyone. Teenagers filled that place with all those pop acts like Wham! What if his girl were there?

He headed to the bedroom for the phone extension. Thank God for operators. He held a number in twenty seconds.

"You want us to make an announcement for a child?" a stadium voice repeated.

"Please."

"Call the police."

"It's not like that," he said. "But it's important. I need to reach her."

"Sir, we can't make every announcement. It must be an emergency."

"Aren't you the city of brotherly love? Chevy Chase announced an organ donation was waiting for someone. You all may have saved a life today."

The person huffed. "All right. Quick."

"Can you say, 'If your name is Rhiannon, born April, 1971, and you're looking for your parents, call this number'?"

There was a long pause. "Funny, that's the second time I've heard the name Rhiannon today. Look, we'll try to do announcements at the end, but no promises."

Glued to MTV the rest of the day, Cal ate in the living room with Judith as she read. He watched U2 rock Wembley, Bono belting out a twelve-minute "Bad," holding the mic out for audience singalong, a sea of thousands of arms swaying and clapping. He wondered if Nainsi was in the crowd. When he heard Bob Dylan, Ron Wood, and Keith Richards perform "Blowin' in the Wind," and "We Are the World," to close, he waited. The vee-jays spoke about how Queen crushed it in London—Freddie Mercury started with vocal warm-ups with the crowd—and stole the show.

He waited by the phone all night. Judith fell asleep on the couch, and Cal nudged her to the bedroom. Pauley clicked and whistled from his room. "Goodnight, Pauly," she called.

Sunday, he woke to a Tequila Sunrise. He showered and chose khaki shorts and a wrinkle-free short-sleeve shirt. He combed his hair and brushed his teeth, careful not to wake Judith. He brought in the *Post*, checked scores, and got into the family boat. He flicked on the car radio, and as he searched for the classic rock station, he sang "If You Don't Know Me By Now," like Teddy Pendergrass sang in '72. He'd gone on stage yesterday in a wheelchair, with Ashford & Simpson, in his first appearance since an accident caused his paralysis. Yet Pendergrass had spoken of gratitude, and it felt inspirational. Life was unexpected and all we had was now.

He sang as he drove for a good while, landing at a place he hadn't seen in fourteen long years. Mass had just ended, and he dodged cars racing out. He parked in the back. He smoked his last one ever, snuffed it out in his ashtray, and threw it out the window. For fifteen minutes listening to the radio, he prayed for courage.

Then he walked up those imposing steps to St. Ronan's Catholic Church.

46

"Shining Star"

Nainsi, August 1, 1986

Phone Transcript

Father: How was your year in London working for Live Aid? Did you meet U2 or McCartney? Did you see Queen?

Nainsi: They were all amazing! I even met Princess Diana!

Father: Wow! What's she like?

Nainsi: She was so gracious she said hello to *me*—and I got frazzled and bowed!

Father: Ha. Wonderful. So, what's happening with Killian? As I remember, he threatened ugliness when you moved to London?

Nainsi: He refused to move to London with me, but with customers in the UK, he did fly out and see me each month, so it's fine. It's for better or for worse, right?

Father: Where are you?

Nainsi: Home in Dublin weighing offers from artists and labels here, and I'm happy at being back home. Killian said he might even consider moving to Dublin for his business—not necessarily me. [chuckle] Guess we're '80s yuppie DINKs.

Father: Yuppie DINKs?

Nainsi: Young urban professionals, dual income, no kids. Though I'm staying in my family's house in my old room, saving cash as I consult with artists by phone. It's actually lucrative, and it lets me help by taking care of the house, cooking meals, taking Liam to doctor's appointments and physical therapy. Gives Auntie a break, yet she still comes by. But long-term, maybe I'll move back to LA if doors will open for me there now with all this experience? Because we're thinking about starting a family now. Doctor said at thirty-four, my clock is ticking. I wonder if a baby will help fill the eternal hole in my heart? I still miss Rhee terribly. I just want to love her, help guide her, live near her, anything she'd let me do to care for her. Do you know what I've learned? What good is success if you can't share it with the people you love? For me, that's Rhee. And I'm trying harder to reignite the marriage with Killian too. After London, I flew back to LA with him for two weeks together. We ran around like old times having fun. Caught a show at the Troubadour—his choice—Guns and Roses. All this time apart mostly did us good.

Father: Mostly?

Nainsi: He only got mad at me once.

Father: His business again?

Nainsi: We were running errands, and he stopped at a warehouse. He said to wait in the car, but I got bored after twenty minutes and wandered in. I could hear raised voices talking in the back office, so I waited outside. But things got too heated. Shouts about gunpowder! Strange—he deals in religious knickknacks and statues—but I overheard words like small and folding stock, high velocity, ammo, explosives, a defective shipment on the QE 2.

Father: What else did you hear?

Nainsi: Or what I didn't hear. Nothing about holy statues. Mostly gunpowder.

Father: How did this end?

Nainsi: I backed away to the car and he stormed out with clenched fists and a red-hot face.

Father: And?

Nainsi: I asked what happened. He screamed it was none of my fucking business—sorry, Father! —and he can run his *successful* business with his customers just fine. And that was that. A shiver crawled down my spine.

Father: That's the Holy Spirit's talking to ye. Extra poems, prayers, and promises as you go forth, my friend.

47

"I'm Not in Love"

Cal, December 24, 1986

Cal and Judith walked the frozen food aisle looking for an ingredient for her tantalizing eclairs recipe, just as a woman dressed in a black leather skirt, black stilettos, and a low-cut ginger blouse turned into the aisle. "Heather?"

Heather lit up when their eyes met. "Cal, hi! Is this your wife? Hi!" She extended her festively manicured hand.

Judith nodded hello, barely grasping fingers.

"This is my favorite Quincy's bartender," Cal said.

Judith's cordiality turned to a scowl.

"Stop by Quincy's tonight for a holiday drink?" she said. "Yes, it's open. I'm headed to work."

"Great idea." He turned to Judith. "How about it?"

He longed for boisterous bustle on Christmas Eve, comforting family traditions, presents under the tree in the morning, and the goodwill toward humanity in the air. With no family—her parents never visited—the last thing they wanted was a childless house Santa skipped.

He'd never told her he asked at St. Ronan's "for a friend," if anyone had brought in a baby girl on August 7, 1971, "for help." The secretary looked perplexed. She'd check with the woman who ran the cry room and with the sisters and priests. Unfortunately, she explained, the church had had a flood, their file cabinets ruined, so records, newsletters, and correspondence was unsalvageable, so it was up to human memory. She asked for his number, but he said he'd call back. When he could afford a lawyer.

When Judith had accepted they wouldn't have a biological child, Cal had said they should look for Rhee. "She's fifteen now. There's three years to cherish before adulthood." In his eyes, he'd agreed to Judith's wishes to build a family first before he found Rhee. Now he wouldn't wait anymore.

"It's a terrible idea," she had said, shooting him a look. He shouldn't waltz back into her life now, disrupting high school angst, exams, part-time jobs, college planning. "It's tumultuous growing up. Wait until she's an adult and finds you. Her choice. And by the way, affording a lawyer with our astronomical bills already?"

He'd brushed it off this time, saying, "I don't care. Life is short. We wasted so much time." A guilt wave rolled over him when her eyes watered. "I'm sorry. That's not what I meant. Just, I've missed Rhee's entire childhood, for us, like you asked, and now... I could still say I'm sorry, try to be part of her life somehow. Don't you get that?"

"It's to ease your guilt? Or is it for her?" she had said.

He met her gaze. "I want to make sure she's okay. Give her a second family, if she'll consider us."

"God didn't want me to be a mom," she'd said. Untrue, he said, but compassion for her flooded him then, and he wondered if he was being punished by God for abandoning Rhee. *He trusted a stranger to find her a family!* He hugged Judith and suggested they research adoption lawyers. She turned and brought the bird from his room to watch TV with them. Pauly liked *Alf.*

"So, Quincy's?" Cal awaited Judith's answer. This Christmas would be like the previous ones—no cookies for Santa. No kids tearing open presents as a fire crackled. It'd be the two of them eating a pork loin, him hitting the eggnog early and often. If he couldn't smoke anymore, he wanted to at least indulge in libations at Quincy's and forget misery tonight. "Please?"

In something of a Christmas miracle—like the show he saw with Mama when Carol Brady got her voice back—Judith unfolded her arms and agreed to the last-minute social outing. Cal kissed her cheek.

At Quincy's, the atmosphere warmed Cal. "Last Christmas" blasted from the sound system, and laughter bounced from each corner. Colorful lights wrapped around the bar, and a brightly lit tree shone, decorated with beer cans. A Santa Claus statue, manger, and a lit menorah perched on the bar.

On break, Heather sat down with Cal and Judith at a corner high-top. Before long, she and Cal fell into stitches, reminiscing about ten years at the bar and filling in the blanks for Judith. She nodded politely, sipping apple cider as the designated driver.

"Remember when Jorge told off that weatherman?" Heather said, and Cal slapped his leg, laughing so hard he cried. Exactly one hour later, Judith touched her dainty watch, the cue for wrapping up social niceties like small talk in a funeral parlor. Fair enough. Hugging Heather goodbye, he wished her a merry Christmas, while Judith bolted for the exit.

As Judith drove home and he stuffed a Three Musketeers into his mouth instead of a Pall Mall, she asked, "Did you ever sleep with her?"

"Stop with the jealousy," he said. Not that he hadn't considered when, a few years ago, he'd been drinking with Sarge and the guys at the bar, talking about the rail-thin elderly man who'd fallen unresponsive. In his run-down studio apartment where the TV blared and newspapers were stacked to the ceiling, Cal realized the cupboards and the fridge held nothing. This man was dying of *hunger*. The IV he'd drawn had saved his life as they whisked him to the hospital, but the sad, lonely scene ate at him. The man was only alive thanks to an alert neighbor who called when she hadn't seen him in days, he said as Heather made his next 7 & 7 before her shift ended.

"Awful. Sorry for all the trauma you all see," she said, putting on her coat. "If you ever want to talk more…"

He and the guys pounded another round, and he excused himself to a pay phone. "Stopping at a diner, don't wait up," he said, and he grabbed his jacket and rocketed out the door to 7-Eleven. He bought a bottle of wine, and in line he gazed at the lights of Rosslyn. If only he and Judith had a city view like this, instead of sprawl and a bus stop. He sighed. It didn't matter. Rekindling with Judith felt monumental. He grabbed the brown paper bag and exited, the bells jingling on the door as he weighed whether to show up at Heather's place to talk or forget it. Then his stomach dropped.

"Judith! What are you doing here?"

"It was my turn to get the bottled water for work…" She'd looked at the liquor bag, an apprising stare coming to her eyes. "You?"

"Just thinking about shooting the breeze with a friend."

"Bringing her wine?" Her voice held a sharp tone. "To a diner?"

He stammered. Her lips pursed. "Let's go home," she'd said. They never spoke about it again.

"Can I ask something?" he said now from the passenger side as Dan Fogelberg's "Same Old Lang Syne" drifted from the car radio and the annual Christmas Eve drizzle fell on the windshield. "Were we just a science experiment for procreation?"

"You chose fifty ways to leave your liver." She pulled into their drive-way, hit the brakes, threw the transmission into park, and their torsos bounced forward.

"Man, c'mon. Low blow."

"Is it?" She took out the keys and turned to face him, a flash of anger in her eyes that settled into something sadder. Emptier.

"No, we never slept together."

She slammed the car door and marched in. When she opened the door, the silver garland wreath and purple bow jostled, and he shut it closed behind him. Judith checked on the bird and hung up her coat. "You were at the bar last week when I got my award."

"What award?" He vaguely remembered her chatting about Administrator of the Year.

"Remember? The execs said I had made a difference in streamlining procedures, saving them money. The program I started for members is growing, getting praise, and you still haven't said two words acknowledging my work."

"I'm sorry," Cal said, feeling an inch tall. He slithered to the kitchen to scavenge for a beer and brownie. "I'll Be Home for Christmas" played from the radio.

Judith turned on the clear lights on the white artificial tree. "You don't even know I started volunteering at the bird sanctuary. Or that I adore Pina Coladas."

He chuckled. "About that personal ad I took out..." She did not laugh. "It's a joke, Judith. That song? Look, I'm sorry for missing your award."

"You were at the bar having 'just one,' right?"

"Judas Priest, I'm an ass."

She fluffed a candy cane pillow. "You want me to join you at the bar, yet it's asking too much for you to show up when your wife gets an award?"

"I'm apologizing. It's just, I can't make you happy. I've tried. Maybe like Carole King says, 'It's Too Late,'" he said. "Should we be married anymore? There's nothing we share. Just this house and our damn bills. Twenty-five thousand dollars of them. We don't even share something simple like blasting albums. The silence here is killing me. It's like we're not alive."

She threw the pillow into the ice-gray wall. "Did you ever ask yourself why you hate silence, Cal? What are you running from?"

He paused for a few seconds. "Music is always there for you. And is fun and escape so bad? You like it deathly quiet—like a funeral home."

"Stop. The bar is talking now."

"The bar is a happier home for me."

Don Henley begged "Please Come Home for Christmas," on the kitchen radio she'd only left playing to deter burglars from stealing presents. Cal stepped to their bedroom and pulled out the Browning from his dresser. He walked back, pointing it down at the worn beige carpet. "You never asked me about my week, either. It was hell. Dealt with a teenager who wanted to blow her brains out, but we got her to a psych ward."

Her eyes widened, staring at the gun. "What are you doing?"

"The world sends signs I'm better off dead. If you're so unhappy you should be the one to shoot me. Plus, you know where to get a discount on a coffin." He thrust his hand toward her, the gun atop his palm.

She bolted to their room.

He flipped the empty gun onto the poinsettia tablecloth. *An asshole move*, he thought. He exhaled and poured a self-loathing double and plopped down by the mail. A Christmas card from the dentist. A Jelly-of-the-Month Club offer. The fertility center payment plan. It'd take them fifty years to pay off the failed attempts. One good letter, though. A decade later, his contract with his record company was severed. He gave up future rights and royalties and repackaging his song, but they couldn't sue for failing to produce an LP. A pain in the ass, but it was over.

So was the chance the song would find Rhee, and now his song, like his hope, was DOA. He whipped the mail into the trash can, put his head down on the table, and closed his eyes.

When he awoke Christmas morning, slumped over like his old man, the firearm was missing. Judith had replaced it with an egg soufflé.

"Eclair?" she said.

Cal's eyes narrowed. He stretched, rubbed his back, and took the luscious pastry. "Thanks." He glanced at the side window at the dead grass near the birdfeeder. Under it lay a fresh hole, a trowel nearby. Much like him, she buried pain. Today it was his gun.

He set down the breakfast treat and dashed outside without his shoes, the muddy wet ground seeping through his crew socks, and he groaned. Like every year in Virginia, it wasn't a white Christmas. Raindrops fell in a misty fifty-degree drizzle. It wasn't the reassuring "Kentucky Rain" anymore. More like the song, "November Rain," a slow drone of life without love. Maybe he didn't deserve it. It was a death of sorts, and Cal and Judith couldn't figure out how to birth life.

His cold, dead firearm dug up and recovered, he stripped off his wet socks at the doormat. The gun was marched back in his dresser, socks deposited in the hamper, and last night's fight was ignored the rest of the day.

As turkey aroma wafted from the oven, he poured mimosas in snowman glasses, and she brought out Pauly's cage. "Pina Coladas later," he said. The cockatiel hopped onto the coffee table and flew around, landing on Judith's shoulder as they exchanged presents. She gave Cal a blue crewneck sweater, a toolbox, and an electric razor for his new beard, new socks, and underwear. He gave her cookbooks, knitting needles and yarn of every hue, *Crocheting Today*, and a necklace made of amazonite, a stone representing hope. Twelve-year-old Pauly got millet, sunflower seeds, berries, and a toy.

Christmas night, after he fixed her a pina colada, he asked her out to a movie. She declined, saying she didn't feel *King Kong Lives* was remotely festive, and would read by the fire instead. "True," he said, and walked solo to the only other open place, Quincy's. A spiral-permed young woman there asked why he looked familiar. He didn't recognize her, but he'd responded to so many calls. They introduced themselves, and he was shocked when she asked if he sang, and he nodded slowly. Recognition flashed in her voice and gigantic eyes. "No way. Cal Leonard who sang "Girl It's All for You?" My mother just bought it *again* in a cassette single. She *loves* that song."

"She's the one," Cal cracked to her giggles. "Wait, when did it come out as a cassette single?" She laughed again, batting at his shoulder. He was thirty-six, or eighty-six; she was a few years past twenty-one, at least. He had socks older than her.

She recited his own lyrics, remarked he was ruggedly handsome, and asked him about fame. Unrecognized since his tour, he sucked in his once-taut belly, with more burgers and beers behind him than work-outs, and embellished answers. "Carson wanted me on the show, but we couldn't agree on a date..." His ego hadn't been stroked in eons.

She fluttered her eyelashes, listened to stories of the road—that one time—and said she had an idea. What? Cal seen, heard, *and* given a Christmas present for a painkiller? The irony was he wanted to call his best friend Judith and say, *found my first groupie!*

The woman whispered, pulling out a picture. Her breath felt thick against his ear. He stared at the photograph. A smidgeon let down, but he adored the photo. Hell, yeah.

He knew exactly what he was doing. He hopped in her car, the two yakking easily down I-395 with Christmas tunes on the radio. The mood was changed, though, when he glanced in her rear-view mirror and his heart skipped a beat. Judith's silver Toyota. She'd tailed them in hot pursuit like a warden in a prison break. Cal gritted his teeth.

They arrived at a raised ranch in Springfield. Ignoring Judith's car entering the dead-end street, he walked to the young woman's front door, and she called inside. An attractive woman in her late forties appeared, putting her hands over her mouth, giving Cal an enormous hug. He signed an autograph, too. But then Cal opened his wallet, forking over a hundred dollars he'd just withdrawn from the ATM before Quincy's. Money should pay bills, but the eyes had won him over. Love at first sight.

Several basset hound puppies soon crawled over him. One snuggled into Cal, licking him with gusto like he was beef, scaling his feet, jumping on his ankles. The One. "She'll love this present. Finally, perfection." He scooped him up, hugging the puppy, and they gave him special puppy food. "I love him already. Thank you."

The young woman jimmied a flashbulb on her camera and snapped a picture of her beaming mom hugging Cal, cradling the puppy. "Can't wait to get this 110 film back in ten days, double prints. Cal Leonard!"

"Glad I could make someone's holiday." He looked to Judith's car, lifting the wriggling puppy, waving his paw. "Might as well meet our new baby, Judith. Pauly's got a brother!"

Judith gave him a lift home, and when they got inside, she cuddled the puppy, saying she'd keep Pauly in the cage in his room for now, until she researched introductions. She kissed the dog. "He's the baby I never got to love," she said. His heart pinged as he jotted a list of dog care items to buy. "This is a wonderful present for us, thank you," she said, unfolding the unused playpen. Cal wasn't sure if it was for him or the pup. "You know, I did trust you, Cal."

"Funny way of showing it, trailing me." He placed the dog in the pen and grabbed a beer from the fridge. "Why are we going through the motions? Know when to fold. Have you learned nothing from Kenny Rogers?"

"Let's try again. We'll do better. It was all so hard, for years, the tests, medications, appointments, the crushing conclusion," she said. "First let's pick a name for our baby."

The adorable long floppy-eared doggie with sad eyes ran zigzags and frolicked.

"How about 'Black Dog' like Zeppelin sang? What Churchill called his depression."

She shook her head. "He's tri-colored."

"How 'bout Boo, for that old '70s song. Probably another one-hit wonder who fell into obscurity, keeping the missus happy."

"No." A rebuke flooded her tone. "No to a separation and no to Boo—he's not scary." She leaned down, petting and kissing him—the dog, not Cal.

"Should marriage be this hard?" The dog was devouring chow like Cal would a ribeye at Morton's Steakhouse. "Let's call him Mort." He scooped him up in his lap and clicked the channel for the score of the Christmas Day NBA game.

"Mort is the Latin root of mortal, meaning death," she said.

He sighed.

"He'll bring us back to life," she said. "Because marriage is a legal, binding partnership until death do us part."

"You get an A in funeral law." He petted Mort for a minute. "'Happy Christmas, War Is Over.'"

Mort peed on him.

48

"Sail On"

Nainsi, June 1987

It was one of those delicious spring afternoons in Dublin where magnolia trees, hyacinth, and tulips bloomed, and a chorus of purple and yellow croci peeked out from fields. Nainsi sailed down the motorway to the M11, wind whipping her hair, in route to meet with an up-and-coming musician. She'd always recall where she was when she heard the news.

"The U.S. FBI, ATF, Customs, LAPD, and Interpol, working with investigators from Britain and the Republic of Ireland, have disrupted a smuggling operation of the Provisional IRA, the guerilla wing of the IRA, of small arms to be used in terrorism," a radio newscaster said. "Authorities say the gunpowder for ammunition and explosives was smuggled in the hollow of holy statues." Then they listed those arrested.

And one was her husband.

She swerved off the road, coasted on the shoulder a hundred feet before she braked, her heart speeding as fast as the cars and trucks barreling by. She tried to catch her breath as she gripped the wheel tighter. This "till death do us part" vow she honored turned her stomach now, and a wave of nausea ripped through her.

Like a music video, their fourteen years together flashed like a montage. Red flags waved: A devout lad from Ireland with a bod like a Chippendale's dancer breezed into the Groove-y Lounge, a Mope-a-cabana at a Motel California. Mr. Hot Stuff had used those Temptation Eyes to woo her with the Troubadour. When Mr. You Wear It Well proposed at the record store in a sharply tailored suit, he wore an *apricot scarf*. Of course. He was so vain. Had she learned nothing from Carly Simon?

Everybody played the fool, but there on the highway she lambasted herself for blowing off her intuition throughout the years-long engagement, flying back into his arms every time, and *marrying* him when she was ambivalent, especially when he wouldn't consider her career, move, nor talk about her love, guilt, and hope for Rhee. She'd ignored the warnings of Father M that something might be wrong. She'd *wasted* years when life was short. Had she merely distracted herself from who she wanted most in her life?

She punched the wheel as the whirl of traffic noise filled her ears like surround sound. A truck's horn blared and jarred her.

A minute later, she gasped again, and her hands flew up to her mouth.

They'd last seen each other for a long weekend two weeks ago. She'd gone off the pill.

49

"I Wanna Be Sedated"

Cal, 1987

In a drab burlap chair in a lawyer's waiting room, Cal crossed his legs at the ankles. The electronic waterfall on the counter tried to calm nerves, but it made him want to pee. A clerk scurried by. Gentle music played faintly from ceiling speakers, but the bland, slow instrumental was horrifying. *Please tell me that's not AC/DC's* "Highway to Hell," *on Muzak.*

Judith had sent him to this pricey attorney who she'd called about adoptions. Cal was meeting the lady on a late lunch break. He would ask about adoption, yes, but also spill about Rhiannon and beg for advice on that too. This was one hour of free consultation after all.

The slow cover mercifully ended and "I Got You Babe" now played as an instrumental. It wasn't much better. His mind traveled to when the Ex-Candles sang the Sonny and Cher song at a county fair. He closed his eyes and was back there again. His fingers are plucking the guitar, his throat and lungs finding the notes, his eyes darting past the young kids to Nainsi's beaming smile. Another hokey instrumental started. His eyes flew open at the tune.

He rolled his eyes and groused. "For the love of Judas Priest."

No, it can't be. He hadn't heard the song in ten years. He winced at the barely identifiable instrumental—the intro, mangled. The bridge, chopped. The melody, peppy. The refrain, jubilant. It was plain wrong, offensive really, far from an apology. *For crying out loud, is that an accordion?*

"That's...my...song," he mumbled to the receptionist, pointing to the speaker.

"Never heard it," she said. "My mom might know it, though."

"You don't say."

The piece felt vacant. It begged for lyrics. After all, it was his story. Her story. His love for his little girl. He never said her name in the song, but...what did it matter now? She was gone, just like his voice, words, royalties—*that stupid severed contract!* —MIA.

He reached in the pocket of his flannel shirt for the flask. If he turned his back, the receptionist wouldn't see him drink. He could numb the mocking. *You don't even know where Rhiannon is.*

He listened to the song forgotten by the world now played like a polka. The piece never garnered the acclaim that "Rhiannon," by Fleetwood Mac did, but his little song still meant something to him, a nobody from nowhere.

The elevator music ended. Offices with these puke-colored chairs all around the country had now heard his apology song as a happy instrumental waltz. They could gavotte to an accordion joyfully playing out his deepest regret and sorrow. *Great!*

How could he have done that, indeed?

50

"What's So Funny About Peace, Love, and Understanding"

Nainsi, September, 1987

Phone Transcript

Nainsi: I'm trying to reach Father McKenzie?

Woman: He's not here. Who's this?

Nainsi: Nainsi Murphy.

Woman: Sorry to say, dear, he's been terribly sick.

Nainsi: Oh, no! Is he okay?

Woman: Quite ill. In the hospital. Harder to recover in your late seventies, but praying he'll rally.

Nainsi: Oh I hope he recovers quickly! Sending all the poems, prayers, and promises in the world. Who's this?

Woman: His wife, Dana.

Nainsi: [cough] Wife?

Woman: Aye. We've been married for fifty years.

Nainsi: What? I mean, congratulations...but...a married priest?

Woman: The Protestant tradition of course. Nainsi, did he ever tell you he left the Catholic priesthood after we met in our twenties? He loved it there, and it broke his heart, but then he went to the Church of England seminary in Northern Ireland and then—

Nainsi: He never spoke of that...I just assumed he was a retired Catholic priest...

Woman: Sounds like him, not talking of his background. He meets people where they're at. Humble, isn't he? A man of service, putting the needs of others first. He doesn't look to change your—or anyone's—faith. He's supportive of all legitimate religions promoting peace and allowing questions, dialogue, and connection with loved ones.

Nainsi: You're right...listening was never about him. Helped me find my own answers. Come to think of it, he never gave me sacraments...

Woman: That's him. But yes, our background is a curvy path. [chuckle] We—I've become a deacon trained in counseling— moved to the U.S. and served in various denominations and non-profits, until he retired as a police chaplain. Though he never really retired. Our life's work is supporting all who seek peace, doing our part for world peace one person at a time. Is this an emergency or are you in crisis, dear? Did you need someone to talk with today? I have a few minutes before I head back to the hospital...or I can refer you to some wonderful Catholic priests we know...

Nainsi: [pause] So, Father McKenzie was a Catholic priest-turned-married Protestant priest and chaplain, from Northern Ireland, who has been counseling a Catholic from Dublin who's separating from someone facing prison in LA? [nervous chuckle]

Woman: Why, that sounds right! And we've grand plans to move to Scotland for our third act. We want to host discussions on peace and unity throughout the UK, Northern Ireland and the Republic. Anyway, enough about us! You called to tell him something, dear?

Nainsi: When we last talked I thought I might be pregnant—but tell him I'm not. And while it was all wrong with Killian, it's hard to accept you'll never be a mother, and it's my own fault. Oh, how I miss her. Every single day...

Woman: I don't know your specific situation, but we weren't parents either, and we led fulfilling lives caring for others like they are our kids. And I know for sure you, especially, are like a daughter to him.

Nainsi: [long pause] I feel the same about him. He's been like a rock to me. I can't bear to think of him being sick. Doctors say he'll recover, right?

Woman: [longer pause] Pray for him to beat the odds...

Nainsi: Oh yes! When I get off the phone, my first prayer is Hail Mary and then I'll talk to my own Ma too. Meanwhile, can you please tell him how much of a difference he's made in my life? As I do music promotion work, I've started working on my master's degree in music therapy. He always urges the greater good, and I'm volunteering at a domestic violence shelter too, hosting support groups with music to help women share their burdens. It builds such rapport and connection. It feels more meaningful than anything I've ever done, and it's all thanks to him. His belief in me, despite all my terrible choices, despite me not deserving anything...

Woman: Oh dear, it's never about earning or deserving love...

Nainsi: I know. When I become a music therapist, if I could be half the counselor he is, one who never judges others—

Woman: You will. We're given love and compassion freely. We can give it to others...

Nainis: One last thing, the most important? Tell him I forgive him. I figured it out. He tipped the police about Killian, didn't he? When I heard clicks on the phone, I bet the feds wiretapped our conversations. They could still be taping to check on my involvement, but I told them the truth—I never knew what Killian was doing. It'll be hard to hear our talks in court, but did Father McKenzie tell them because Killian's criminal operation endangered innocents—and me? He always counseled caution to me, wanted to protect me and all people, so ...did he do it for the greater good?

Woman: I only know we're both about helping people know they're not alone, and we're all one...

Nainsi: I hope he recovers. I can't bear—no, I can't even think it—if—

Woman: I know, dear. Please take care, all right?

Nainsi: [sniff and a pause] Send him my love...

51

"Don't Do Me Like That"

Cal, October 1987

The lawyer in a navy power suit, shoulder pads, and killer black pumps flabbergasted Cal.

"Calvin Frank Leonardowski of 7171 Maple Street?" She flipped her big hair, standing up to offer a firm handshake. Something about her greeting him with his address was off-putting, but he supposed attorneys were formal.

"That's me."

"Have a seat, please." She put on her glasses and handed him a packet of papers. A fax cover sheet held Judith's signature. He expected a song and dance first over the adoption information, but whatever. She said, "You've been served."

"Excuse me?" His eyes dropped like his gut to the papers. His secret must've caught up to him. Had the St. Ronan's secretary turned him in for an illicit adoption, or had Judith slipped? He was *toast*, being prosecuted for child abandonment, recklessness, or—*wait, have they found Rhiannon?*

His pulse quickened. He skimmed the legalese as the lawyer peered at him. *No, no, no.* This wasn't about Rhee after all. Judith had sued him for divorce! This esquire was *her* attorney. *What the--?*

"Nice trick." He jumped to his feet, and a barrel of questions flew out the door with him. A fall chill greeted him outside after the storms blew through last night and he slid on the wet pavement. "Freaking rain." He kicked his tire, jammed the key in the door, and unlocked.

On the drive home, he vacillated between rage and fear. The marriage had been rocky, but he thought they were trying again. He'd asked more about her work. He'd given up smoking for her!

At a flashing red light, a car honked when he missed his turn. "Oh, shut up!" Putting his middle finger out the window and accelerating, he planned how he'd try to save them, because she was all he had. He'd book them a vacation. Read those dull marriage books she'd recommended. His car hit a pothole and he cursed again before he plotted an about-face on all he'd neglected. He'd become a better handyman to her fortress. Spruce up the yard. Mow before it got a foot high. Stock the once-cherished birdfeeder with black-oil sunflower seed, suet, or safflower to lure cardinals. She always described each robin or bluebird who visited, even the winter wrens who roosted, so he'd try harder to converse about sparrows. Mail a donation to the Audubon Society. Fix stagnant airflow in the bedroom. *It was stifling*! They were a walking "You Don't Bring Me Flowers," so he'd stop by that Route 50 florist. The new MO: talk birds, books, buds, even Brosnan. *Ugh.*

A moving truck was parked in the driveway. Cal scaled the front steps and raced in the open door. Gripping the doorknob, he froze, and his mouth dropped open. The bungalow was devoid of furniture, except his worn recliner, where Mort was lounging, his head slung over the arm. *How long...?*

Judith held court before a team of burly men who stared blankly at sketches. "If you look on the graph at the map and key I made, you'll see rectangles for bed and sofa, squares for tables, parallelograms for bookshelves, and trapezoids for desks. The lamp is marked with a rhombus."

"What the hell is a rhombus?" he said.

She finished her instructions to the men, and she lowered her voice. "Sorry, I know it's a shock, Cal. And it's a parallelogram."

"Divorce by fax? We ate dinner together last night, Judith, you could've mentioned it somewhere between the pork chops and freaking kale."

"You know I abhor confrontation. I'd hoped to be gone by now, but the movers aren't as organized as me."

Two young men smirked, picked up boxes, and marched away.

"C'mon. This feels sudden."

"I'm never hasty," she said.

"I had no idea that—"

"We've been in decline for years, you often said." She spoke in a mortician's monotone. "Our bodies reiterated we weren't working. And I don't have forever to find someone else."

"So, that's it?" Movers marched out of the bedroom with their king-size bed and the hideous paisley bedroom comforter he hated, and the turquoise Egyptian cotton one million thread count sheets he'd miss. Cal would apparently sleep on the hardwood floor. "Look, we just celebrated our tenth anniversary—"

"*You* celebrated our ten-year anniversary—which is a gift of aluminum or tin, by the way—with buying everyone at the bar beer cans? Saw it on the credit card bill."

"What was I supposed to do? Go to the library with you?"

"They have great book talks there." She cautioned the men moving the dining table. "It's over, Cal. I submitted my resignation. I'm moving back to Oklahoma."

"You know your parents haven't visited in ten years, right? Don't think they miss you." It was a low blow, her sore spot.

"Maybe I'll find a handsome cowboy there with a big strong sperm count."

Cal would've whipped something at the wall, but he stood in an empty house. She'd legit taken him to the cleaners. A mover grabbed a pizza slice.

"We're a longtime duo, like Ike and Tina—er, not them—Captain and Tenille? Peaches and Herb?"

"Who?"

"You don't know the pop pairs?"

"You don't know birds."

"I love the Byrds." He stroked his graying facial hair and patted his beer belly, worse with each passing candy bar instead of cigarette. "Fine. *Beauty and the Beast*. You're the babe. I'm the monster."

The beloved Disney tale sparked in her eyes, and even Mort shot straight up in the chair. "Cal, you know something? You never called me babe. In all this time together."

Had he never...? Guilt perched on his deadened heart. He'd called Nainsi babe back when he was young, naïve, foolish, in love, and they held each other tight, as if for dear life. "Then I'm changing that. I'll play you 'Babe' by Styx."

"We both know I'm not the babe you think of. Like her. Or the bleach blonde bartender."

He deserved a jab, but why hadn't he complimented her? Judith was still Ivory-girl pretty with her porcelain skin, unblemished like an air-brushed model, emerald eyes sparking a luster of goodness. When her blondeness had faded into a brown sheen—she refused hair highlights trying to conceive—why hadn't he said *you're a beautiful babe whatever shade, inside and outside*? He looked at her as the daylight streamed in from the bay window, highlighting her chic new side-swept haircut. "I'm sorry."

He felt the same strike of being inept at love as when Nainsi left. He wondered if he didn't feel the same fiery love and passion as he had the first time, because he was afraid to be abandoned again, so needing safety, he'd clung to Judith. Their fearful complacency wasn't fair to either of them. Could they try one last chance—before the movers took away his MTV? He wasn't ready to end the dream for a family.

He pulled her soft hands close, searching for the right words that always eluded him.

She gazed back at him, giving him a glimmer of hope, and then she pecked his cheek. Out the window chirped a yellow bird, and her attention turned to it quickly. "Oh! The American Finch who visits, that canary yellow bird, or, well, a shade more saffron. See the black cap? It's a he. I'd like to think he's coming to say goodbye. Tweety, I'll miss you."

"Geez, that bird is small. How did you see him, hear him?"

"You look. Beauty. Nature. Calm. All evidence life goes on, even when things are difficult."

"He's not Tweety. He's Woodstock. Mort is Snoopy."

"We're just different people, Cal. We had a nice life. But it can be nicer for both of us."

"But our overture isn't over yet." He paused. "We're a couplet, heading to a crescendo, growing with time and harmony?" Silly, sure, but his middle name was regret. They needed more time to change. Lasting love still seemed elusive. The soulmate stuff was bogus, but he once asked if she even wanted bliss. "No," she'd said, "Marriage is about having someone when you die." *Judith had been living to die!*

She scanned the room for her last things, and anger began to creep over him. *Rhee.*

"But I kept true to my promises for a decade, dropped the music career and held off looking for Rhiannon for *you*. That's *my child*! You could've been part of her life too." His sacrifice was for what, this broken partnership like a tangled cassette? You could use a pencil, but should you bother? What time he'd wasted—for them to build their family first. Rhee was his family, too, on hold for Judith, who was leaving him just like Nainsi did. He'd lost *everyone!*

"You tucked the past away for us, giving us a fighting chance, and I'll always thank you for that. But it didn't work, and we must move on."

A mover asked to use the bathroom, and she nodded and walked away. The man looked at Cal. "Saw your service souvenir. I was in 'Nam too. Sorry to butt in, but I couldn't help overhearing. Want some advice?"

"No."

"When my wife died, know what saved me? A project, man. Started fixing up cars, got out my model car collection too."

"Thanks for your service, brother." He rubbed his temples and exhaled. A toilet flushed, and faucet sounded. Movers filed outside. With the pizza. She reentered to fetch her clipboard.

"Judith, we can't do life alone."

"And there we have it."

"Plus, I'll miss your organization. Seriously, you color-coded the closet. Collated your recipes. Spices alphabetized. What day does trash come?"

Judith's tone softened. "Tuesdays, about seven thirty-five. Look, you got the house, and I left you a place setting, pot, pan, and a recipe book."

"Not Julia Child's. Too hard."

"No, I made one for you. Wrote out recipes for my mom's potatoes you love, my homemade brownies you love, and your mom's chili recipe from your memory." Judith went to Pauly's bedroom and emerged holding his cage. The bird whistled. Cal whistled back, opened the cage door, and stroked him goodbye. "Aw, I'll miss you too."

"The thing is," Judith said, her tight voice echoing in the hollow house, "you loved the idea of a family." She took off Mama's ring and handed it back. "As did I. We're more alike than we thought."

He stared at the silver ring in his hand, and he looked around at the nothingness that now weighed on him. Their life had been heavy on "attachment" love, said a marriage counselor who hadn't helped one iota, though she sure left a hefty bill behind.

"C'mon, Mort." She opened the door. Mort jumped down from the recliner and followed her.

"No! No way in hell!" Cal strode to his side like a bodyguard. "I'll fight you on this one. Take Pauly, but I get Mort."

"We'll have to go to court for him, then. Goodbye, Cal. The best of luck to you. I love you, Mort. See you someday soon." She kissed Mort's snout and walked out.

Just like that, with nothing to show for ten—or a hundred—years together, Cal was abandoned again, broke and broken, with only a recliner, kitchen table, radio, TV, the unfinished basement man cave, a crammed attic of clutter, and a thousand bills.

An engine fired up.

"Oh, for crying out loud." He could see Judith backing out of the driveway with their only car, the Lincoln Continental. For a family that never happened. He needed a drink. Or seven. *And where the hell is my Mustang?*

Mort laid down, and they sat on the floor together. He was Cal's saving grace. Calvin Frank Leonardowski, spousal defendant, may be down and out, but at least Mort was right here, right now. "She'll get you when she pries you from my cold, dead hands," he said.

Part III: "I've Got a Name"

52

"Alone Again, Naturally"

Cal, January 2, 1988

Funny how life changes on a dime—or, in Cal's case, a dollar—catapulting you into another world in little ways that look harmless: a lump the size of a pea. A concert. An official letter. Words roughed out in barracks. A stranger at a laundromat. January second held one such moment for Cal, a dismal yet mammoth day.

Cal woke up on his cheap new futon bed in the living room to Mort licking his hand and whining. With head pounding from Quincy's last night, he rubbed his temple with one hand while patting the dog with the other. While remembering charging rounds for strangers before he staggered home and crashed, pain shot through his neck. What a dumb collegiate-like bed purchase of this sheetrock for a six-foot-one, two-hundred-pound, thirty-six-year-old man.

Cal's head hurt worse when he saw three inches of white stuff outside. Steve and Isabelle shoveled their driveway and scraped ice from their cars, which he should do—if he had one. He'd been taking the bus to work, one rung in Dante's nine levels of hell. Cal pulled on sweats over his boxers and shuffled to the kitchen, Mort's puddle greeting him. He squinted at the microwave. 11:07 a.m. He apologized to him and wiped Mort's mess. He hitched the leash to his collar, threw on his coat and boots, and opened the door. When he stepped onto the icy stoop, he slipped into a freefall and tumbled down the three stairs and crash-landed worse than the skier on Wide World of Sports. He lay in a snowdrift assaulted by the bitter cold air and wind. Mort peered down, unscathed, then licked the snow off his face.

"You okay?" Steve yelled.

"A gauntlet of death over here," Cal called as he picked himself up and headed back in. He craved an Irish coffee and opened every cupboard finding alcohol but no coffee. He fed Mort, told him to staff the fort, and trudged to the dollar store at the corner. He traipsed through the aisles, grabbing generic instant coffee, pretzels, a pack of one-ply toilet paper, and a toilet plunger. With arms full of crap for the crapper, that's when he saw it.

Surprise! Next to the plungers sat a stack of CDs labeled "Sultry & Sorrowful One-Hit Wonders of the '70s." He squinted at the CD's miniscule text before doing a double take. His stomach dropped. Was that a tiny picture of *himself* singing, among eleven other pictures? *What in the freak?* Sorrowful. Great. Cal was officially deemed a sad sap. A sultry one, but here lived Cal in the dollar store with his sexy, pitiful self, having an existential moment, finding his song sandwiched between Terry Jacks' "Seasons in the Sun," a wrenching song about dying goodbyes, and Henry Gross's "Shannon," about the death of Beach Boys' Carl Wilson's Irish setter. Good songs, but Cal fell smack dab in the middle of misery jams.

He shoveled his own forgotten cheap tune into his arms and ambled to the register. One five-dollar bill for this sad sack of glory. He wouldn't even get royalties on this CD, the fifteen cents he would've gotten from his own sale.

"That's my song," he mumbled at the register.

"The first dance at your wedding?" the teenager asked.

"No," Cal said. "Not even that."

One. Hit. Wonder. The moniker mocked him all the way home. As he lugged his bag on the mile trek through wind, snow, mud, and ice, he re-evaluated the shambles of his life. A chaplain at work had called him a "tortured soul with low-grade depression," even though he'd been a loyal spouse enduring *bonds* of matrimony. He should get a *medal.* These days, he only got out of bed because injured folks counted on him—and because happy hour afterward with coworkers awaited. Over a shot and a beer, or five, Cal admitted that he missed his best friend. Sarge said he was a "good, decent man of honor."

But Cal didn't feel like one. He was a lot of exes—soon-to-be ex-husband, ex-father, ex-son, Ex-Candle, ex-boyfriend, ex-soldier, ex-singer-songwriter of a number thirty-nine hit. One and done, like Evan warned. An ex-musician with no rights to his single, one whose apology didn't reach his daughter, and a dude currently labeled as a has-been at the dollar store. *Next to toilet plungers!*

He made the horrendous instant coffee. Spotting this CD demanded adding the fine whiskey he'd saved for "someday," like when Judith got pregnant, or they adopted, or he found Rhee. A special bottle, just like his old man had saved. He pulled the treasure from a high cabinet and salivated. The bottle awaited with a yellow sticky note from Judith.

Cal, save yourself. Alcohol won't fill the hole inside you.

After her Christmas card, which was only a love letter to Mort and a reference to joint marital property, this felt a condescending blow. Sure, he'd checked out, self-medicated every day since Mama, Nainsi, Rhee, Vietnam, marriage, infertility, separation. Drinking had no expiration date, yet it returned only hangovers, bad judgment, zero solutions, relationship problems, costs, and feeling sick and ashamed.

Judith was right. He might not have loved her something easy, fierce, like he did with Nainsi, the passionate love that brought baby Rhee.

Maybe that kind of love only came around once when you were young. Or was love actually this long-term loyal partnership, missing passion because he passed out every night, numbing tension and trauma? Didn't matter what kind of love, it always ended. In engulfing pain.

He'd forgo the drink. He didn't owe a day without booze only to Judith. He owed it to Rhee, too. He needed to figure out how to find her, without this fuzzy cloud.

Yet by the five o'clock cocktail hour, Cal shook. Only one way to relieve that. He walked to the fridge, where a case of beer greeted him. He perspired. A snow-blower roared in the distance. The weathercasters on TV, sponsored by the DC-area grocers, spoke in a giddy tone, drunk with delight at storm desks.

Cripes, he'd been numb since 1970, so maybe he didn't owe a decision to Mama, Judith, and Rhee, but to himself. The one who'd been there all along. The stark reality of drinking every single day and sky-high tolerance hit him. Could he even live without this crutch?

No. Alcohol was the only thing left. The only thing he *could* ever count on. It didn't leave him, merely numbed and distracted him. Always on the shelf looking sleek and sumptuous, he could at least trust it. The next thought shot through him like a .50 caliber.

But it lies to you.

A helicopter's rotor blades sounded. "Goodnight Saigon," Billy Joel sang from the radio, each sound bringing him back—screaming back. The bodies. The battles. The blood. The soldier's prom picture in his pocket.

"The war, if it wasn't so...what if I still had Rhee..." Trembling, Cal scratched Mort's head and his shoulders dropped, as if the burden—survivor guilt—was too much to lift again, the crush of weight too great. A deep breath failed to calm him. Instead, he heard the bombs and moans on the battlefield. Felt his nineteen-year-old strong arms that once lifted weights in Mama's basement lift a burned eighteen-year-old onto a stretcher. Smelled the melting flesh and scorched earth and rotten vegetation and gunpowder. At that split second, his knees buckled and he collapsed to the cold tile. Then, for the first time since Vietnam, Cal let out a guttural cry, a wail that could be heard by all the neighbors in Arlington, perhaps even the soldiers guarding the Tomb of the Unknown.

He grieved for so much those next hours. His drunken choice at nineteen berated him first. Then, unrelenting grief flooded him for the guys who did not make it out of the war, like Terry, and for all the people he'd lost in three years. He grieved all the toys long gone, too, like the Mustang and Mama's Beatles eight-track, Daddy's Armstrong and Sinatra albums, records he'd pawned on the way to the war, even their furniture in the townhouse that he'd sold and sent anonymously to St. Ronan's. Cal pounded on the floor. *Just. Kids.*

He grieved Judith's patient love and friendship, but also the passionate love they never knew. An abiding, joyful love seemed too hard. Should it have taken that much work? They'd never known the love he'd felt with Nainsi, or like his parents or Steve and Isabelle had. Even with good intentions, love slipped through his fingers. Cal mixed so much sorrow, loss, and regrets for their troubled union that he expelled a reservoir of tears trapped over a lifetime. As dusk crept through, he made one last promise.

"For the first night since the war, I won't drink tonight," he said to the white paint peeling on the ceiling, his back feeling the chill of the kitchen floor. Mort tried to lick his tears. That the dog still loved him like a rock, no matter what mood he showed, gave him pause. "The thing is, Mort, I should've called Judith a babe in the last ten years. Neglect was my fault. We weren't the best match, but I drank away our life. I'll be better for you."

Cal stood and tossed the case of beer one-by-one into the garage trash can like he was shooting baskets. He burrowed the last one under his recliner for an emergency. Then, he loaded bottles of whiskey and vodka into his arms. He stepped into the uninhabited room that was supposed to house a nursery and pushed up the drafty window. As frigid wind blasted him and Mort watched at his side, Cal pitched each bottle at the bare tree, shards raining down the once-beloved birdhouse from Topeka, disappearing into the thin blanket of snow.

Next, he flipped through the phone book. A: Adoptions, Catholic. He dialed with trembling fingers and wiped his sweaty forehead. It rang four times before he left a message on the answering machine.

"Please call," he may have said, as all limbs shook. "It's life or death."

53

"Every Time I Think of You"

Nainsi, January 2, 1988

Nainsi may have been thirty-six years old, and it happened almost seventeen years ago, but sometimes the memories snuck up and shut her down when she least expected it. "Remember your biggest mistake?" life taunted via a song on the radio. A touch of a quilt. A bank statement for Rhee's college savings account she'd started years ago. She could distract this pain with work like usual—but regret always returned. Today, 8:15 a.m., it pulled up a seat at Ma's table as she gazed out the window at snowplow trucks. She walked over to Ma's kitchen radio—she'd cherish it forever—and turned up Cher's new song. Her voice was all it took for her heart to pound like the wind gusts shaking the door, the memory so vivid.

They were in a barn, the Ex-Candles playing at a fair. A young couple requested a song. He was shipping out tomorrow, to Fort Benning, then Vietnam, he said as he wiped away his girlfriend's tears with his thumbs. The recruit looked only at his girl, clutching a prize teddy bear, as they choked out "I Got You Babe." As Cal sang to the thirty people moseying around the barn, toddlers dancing with cotton candy, kids jumping off haystacks, the two with the teddy bear slow-danced. Cal flubbed a few notes, Troy missed a cue, and Terry forgot lyrics, but the young couple didn't notice. Their adoring gaze seemed like how Cal's dark eyes made love to Nainsi's from the stage. She'd blown him a kiss. It was the first time she felt Rhiannon flutter.

"Time goes by too fast," she said, looking at Ma's framed portrait hanging in the wood-paneled family room where Liam read. "So why do we give up and walk away from people instead of working things out?"

"Did ye say something?" her brother said.

She wanted to admit to her family someone was missing. Ma and Da's first grandchild. Liam's niece. No one knew why Nainsi set out two extra place settings every Easter, Christmas, and April fifteenth, but it was for Ma and Rhiannon.

"What song is that?" Liam asked.

"'Turn Back Time,' by Cher. She's making a comeback." Nainsi's voice trailed off. She could still see Rhee reach for a rattle, the beat going on.

How could she have done that, indeed?

54

"All By Myself"

Cal, March 1988

The home Judith wanted quiet once and for all was quiet once and for all...and it was unbearable to Cal.

The detox malaise had been brutal. Shakes, sweat, cramps, and muscle aches beat him up, and he'd called off work. It wouldn't be fair to those who needed him in the ambulance, so back and forth he went between bed and toilet for seventy-two hours.

In this shape, he'd gotten a call back from the adoption agency. His faint voice barely mustered the strength to ask if someone anonymously handed a child to someone, where would the baby go? Social services and authorities can ensure care until they place the child with an adoptive or biological family, depending on many factors, a kind voice had answered. He'd feared all along she'd bounced around foster homes. He prayed her life was one of stable love instead.

"Hypothetically," he said, "if it was at a church, would the church approach this agency?"

The person answered, "Not necessarily."

"Would you have records in the region if they did, say, from 1971?" He shouldn't have blurted that out, but he was coming out of a fog, an unraveling of sorts.

"Yes, but it's not that simple...the eighteen-year-old adoptee has to request—" was all he heard in his grogginess. He'd guessed that. She wouldn't turn eighteen for another year. His immediate hopes dashed with each gulp of ice water, he left his phone number if anyone asked.

Back at work, long days stretched before him, harder when cohorts asked about happy hours. He craved the social connection, but he couldn't imagine *not* imbibing. It'd be like passing up a hot glazed doughnut, which he'd never done. He conjured up excuses for two months, scarfing down frozen pizzas at home watching MTV. "An eight-week flu?" one coworker said. Another asked if someone died. People brought over casseroles. Others offered unsolicited advice. *Anti-depressants! Work out! Date! Sleep! Eat your spinach! Drink celery juice!*

He'd gagged. They meant well. But they hadn't stopped drinking before and hadn't lost everyone he had. How would they understand half of grief was wading through the things you should've done when alive? Grief could sometimes be spelled g-u-i-l-t.

One day, as spring cherry blossoms bloomed on the tree lawn, Sarge drove up to his house with a six-pack. "Here you go, buddy."

"Skipping happy hours. On a diet." He handed the beer back to Sarge. A funny thing happened. He survived. Sarge didn't even make it a big deal.

"Hey, this support group meets in my church basement," he said. "Maybe—"

"Talking about problems sounds terrible."

"Suit yourself." Sarge guzzled the beers as they watched the Washington Bullets game. The brew looked awesome, so Cal reminded himself addiction was a physical—not a moral—issue. To remind himself he thought of the teenager who'd almost died last week. They'd responded to a call for an addict fresh out of rehab who'd overdosed. No one told them after rehab, if they went back to using the same amount, it'd kill them. Their bodies couldn't withstand it after getting clean and sober; they could OD from a small amount. They saved the boy with an injection. He hoped he'd stay clean. While Cal wasn't a heroin or prescription addict, it didn't matter the fix. He didn't want to backslide after this long. Promise to himself, Judith, Rhee, and Mort intact, he sipped a soda.

Mort suddenly galloped to the backyard—albeit slowly, but as fast as his short legs could carry him— and barked. Cal moseyed up and investigated. "Protecting us from killer geese?" He patted him as they watched a yellow bird swoop down from the birdhouse, pecking at the shards of glass, nibbling under the tree. The snow had melted, and Cal could see he'd forgotten to clean up after his bottle-whipping escapade. He lifted the old drafty window, but the bird flew away.

"What are you doing?" Sarge asked.

"Didn't want the finch to get hurt." Cal got the broom from the garage and went outside to clean up the shards of glass.

Later, on his way out, Sarge said, "Never told you this, but my brother was a Huey mechanic in 'Nam. When I met you and you said you'd worked medivac, that's all I needed to know. You all made amazing saves. Like, a million, ain't it? Rescuing our wounded, braving it all, I said to myself, 'Self, he'll be fine here.' A hero day in and day out. But never in a million years thought you'd worry about a bird."

"It was my friend Woodstock."

"What are you, Snow White?"

They joked some more, and as he pulled away, Cal scratched his head. *Hero* category for Cal? Hardly. He couldn't save his parents or his buddies Terry and Giuse or all the brothers on the battlefield. The clock ticked. How could Judith stand this silence? He equated it with the somber silence accompanying a coffin lowered to the ground. But it was the sound of music that had spoken to him since he was a kid, noise that shot to his soul and shook him to life.

The mover had said he needed a project. Too much time on his hands. He knew it, Styx knew it. He glanced at the door that was ajar. What if he turned that barren nursery room into a room bustling with noise? He could fill it with tunes from the '70s, specifically, a nod to the last time he felt—what, exactly? *Alive?* He'd recreate the time of hopeful youth, before his draft number was up. When a concert stretched through a July fourth weekend into an endless summer of sun and skin and fun.

"If I unpack my guitar, too, can I remember all the chords, riffs, frets, licks?" he asked Mort, as he planned to bring up his stereo from the basement, crank his raucous music here, drown his pain daily. Sure, the guitar strings would bust as soon as he plucked, but the room could be an ode to happier times, the last time he felt peace, love, and music. Rock music had saved his life, bringing him Rhee. Just remembering her toothless grin, the way she smiled, a light so bright, plucked at his heart.

This new '70s room begged to be a nostalgic tribute to a mid-summer night. Nainsi and Rhiannon lived in this era, untouched by time, seared into his memory. He'd never forgiven himself, but this room should not hold that sorrow. The room would hold life. He'd hang on to the old songs here to lighten his load. Spiff up the room, scour used record stores, collect old albums, and blast them. Survive.

"Wasn't music better then?" he asked Mort, who'd trailed him in. The dog refused to be in any room Cal wasn't and plopped himself down at his feet. Cal scratched behind his floppy ears and then turned. Mort sighed and followed him to the kitchen, where Cal dug out a yellow pad.

Judith, it's no one's fault, really. "We Just Disagree," goes a song from the '70s. Our wounds bled and scabbed over. Scars prove we lived. But you're not getting the dog.

55

"I'm Every Woman"

Rhiannon, April 30, 1988

After Gert had taken all twenty-four Kodachrome pictures of film, and kissed her forehead goodbye, Rhiannon stepped into the parish bingo hall, dressed in the gently-used red gown and a white carnation wrist corsage. She patted her bangs, teased six inches high, hair sprayed and preserved for eternity as "Walk This Way," by Run DMC and Aerosmith greeted them. Purple streamers, balloons and signs carried school-approved song titles like "Living On a Prayer," "Higher Love," "Faith," "Yah Mo B There," and "Greatest Love of All." Vases of fresh wisteria dotted lavender tablecloths, softening the stink of last night's fish fry.

"'Push It!'" they shrieked as they raced to the dance floor on Salt-n-Pepa's cue. As Rhiannon's mix tapes blared, they danced with joy—most kids did, anyway—and she smiled in satisfaction, having spent weeks curating the five-hour '80s playlist, weighing each selection like an SAT answer, loading their Footloose class with Prince, Whitney Houston, the Boss, Journey, Wham!, Michael and Janet Jackson, INXS, Tina Turner, Kool and the Gang, Joan Jett, Survivor, Lionel "Dancing on the Ceiling" Richie, Richard Marx, and Air Supply. She'd snuck in '70s Saturday Night Fever, ABBA, and Grease.

"Shout!" they echoed Tears for Fears as guys in tuxes—the all-girls school had fund-raised to bus in all-boys St. Thomas-- stepped off the bus, ogled, and goofed off. "It's Raining Men!" they sang, watching the boys teetering on the perimeter, gawking before they joined in. The hall full, laughter abundant, the teens danced the night away under a disco ball.

Later, when the lights lowered, the chemistry teacher walked to the mic. "For Class of '89 junior prom queen, the teachers choose the brilliant Sara Smythe!"

Sara screamed so loud it was as if Jon Bon Jovi himself had strutted in and kissed her.

"'Sara'! 'Sara Smile'!" Rhiannon hugged her best friend. Everyone swarmed Sara as they crowned her with a tiara and gave her flowers that looked suspiciously like they swiped everything off the Mary shrine. Sara sobbed and rambled in a speech like she'd gotten an Oscar, and guys inched closer amid cheers and applause.

Five minutes later, "Lady in Red" by Chris de Burgh played. A cute six-foot guy with glasses, warm brown eyes, and a halfway clear complexion, strode over to them. He hadn't danced yet, his black tux, shiny purple bow tie and rose boutonniere intact. Rhiannon had seen him somewhere before.

"You've another admirer," she whispered to Sara, who was shaking, waving, accepting bouquets like Miss America.

He held out his hand.

To Rhiannon.

She froze.

"Wanna dance?"

"Me?" She was as shocked as when Gert showed up at Live Aid.

"Go," Sara whispered, smelling a rose and adjusting the crown before her line of suitors.

"Of course, you," he said with a throaty laugh.

She looked at him quizzically. What? Guys only crossed rooms for Sara! "Sure, I guess?"

They clasped hands and fell into step, his other hand resting on the small of her back, causing the chiffon fabric to tickle her skin. They didn't speak for a minute.

"Been wanting to ask you to dance," he said.

"Because it's 'Lady in Red' and I'm wearing a maroon dress and have auburn hair?"

"Well, that too. Whoa, that dress, killer, man."

Heat rose to her face.

"It's because I've wanted to talk to you for, like, a year. Finally got my nerve."

"*Me?*" She stepped back and looked into his dark brown eyes. "Have we met?"

"Girl comes into a record store once a week. Boy who works there notices her albums—and her."

"Oh, my gosh!" she said with a wide smile highlighted by the ruby lipstick Gert gave her. "You work Saturdays?"

"Yeah. Hi. Nick Lowell."

"Like Nick Lowe from the song 'Cruel to Be Kind'?"

"Exactly. What's your name?"

"Rhiannon."

"Of course."

They laughed, though she could predict the conversation next, and the existential crisis that came on afterward. It was the same every time she met anyone.

Rhiannon, like the Fleetwood Mac song?

Yeah.

Your parents named you after the song?

No. Born before it came out. And I don't know who my parents are.

They say Stevie Nicks wrote it about a Welsh witch.

Supposedly.

Are you Welsh?

Who knows my heritage?

Are you a witch? [Person laughs at his own joke.]

But he didn't ask the usual banter. He said she was probably sick of the song question, and she seemed different, more down-to-earth, from the song's character. "Except, you're pretty like Stevie."

She couldn't have been more shocked had Lindsey Buckingham himself played her a guitar solo. She blushed and asked his favorite '70s singer-songwriter.

"Don't know if I have just one, but James Taylor's cool."

"For some reason, I've always been drawn to JT." She could smell his Drakkar Noir, which she only knew from magazine inserts. "Love 'Fire and Rain.'"

He said he loved "Carolina On My Mind" most, and, by the way, would she go to the James Taylor concert with him this summer?

That was it. Bit by the smitten bug. Butterflies fluttered inside as they danced. Though soon the slow songs ended, and they pulled apart. Kids poured onto the dance floor when "Bust A Move" played next, and they joked and mocked their own dance moves.

But when "Papa Don't Preach" came on and the class chanted lyrics, the nuns and parents shut it off. She looked at Gert's Timex for the first time all night. It was eleven thirty, and Gert had set curfew at midnight. A rare reprieve after being grounded for three years.

"Can I give you a lift home?" he asked.

She dashed over to Sara to say she wouldn't be carpooling home with her parents. Sara nodded as she held hands with a jock. Rhiannon climbed into Nick's Camaro, and they zoomed off into the darkness, JT cassette blasting through a perfect seventy-degree night, a million stars twinkling in the sky. How Sweet It Is!

By the time they pulled into the gravel driveway at 11:59 p.m., just after they launched into a game they created—name songs that make you feel you're chilling out on a boat? -- the kindred spirits hadn't stopped talking timeless tunes. "Bummer tonight is ending. It was fun," he said as he parked, came around to the passenger side, opened the car door, and strolled to the front door.

"Yeah." She smiled, her heart pounding.

They stepped on the stoop. "Coming into the store Saturday?"

"Is Robert Palmer's album on sale?"

"You'll have to come in to check." He inched closer. Her heart tried to thump out of her body. "You smell good."

"Oh...er, Cher perfume sample?"

He brushed her feathered bangs away from her face, but even after the dance and the fresh air, the sprayed hair stayed matted and moved in a clump. Did she look like a dork? A trickle of perspiration rolled down her back, just as he leaned in for the slowest and deepest first kiss in the history of ever. Please, don't let this end!

But it did. The porch light flicked on. Then it went off. Then it went on. And off again. It flashed every five seconds, not like it had burned out, but like morse code. They laughed. Rhiannon could never tiptoe in past curfew.

"Goodnight," she said to his grin, which now carried lipstick smudges. He jumped off the stoop and even waited to back out his car until she opened the door and waved goodbye. She couldn't stop smiling. She was lost in lust.

Until she stepped inside. She gasped.

There in the foyer, under the light switch, Gert huddled on the floor. She was pale, her face drawn. She held her chest and caught her breath. "I had to crawl to the door...I'm so sorry, Rhee...not on your special night..."

"Did you fall? Is it your bad hip?" Rhiannon touched her clammy forehead.

"No, I just don't feel good," she said with a trembling voice, her weak tone morose. Tears welled in her eyes, absent their *joie de vivre,* and her cheeks lacked the usual ruddy pep and vigor. "It's probably indigestion. But it hurts like the dickens."

She held her breath when Gert lay down on the indoor welcome mat. Boo barked, and Ezekiel purred. "I'm so sorry to trouble you tonight, dear-heartie. What a joy to see you dressed up. We got such a good deal on that dress, remember? Only seven dollars, tax forty-nine cents..."

"Shhh. Save your energy. You're okay. Hey, Ezzy, Boo, she's fine." Rhiannon stroked Gert's ashen arm and petted their babies. A strange maturity descended on her when she walked to the rotary phone, dialed 911, spoke in a calm tone, and filled her a water glass.

Gert asked for the statue, and there they sat, mumbling the rosary in a tight family circle, Gert, Rhiannon, Ezzy, Boo, and the life-size, red-cloaked child Jesus statue.

Rhiannon added a silent prayer— to make the ambulance speed like a demon.

56

"Stayin' Alive"

Cal, May 1, 1988

Cal's hands made the new '70s music room breathe. Whenever he fought cravings, he dove into the project, painting the room a "sassy, sunny saffron," as Judith had called the hue of the bird Tweety-Woodstock, but he chose it for the saving grace of a sunny, deathly hot concert that had saved his life. He pulled up the beige carpet, sanding the hardwood underneath, and charged a brown shag area rug and a modular couch at a discount store. He'd hung his framed single from the record company, and a Billboard chart week at number thirty-nine, above several shelves he built. Albums from neighbor Steve's latest garage sale, flea markets, and thrift shops lined the shelves. He tacked up a few tour pictures, too. When he was at Goodwill, he'd picked up an Allman Brothers album and a magnet with the Serenity Prayer. He tried to memorize it as he stood in line, but a teenager stood holding a Robert Plant solo album, and it nudged Cal, like he was looking at himself at that age. When the kid said he wanted to take it to the Boys and Girls Club, where he went afterschool since his mom had died, Cal's heart sank. He recognized the immense sadness in his eyes, and he patted him on the back. "I'm so sorry," he choked out as he paid for the boy's album. "Lost my parents as a kid too. Sucks. Promise me you'll hang in there?"

Cal was listening to Journey's '70s stuff last night, flipping through his growing stack of a hundred classic rock albums, when he stepped over Mort to turn up "Lights." "You and this project are keeping me alive, buddy," he said. He hadn't drank in four months, because every time he looked in Mort's forlorn eyes, he pictured him orphaned, alone in a shelter if he'd drunk himself to death. Mort's pathetically cute looks, like he was begging for treats, his baseline MO, kept them both alive.

He cracked open a soda can, grieving the hard stuff. He visited the pantry often, stuffing his regrets and emptiness into his mouth with beef jerky or candy. Sometimes he took his cue from Mort and napped; sometimes he watched anything shot, hit, or dunked on TV. Cal coped with a new sober life alone by baby steps day by day, by moving ahead, like Judith always said, yet living in the moment like he and Nainsi agreed. Every day after work, he nuked a frozen dinner and toiled in the room. It felt victorious when he demolished the drafty window, replacing it with an energy-efficient one.

"Needs more in here, huh, pal?" Cal headed to the basement for the crown jewel, Mort trailing him on his heels. After batting through a cobweb stretching from the ceiling, Cal saw it, right where he abandoned it during the anniversary dinner six years ago. Dust rested on the case, and he sneezed as he unlocked it. The beautiful '71 Gibson acoustic guitar. He stroked the curve of the bout and the once-sleek oak face. Bringing the guitar and case upstairs to the kitchen, he took a damp rag and polished it. He gripped the neck. "We meet again, The Hendrix. Missed you."

He fiddled with the tuners on the headstock, then played a few chords from top to bottom. He plucked the EADGBE notes. A string broke, and he fixed it, but it was still out of tune. He'd get it restrung. He played a pentatonic scale, tried a dyad, then a triad. Worked his way through chords, barre chords, power chords, changing octaves and pitches. An hour later, he'd immersed in tabs, frets, and bends, feeling the vibrato, and looking for old sheet music and fretboard diagrams. How did "Lay-la" go again? He strummed for two hours, attempting parts of "Amie" from Pure Prairie League. "Take It Easy" by the Eagles. Frampton's "Baby I Love Your Way." He butchered the licks from Heart's "Crazy on You" and Hendrix's "Purple Haze" while he was at it. As Troy and Terry said, *"Now you're getting cocky, pal."* He was no Santana. He warmed up his voice and jokingly tried to sing like Steve Perry, but it wasn't even close. Even sang a few songs he, Nainsi, and Rhee slow danced to in a newborn fog stupor, like the Beatles' "Long and Winding Road." What about the toughie, the song he wrote for Rhee? Too painful, but he'd plucked rusty strings on everything else so hard his fingers burned. Raw and reddened, it'd take a while before he built up calluses again. Session over, he placed the guitar upright. It looked right in the room, as if The Hendrix said welcome back.

"Thanks," he said, and Mort looked up. "Judith liked silence, but I hate it, pal." Cal scratched Mort's tummy. "Except for when I tried to serenade her but got blitzed, that guitar's been MIA for a decade. But it was life."

***

After Cal scored a Guess Who album at the used record store, he got his guitar restrung. Then he walked into Quincy's, the neighborhood bar and grill he'd deserted in sobriety.

He missed this place. He'd left at a time he most needed brotherhood. But being here was like visiting an old home again, but a battle raged in his head: should he go, accepting the inviting familiarity--or not, fearing the kiss of a cool drink on his lips. His first steps crunched the peanut shells on the floor, and it was like a call to action. A buddy lifted a draft beer mug. "Leonardowski returns!"

"Hey there." Perspiration dripped down his forehead. The amber ale looked so refreshing, he salivated. His nose honed in on the malts and hops. A cold pilsner or a pint of stout would slide down his throat smoothly. But he'd been dry, and if he learned anything from Fleetwood Mac, he couldn't break "The Chain."

Heather dropped her dishrag. "Hey stranger, how long's it been?"

"A hundred and four days. Hi, Heather. You look great. Still like Blondie."

"And you still look like Johnny Cash's cousin. So, what'll it be? Double shot of Jameson, chaser of Guinness? Fond of the drinks of Ireland, I recall..." She walked to fetch a frosty mug, her tight outfit trumpeting her figure.

"Nothing for me, thanks." The bar quieted. Forks dropped. It was as shocking as if Calvin Leonardowski announced a presidential bid.

She brought over a soda and embraced him, and he eased. It was the first time in years any woman, including Judith, had touched him. Not that there was any reward for staying faithful. But if he could resist Heather for years, he drew on his resolve to not drink now.

"Since you have live music here, was wondering if you needed someone to play?" He pointed at his guitar case.

"I'm the manager here now, why don't you play me something? Say, remember that night when the guys discovered you were 'Cal Leonard' and teased you mercilessly about your song booted off the charts by 'Disco Duck?' So funny. But would you believe I recently saw it at the dollar store?"

"How is that damn duck doing?"

She smiled. "You know I'm talking about your excellent song. The best one on that CD. Love me some sultry songs."

"Thanks for not alluding to the 'sorrowful' part," he said. "Me and Randy Vanwarmer."

"Who?"

"Exactly."

She gave a gentle smile.

"He wrote "Just When I Needed You Most.' Solid songwriting, good musicianship, but where is the poor guy now, besides this CD?"

"Working his tail off on his next hit. By the way, none of us ever heard you play your song live."

He brushed it off and strummed a cover, "Taxi," the Chapin song of two old flames. Soon Heather's gaze cast far away, hopefully not on the twenty-dollar tip he once left her, like in the song. His joke had fallen as flat as the soda now.

"Your voice sounds good. Now play your song?"

No. He didn't want to be reminded of his girl. That wasn't why he was here. His hope had been dashed of late. The Catholic agency and St. Ronan's secretary had no information, and a PI wanted a hefty retainer. "Sorry. That's all I got today." What was he doing here, like a hotshot? "You don't have to be nice. I don't sound like before. Rusty, I know."

"I enjoyed 'Taxi.'" She wiped off the dust on his guitar case. "And if you make me, a hardened, middle-aged divorcee, feel something, you'll make others."

"That's why I'm here." He slugged the soda and looked around. The dartboard was gone, replaced by a sports screen. It felt genuine here, unlike pretentious DC yuppie bars. "I just want to play again. Just to play. Here."

"Are you free Sunday nights from six to ten?"

"What if Washington's playing the four o'clock game?" He winked.

"We get an over-forty crowd who likes soft rock tunes from seventies and eighties. Aim for nostalgia. A hundred bucks a show, tips, and free meals sound good?"

"Thank you."

"You're way too young to fade away."

"Thanks." She called herself hardened, but she wasn't. How kind to listen to his bludgeoning of songs.

This gig would help to keep busy outside work. He'd missed the feel of that old six-string. His fingers had found guitar instead of a drink again, and that sparked a weird energy. He'd always quelled his emotions with booze, but now they bubbled up often.

On the walk home, he created a setlist with crowd-pleasers like "Brown-Eyed Girl," "Sweet Caroline," "Maggie May," and "Margaritaville." He wouldn't play "Rhiannon," nor would he play his own hit for his girl. Everyone assumed he penned "Girl..." for an old lover. Evan had leaked that by design. His buddies and Heather, when they discovered he'd been a singer, thought the hit was for a girlfriend who got away too. But all had misconstrued the song; "Girl" was literal. He'd done his only child wrong.

It'd rip through his heart if he sang it again. Without self-medicating, he'd have to feel this sorrow. No, thanks. He didn't want to revisit wartime with the B-side "Spit" either. Now that he wasn't drinking, all the wounds and losses felt rawer, like he needed stitches.

Covers only, it is.

57

"Just My Imagination (Running Away with Me)"

Rhiannon, May 1, 1988

In the dress that hours earlier Gert had said was "to die for," Rhiannon paced in the hospital waiting room, wobbling in her plastic hollow heels.

"For Gertrude Jaymes?" said one of two doctors scrutinizing clipboards.

"Yeah, how is she?"

"I'm Dr. Corneil, a cardiologist. This is the chief resident, Dr. Julia Forsythe. We were just in the cardiac cath lab. She had a mild heart attack because of a blockage."

Rhiannon's stomach dropped.

"But we placed a stent and performed an angioplasty to open and expand the clogged artery. It's like a balloon. Worked perfectly."

She exhaled. "Thank God! Thank you! When can I see her?"

"The procedure was under heavy sedation. She's awake, on Valium. You can see her for a short time in recovery. We've immobilized her with weighted pillows—sandbags—to ensure clotting. Keeping her still.

While she tolerated the angioplasty well, because of her age and weight, we'd like to keep her another day as a precaution. She'll be fine," he said. "But we encourage her to work with her physician on a weight-loss program, like walking, maybe swimming, and a low-fat, low-sodium diet. She'll leave with a regimen of beta blockers, aspirin, meds to keep platelets from clumping, cardiology check-ins."

She thanked them as they pointed to the recovery room.

She recoiled at Gert buried under the wires and weights, and her own heart fluttered. Her energetic, round face was gaunt. Gert's eyes opened at her voice, but seemed sunken, the dun hue a weathered brown like an acorn. Her swollen hand, taped up with an IV, lay wedged between sandbags. For the first time, Rhiannon saw sturdy, invincible, spunky Gert as old and vulnerable, and her frailty saddened her.

"Her vitals are stable," the nurse said, seeming to read her tight, stricken reaction. "You can talk for ten minutes, then we'll move her to a room. She'll be stronger tomorrow."

"Hi, Gert. I'm here." Rhiannon bit her lip as the heart monitor beeped steadily. "You came through like a champ. It's okay."

Gert's gaze settled on Rhiannon. "The Holy Infant saved me."

"Amazing. I'm so grateful. You're going to be all right, Gert."

"This bad luck is because I opened the umbrella in the house, right after a black cat had crossed my path, after I broke that mirror last week! I'm a dingbat." She furrowed her brow. "Did you call Father Joseph?"

"No, you don't need last rites. You're going to outlive me. Your recovery has a great prognosis with this new hardware for your strong heart."

She closed her eyes again. "Father never checks on me."

"I know."

"Well, there are many parishioners in need. I'm no one special." Gert reopened her misty eyes. "But my secret? I've crushed on him."

"So, Valium is truth serum, just like General Hospital." She smiled. "And I know."

Gert's eyes showed a longing, yet resignation, in the confession, her face pinched, her body blocked from writhing. "I wasted decades pining for him. Silly me. It's not The Thorn Birds."

Rhiannon stroked her arm. "He should've seen the beautiful, loving woman with a heart of gold right in front of him."

"Rhee, remember when you got off the bus and caught me in your room vacuuming, dancing to Tom Jones, and I said that only happened once?"

"Yeah?"

"When you were at school, sometimes I played albums from the library, dancing to romantic, dapper crooners like Dean Martin, Perry Como..."

Rhiannon patted her hand softly. "Good for you."

"No, not good for me." Her eyes shrunk, etched with sorrow. "I spent a lifetime loving men who didn't love me back. It's lonely never waltzing since the second world war."

Rhiannon's heart twinged. "I'm sorry. How I wish you had someone. There's still time. Sara's grandfather is a widower—"

"Oh, no, silly. It's about serving others, not yourself." Gert's eyes lowered. "Besides, the Lord is my strength and song."

She exhaled. "It's not selfish to want to love and be loved on earth. It's human. It was fun just talking with someone tonight, you know?"

"Please tell me about prom, dear-heartie..."

"Tomorrow. Just know I love you. Because you 're-signed my lease' each year as my foster mother, guardian, whatever you called it, I never had to bounce around homes. You're my mother, even if you don't want the name."

"I wanted to leave open the door in case your parents came back. I raised you as a daughter of my heart while I prayed God would guide you to learn your family."

"You and Boo and Ezzy are my family. My biological parents are dead. And I never even heard God say who they were. All that praying, and nothing."

"You heard risqué lyrics instead."

She smiled. "Easier to hear."

Gert's chuckle was raspy. "Heavens, the songs coming from your room! 'Only the Good Die Young'? 'Kiss You All Over'? 'Lovin' Touchin' Squeezin''? The sounds of 'Love to Love You Baby,' oh my, the sisters were over for tea, and I was red as beet juice! Then last year, when I heard you play 'I Want Your Sex,' that was actually my first heart attack!"

Their laughter bellowed, bounced around the room, and drowned out heart monitor beeps.

"Sorry to horrify you."

"I marched to the crucifix on the wall, pulled it down, and baptized your room with it."

"Ha! You're full of secrets today, Gert."

"Music was always your language, comforting you. That's why we picked the confirmation name and middle name of Saint Cecilia, and I prayed music would guide you to your truths."

"Oh, I called Sister Mary Pat. You're on mass intentions. The Pope is probably praying."

"Ask them to pray for your parents too. Your dad. A tortured soul when I—" She stopped.

Rhiannon's eyes widened. "What?"

"Oh my." Gert's eyes cast downward and a few more beats of silence followed. "I've never told you..."

"Hmm?"

"This will sound batty, but...over ten years ago, getting a root canal—I may have been delirious—"

"What?"

"On the radio at the dentist's office, Mr. Casey Kasem announced a song and briefly talked to the singer who was a veteran of the war. You know how I never forget a voice? Thought I heard the singer's gravelly voice before. So, I listened closely. The lyrics struck me. The song felt like an apology to a baby, like a father who got drafted to Vietnam. I thought, it could be. There was a guitar pick in your diaper bag, Rhee…"

"You said they left me in a bassinet with a note. How would you know his voice?"

"I—I—owe you the full truth. The secret I've confessed in the booth for seventeen years. A young man handed you to me. He'd called me first, loopy, slurred words, stench of alcohol, sad, in great distress. I guessed he'd been drafted and feared he wouldn't come back. He wanted anonymity, so the loss wouldn't hurt you, he said. Oh, I feared your pain in knowing he handed you over blindly. Why, you'd feel like a donated can of peas! My intentions were to spare your feelings, and honor his anonymity, so I said it was a note. I wasn't sure if he was asking for babysitting or an adoption, but clearly you needed someone as a guardian right away, stat. But yet I didn't take you inside or to an agency because, well, I wanted you. You, Rhee. A precious baby when I didn't get to be a mother, was like a gift from God. And St. Ronan! Heavens, I didn't know what to do, but wanted to keep you safe first…"

"Are you serious?"

"I waited out the war for four years. When he still didn't come back to claim you, I figured he died like he feared, but I signed papers that he chose me as your guardian. A few years later, I heard this song, and something about it…so I wrote to Mr. Kasem. When I didn't hear back, I called LA information. Operator put me through to a secretary. They couldn't give out addresses but said they forwarded my letter to Asheville, North Carolina, where they reached him for the interview. If it was your father, once he got my letter, he'd want to know you were okay. After all, I just did the longest babysitting job in history! That's why

I never adopted you. He might've wanted you back, and you belonged with your daddy. I was torn, so prayed for a sign." Gert's tears streamed, breath quickened, and nose ran. Her face flushed and voice grew robust.

"My father might be alive?"

"Mr. Kasem mentioned the singer wanted to travel to Arlington Cemetery someday, so I thought if it's him, he could go to the cemetery and meet us on the same trip. Saving two birds with one stone! So, I invited him to Bob and Edith's Diner for your seventh birthday. Remember? That day you got the record player and albums?"

She gasped. Page one of her music diary, the surprise guest who never showed, and the free records that comforted her childhood. "You never told me we'd be meeting—him?"

"Because what if it wasn't him? Sure enough, he stood us up. He's either a cold son of a gun—or it wasn't him at all, and he died in the war like perhaps he feared. All the boys were coming home in body bags, Rhee! I prayed for a sign of what to do. I couldn't have you thinking he left you *twice*! When I heard you playing Let It Be—my answer."

Rhiannon's jaw dropped.

"Time to rest, Mrs. Jaymes," the nurse said. "Miss, we're moving her to a room. We'll take good care of her."

"Wow, Gert, so many questions. Okay. We'll talk tomorrow. Sleep well."

"Don't worry, it's not him. He would've come to his daughter's birthday, for heaven's sake. Goodnight. I won't dream about Father Joseph. I'll dream about tossing my girdle at Mr. Tom Jones instead."

Rhiannon blew her a kiss. "We'll go to his next concert."

"See you tomorrow," Gert said, her face no longer anguished, her cheeks brightening.

Stunned, Rhiannon walked down the hall with her mind spinning. Tonight, she planned to write the immortal Marvin Gaye's song in her diary, "Mercy Mercy Me." Tomorrow, she'd ask Gert for facts.

58

"Come and Get Your Love"

Nainsi, May 1988

After a rough day promoting an up-and-coming artist, Fiona Falini, who insisted on TV placement on *every* morning show in Europe, Nainsi met up with half of her family at a pub with grand fish and chips. Da came from the Boxing Stadium, Michael from the Guinness factory line, his pregnant wife Cara from teaching primary school, and Auntie—whose boys had moved out—from her house. Nainsi's bachelor brothers Vincent, Ian, and Liam—in their twenties, a banker, an auditor, and a computer programmer—had cooked up a triple date, a homemade dinner for triplets they'd met at the passing of the peace.

"I'm exhausted!" said Auntie, ordering another round for the table. "I made lobster bisque and homemade rolls for them. The boys better have a second date with those girls."

"You cook just like Ma did," said Nainsi. "It's the best."

"Our mother taught us how to feed our men. Just didn't know we'd be feeding the same men!"

"What would we ever do without you?" said Da, rubbing the scars on his jaw.

"I got the next round," Michael said as the waiter brought the second round of lagers.

"Ah, my virgin daiquiri," said Cara, holding her back.

"How much longer?" Nainsi said.

"I'm on week thirty-six. Four more weeks--if I survive."

Nainsi gulped the second pint. "That's the worst. How I remember! You can't sleep or get comfy, you're peeing all the time, your emotions are roller-coaster, and you're out of breath and waddle around. Cara, you make it look like it's easy, but that last month is sure a killer."

All eyes darted to Nainsi.

"Oh, I mean, a friend in Atlanta—LA—or Branson or London? —once said—" But it was no use; they stared. Studied her eyes. Deciphered. Awkward silence pervaded.

She stumbled through more words and backpedaled, but she stopped. Nainsi was a grown woman now, not an ashamed teenager. She didn't want to deny Rhee's very life anymore. Her child wasn't shame. She only spelled love.

"There's something I never told you all. A deep pain in my heart." She took a breath and slowly unburdened her heart. "Her name is Rhiannon." She didn't blame them for being devout and unable to hear the news back then; instead, she blamed herself. She talked about how *she* didn't want to be an unmarried teen mom in 1971. She'd chosen education and career instead of family, longing for the life Ma never had, when she thought she had to pick one. She couldn't do it all at nineteen, and maybe it was wrong to choose her dreams over her baby and first love a long time ago, for a promise to herself and Ma, and for that she'd confessed every day. It was a profound sorrow that still haunted her. She couldn't forgive herself. She said how she talked to a counseling priest through the years who'd helped with the weight she carried, and he opened her eyes—about Killian too. Was this choice too much to bear? It was. And while she hoped they didn't condemn for the secret she'd hidden, she asked for forgiveness. But if there was one thing she wanted—one measly thing—-it was not their acceptance.

She wanted to see her girl again, to wrap her arms around her and say she was sorry, that she loved and missed her. For always.

The waiter filled the glasses of the family in rapt attention, asking tons of questions. Nainsi feared ridicule and criticism would greet her, but weirdly, compassion emanated from the table. Perhaps they saw religion differently now, a comfort in trials instead of a judgment, Nainsi wondered, or perhaps it had spoken to them with just plain love. Perhaps a maturity had settled, or perhaps Da's scars had crusted over, kept by the Troubles. Perhaps their hard edges years ago had been softened by time and tragedies; maybe a knowledge prevailed that no one can avoid regrets and "what ifs." By now, unlike in the cockiness of youth where they took time for granted, all had known troubles within the Troubles.

"I'm sorry that because of me, you don't know a grandchild and niece," Nainsi said, wiping the tears that rolled down her cheeks. Auntie squeezed her hand. Nainsi appreciated there was no religious scorn or piety here and now, only care. Over the years, in the darkest moments as a, well, broken-hearted birth mother, she asked Ma's, Liam's, and her favorite saint, Mother Mary, for strength for the longing, sorrow, and guilt that choked her throat from a simple song. Tonight was no exception. As she said a silent thanks, Michael and Cara hugged her. Dishes clanked, people chatted, and waiters flew by, but table five fell quiet for a few beats.

"You should find her," Da said.

"We'll help you," Michael said.

Support felt nice for a change, but she couldn't wallow in it. Da had cleared his throat, his signal for a burst of rare emotion. Something more was happening.

"Nainsi, you just gave me courage. Everyone, I've a secret to share, too. Ma's sister here—this wonderful, godly woman Mary Louise—and

I have been, er, *together*, for seventeen years! Let he without sin cast the first stone." He let out a belly laugh and raised his glass. "Sláinte!"

Nainsi's mouth dropped open. Michael and Cara burst out laughing. The mood turned jovial.

"Oh, for Pete's sake, Jack, you've gone mad! Kids, you know that concussion made him talk crazy," Auntie said. But she blushed.

"Feels good to get that off my chest. No denying us anymore, sweetheart! Poor Nainsi couldn't even tell us she had a *baby*. That's how uptight we all were, for crying out loud. And because of that, she married the next guy—an asshole! So, no, we can certainly admit that at first, we met after work downtown, which is why I was walking there when the statue exploded! And yes, I've confessed this!"

Everyone gasped.

"But I want to rendezvous with you for the rest of our lives. Kids, I will always miss Ma, my love, Mary Rose. May she rest in peace. Mary Louise misses her love Paddy, may he rest in peace. We pray for them every day. But we have found a beautiful love together."

Hearty hugs and congratulations traversed around the table.

"Jack forgets God gave him an edit button," she said.

"Forgets? Except for my dang ear and scars, nothing wrong with my memory or any part of this sixty-year-old hunk of burning bod!"

Mary Louise turned as red as her rouge.

He stood. "If I drop to one knee, I won't be able to get up, but I'd like to ask you officially to marry me?"

Mary Louise jumped up and burst into tears, which no one had ever witnessed before. She'd always been as stoic as a statue. "Yes! I love you, Jack. And I love all our kids!"

They kissed. Hoots and hollers erupted from tables. The waiter appeared with bubbly.

"We knew all along, Da," Michael smiled, raising a glass.

"Sláinte," said Nainsi, raising her glass too.

"We'll never ever forget Ma," Auntie whispered to Nainsi and squeezed her hand.

"She's happy for you both," Nainsi said. "You know I talk to her sometimes? Mothers and daughters never forget each other."

Do they, Rhee? Do they, baby girl?

59

"I Will Always Love You"

Rhiannon, May 1, 1988

When Rhiannon awoke after three hours of sleep to the telephone's ring, the clock read 5:47 a.m. Gert the early bird must be calling to remind her to feed Ezzy and Boo. The ringing stopped by the time she reached the kitchen phone, so she let out the animals, fed them, showered, dressed, and left.

The elderly hospital volunteer ushered her into a makeshift office, decorated in diagrams of heart chambers and organ donation brochures, where she waited until doctors entered with bloodshot eyes.

"How's she doing?"

"We've been trying to reach you," Dr. Corneil said. "Mrs. Jaymes suffered another sudden coronary. She didn't recover. We're truly sorry."

"Oh, you're mixing up your files. I'm here for Gertrude J-a-y-m-e-s."

"Yes, Gertrude Jaymes. We're sorry. We did everything we could."

Her hands flew to cup her mouth, and she jolted like defibrillators came at her own heart. "No. She bounced back yesterday. You said she'd be fine. She was here. At the hospital."

"Risks happen after any procedure," the resident said. As they explained cataclysmic cardiac events, Rhiannon only pictured Gert dancing with the vacuum cleaner, a.k.a. Perry Como. Her knees buckled. *You never thanked her for the prom dress. You never said goodbye.*

"You said we needed to bring down her cholesterol? Cut the salt. Take meds. You don't die from another heart attack while you're *in* the hospital!"

While the doctors rattled off medical terminology, VH1 played in her head. Tom Jones's "She's A Lady" echoed, along with "Lady," by Little River Band. "Lady," by Styx. "Lady," by Lionel Richie, sung by Kenny Rogers. "Three Times a Lady" by the Commodores. Gert was all of them.

"Yes, you can do something for me," she called as they walked away. "Call Father Joseph. He can do last rites now!" She turned and walked the hollow halls in a daze. Panic wormed its way in with each step. *What now? Where do I go? What do I do? I don't even have a job and can't pay for all the things Gert complained about, the electricity, groceries, gas, and insurance. Do I quit school to get one? Will I be homeless? How do I set up a funeral? Does it cost?*

The shock spiral landed on just wanting Gert back right now. The blow shut her throat, and she could barely swallow. She must get back home to break the news to Boo and Ezzy. They'd whimper and cry, for they didn't have anyone either, but she would mother them *now and forever.* Then, tonight, if she survived this shock, she'd play Lady songs and write in her music journal.

Lady, she'd write. *Gertrude Jaymes, the best lady I ever knew. Mom.*

60

"I Believe in Music"

Cal, May 7, 1988

At Quincy's, Cal loaded hot sauce on wings and dug in just as Heather approached with a clipboard and sat down.

"Cheers." They clinked water glasses. "Lemme have it, boss." He was ready to be fired in his first review. His opening weekends drew crowds of only thirty-five with his covers. A few people even danced, but they were blitzed.

"People like to reminisce. They like nostalgia." With her drawl, on-coming bad news seemed kinder than Evan's.

"Thanks, hon."

"Oh, I'm hon now? I was 'Hey, you, gimme another drink' for years."

"That's not true, Holly."

"Heather."

He winked. "If I get canned, do I still get free potato skins?" He tapped his foot to "Wheel in the Sky" in the background, perfect for how his life felt lately, topsy-turvy without his crutches—Judith, cigarettes, and alcohol.

"But here's what we learn from Steve Perry," she said. "You need to feel your heart to sing. Frankly, you sing like a robot, sugar. Like you're not totally here. You're talking at the audience."

"Ouch." He wiped his face and hands with a napkin.

"You're wondering why the hoopla isn't following you again? The fog lifted, but you're still bottled up. Trust the audience. You're going through the motions to keep busy, but your eyes are vacant, like no one's home."

He looked away to the big screen TV and ran his hand through his new short haircut. "This beats therapy. I don't even need to talk."

"You haven't played your song yet. Start there. Let pain spark you and your voice deliver that energy."

"I'm mulling over the psychobabble. Like an irresistibly sexy, brooding artist..."

"When you sing your song, you tell your story, you show your vulnerability, and your voice is authentic."

He twirled the straw. "I'm avoiding reliving *Girl* or *Spit*."

She took a sip of water. "Your story might help someone else."

"Know the funny thing about loss? It's not just one. It triggers you to grieve all the people you ever lost. Like you're bobbing in deep water, but regrets are holding you below." He'd never shared painful feelings like that before—drowned them instead—and the nakedness made him put his elbow on the table and cover his mouth.

"Write about that."

"If you only knew the half of it." Rhee must *hate* him. Judith said he shouldn't wreck her peace in her teen angst. What if the world's best family had adopted her, and she didn't know of him? Should he wait until she was an adult and found him?

"So, I'm not fired?"

"Not yet," she said.

That night, unwinding to Van Morrison, a memory drifted through of Nainsi cranking this album, and Mrs. Henderson knocking like in morse code, her cue to turn it down.

Mrs. H! She'd been the one to give them the number of the church volunteer friend to babysit. That was the number Cal called in a drunken stupor, stammering, "Ain't never coming back alive," asking about finding someone to take her. That woman had shown up to St. Ronan's blindly—not even her church—simply because he asked. Cal had put too much trust in this stranger, handing over his precious baby, hoping she'd find her a family. His drunken idea mixed with blind faith could've gotten her killed. Sold. Neglected. Trafficked. Abused.

What a longshot, but he could look for Mrs. H's son, who might remember his mom's acquaintances, and maybe he could trace leads. Why not? He called the operator—and every Henderson in St. Louis.

The fortieth call, the man—who must've been in his late seventies—listened to Cal's ramble and said, "Yes, my mother lived in Manassas in the early seventies, until I moved her here to St. Louis."

Cal sharply inhaled, his hand flying to his mouth. "What? You're Mrs. H's son?"

"What can I do for you?"

"Geez. Am I happy to find you. First, I'm sorry for your loss. She was a good lady. Wondering if she'd ever spoken about her friends? I'm looking for someone she knew, from another church, actually, to begin a search for—someone."

There was a long pause. Cal repeated the question.

"You're aware she's alive? You can ask her yourself."

What? He sat stunned. She had to be in her late nineties.

The phone rustled, and a loud voice picked it up. "Why, Bill tells me it's you, Calvin! What a pleasure to hear from you."

"Mrs. H! It's great to hear your voice," he said. She chatted about doctor's appointments, kids, grandkids, great grandkids, like no time had passed, but long-ago memories caught in his throat. How could he tell her?

"Wait, this dang hearing aid..." She stopped and fiddled with the phone again. In a normal tone, she said the biggest surprise of all. "I ran into Nainsi a few years ago, a bigshot now. Sorry to hear you're not together anymore, dear. You were a sweet couple."

He gasped, as if Jimmy Page had called him to play a few chords with Zeppelin. "You saw her? Where?"

"At a show in Branson, of course. Silly! Don't you keep in touch for Rhee? By the way, can you mail me Miss Rhiannon's picture, please?"

"We'll get to all of that, but I'm calling because I first need a name to help with something with her. Do you remember you once gave us the name of a volunteer to babysit, but she lived an hour away, so we didn't?"

"Rhee's a little old for a babysitter, isn't she?"

Cal chuckled. "The woman helped me with something else."

"Let me think. Was it..." Her voice faded. He could hear a family on *Family Feud* ring a bell and shout answers. "The name Gertrude rings a bell."

"Yes, that's it!"

"She never said no to anyone, volunteered outside her diocese."

"What's her last name?"

"Oh, dear, I do not remember..." She spoke slower. Said she was tired. Excitement unsettled her.

"Okay, that's a great start."

The call waiting clicked. Why had he agreed to this new annoying feature? "Hold that thought." Cal toggled over. "I'm on the other line, can I call you back? Unless you're a telemarketer—"

"This is Marissa Warner from the TV show *Solid Gold*," the woman said. "Looking for Cal Leonard."

His hand flew up to his mouth. "Hold on?" He went back to Mrs. Henderson. "You were saying?"

But Mrs. Henderson was gone. Exasperated, he flipped back. The producer explained how she'd received a '70s one-hit wonders CD in the mail that was good, so she'd pitched a '70s one-hit wonders medley show to the powers-that-be. Would he fly to LA for the taping?

This last minute of his life was dizzying, like a line drive had cracked his forehead. He shook with Evan's parting words: *Second chances never happen in the biz.*

"It's not much money," she said. "But it may spur sales of your CD."

"Don't remind me," he said. How asinine to give up rights to "future repackaging of the song." But how would he have known? He couldn't predict life. Just like he gave up his parental rights long ago, but he didn't know he'd survive Vietnam, then spend years burying it all. He believed he and Judith would have two-point-five kids and a white picket fence, his daughter would join them, and they'd live happily ever after. "Yes, I'd love to do it. Thank you for the chance."

Marissa explained he'd appear after being introduced by Marilyn Mc-Coo, perhaps lip-sync a verse of his hit with others, or, after Nina Black-wood would interview him and other, er, *former artists* from *long ago*, he'd sing.

"When?"

"Firming up details, but we'll get you the info soon," she said. He gave her his address to mail the contract. He didn't own a nifty fax machine yet.

He floated to the music room. Mort jumped and curled up on the couch as Cal loaded his own one-dollar CD in the player. "Mrs. Henderson, Gertrude, a highfalutin' Bigshot Nainsi sighting, and now *Solid Gold*, I'm dumbfounded. National TV!"

Mort closed his eyes. Cal nudged him. "How can you sleep? Didn't you hear me say *national TV*?"

This rare second chance to resurrect his music career, singing a song of remorse, was a second chance for Rhiannon to privately hear it and contact him, if she wished, now that she was older. A pipe dream, coming true? He shivered.

61

"I Love You, I Honestly Love You"

Rhiannon, May 7, 1988

Gert is dead. Three words looped in Rhiannon's head during Fr. Joseph's homily about Gert's personification of love in action. She crossed her arms. How hypocritical of him to not visit an adoring parishioner and volunteer for *decades*—especially in the hospital.

The sisters across the aisle fished tissues out of pockets and wiped their tears. Faithful customers bawled in the third pew, probably wondering who to order from now, she smiled. Gert was everyone's anchor. She felt like "Little Orphan 'Annon," untethered and lost now. She'd never seen it coming, being alone at seventeen, and her mind whirled. While it stung Gert had denied the title "Mom"— "if God wanted me to be a mom, Bert and I would've had a baby"—each muscle in Rhiannon's body ached as a daughter. But did she deserve that title? She must've disappointed Gert with her 2.5 GPA; the band or athletic or volunteer scholarships wouldn't call her name either. No college for her. More importantly though, no one was there to hold her hand at the moment of death and pray her soul into heaven. How could she forgive herself?

As Sister Jean sang "Ave Maria," and the sun filtered in from a beautiful stained-glass window, she wondered why she'd never noticed the majesty of this song before. Her mind's eye saw scenes of Gert's kindness at that moment. Gert letting her stay up on Tuesdays until nine o'clock for *Happy Days* and *Laverne & Shirley*. Stuffing free ketchup and sugar packets into her purse. Making a pot roast for parishioners with a new baby. Giving her *Jesus Christ Superstar* for her birthday. Gert mixing metaphors and co-mingling scripture and superstitions. "If ye have faith like a mustard seed, you can move mountains if a black kitten doesn't cross your path and step on a crack."

After the funeral liturgy's closing dirge, "Be Not Afraid," people swarmed Rhiannon in the church vestibule offering condolences, but when the first set of warm eyes locked with hers, she drew a breath.

"Hi, Rhiannon," Nick said.

She stepped into his hug, burrowed her head in his chest, and teared up at the gesture. "A class tact," Gert would say, because she messed up sayings, which as a kid annoyed her, but now, what she wouldn't give to hear her voice. "Thanks for coming, Nick Lowe. You're not cruel after all."

"My mom saw the obit. It's like, sad, you know? I'm sorry."

Someone pushed forward her hand to offer her condolences, and Nick stepped back. Rhiannon frowned at the intrusive random lady who wore a tailored black dress, immaculately dressed for a royal funeral, a veil attached to her hat that covered a severe bob. "Sorry for your loss and to meet under these circumstances, but I'm Samantha, your real estate broker. The market is heating, and Gertrude had inquired about selling the house to fund your college. So, since you'll be going into your senior year," she handed her a card, "let's talk. I can walk you and your new—guardian?— through everything, of course. I'll be by Gert's house later for the gathering."

"Huh?" Rhiannon scrunched her brows as her eyes darted around for Nick, but he vanished.

Sister Jean whispered, "Don't worry, we'll take care of the reception—and everything else."

"A reception?" Rhiannon said, whispering thanks to Gert's friends who had taken care of everything since Gert's death. Her eyes narrowed at the agent. "You want to talk about the house? I don't know anything. Like, I'm seventeen? I've never buried anyone before. I didn't even know everyone's coming over."

"Aw, you poor thing. Prayers." Samantha offered a fake hug and strode away, dipped her fingers in holy water, and crossed herself.

Sister Jean patted Rhiannon's arm. "Hullaballoo to her! Ignore her! Don't you worry, dear. We got you."

She still couldn't catch her breath in this blur of people and questions, but gratitude swelled in her throat.

***

Holding a highball in one hand, a pint of Guinness in the other, Fr. Joseph cracked a monologue in the kitchen to an audience of parishioners, shelter friends, neighbors, customers, and Gert's handyman. Though Mrs. McCreary across the street didn't come over, their lifetime grudge still solidified in death. But at the dinette with the Infant of Prague statue—where Gert once spilled hot chicken soup on the unflappable statue and apologized to him—laughter bellowed. People poured from a two-hundred-gallon drum of coffee. Trays of chicken wings soon evaporated. Someone—rumor was Fr. Joseph himself—had bankrolled the cases of beer, wine, soda, in coolers in the backyard. Sara's family filled up counters with cookies. The sisters placed heaping casserole pans for a thousand on the stove, the buffet line spilling into the garage.

The real estate agent, still wearing the designer black dress that went "from funeral to cocktail party glam," she'd said to the man accompanying her, commented on the elderberry hints in the Pinot Noir. This woman was clearly here to sell, and Rhiannon rolled her eyes, thinking about how Gert detested money blown on expensive wines instead of giving to the hungry.

Rhiannon realized there was no background music. Ironically, her journal entry today had been "American Pie." Losing Gert felt like the day the music was dying. If Don McLean's song was about the death of innocence, she agreed; she now marked life before and after Gert's death.

Rhiannon put in a mix tape she'd made for Gert of her crooner crushes, cleared her throat and raised her cola. "To the best lady I ever knew."

Everyone raised drinks. "Hear, hear!"

"Can we talk to you?" Samantha and her colleague took her aside. "So, if you list with me soon, I'd recommend fresh painting in white. A pink house is terribly dated."

"Are you kidding?"

"Also, clear the clutter, love." Samantha pointed to Gert's figurines.

"Her *saints*? No. She spent a lifetime with them. She dusted them."

"Buyers won't identify with another religion. They won't feel like the house is theirs with a giant"—she looked at the enormous statue staring back steady as Gibraltar— "red cloak staring at them."

"Boy child Jesus? You tell him, then—I'm not getting struck by lightning. Gert called him our miracle man. And, um, I'm not selling the house now. I need to live in it."

"I'm sure you'll live with your—guardian? So you can sell this as I'm sure she's left it to you. We'll grant you a little time in this hot spring market but, decide soon to sell, by this summer," said her cohort. "And we'll list for five percent instead of six percent. We'd hate for you to ride out this market and it burst like a bubble and your college money is *poof*, gone."

"This is all too soon." Her voice cracked. "Like, I'm seventeen, I said."

"How will you get through this year—and then what will you do for your future?"

"The sisters said I'll get up every day like usual and finish boring school."

"Oh, you're young. That's why you don't see long-term. You don't seem to get the tumult of social services."

"What?"

"If you don't have relatives, who will care for you?"

"Her lawyer Mr. Woodson from church will tell me everything."

"Hope she *has* a will and everything ready, so you don't go into the foster system this year. Who knows what happens there to an underage teenager as lovely as you..."

It was precisely what Gert said she'd originally feared; Rhiannon would have no one. Her pulse quickened.

"Just don't want this house to be an undue burden on you with that discombobulation." Samantha finished the wine. "Just trying to help, love."

"Gert's *home* isn't a burden. I wouldn't have had anything if it weren't for her."

"Yes, but," said Samantha, tucking her bob behind her ear, "the market's on the uptick."

What would Stevie do?

"Ma'am, I gotta go." Rhiannon dodged into the kitchen. Sister Mary Anne wrestled with pulling out a full trash bag.

She took it. "Sorry I called you Sister Golden Hair a long time ago and you were stuck with that nickname and teasing forever. You always looked out for me and loved the whole class when we weren't so lovable."

"Oh, I didn't mind the name—that much."

"Good. Sorry." Rhiannon weaved through people in the garage seated in folding chairs and pulled Sara outside for fresh air. A loop had played in her head, like an overplayed song: *Gert is dead. My father may be alive.* Her abdomen churned with the questions from the real estate agent about the house and foster care, and she felt light-headed. Dizzy, she raced to the wastebasket, and to the audible gasp of folks eating in the garage, she threw up the only food she'd eaten, three bites of casserole and a cookie.

"Sara, I need to leave," she choked out, blotting her mouth with a napkin.

"Go lay down."

"No, leave *here*. I see Gert everywhere."

Sweat started beading on her face. The muggy summer night felt sweltering, and it made her think of *Hot August Night*, Neil Diamond's best live record and, in her opinion, his seminal album. He'd taken a sabbatical after that historic concert run at LA's Greek Theatre in 1972 for solace and analysis. If it worked for Mr. Diamond, it would be good enough for her. "Need to clear my head. After my last final, can you and your parents stall county social services if they show up here? Oh, and that Samantha lady too."

"We got your back," she said. "Totally. For sure."

Ezzy purred against Rhiannon, while Boo wagged his tail, begging table scraps from the garage crowd content to stuff him silly.

"You two will not be alone. You'll come with me." She petted them, thinking of her next diary entry, maybe "A Cool Change." But when the sound of explosions ripped through the still air, the day's live fire from the Quantico base jostling her, pounding deep inside, she chose another song. "That you, Bert and Gert? You two World War Two heroes finally dancing again to 'I'll Be Seeing You' up there?"

62

"Take A Chance On Me"

Rhiannon, June 1, 1988

Near the Biltmore Hotel signs in Asheville, North Carolina, Rhiannon stopped at a diner advertising grilled cheese, tomato soup, fries, and a soda for $4.99 because it was like Gert's comfort food. She took a counter seat, her wallet flush with $500 from Gert's savings bonds. As Rhiannon hoped for a six-night research vacation with a library nearby for genealogy research, she asked the waitress about cheap accommodations.

"How old are you? Where's your mother, sweet thing? Stay away from the cheap motels," the woman said, but kindly pointed her to the hostel at YWCA, fifty bucks a week, and the library.

"Why didn't I think of that?" She mouthed the YMCA song with hand motions. "And thanks for letting Boo and Ezzy play in the fenced area behind the restaurant. You all are nice!"

"Not that nice. All y'all hear that morning DJ break down this mornin'?" said the customer two seats away.

"Oh, the WHAP-Happy-FM gal, who ain't so happy? Bless her heart," the waitress said.

Rhiannon asked, "What happened?"

"DJ up and lost her marbles, ranted she was sick of faking happiness at the 'WHAP, the Happy '70s and '80s Mix.' A door slammed, and dead air. Talk of the town."

"She quit a dream job like that? Wow, I love '70s songs. It's my thing."

"See if they need an intern, sugar. They're a hop, skip, jump away."

Interning in high school? She looked out the window, grabbing a handful of free jelly packets like Gert always did. A marshmallow puff cloud hovered over the majestic mountain backdrop in the bright, mid-afternoon sky. A breeze shook the lush green leaves on the trees. Gert's voice said, *what do you have to lose, dear-heartie?*

"Can you watch Boo and Ezzy a little longer?"

***

Streets decked in hanging geraniums, historic brick churches with red doors and towering steeples, and bright window boxes of petunias and peonies charmed her. The studio's window faced quaint cottage storefronts of a bookstore, pharmacy, five-and-dime, gift shop, art gallery. Family businesses peppered the landscape; shoppers seemed to have known each other for decades. She found the station, took a deep breath, and pretended it was *"WKRP In Cincinnati."*

She knocked three times for luck. "Rappers Delight" from 1979 played through outdoor speakers as a disc jockey in the studio window danced in his seat. She opened the door with a little jig. "Girl can't help it," she said under her breath. "One dance a day keeps the nerves away." A good-looking sandy-haired guy in his mid-twenties stood near the door and greeted her with his mouth full. He wore a navy cotton t-shirt revealing huge biceps, Rhiannon couldn't help but notice. Juggling tapes, he stuck a pen behind his ear and finished chewing. "Sorry. Vending machine lunch. Kenneth Crenshaw, station manager. Howdy, can I help you?"

"Do you do tours? I'm in town doing research."

He pointed behind him. "Okay, tour. Don't blink or it's over. Besides the studio, supply closet and bathrooms, there are four rooms—studio, my office, conference room, and the pit where staff works, like the engineer, promotions director, intern."

"Interns?"

"Ah, you're here for that? You college kids can leave resumes and reels here."

She fidgeted, having only read announcements over the high school PA.

"You're a broadcasting major? What school?"

"Uh, up north, in Virginia."

"UVA? Virginia Tech? William and Mary?"

"Makes me think of 'My Old School,' by Steely Dan," she said.

He smiled. "You know that song?" They walked past pizza boxes into a small office. He slid behind his desk stacked with tapes and offered the folding chair. "Why should you intern here?"

"I love the seventies tunes so much, I'd help you for free."

"Don't devalue yourself. You're female. Demand pay," he said. "Now, having said that, I can't pay any interns, male or female." He chuckled. "But if I select you, I'll fill out your college forms for credit, and the work will give you experience."

Getting college papers signed would be great if she were *in* college, but she was still in high school. Besides, she'd never afford college. Her smile faded.

"You work at your college station?"

She looked down. Her milk crate of albums under her stereo, and her hardy, hearty music notebook flashed in her mind. "Not yet. But Gert said my quirkiness was hearing life in seventies song titles for some reason. It's like, I can pick songs for people, like peanut butter to jelly."

"Huh." He crumpled up a letter, shooting it into the wastebasket, and leaned back in his chair, putting up his non-name-brand sneakers, much like hers. "That all ya got?"

"I created mix tapes for my prom, orchestrating each minute of the five hours, and everyone danced. I dedicated a song for parent chaperones and alumni, who gave money to the school that night. Four hundred dollars! And my tapes saved our class hundreds from hiring a band."

"Boom, three-pointer," he said. "Always lead with what you can do for the bottom line. Here we're just trying to avoid bankruptcy."

"Yeah, but music helps people too. Like, one of Gert's friends works at a nursing home, and I taped albums from the library from the forties for the residents. The nurse said the nostalgia comforted them, and they remembered happy stories."

"Nice."

"I'd love to help here. It'd be a dream. Like, totally."

Keith moved his coffee mug on his desk and picked up a Pat Benatar album. "'Hit Me With Your Best Shot,' kid. What's your schtick?"

A schtick? Huh? She looked around. *What would Pat or Tina or Stevie do?*

"Hello?" He waved his hands.

Lionel's song flashed in her mind. She'd written "Hello" in her orange notebook—page twenty-seven--about the time she showed up in a science class that was cancelled, and she kept calling, "Hello?" looking for the absent teacher.

All at once her music diary barraged her, an autobiography of sorts. Her only resume. Page one, 1978: She'd written "Mamma Mia," and "Papa Was A Rolling Stone," because she didn't know who they were. Each page held a song yoked with a memory. The notebook was a literal soundtrack of her life. Her *schtick?*

"'Hello Again'?" Keith said.

"'Hello It's Me,'" she said. "'New Kid In Town.'"

"'You Haven't Done Nothing.'" He smiled.

"'I'm a Shining Star.'" She couldn't even say it with a straight face.

"'You're No Good.'"

"'You Ain't Seen Nothing Yet.'" She straightened her slumped posture. "'I Am Woman.'"

"'Jive Talkin'?"

"'That's The Way I Like It.'"

"'Can You Play That Funky Music'?"

"'With A Little Luck.'"

"'What A Fool Believes.'"

"'Killing Me Softly.'"

"'You Don't Have To Be a Star (To Be In My Show).'"

"'Hey Won't You Play Another Somebody Done Somebody Wrong Song'?" She could converse in '70s song titles all day, a plethora lodged in her brain.

"'Silly Love Songs.'"

"'The Gambler.'"

"'I Can See Clearly Now.'"

"'My First, My Last, My Everything.'"

His smile widened. "A complete conversation in song titles. You know your stuff. Lots of number ones."

She soared, aplomb with song confidence; she trembled, dizzy with the terrifying array of buttons. What if she pressed the wrong one and they'd go off the air? What if she did this at a commercial, and the advertiser would freak and she'd be fired day one?

"But without experience, afraid you're not ready for an intern slot here, Miss—?"

"Rhiannon. Oh, fine, I figured that."

He coughed. "Rhiannon?" He gazed out at the street, a slow smile coming to him. "Yay...you've just given me an idea. Look, I don't have time to sift through intern applications and needed help yesterday, and you're…soulful."

Page thirty-two, "Soulshine" by Allman Brothers. She'd written *Shine for others, so they can see a way ahead. Like Gert.* A lump came to her throat.

"I'm in a quandary. You're young, but quick, with chutzpah. Takes gumption to stroll in here," Keith said.

She *was* ludicrous to try. A moron. "Goodbye Girl" by David Gates even played from the studio.

"What about a trial internship for the seventies morning show shift? If you can work five a.m. until one, Whiz Kid Wesley—who runs his college radio station—can train you. Two months on-the-job crash-course, but if it's not working, we'll free you up for vacation."

She looked away, trying to do the math. She'd work hard to stay. She could use all the savings bonds for the YWCA stay and gas for the return trip, and she'd already brought along food for Ezzy and Boo. She eyed the pizza boxes and vending machine. She could live on one meal a day. *Holy Gloria Gaynor!* "I Will Survive."

"You got the first rule down. We keep a positive atmosphere, treating listeners like we're family, the background music for their lives. Now, 'Don't Go Breakin' My Heart.' Make me proud. And thanks for the great idea you gave me. See you tomorrow, Rhiannon. Topped out at number four in '76, prior to *Rumours* in '77, number one for months."

"Thank you! 'I'll Be There!' Rad." She shook his hand goodbye, grateful to intern by morning, research in the library by afternoon, far from the house missing Gert—and all the other worries. Who knew, maybe they'd let her wash dishes at the diner for free food.

Stepping into the muggy afternoon, she remembered the Robin Williams movie where he played a radio announcer in the Vietnam War. Was her father a soldier there or a singer here-- or both? Was it silly to chase Gert's words here? "But a piece of me always felt missing, and I want to know who I am," she told Boo and Ezzy when they were reunited in the diner's backyard. *Good morning, Asheville.*

63

"Sing A Song"

Cal, July 1988

Waitresses flitted about the jammed-packed Sunday night crowd. A hostess informed people of a forty-five-minute wait due to capacity with the fire ordinance. When Cal squeezed in at the bar chowing down on fried onion rings and a half-pound rare burger, he asked Heather how this happened, as last Sunday topped twenty-five people.

"Conference at the hotel next door checked in. I tipped the concierge to say *The Cal Leonard*—singing his *mega* blast-from-the-past-hit, "Girl It's All For You," is performing here to five-star reviews."

Cal's mouth dropped open, onion sliding out of the fried casing, ketchup dripping onto his t-shirt. "What five-star reviews?"

"I give you five stars, darlin'! Don't let down two hundred and fifty people here."

He will tape a show on national TV soon, unbeknownst to anyone, but it would be a lip-synced verse in a studio. A camera was one person, easier than a crowd. But singing his heartfelt song *live* here, after all this time? Feed his soul into a shredder. Cal's stomach churned. Back in the day, he tossed back shots pre-and-post-show for courage. Sober, he could taste the fear, like the greasy aftertaste in his mouth. What if he tanked?

"People have their picks of live music at venues around here. Between Cap Centre, Birchmere, 9:30 Club, Wolf Trap, Monsters of Rock—Metallica, Van Halen, Scorpions—playing at RFK, that we're getting people *at all* is a win. People remember you."

"They're drunk."

"*Girl* and *Spit* are beautiful songs. It's a good night. Let's go, *The Cal Leonard*."

Sweat dampened his shirt. He needed to rehearse before live people who weren't forgiving basset hounds. Shuffling to the stage sans an intro, only the sound of silverware clattering, he clutched the guitar's neck for dear life. It was now or never. "I'm Cal. Thanks for coming."

Kind applause. Someone lifted a frosty brew to a smattering of claps and a "woohoo!"

He straightened, bracing his fingers on the first fret. His stomach churned into a queasy ball. A nausea wave rolled over him, his gut seized, and he cramped like he was detoxing again. He bolted to the restroom and the crowd fell into a confused chatter. He locked the stall and clutched his stomach. *The zero-star review would say Almost Cal Leonard of that almost famous tour, who almost had an album once, almost played his old song last night...*

Heather led a crowd chant. "We want Cal! We want Cal!"

When his stomach calmed for five whole minutes, he washed his hands, sprayed a can of deodorizer, and slunk back to the stage. "Going to level with you—got raw nerves singing my own songs. Haven't played them in years. But now that I quit drinking, nothing hides me from my feelings and choices—like two dozen onion rings."

Laughter boosted him, and he said, "Here's a song you only hear in elevators, hospital waiting rooms, and attorneys' offices now. Don't ask me how I know."

When more laughter settled, he shared how he wrote the first words in the Vietnam War. He played the first chords of "Girl..." and before long, choked out the refrain that dwelled deep in his soul, *"Ain't never coming back alive..."*

The chorus lifted him when the audience sang along. His mind traveled, picturing his little girl eating her fist that day. A lump lodged in his throat, but the crowd brought him back to the moment and carried him through to his last note. When they went wild with applause, it was like getting thrown a life vest. It felt as good as when he volunteered on Wednesdays at the Boys and Girls Club to teach kids guitar. He only wanted that kid from Goodwill to know he wasn't alone, and he'd survive another day. Yet a funny thing happened when helping those kids; Wednesdays helped heal Cal more.

Goose bumps crawled up his arms from the applause. Cal rolled the momentum into singing "Spit," outside that airport, alone, mocked for duty, but this time, the applause consoled him and perhaps time softened things. Men with motorcycle t-shirts and veterans' caps marked "Rolling Thunder" hollered and pounded on tables. People tossed ten-dollar bills in his guitar case.

He took a break, walking directly to a couple who waved him over.

"Our son was killed in Vietnam," they said. "Thanks for honoring our soldiers."

Cal took the cash from the guitar case and handed it to Heather for the couple's check. Then he played covers for the next three hours, to mad love. Live connection lit him up, he couldn't deny. He closed to a 1974 song sung by Mac Davis, "Stop and Smell the Roses," and breathed in thanks. Music had pulled him into the here and now, and it was one mighty fine night.

When Cal got home at eleven, the phone was ringing. He hoped it was details on the *Solid Gold* show, but it was Heather. "See what happens when you share your story? You connected with others. It may hurt to sing your stuff, but it's not about you on the stage. It's about the audience. They derive their own meanings. That couple didn't hear *your* story. They heard their own."

"Were you always this smart?" he said.

"What if you make people feel a little less alone?" She cleared her throat. "Anyway, you should write again from your heart. We'll pack them in."

"You're good to me," Cal said.

"Just trying to make money off you."

Winding down to Styx's *Grand Illusion* in the music room that night, soaking his callused fingers in vinegar like he did on tour fifteen years ago, he stared out the window at the night sky. A crow nibbled at the barren birdfeeder. Cal still forgot to stock it. He jotted down, "Buy seed."

Cal scratched behind Mort's long ears. "You miss Pauly? So do I. Who knew I'd miss that dang whistle?" Cal raised the volume on "Fooling Yourself," at the first note of Tommy Shaw's guitar. The song would sound awesome with better speakers. He'd bought a surround sound system once, the latest and greatest speakers. He told captive Mort the story. Once he told Judith he'd bought them a surprise. With a glint of hope in her eyes, she seemed excited. Until he said it was an audio surround system. Her face fell. "Not for our living room," she said. He said, "We don't live in a library. How about in our room?" She said the wires were too ugly, and their bedroom was minimalistic. He cracked, "Yeah, I got *that* message." She suggested he hook it up to his basement CD player. He disagreed, because it was unfinished, but she persisted. "I like it quiet. The bird and street noise is plenty noise up here." He accused her of shutting out the world. "Isn't that what a home is for? Work takes all my energy. I'm drained." He folded his arms. "If I want to unwind by blasting music, it's not a bad thing." She said, "Unwind, or pass out with booze?" Cal said thanks for the idea, and bailed, trudging the mile to Quincy's to get hammered. Heather nor his friends were there, but he drank heavily. Staggering home, a note greeted him. *"Darling—it can work if we rig it up in the basement."* What the hell? A surround system in an unfinished basement was like a jukebox in an outhouse. It was a standstill, like DC gridlock between Democrats and Republicans. What he didn't know was her grand scheme. One morning, a handyman showed up to quote basement drywall installation. Cal *could* finish the basement himself, but he'd never found time. But he didn't want Judith's compromise; he wanted music *now*. Neither relented, the unopened surround sound system untouched.

"This house has been silent for years, Mort. Enough." Cal trekked to the garage storage space for the audio system. He climbed the ladder to the crawl space and shone the flashlight. A shoebox marked in Judith's writing lay next to the sound-system, marked "For you." He hauled them both to the kitchen. A packet of letters sat on top, tied in a pink bow.

He scratched his head. Ah, when Judith asked him to walk away from it all, she'd said fan mail had arrived. With all the hoopla of halting his career, he'd forgotten about it. Fan letters would be a kick now. He opened and read gushing letters from teenagers and women who saw his tour. It made him smile as he picked up the last two letters, with another note from Judith attached.

*Darling, these arrived as we've started our life together, and
I want your attention with our family.*

Let's move forward. I love you.

His eyes rested on the first letter, addressed to c/o Casey Kasem Show, forwarded to Asheville. Then, he dropped to his knees.

August 1, 1977

Dear Sir: My apologies for whiting-out mistakes on this
old church typewriter. During a recent root canal akin
to medieval torture, I heard the radio show playing, *Mr.
Casey Kasem's Top 40,* to whom I'm sending this letter,
in the hopes they forward it to you. They played a lovely
song, but I did not catch the exact title nor a full name.
Maybe it was the painkiller, but both lyrics and voice
sounded exactly like someone who left his baby with me
at St. Ronan's in 1971. I never forget a voice. Is it you?

Mr. Kasem referred to the B side song and said you wanted
to visit Arlington Cemetery, which is only thirty miles
away from us. My Bertram is buried there. There's a diner
near there, on Columbia Pike, with a jukebox. Since she
loves pancakes and popular music, would you meet us
there at 11 a.m. on her birthday? She'll wear her Sunday
finest, hair up in pigtails, so you know it's us. If you'd like
a visiting relationship first, as a transition, I'll consider.
She's a loving child. I fall short as a cool, hip guardian,
but the saints protect us. It may be a frugal life, but the
Good Lord provides. Please keep this letter in confidence,
for Rhiannon's sake. Also, we're not asking for money.
Thank you. Sincerely, Ms. Gertrude Jaymes

His breath caught at the image of a little girl waiting for her daddy who never came. She'd written the letter over eleven years ago. He could've enjoyed a decade with his daughter!

How could Judith have kept this letter? In her quest for their children, she didn't understand his deepest regret. Or maybe she did understand longing with empty arms; if she couldn't love a child, why let him? The Virginia postmark and return address showed they lived forty miles down 95. He picked up the dog's bowl and whipped it at the wall. Mort jumped up and barked.

One glance at the handwriting on the second letter with a postmark of LA, his stomach sunk. Addressed to his record label, the mail was forwarded to Asheville, too. He even caught a faint scent.

Chanel No. 5.

October 1, 1977

Dear Cal/Calvin/Callum/California—

Dia dhuit! You're a rock and roll star! I TOLD YOU SO! When I heard your song on a 45 at a record store, I fell over. I LOVE IT! Grand! A hint of Allman Brothers, Hendrix, Richie Havens—sounds like Atlanta to me. I don't have the right to ask, but who was the song for?

Remember when I said someday, I might write 'I've made the worst mistake'? I was young, scared, depressed, too far from home. I've made a mess. You've moved on, probably found someone amazing like you deserve, but please know I'm sorry. I'm so broken!

How's our little girl? At six, what's she like? Does she still like James Taylor? I understand if you don't want to talk to me, but I'm writing because I want to see our precious pumpkin. I've never forgiven myself for leaving, but deep in my heart I knew she'd be best with her daddy. But will you visit with Rhee— either LA or Ireland, Disneyland or the Dublin Zoo? You'd love O'Donoghue's where Dubliners started. A fabulous band of lads called U2 is playing there.

I miss you both. I don't deserve forgiveness, but please, write back, so we can start to talk. I long to tell Rhee how much I love her, and that I'm sorrier than sorry. Please kiss her sweet face for me? Nainsi.

This time Cal yelled out, like Rhee cried when he left her, the jarring, guttural sounds of a lifetime without the people you love. He spent the next hour sitting on the floor, anger pulsing through him, feelings mired in regret, as the radio blared Metallica. His mourning was not for his losses anymore, but for the life he never lived. The one he *almost* had.

Dammit. Dammit to hell.

If there was ever time for a triple shot, it was now. He moved to lay on the music room couch, seeing an alternate life. Nainsi accepted his mom's ring, welcomed him home from the war, and they raised Rhee together. She loved her incredible music business career, and his one hit became five; they moved to the Cliffs of Moher and watched their grandchildren. What if he received the letters from Gertrude and Nainsi in 1978, when they came?

He thrashed around. At 4:44, when the kitchen radio played "Reelin in the Years," he ticked off his missed milestones like a Bingo card. Rhee's first bike ride. First communion. First dance. First concert. Bingo Ringo, he missed them all! Seventeen years, absent. Every loss felt like aftershocks. Lost loves, lost children. It was the ramblings of a broken man. His shame flared. Nainsi had walked out but entrusted him with *their daughter* to raise.

Heather was right. He wasn't drunk, dishing jokes at the bar anymore, but he had only been dry, feeling life scenes only tangentially. Cal had been playing a soundtrack, but not *feeling* the music deep within anymore. He'd avoided playing music for the last ten years, hiding behind Judith, but he hadn't wanted to *feel*. Safety was a cocoon of numbness. But now, it was out.

He found a pen and a yellow pad. Like he did in Vietnam, and on the plane, he scribbled feelings onto the page. *Brave Cal* had always done what others had asked but came up short. *Almost Cal* met everyone's needs—almost. On the page he ranted, exorcised demons, blurted fears, remembered love, the feelings becoming lyrics that begged for music. He chose a C major key and strummed his guitar, mixing chords, frets, and licks, jotting notes, bridges, chord progressions, erasing the noise. He was no Paul Simon. But the page was safe. No one died songwriting.

When the sun rose much like the hazy sunrise of an Atlanta morning, he'd written his life's song. What did he lose by songwriting again, pouring out his soul? What's the worst that could happen with it? He looked around his empty house. Mort was all that mattered. So what if people mocked Cal? *Bring it. Mort will still be here!*

Cal put his guitar away and hooked up the surround sound. He lay back down on the sofa in the '70s room to Boston's "More Than A Feeling." Sleep came at 6:17 a.m.

On Sunday night, when he debuted "Mourning Regrets" at Quincy's, he sang the ballad of his life slowly, the story of a hero WWII dad and a mom who said he was brave, but he'd rather not be. He'd rather have love back—his only child, parents, close friends, a career he loved, and...someone to share all this love. When he sang the refrain, a bullet tore through his heart.

It's the government letter/ it sure won't get better

It's the lady at St. Ronan's keeping your girl alive/ It's a godforsaken unholy Easter drive

It's the music you play to cope and fight/ It's the gigs at the bar and the songs you write

It's Number thirty-nine, on American Bandstand/It's an Asheville wedding with no band

The girl waiting for her daddy at a diner/The woman waiting for forgiveness to find her

If only you could've held them in your arms forever/How you should've played the music now, not never

So you live with regrets of the road not taken/ only to find the road less forsaken.

Three seconds ticked silence. He felt bare and he swallowed hard. Well, he didn't write the song for others anyway. Creating was for him. He'd realized something when writing it. Through the years, he became a man not by a legal age but by showing up for others when it counted. By kneeling next to Daddy and turning up Roy Orbison. By holding Mama's hand at death. By patching up his wounded brothers in Vietnam. By praying for the dying soldier who asked, by bandaging ailing people in Arlington, by trying to save the marriage, by reaching out to another orphaned kid, by volunteering to teach guitar. He tried to help, even if no one understood his life's song. His journey was forgiving himself and caring for another.

His face flushed at the subdued crowd. His rhymes were lame. Not his forte.

But a crackle of thunder erupted before the crowd's resounding applause bounced off the walls. The audience roared an acceptance to his vulnerability so loud it buoyed him. His story resonated?

"Thank you," he said with a grateful mic drop, walking off the stage to Heather's hug.

"You're a regular Harry Chapin, darlin'."

Cal floated that night, having dispelled and survived feelings. Seems they were universal after all. He wasn't in a holding pattern over disaster zones anymore; he'd evacuated from heavy fire. Cleansing his heart and mind oddly lead to Judith's credo—*Move ahead. Live again.*

When Heather gave him a lift home, he admitted it felt invigorating to be writing and playing music again, and because of it, he hoped to find a loved one he deeply missed.

She didn't pry, offering, "Things are looking up for you. Why not ol' Cal Leonard/owksi coming back from the dead? Beach Boys just had 'Kokomo' as a number one, and even Donny Osmond hit with 'Soldier of Love.'" She turned up George Michael's "Faith," on the radio, steered the car into a fried chicken drive-thru, and dropped him off at his empty bungalow.

Mort greeted him with slobbers and wagging tail, and Cal plopped down with fried chicken and MTV. That was when the phone rang, and his dinner skyrocketed to Mort. He wished he'd let it ring instead.

"I know what you did," the voice had said.

The jerk seemed to know the song's truth, his words preying on Cal's self-loathing and agony. He threatened to tell the press at Cal's come-back, to reveal the secret of Cal's greatest regret.

No, no, no. He'd always wanted Rhiannon to recognize the song privately, to hear his heartfelt apology and choice was for her to have a better life and find him when *she* was ready. Cal didn't care about his reputation. Only about the sudden invasion of the world learning it publicly alongside Rhee—and Nainsi who gave her parental rights to him to raise their child. Their lives and identities would be used as entertainment fodder, all for this dude's greed. That kind of spotlight glare would be ugly. The way the man sneered, "How'd you like that, *Cal Leonard*?" made his skin crawl. He needed cash fast to buy him time.

Highs and lows made strange bedfellows, like the universe balanced itself. Nainsi always said it was Murphy's Law, that the other shoe always dropped. Cal had been pulling himself up lately—a rare second chance with music—of course it would come crashing down.

64

"FM (No Static At All)"

Evenings, she researched articles in the *Asheville Courier Journal* at the library for any leads on her father. She visited music stores and asked about the green guitar pick from the diaper bag. She contacted every musician in the phone book, asking if they'd had a child on April 15, 1971. "Uh, not that I know of..." they chortled. She found an ad for a place called Duncan's that had open mic nights in the '70s. Faulty wiring burned it down.

By day, she toiled at the station, which wasn't WKRP after all, yet she still loved it. She answered the phone, chatted with listeners, assisted talent, and learned about markets, audiences, promotions, shares, ratings. Work flew by in a blur, and she said, "What am I doing?" a million times. Whiz Kid Wesley gave her a radio crash course on the Otari reel-to-reel tape machine, the mixing board with all its buttons and switches, and the cords, wires, disc players, and reels. The microphone reverb threw her off. He also showed her how to load pre-chosen songs cued in the Selector. She compensated for zero tech wizardry by being genuine when she answered the listeners' line, found them perfect songs and wrote dedications. Wesley said, "Where'd you go to school, again?" She flinched with imposter syndrome when she answered, "Virginia."

One day, with one month left in the summer internship and $79.42 left, Keith called Rhiannon into the conference room, and she entered to many unknown faces who had just been hired. "We're in a new era for WHAP-FM, the best mix of the '70s and '80s. So, congratulations, all y'all are the new DJ muses for WHAP Muse Radio!"

Everyone broke into applause as he introduced Jolene, Brandy, Mandy, Daniel, Beth, and Rhiannon to work on '70s shows, and Billie Jean, Gloria, Sherrie, Jenny, Jack, and Diane, for '80s shows. "Branding, it's the innovative marketing of the future," Keith said. "We're now Muse Radio. Your names will make listeners think of us for their seventies and eighties destination on the dial. The fresh buzz will draw talk and audience, but your music knowledge and enthusiasm will keep people tuned in. Thanks to our summer intern Rhiannon, who unwittingly gave me the idea."

Huh? Me? She sheepishly smiled at the idea her name spurred a marketing strategy, but she liked her name brought a tribe of people who shared names with songs. But more practically, she owed Wesley for his tech help, and Sister Jean for becoming her "faculty advisor," writing up the first-ever high school summer internship program.

"Let's 'Turn the Beat Around.' Think first-place ratings, or I'm hiring again. No pressure." Keith chuckled. "Let's start with creating compelling rockumentaries to play weekends or overnights. Ideas, anyone?"

This was her kind of challenge, all right. She brainstormed how the '70s were a rich musical time. Gert once said maybe she looked for clues in the music of the times just to understand her parents. Regardless, she'd loved researching music history at the station, sifting through files of record labels' press releases, reading old *Rolling Stones*, making source lists for producers. She jotted down: *Protest music. Beatles break-up, go solo. "Ohio" song- Kent State, students there were Joe Walsh, Chrissie Hynde, DEVO; Elvis's death; Lynyrd Skynyrd plane crash; rock festivals.*

"Woodstock?" Daniel said.

"Overdone," said Brandy.

Since Rhiannon had been researching if her father was a soldier, it was first on her mind. She cleared her throat. "What about soldiers at another rock festival?" Her voice quivered. "Like, if the angle of 'singers protesting *through* music, *in* counterculture,' has been done, what about military in the audiences? We could find out what *they* felt, before and after they served, at festivals? Did those drafted or enlisted feel personally supported by the music before and after the trauma of war, or have their feelings changed over time?"

"I'm listening," said Keith.

"It's like, some people hear music, but others *feel* it, and their lives are intertwined. It must hit home with many vets, brings them square back to that time and place. I mean, war was *their* actual lives." Her voice gained speed. "So maybe we ask them what they thought of the music then?" It fell silent and she dropped her shoulders. "Well. Whatever. But, for sure, some people use music to hear and be heard. It's like their language. Totally."

"Vietnam War was a tumultuous time," Gloria said. "Who wants to reminisce about that? It wouldn't pair with the WHAP-happy brand, right, Keith?"

"Kind of woo-woo from an intern." Billie Jean smirked. "You studying psych?"

Slouching in her seat, she felt a "less-than" stab of an orphan, an unwanted child, a girl with a blank family tree poster and no date to the Father-Daughter Dance or Mother-Daughter Tea, a middle schooler with no family medical history, a kid who wasn't an athlete or scholar. She was just a teen with tunes, whose only family now was Boo and Ezzy, an unpaid temp high-school intern sitting before radio professionals. "Sorry," she said.

"Never apologize for yourself! Y'all, I'm with Rhiannon," Mandy said. "We respect people by hearing their stories, not just hearing ourselves talk. It's a good idea."

"C'mon," Eileen said.

"Okay. Let's rock and roll," Keith said. "The first rockumentary will be Rhiannon's idea, Vietnam veterans at a rock festival, preferably a southern one. Rhiannon assistant, Jolene producer, Brandy talent. Everyone good?"

Rhiannon raised her eyebrows. *Really?* She channeled the philosophers Ann and Nancy Wilson. "OK. Straight on!"

Within days, Rhiannon studied Monterey in 1967, Woodstock in 1969, and Altamont Speedway Free Festival in 1969, which turned violent with deaths. An alphabetical search meant Atlanta Second International Pop Festival of 1970 turned up first, and she learned "Southern Woodstock" included Allman Brothers, BB King, and Hendrix. Atlanta articles told of the hundred-degree scorcher on July third until early morning the sixth. Pictures showed crowds, traffic, and revelers transfixed by Hendrix and fireworks. One newspaper photo showed a couple sleeping under a tree. The guy looked a bit like David Cassidy, and the gal's red hair like Bonnie Raitt. "'Every Picture Tells A Story,'" she told Jolene as she read the caption—*Byron, Ga.-Two concertgoers sleep in the early morning at the music festival, despite soaring record temps. Cal Leonardowski, 18, of Manassas, Virginia, and Nainsi Murphy, 18, of Dublin, Ireland, rest before today's line-up that includes The Jimi Hendrix Experience.*

Then she remembered another concert, and her heart plunged. She'd left town so quickly, she'd never told Nick—and missed the James Taylor concert. Her first date—and she'd blown it. Ugh. *Who splits like that?*

There was no time to mull the ill-fated romance as she worked a hundred hours on the rockumentary. She tried to reach the couple photographed at the Atlanta festival, but no luck with Dublin, Ireland, listings, nor Virginia. She gave up when she found a local Vietnam veterans' group who invited her to the VFW to interview them about their memories, and she liked the experience of hearing their stories.

One day at work, she saw a record company's information for a "One-Hit Wonders of '70s" CD. A blurb about the song "Girl, It's All For You," said it charted at number thirty-nine as singer Cal Leonard's only hit, but also mentioned the single's B-side, "Spit," as a returning soldier's story, so she scoured stores to no avail. *Would someone please invent a library of videos and concert footage for every song ever?* At her last stop, a used record store, she found it. The old 45 lay in a clearance bin. Back at the station she listened to the moving saga of a returning veteran who'd been drafted and treated like a pariah. The deep vibrato mesmerized her, the lone acoustic guitar perfect for her story. Unfortunately, she couldn't find any information on the singer-songwriter Cal Leonard.

Rhiannon outlined a script, sharing one last idea. After all, it was why she came to Asheville. She pled her case to Jolene, Brandy and Keith, and she cheered with hope when they granted her one on-air minute. In the studio, she put on the cans and leaned into the microphone to record.

"Hi, listeners. I'm only the intern, but here's why this piece means so much to me. I don't know anything about my birth mother, but I was left by my father as a baby at a church, given to my late foster mom who guessed he was drafted into Vietnam. In the seventies, she heard a voice who sounded like him sing lyrics that would fit. I'm trying to find that song—without a title or name. Seventies songs always called to my heart for some strange reason, but now it turns out an old unknown one might be important." Her voice stopped quivering, oddly empowered, and she questioned why she'd carried this as *her* pain, *her* secret. "So, if you know of someone who handed his baby to a stranger at a Virginia church in August 1971, or you know the song, please let me know."

After it aired, a sister station in Charlotte picked it up. A classic-rock loving pastor in Fayetteville asked to play it in a reconciliation sermon. The program garnered dozens of letters.

Served in-country two tours. Went to a festival and someone who disrespected me, so I punched him in the gut.

You haven't lived until you drop acid for $1.

Rhiannon, I was adopted too...

Though compassionate, no one knew the story. She'd hit it with her best shot, but she missed the basket. She hung her head in defeat.

On her last day, after she thanked each person, grateful for the internship knowledge and advice, Keith called her into his office and said he had a surprise. Rhiannon closed her eyes and wished for cake.

"Rock and Roll Hall of Fame Museum people called," he said, when she opened her eyes and saw Jolene and Brandy standing there too with smiles.

"Thought they didn't build it in Cleveland yet?"

"They haven't. But this year they inducted—just some little bands you may have heard of—Beatles and Beach Boys? Dylan? Supremes? Last year Aretha, Smokey, and Marvin—"

"Cute. Okay?"

"They're collecting information, curating future exhibits. Figured they'd do one on rock festivals, so I sent them the piece you conceived and helped produce on Atlanta. They want to use it as audio background, maybe even next to a Hendrix guitar."

"What? The piece might play at the Rock and Roll Hall of Fame?"

"Yep! Congratulations team!"

She gasped and Brandy and Jolene screamed. They all hugged and jumped up and down together. All she ever did was feed her inexplicable call to '70s tunes. Follow her ears. Lend her voice and story. Shared her passion. And now the Hall said the idea and work mattered? She was just a girl with a music diary.

"It gets better for you, kid. Reporters Of Rock are hosting a gala at a hotel near the Hall's future site—"

"I've my prom gown Gert bought me!"

"Well, no, we aren't invited to the gala. But the Students Of Rock chapter are having a recognition ceremony next to it, honoring media interns, business casual kind of thing. I felt bad you worked for free, so I sent your name to be recognized. You helped bring our little station national recognition, kid. You have a bright future. Our promotions director is sending out a press release now. Pack your bags. We're going to Cleveland!"

Her smile widened. "Cleveland Rocks," she sang.

Her grin faded in a fast minute, though. A pang of grief hit, because her first instinct was to call Gert. When she came home exhausted after dishing out lunch daily to the homeless, she soaked her feet, saying, "No biggie. Serving people is why we're here." Gert, who cooked spaghetti dinners for the parish. Knitted baby blankets for infants born addicted. A widow who cared for a random unwanted baby, unexpectedly single parenting through her sixties to late seventies. She'd done nothing worthy like Gert did, so when a veteran at the VFW thanked Rhiannon, saying no one had ever asked about his story, she teared up. When she saw his obituary in the paper a week later, she could only hope she made him feel heard, his story told thanks to music. Her throat tightened, and the *Mary Tyler Moore* theme song played in her head. If she had a hat, she'd toss it up. All the way to Gert.

65

"Turn the Page"

Cal, July 28, 1988

After the extortion call, Cal clutched the beer bottle he'd hidden. He'd missed the cool liquid slide down his throat. He needed this smooth numbness badly. He twisted off the cap using his T-shirt.

Pssssttt, it may have said. *Missed you, Leonardowski.*

Cal raised the bottle to his lips. The beer smelled divine.

Mort stared daggers at Cal because the tennis ball had also rolled out from underneath the futon. Mort waddled over to the ball, gobbled it into his mouth and shuffled back over and dropped it in front of Cal. The ball bounced onto his foot.

"My moment of reckoning. Drink or play with you? Am I hearing 'Cat's in the Cradle' from a dog right now?"

Mort cocked his head.

Cal gripped the lukewarm bottle tighter. It'd taste so nice. *Talk to me, buddy*, Cal thought it said. *Let me help you.*

"Liar." Cal took the emergency beer and stepped to the garage. Like he was Larry Bird, he made the most spectacular three-pointer into a faraway trash can. The power felt good in that one simple act.

He picked up Mort's ball and pitched it across the largely empty room. The game lasted for fifteen minutes, enough for the desire for drink to subside, and his nerves settled. "You know, pal, since sobriety dissipated the brain fog, we both know who made the phone call, don't we? I'll take care of that little weasel, all right."

Mort looked around. He did not like weasels.

"But first, I can only rip away his threat if I'm still a nobody. Make the story a non-story, one editors don't want. Because tabloids at her door, the world finding out as she does, throwing her into a public spotlight, as if *she* was my shame and regret, petrifies me more than anything. She is not the story."

He'd slept on his decision and dialed *Solid Gold* the next morning. "Marissa? I need to cancel my appearance."

A beat of silence. "You'll give up your chance at a comeback? We've been considering this segment for the season opener."

"I'm sorry. You've been great. Thank you for the chance. It helped me believe in myself again."

"If we're being truthful, there's rumors we're not getting renewed. But I'll keep your info for other things in the pipeline."

He'd wished her well, thanking her for her professionalism.

Then, he walked to a place in his neighborhood he'd never visited. Before a brick building, he breathed in the fresh-cut grass, admiring the perfect edging at the swept sidewalk and the petunias and marigolds blooming below the sign, "Welcome to your neighborhood library. Since high school was the last time he walked into one, he wondered if, like when Merv's people called, they'd find him an imposter. "You don't know *the Reader's Guide to Periodical Literature*?" the librarians would mock. Plus, Judith had taken her library card. *I'll be unarmed!*

Inside, the scent of knowledge smelled like maple trees, mustiness, and fresh reams of paper. Bound volumes of books lined the walls, shelves to his right holding reference books, law volumes, and phone books, and a gigantic card catalogue loomed monstrous. A librarian in a leather suit pointed him to information galore, the hip woman far from Mary the imagined spinster in *It's A Wonderful Life*, as if an advanced degree in library science was a bad thing. She led him to microfiche of local newspapers and flicked through, explaining indexes. "You're a godsend," he said as he began to scan for any mention of Gertrude Jaymes or her return address from 1978.

Minutes later, his hands flew to his mouth.

> **Jaymes, Gertrude**. Gertrude Jaymes, 78, was laid to rest at Our Lady of Perpetual Help Cemetery, following a funeral mass at St. Joseph's, where she served as a volunteer throughout her lifetime, serving lunch at the homeless shelter every day for almost fifty years. A top-selling Savon Lady, she often bought bath and beauty inventory for disabled, destitute, or disadvantaged people. A widow to Bertram Jaymes, killed in action at the Battle of the Bulge, Gertrude raised a "daughter of her heart," Rhiannon Jaymes, Ezekiel the cat, and Boo the dog.

Sorrow flooded him at first, but then—peace for the first time in seventeen years. His daughter had a permanent, stable home with a good mother after all. She hadn't bounced around foster homes like he feared. She seemed loved, all he could've hoped. His heart pinged with empathy, for Rhiannon's loss as a seventeen-year-old, much like how he felt bereft at eighteen.

A memory overtook him, when Mama gave him the Mustang and they took off on that first and last cruise. He pulled into a gas station after the Beatles song "Two of Us" ended, and attendants raced out to pump the gas, clean the windows, and check the oil.

Mama took a deep breath, ejecting her tape. "Love the smell of gasoline," she said and reminisced about her family road trips as a child, and how strange it was that little things like this take you back, maybe to comfort us. She pushed up her sunglasses. "Cal, you won't be alone," she said softly. "I'm still going to be sending you love in the smallest of ways." He looked at her. Tears were streaming down her pale face, and she wiped them away. He didn't remember her exact words next, but the gist rushed at him.

Hit the gas on the Mustang and blast the tape and roll down the windows and put the sunglasses on and soak up the sun. My sweet son, I'll never leave you, because I'll be in the sun's rays through the raindrops. I'll be in the pile of gold and orange autumn leaves we used to play in, remember? My prayers for you will be flickering in that candle flame. I'll be cranking the volume of your favorite tune. You better believe I'll be your back-up singer when you strum that guitar, and in the notes Sinatra croons when a Summer Wind blows in. I'll be weeping happy tears in the first pew at your wedding, and I'll be the gentle kiss you give your baby's forehead as you welcome him to Armstrong's wonderful world. I'll be dancing in that blue sky and puffy clouds with your father, and we'll be whispering in your ears that we love you for always. We'll wait for you to have your big, brave and messy life first, but when we reunite someday, a long time from now, we will hug you again with all our might. It's going to be okay. I love you, my son. Forever.

"I love you too Mama but—" He swallowed hard, inched back out to traffic, and hit the pedal to the metal. "You're not going anywhere, okay?"

"I know, I'm going to beat this," she said, her voice swallowed out in the wind's roar.

The memory choked his throat. In the haze of grief then, he'd buried the memory as too painful. Now, it hugged him as tight as a beloved classic lyric.

A blurb in a suburban weekly paper pushed him to the present, right to her.

Students Of Rock will recognize local resident and up-coming HS senior **Rhiannon Jaymes** at a ceremony held at the future site of the Rock and Roll Hall of Fame in Cleveland. As an intern for WHAP-North Carolina, her story on veterans at the 1970 Atlanta Pop Festival will be used in a future exhibit.

The Atlanta festival? Did she *know* of her parents? "Hold on. The future Rock Hall?" Cal's smile turned into a beam which turned into a joyful jig. Though elation was hard to pull off in a library. All he could do was ding a tiny bell, and the librarian came running. "How do I make a copy of a microfiche article? My girl's getting an award!"

***

After a public transportation nightmare to Gertrude's address—a bus to the orange line subway, changing to the blue line, another bus to Dale City, followed by a thirty-minute cab ride down a jammed I-95—Cal rang the doorbell of a little pink house with overgrown shrubs and a sagging roof.

His heart sped as he waited on the stoop and wiped the sweat from his brow. The three-foot-high lawn needed a mow. A Mother Mary statue stood nestled among some weeds. Rolled-up newspapers laid in the gravel driveway. *Catholic Digest* stuck out of a crammed mailbox. He leaned on the iron railing, peering through statues that lined the front window of an empty living room. The sun beat on him, but a summer breeze cooled him and brought a whiff of the rosebushes. An ice-cream truck with jack-in-the-box bells drove by, and neighbor kids flew outside, shouts of "I want a cone!" cutting through the humidity. He rapped on the door.

Had Rhiannon left Gert's home for good? Is she with Gert's relatives in North Carolina?

He stood as long as he could in the hot sun, and dejected by the empty house, turned away.

On the horrific commute back, when Cal's eyes grew heavy and his seatmate said, "I sleep like a baby," it only made Cal remember.

Rhee was wailing at 3 a.m. Nainsi was rocking her, trying to nurse. He didn't know who'd been crying harder, Nainsi or Rhee, but he wanted to fix it. He trudged into the baby's room, fed her a bottle of formula as Nainsi sobbed. Rhee drank it all in, as they sang "A Long and Winding Road," and "Let It Be," gazing at her parents' faces in their harmony. They laid her down in her crib, crawled out the door, and tiptoed up the stairs. When they dozed off, she started screaming again. Nainsi sighed, jogged and scooped her up, and rubbed her back. She, not Cal, played "Our House," and it worked. Nainsi cuddled her as she drifted off. At the base of the stairs, where a little boy with footie pajamas once watched his parents dance, Cal gazed at them lovingly, rejoining them in a family sway. It was the last slow dance they'd ever had.

When he got home, he called Nainsi with the number Mrs. H gave him when he'd called her back. He needed to come clean to her, too, even if she had left them and never looked back. She'd entrusted him to raise her. It was time to confess.

But the number had been disconnected. There were no other listings in Branson, Missouri, area. He whipped the phone receiver into the wall.

66

"Looks Like We Made It"

Nainsi, July 30, 1988

Between her impending divorce, graduate classes, promoting artists, helping Liam, and planning Da and Mary Louise's wedding, frazzled Nainsi walked into closing on the cottage with the wrong papers. She'd grabbed the file that said "Cal" instead of "Closing." She offered an apologetic smile at the men seated around the conference table in the windowless room. One pushed up his glasses with an apprising stare at her sundress. She hadn't had time to change. "I'm sorry, but I must race home to get the right paperwork. Been saying for years we should invent phones to carry—wouldn't that be amazing?"

The men checked their Rolexes.

"The check for the down payment is in another file. Could they please invent banking on those phones, too? Ha! So, can we kindly postpone so I can get the right file? An hour tops!"

"We have other appointments, Mrs. O'Brien."

"It's Ms. Murphy. Twenty minutes then? If I call my family, someone could race over here with the file. Please?"

The banker shuffled his papers. "We don't have time. Call my office for another appointment. Good day." He left with a nod. The other suits followed suit.

Nainsi plopped down and buried her head in her hands. When she opened her eyes, she eyed the file. She hadn't seen these copies in years, except the recent one. Her letter-writing campaign—with the electric typewriters in the campus library—was a decade ago. Maybe part guilt for leaving Cal and Rhee, part hope the appearances would boost his career and bring them more cash, part brimming with ideas from Promotions 304 class, but it was the least she could do. She flipped through the letters.

Dear Mr. Dick Clark:

Have you heard the incredible new song, "Girl It's All For You," by the hottest new singer-songwriter-guitarist to crack the Billboard Top 200? Enclosed is the 45. Hauntingly beautiful in lyrics and sound, Cal Leonard is a voice that carries longing and loss authentically—but also hope and resilience, a vulnerability so unique to the charts that it'll be remembered for years to come. As his former manager who gets nothing for this, I believe in him that much. I've seen him perform in small venues and he's the real deal. Trust me, CAL LEONARD will be BIG. I'd hate to see you miss out on a booking—his availability is limited. Thank you. Sincerely, Ms. Nainsi Murphy, Promotions, Los Angeles.

As she looked through copies of other letters she wrote—to Mr. Merv Griffin, Mr. Casey Kasem, Mr. Glen Campbell, Mr. Johnny Carson, Mr. Mike Douglas, Ms. Dinah Shore, Mr. Dick Cavett—she remembered photocopying the letters at the library, making a chart to track them, buying 45s from her own record store with bulk and employee discounts, and packing materials to send each letter and record. What a project.

Nainsi spotted her most recent letter, from just this year. She'd written it when she saw Cal's song on a compilation CD in a drugstore when she was buying a panty hose egg. The display made her smile how Cal's song hadn't vanished into the annals of time. The music was solid gold.

Dear Solid Gold producers:

Please consider a segment on these fabulous one-hit wonder songs from the '70s. They're not forgotten. Appearing on your show could spur sales for these talented artists and reinvigorate careers. As his former manager, I'm awestruck by the gorgeous "Girl It's All For You," by Cal Leonard, but please listen for yourself. The vocal and acoustic is intimate and lends itself to stunning choreography for your show. Thank you for your consideration! Best, Ms. Nainsi Murphy, NM Promotions

Nainsi sighed, stuffing the Cal promotions file back into her briefcase, wondering if he'd ever gotten a call from *Solid Gold*. Who knew? Her mind traveled to what she'd enclosed, just in case they reached him. She'd asked them if they'd kindly forward a note and a few items she'd still had of his.

A long time ago, I tried to return these to you, but they came back, she'd written. *I'm sorry, Cal and Rhee. You're in my heart. Nainsi.*

67

"If Not For You"

Rhiannon, August 4, 1988

Perspiration trickled down her torso as Rhiannon drove I-95 north away from Gert's house. The stop there in a closed-up house without AC felt like a sauna on the equator. Boo galloped and Ezekiel pranced, searching for Gert, while she took a cool shower, dressed, unpacked, repacked, and played the answering machine. Telemarketers, Sister Jean, Gert's lawyer, a social service "courtesy call," and a call from Nick greeted her. Her heart had pinged for missing the JT concert—and her one chance to hang out with Nick. She was an _idiot_.

She took Boo and Ezzy over to Sara's, said hello, goodbye, and thanks, and headed up 95 on the seven-hour drive in Gert's 77,589-mile 1970 Pinto. First, she'd stop in DC for what she knew she must do. She sped past the dizzying array of Beltway exits, slowing in jammed lanes on congested 395 north. At least she appreciated Gert's atlas. _Gert had correctly predicted map-reading the most important skill of the future!_

The gray skies unleashed a downpour, and she flicked on headlights, slowing to a crawl. After she crossed over the 14th Street bridge into the District, she turned onto a jam-packed Constitution Avenue, inching slowly ahead. Frazzled, she inched around the Mall, twice, before she issued a prayer to the patron saint of tight parallel parking and found a spot without hitting another car. She grabbed her umbrella and ran straight to the Vietnam Memorial Wall.

The 58,000 names, those who died or were missing, made her pause. It was overwhelming, names beginning flush to the ground, and as the walkway dipped, the sleek, black granite grew larger, wider, all-encompassing. She walked toward the west panels, the 1968 to 1975 half, moved by the smooth black Wall honoring the sacrifice of so many, seeing the mirror-like marble reflect the peace of the nearby trees, lawns, and monuments. She looked at the wreaths, flowers, mini-flags, and pictures left along the wall, now getting soaked. Even in pouring rain, people took paper and pencil and etched over loved ones' names, the rain dropping on their sad souvenir like heaven's teardrops. Touching names on the panels from 1971 to 1972, she leaned close to the Wall, like going in for the goodbye hug from her father. "Is this you? Or is this you?"

Rhiannon prayed for him there, and then all the souls lost in all wars. A wind gust blew her umbrella inside out, and she got drenched just as quick. She ducked into a tent near the Lincoln Memorial where a man with an MIA cap smoked. "Mind if I sit here?" He said for a donation, she can sit wherever she pleased. She plopped into a camping chair and, fishing through Gert's tote bag, handed him her last roll of dimes. She pulled out a pen and the trusty orange music journal, flipping to the last page she'd saved, and began to write her last entry. Forever.

"Dust in the Wind"-Aug. 4, 1988

I always wanted to know who and where you both were,
and why you left me on church steps with a stranger.
When Gert said she may have heard you in a song, I tried
hard to learn your—our? --story, even put the call on the
radio. I asked veterans, called every musician in Asheville,

checked old newspapers, called the church, even tried to trace the guitar pick! No one knew anything. It's useless. I'll never know. Gert—who invoked all the saints—must be right: you're both in a better place now. Time for me to let go, or "Let It Be." Goodbye, birth parents. I'm leaving you my music diary so you can know I'm okay in case you wondered. Gert was the greatest, and I'm thankful she loved and guided me! Oh how I miss her, and I wish I had her longer. Wish I would've learned your stories and voices, but it was not meant to be. May you both rest in peace, with all the accompaniment in Rock and Roll Heaven.

"The Best of My Love," Rhiannon Cecilia Jaymes.

Then she ran back into the driving rain, back to the Wall, where she placed the ratty, frayed, tear-stained, soaking wet music notebook of a lifetime—the soundtrack that played her through her life—and nestled it among soggy roses.

68

"This Is It"

Cal, August 5, 1988

Under overcast skies, Heather and Cal coasted along the Lake Erie shoreline in her Fiero. "Didn't the river catch on fire here once?" she asked, as they passed a lakefront airport.

"It was an oil slick in '69 but out in a half-hour," said Cal, having read it courtesy of his shiny new library card, looking at the colorful sailboats and a barge that marked the horizon, and the submarine USS Cod Cleveland, which had sunk twelve ships in WWII. It made him think of his old man. Gordon Lightfoot's "Wreck of the Edmund Fitzgerald," lingered in Cal's ears, a haunting piece etched into his psyche years ago, a true story of a ship—much of the crew from northeast Ohio—that capsized in a storm on Lake Superior, killing all souls aboard.

Heather turned into downtown Cleveland's Public Square. The department store Higbee's and a strikingly high Terminal Tower loomed large above the city. Pedestrians scurried to lunch spots.

When they found a parking lot and got out, Cal said, "Judas Priest, looks about to pour," and tugged at his only sportscoat. Judith had given it to him one Christmas to his less-than-enthused expression, but today he appreciated the upgrade for this affair, though his shirt underneath had sweat stains already.

Heather smoothed her sundress. "We forgot an umbrella for this big day."

"Been a big enough day already," he said. When he'd figured out the caller's motive, it led him to his identity. Who was the only one who knew the real story, besides Judith? Who had the motive to benefit from the publicity of a sensationalized story at the *Solid Gold* appearance, increasing sales of the compilation CD that gave the label—not him—a cut?

"Nice try, Evan," he had said this morning when he called. "Don't you remember what you taught me--there's no bad publicity? You wanted a scandal to sell that CD, which I don't get a penny for, though you do. But try to release the story now. I cancelled my appearance, so the story won't make a splash because I'm a nobody. It's good to be a has-been sometimes. Tabloids won't care, while I get to my girl first." Evan had slammed down the phone. "He's pissed, Mort, I stole his thunder." Mort looked up. He did not like thunder.

"You're going to be fine," Heather said.

"The moment of truth," Cal said as they began to walk. "Thanks for coming."

"I invited myself, remember?"

"You knew I needed the ride. I got this manager who's not paying me the celebrity wages I deserve."

She punched his arm, but the banter and breeze failed to calm his nerves. It was strange: He survived the jungles of war. Lost family and friends. Witnessed horrific scenes of accident victims, bodies strewn over the road. Comforted traumatized children. Faced audiences armed with only a half-decent voice and a used guitar. He'd braved it all. But now, his nerves of steel felt like he'd gulped four espressos. Surprising his daughter would be risky. She may not know of him. Or she may, and she hates him. Should he bail?

"You guys lost?" said a passerby in a Cavs hat and Browns shirt.

"Looking for a hotel banquet room near the site of the future Rock Hall?" Cal unfolded the news article.

The guy pointed and gave detailed directions near the lake.

"Thanks." Cal couldn't contain himself. "My girl's getting an award!"

"A major award?" The guy winked. "Congrats. Stay and catch a ball-game. Outfielder Joe Carter's looking good."

"Can't, the dog's back in the kennel, but thanks."

They walked past signs for the Playhouse, University Circle, and Stadium, and Cal talked of the wild World Series of Rock held there during the 70s. Flags with team logos filled every glance of the sports town. "I root for the underdogs," he said as he filled in Heather on the Browns, one of the few teams never in a Super Bowl. "Maybe next year?"

"Entire cities rebuild. You can too, Leonardowski."

"Right, and Cavs have their eyes on a fourth grader out of Akron, like that'll work." But inside, he wished the resilient, never-give-up spirit in this town could rub off on him. "Here's to renaissance, turning things around."

"To rebuilding," she said.

***

At the Students Of Rock ceremony, his gaze darted around the crowded room. He scanned the front tables. Parents, students, and sponsors sat in folding chairs. A red linen table in the back held refreshment trays and coffee. The teen event meant no bar, and Cal was grateful. Weirdly, he craved a drink to settle the spasms he now felt for the first time because he wasn't drinking. Cal looked at his watch. They'd been late because they'd stopped at Arlington Cemetery at the grave of the soldier whose brother gave Cal a ride to Fayetteville.

At a sign-in table, a volunteer said, "Unless you're family or a Hall inductee, please stand in the back."

Cal bristled. He'd never get musical validation as an inductee, but the deeper truth hurt: he wasn't family either.

69

"I Am, I Said"

Rhiannon, August 5, 1988

From a hotel rooftop terrace overlooking Lake Erie, with a hundred well-dressed people inside mingling to a rocking playlist from incredible speakers, Rhiannon tried to calm her nerves by listening to the rhythmic lapping of the waves below. *Crash, woosh, crash, woosh.* She remembered when she became so obsessed with onomatopoeia she wrote an English paper on it. "See how you hear life! Now you've discovered the on-pee-ya thingy!" Gert said, sticking the B- paper on the refrigerator.

Rhiannon's eyes moistened as she smoothed her stone-washed jean skirt and tightened the big black belt over her oversized purple T-shirt. She touched her queasy stomach, tried to will it still, and stepped back into the meeting room. She stood with legs twisted, crossing her thrift store black sandals at the ankles. "What am I doing here, Keith?"

"Breathe." He dipped hors d'oeuvres into Stadium Mustard. "Hey, I just met a TV and radio host, Cleveland rock legend Michael Stanley, a songwriter who had some songs on MTV in the eighties, sold out a record number of shows here."

"I know who he is. Wow, that's so cool." She loved MSB's song "Lover." Gert even liked one song, a lyric with St. Christopher mentioned.

Cameras flashed from the hallway and their heads turned. As people dressed to the nines strolled into the huge gala across the way, Rhiannon gasped.

"Is that Ben Orr of the Cars? Look, Eric Carmen! Whoa, the O'Jays! Tracy Chapman, what? Get out! Oh my gosh, shut the heck up, that's not Chrissy Hynde, no siree! Wait. WAIT. Tell me *that's not Joe freakin' Walsh*!"

"Hot dang! There's a huge shindig in the grand ballroom for musicians from the region," Keith said.

Rhiannon nodded, noting the program's list of accomplished Reporters Of Rock sponsors. As much as it thrilled her to see celebrities and media types, it reminded her she was a nobody. "This is crazy I'm even here."

"Kid, this was your brainchild, work, and heartfelt plea for your father."

"Stop calling me kid. I'll be eighteen in eight months." Her hands flew to her mouth. "Oh! Sorry, I was going to tell you my age..."

"You didn't think I knew? A very nice nun called me on day one."

"Darn it, Sister Jean." She cracked a smile. "Well. Thanks for taking a chance on me."

"Don't start that game, we'll never finish." From his pocket he pulled out a list he'd written and cleared his throat. He'd clearly wanted to lobby whoever would listen here. "Hey, you know who deserves to be here in the Rock Hall? Chicago. Journey. Foreigner. INXS—"

"Don't forget my sisters Stevie, Tina, Pat."

"Surprise!" Brandy and Jolene hugged her. "Road trip for WHAP Muse Radio!"

"Aw, I'm overwhelmed," she said as she relished the hug and thanked them for coming. Yet glancing at the gathering crowd, her nerves took off to the races. Her stomach churned again and she tasted the peanut butter chocolates she'd devoured from the reception.

Just then, lights dimmed, and a screen lowered. An emcee directed awardees to approach the podium from the left and walk to the masking-taped *x* for a picture as they accept Students of Rock awards. In one minute flat, they began an alphabetical recognition.

When she heard "Rhiannon Jaymes," and the emcee shared details of the Atlanta story, she trembled. "And so, we congratulate Ms. Jaymes and WHAP-FM Muse Radio."

Applause rippled through the room, but Keith, Jolene, and Brandy cheered like it was the Grammys. She weaved her way up to "On the Radio," by Donna Summer. When she stood on the designated spot, the claps subsided, and they shook hands for a picture and the certificate presentation.

Claps arose from the back, and a male voice boomed his congratulations.

Her eyes shot to the back of the room where a tall, middle-aged man wearing a sports coat stood. He clapped like he knew her, but she'd never seen him before. Probably an overeager dad for the next kid. Standing on the masking-taped *x*, Rhiannon accepted the award.

The crowd quieted, yet the man still clapped. Rhiannon's heart beat fast, adrenaline coursed, and her face registered heat. *Who is this?*

"Bravo, bravo, atta girl," he yelled, even as the crowd hushed.

The claps continued, to her chagrin, as she fanned herself with her certificate. Maybe this is like one of those laugh tracks on taped sit-coms? They borrow clapping parents for the parentless?

When the emcee asked her something, she shrugged and missed what he said.

She felt dizzy. Hot. Sweat dampened her shirt. Too many people here. Too much commotion. *Why is there no cold air? Why was that man still clapping?* Her head hurt and her stomach somersaulted, quivering from too many free appetizers.

"Good job!" the boisterous man clapped. Again.

Weirdo. Her stomach flipped again.

"The Dawg Pound's here," someone said. Snickers came from a few rows.

Rhiannon stood, fanning herself faster before she swayed. Twice. Then, her knees buckled. She may have whispered to the emcee, "No I don't know him and didn't invite him."

"Should I call security?" he might've asked.

She shook her head. No. No trouble here. She would not be a *burden.*

The clapping proceeded with hoots and hollers. Was that a security guard who entered?

Her heartbeat pulsed in her temple. Her head ached. Her knees wobbled. A wave of nausea roared through. She felt warm, then hot, like stepping into a whirlpool. Then she flashed cold, like she'd gotten out into a freezer. A sharp headache engulfed her.

She must be hallucinating, because now Gert's Infant of Prague statue hovered over the WHAP-FM table, and Gert's voice whispered, "Call Cecilia, saint of music, dear-heartie, and St. Christopher for protection!"

So Rhiannon pled for the saints' intercession. "Don't feel so good," she said, looking at two images of one Sir Paul poster. "Double. Vision."

Like a chorus, Gert, the Mother Mary statue, and Paul's mother answered, "Let It Be." Maybe she heard that?

Her breath caught. She fell limp and collapsed, tumbling backwards, slamming the back of her head on a table. The floor greeted her with another head smack. There was a flash, and she was blinded by the light.

The claps subsided. The man's booming voice faded. Keith's shouts disappeared, and Jolene and Brandy's shrieks were swallowed into a faraway place. Her head heavy, her eyelids heavier, she only wanted to close these eyes.

When she did, she floated as an observer, and she heard a thousand songs and saw a thousand people giving a thousand kindnesses.

Gert buying her record player, and the homeowner who gave her all those albums free that had saved her from the Daddy-Daughter Dance and Mother-Daughter Tea. Keith's break to an orphaned high schooler whose head swam in '70s songs. The wretched ham loaf Sara's mom brought over when they were sick. She saw all the people in her and Gert's world who lifted or bolstered them to feel less alone. But now she wanted time to give back. Time to learn the ropes of the radio and find music to ease people's hearts or let them escape or just make them smile. If only she could survive this excruciating headache.

No, don't take me now. She had things to do, and she wanted to foster or adopt children someday, give a home to kids who needed one. She'd already named one Olivia Gertrude.

Just then, the sunshine of her life, Boo and Ezzy, raced toward her. *No, I won't leave you alone!*

Yet she couldn't fight this feeling, and Rhiannon felt tugged by the fuzziness, sucked in by the unrelenting head pain, powerless to stop this goodbye. She asked her rocking guardian angel if this was it, keep her friends and pets healthy and happy. She'd send them a song sometimes, to let them know she was thinking of them. Apparently, she'd join Gert now.

"Drift Away," Dobie Gray's voice called to her, a favorite upbeat song from the '70s stack, and she began to get lost in the rock and roll before she stopped.

Not yet, Gert! She fluttered her eyes and battled. *Don't take me now!*

But when the peaceful, easy feeling finally overtook her, she succumbed.

Moments later, Joni's Big Yellow Taxi pulled up, blasting her life's mix tape. *Is that "Our House" playing?*

"Wait. I've got to take this call first," she said to Joni. The phone at the radio station was ringing. The caller said, "DJ, what song is for the end of our lives?"

She pictured the titles in her orange notebook. She couldn't answer. Life's soundtrack was too diverse. She cherished too many songs. A life song was not just one played at a funeral or wedding or a birth, but it's other simple scenes you remember. It was the song an orphan played on a fatherless Father's Day, a motherless Mother's Day, a grandparent-less Grandparent's Day. It's the song played in your room after you failed a test, or when you tumbled laughing with your friends at the roller rink, or while zipping home from prom with a sweet guy. And it's the song of a loving widow dancing alone with her vacuum cleaner.

As she faded to black, she leaned into the WHAP mic to answer the caller and play them out.

Listener, DJs may suggest a final song, but it's your story, "Your Song." I might choose "Long and Winding Road," but you may want a different classic, a mix of piercing guitar, strong vocals, powerful drums, a life anthem so varied, it's one for a jam or a dance or cranking the car radio when dropping your kids at school, like "Stairway to Heaven." But if it's hope you're after, play "Here Comes the Sun" written by George Harrison. But, listener? Play the version by Richie Havens, as the sun rose in Atlanta one hot July morning, when it was all peace, love, and music.

70

"I'll Have To Say I Love You in a Song"

Cal, August 5, 1988

Cal's first glimpse of his beautiful daughter with Nainsi's iridescent eyes and slight frame and Mama's bright smile was when the emcee announced her name and she walked with trepidation toward the podium. How he'd missed this girl, now only one hundred feet away. *A lifetime!*

The emcee said, "Rhiannon is recognized as a summer intern for the seventies morning show at WHAP-Muse Radio, North Carolina."

She looked cool but far from confident. Her sandals were quiet as she walked with her head down. She planted her feet dead center to accept the award, but she stood awkwardly, her right hand holding her straight left elbow. She looked as nervous as Cal felt, but a quivering smile lit up her face.

He beamed. The audience applauded. Cal clapped louder, heartily, slapping together his trembling hands with so much force his hands stung. "BRAVO!" he yelled, awed by his girl's award, the pride and emotion swelling in his throat, carrying the clapping as the applause died down.

"Way to go!" His low, rich voice carried louder than the other parents', who had been perfunctory applauding until it was their kids' turns. His felt truer. He'd missed seventeen years of this!

The applause settled.

"In addition, she created and—"

Cal's applause erupted again in his daughter's spotlight. Love swelled in his heart, and gratitude and joy lumped in his throat, and he beat his hands together to slap himself hard. He clapped to make up for a lifetime of absence. How many recitals and lessons had he missed? He could hardly wait to talk with her, to hear of her life. But would she let him in?

Disapproving glares launched Cal's way with each clap. The emcee bit his lip and waited.

Heather nudged him. "You're embarrassing her."

But Cal flashed back to his high school graduation, the newly orphaned boy who only longed for Mama's and Daddy's cheers. He *knew* his girl must feel alone too, with Gertrude gone. He hadn't wanted his child to know grief. *Dammit!* Authentic, loving applause should greet her today. Delight slipped out of him like escaping air from a balloon. "Woohoo!" He couldn't contain his pride, even though he had nothing to do with her success. "ATTA GIRL, BABY GIRL!"

She raised her eyebrows in alarm with a mortified stare that peered right into his soul. He smiled, but his heart hurt she looked confused. The emcee said something to her. Other teenagers smirked at the crazy parent.

"Sir, like, can you hold your applause?" the host said.

"Sorry." Cal zipped it. Rhiannon went pale. What did that student emcee know? Did he ever leave his baby daughter so he could go dodge bullets at nineteen?

"At WHAP-FM, Rhiannon created, researched and helped produce an original piece on Vietnam War veterans at Atlanta's pop festival. They will play the piece as the background at a future exhibit in the 'house that rock built.' Congratulations, Miss Rhiannon Jaymes."

As the emcee shook her hand and handed her a certificate, and the audience officially broke into applause, Cal's breath caught. His eyes misted, even if he had no right to this moment. As the audience's applause wove through the room, he clapped again. His baby. His only child. Finally. He beat himself up for seventeen years. He didn't even deserve to be here, but she deserved every accolade.

"ALL RIGHT RHIANNON!" Cal's voice boomed on behalf of everyone not there—Gertrude. Cal's parents. Nainsi.

Rhiannon fixed her eyes on him, and he gave a little wave. She looked annoyed.

"For this rockumentary," said the emcee, "she also helped create marketing strategy. Station manager Keith Crenshaw said its increased audience shares and advertising revenues."

Her co-workers applauded, and she pointed to them instead.

Cal clapped through it all, louder and longer. He yelled, "GREAT JOB RHEE!" He may have whistled like Pauly the bird.

The emcee leaned into the microphone. "Rhiannon has a cheering squad, so maybe this would be the perfect time to announce a surprise. She's this year's recipient of the one-thousand-dollar college scholarship, from the national Reporters Of Rock!"

Rhiannon's mouth dropped open. "What? Me?" She wavered. Her co-workers cheered. But for Cal? It was as if Elvis, Hendrix, Morrison, and Lennon had risen from the dead and inducted Cal Leonard into the Rock Hall. He'd never been this excited and proud of anything. He jumped up and down, waved frantically, and yelled like he was Steven Tyler. Cameras flashed.

Cal's next shout was worse. "A scholarship, Rhee, you rock!"

Rhiannon shook her head, mouthing "no" to the emcee.

The host looked puzzled, his eyes darting between her and Cal.

Rhiannon seemed to say, "I didn't invite him."

The look on the crowd, enrapt. The look on Rhee, fear.

No, you're safe with me!

"Security," the emcee called.

Parents whispered. The room of future reporters wrote in notebooks. Someone thrust a tape recorder.

"Come with me," said a burly security guard to Cal.

"You got the wrong guy."

Another security officer busted into the room like he was CHIPs' Erik Estrada himself. "Let's go, buddy."

"Me? I'm just cheering—"

"Hey buddy, we can call Cleveland PD and get a disorderly conduct charge if you prefer? Or do we need SWAT?" the guard said.

"I'm a medic who works on a SWAT! I'm happy for my girl—"

Rhiannon may have mumbled, "I've never seen him," but he wasn't sure.

The hotel security buffoons grabbed Cal's arms and dragged him toward an exit. He tried to wriggle them off, and Heather shouted, "This is a mistake—"

"Sure as hell is, I'm her father!"

Rhiannon gasped and her hands flew over her mouth. She said, "But he's dead?"

The room hushed. Pens clicked. Notebooks opened. Cameras clicked. Flashbulbs flicked.

Then, the moment begat a terrifying scene. His daughter dropped, and the back of her head slammed against the table before she hit the ground just as hard. It sounded like a skull crack, maybe two. She lay collapsed on a masking-taped *x*.

No! It was the worst sight ever. As faces registered alarm, he rushed forward, but they held him back. A palpable worry gripped the room. Voices raised and lowered.

"She's unconscious!" Keith called out, kneeling by her. Her radio friends closed in ranks, their cries' pitch climbing higher, a tonality of fear pulsing through the circle. "Any medical personnel here?"

"Me!" Cal yelled. "Let me help her! Get off me!" Cal wriggled harder, security restraining him from checking his girl's vitals. "I'm a medic! Let me check my daughter!"

Someone ran up to Rhee's circle.

No, this would not happen. He lost her for seventeen years. He wouldn't lose her again. Action is quicker than a reaction; Cal learned that long ago. His training taught to act, not react. People froze because their brains were delayed, processing the abnormal. But there was no time. First responders acted instantly, trained to respond to danger.

But what if *he* was the danger? What if all the signs pointed to how he didn't deserve to be on this Earth? He was robbed of everyone, and he still couldn't get it right. Not even to apologize.

Now, the room held a horror that made him drop to his knees and unleash a cry of anguish. Her body was still. Absolutely still.

What had he done? He'd triggered her to fall and crack her skull! What if it was a brain injury that was fatal? His heart sank. Cal Leonardowski had only almost talked to his only child, had almost been there for her, the person he most wanted to help. He couldn't get to her now, when she needed him, and when she needed a medic. Despair pounced on him. After a life of regrets, way more than a few, this was the ultimate punishment.

As the guards jostled him and commotion filled the room, his new song played faintly on an instrumental track for his ears only, with every-one's voices overdubbed. He'd done everything they'd asked. But it was never good enough. He couldn't keep people around. *He* wasn't good enough. He couldn't save anyone. Hell, he couldn't even make anyone happy by trying to make them happy. He shouldn't spare himself!

Cal, be a brave boy. Hold Daddy's hand. I found a lump. Cal, I'm leaving, raise her. Report to the federal building. Serve your country. Forget the war trauma. Wed a nice, safe woman who won't leave. Give up a risky music career. Have a baby. Move. Save the injured. Dull pain and loss with a shot and a beer. Do the right thing, always and everywhere, all the time.

"Almost Cal" had tried to do it all. He'd shown up, but he'd never been able to save the only people he ever loved, and now the only one who mattered, his daughter. He only almost saved everyone. Sure, he'd helped some Arlington citizens. Bandaged up the wounded. Entertained some people. But he was in a loss deficit. A failure at the roulette of life. "Lonesome Loser" would play at his funeral.

"No!" he shouted as they hauled him to the back doors. This was not how this went down. He'd be the deft producer, the solo act, of his last track. It was at that moment, at a hotel near the future site of the Rock and Roll Hall of Fame, where he'd never be acknowledged, that Cal Leonardowski—a medic who couldn't save his parents, first love, child, buddies, or wife—a one-hit wonder who spent a glorious week at number thirty-nine but was usurped by a quack— a singer-songwriter who almost made it to Merv and almost made it to *Solid Gold*— and a dad who *almost* met his daughter but instead harmed her— decided to save the world from himself.

"Rhiannon, listen to 'Girl It's For You'— 'Spit,' was the B side," he yelled, just before they hurled him toward the flashing blue lights.

71

"Your Song"

Rhiannon, August 5, 1988

One whiff of putrid smelling salts and Rhiannon's eyes bolted open.

"I'm an athletic trainer," said a man in a calm tone, peering into her eyes with a mini-flashlight, checking her pulse. "Heartrate one-oh-two, BP ninety over sixty...do you have any medical conditions? Looks like you fainted...Could happen with heat, stress, blood sugar."

"My whole head—" She touched the top of her throbbing head. The room spun. "I was dizzy. This headache in the back too..."

"You got a goose egg in the back. Your head hit the wooden table when you fainted. We're taking you to Cleveland Clinic to check for a concussion with a CT."

"What will it cost?"

"You're too young to worry about that. I'm sure your father's insurance will cover it. Where is he? He sure was proud. A little obnoxious, but proud, huh?"

The scene came back to her in bits. Did that crazy clapping guy say he was her father? The last words she remembered were "Girl It's All For You" and "Spit." She'd used "Spit" in the rockumentary, it was the B side for a one-hit wonder named Leonard. She'd had no time to hear the A side.

"Your shoulder pads saved you, Rhee!" Keith said. "The Browns can use you."

"You should get an award for surviving the awards," Jolene said.

The medics lifted her gurney and wheeled her toward the exit as she rubbed her temples. Fellow students patted her and high-fived her as she passed.

"Before they take me away," she looked at Keith, "can you find that rock historian we were talking to earlier, and find "Girl It's All For You?"

"Now?"

"'Just a Song Before I Go'?"

"Rhiannon's back," Keith called to the WHAP friends, who cheered.

Another intern found the song on a cassette single and a boombox. It seemed Cal Leonard's tune made a rotation on a Rust Belt Oldies station.

"Ready?" Keith hit play, and the first notes echoed through speakers, the clear sound like it was live.

The intro captivated Rhiannon immediately. The ballad started gently, enclosing her in space and time. The calming notes wrapped around her like a quilt, the words simple. "The melody haunting, but the longing tender. It's breathtaking, really. Feels authentic in its apology to her." The singer's rich, gravelly voice bellowed and gripped her, his deep tone holding her untethered mind.

> It was a time we couldn't discuss / when you were stuck
> with us

> When she left my heart was torn/ I held on tighter, was
> forlorn

You needed me but I left/ and ever since I've been bereft

You're all I think about/ you're my deepest doubt

This love is all I have to give/ and it's all I have to live

Girl it's all for you, all for you.

Left you at the church, crying, with your arms out/ just so you wouldn't be alone and without

I was a guy who said/ I knew I'd be dead

Ain't never coming back alive.

Beautiful girl, I'm sorry this is true/ Know this apology is long overdue

I hope you can forgive me/ I hope you can truly see

I didn't want you to be alone like me

I wanted you to have the best life/I didn't want you to know strife

Remember, girl, this love is for you.

Girl, it's all for you, all for you.

With each plain verse she grew entranced. The lyrics hit as straight-forward. Unembellished. Elementary rhyme. Yet the simple song had commanded her attention from the first stanza, carried her to the safe and steady C-minor cradling beautiful girl. Why?

She asked to hear it again, and Keith obliged.

The medic sighed—but she could tell he was listening, as was everyone else. Something about this average song pulled people in. It was like an authentic apology that made the listener lean in. Was it the hurt, gritty voice, or the genuine feeling, or a real person with a story?

Ain't. Never. Coming. Back. Alive.

Goose bumps popped on her arms.

Left you at the church crying.

"Can you play that again?"

"Ain't never coming back alive..." the voice sang. What her father had said to Gert.

Left you at the church, crying, with your arms out. Gert would've recognized that, even in the dental chair. Chills crawled over her.

The lone voice reminded her of Jim Croce's "I'll Have to Say I Love You in a Song," yet seemed more like a powerful lullaby mixed with a mighty guitar riff, like you're hearing a guitarist at the Atlanta festival play to his kid.

Her mind flashed to the Georgia newspaper picture with the woman from Ireland and a man named Cal Leonardowski. *Cal Leonard?*

Something made her count backward from her birthday to the Atlanta festival. *Nine months.*

It was then, in a split second in Cleveland, Ohio, surrounded by photos of the late greats Elvis and Lennon and Hendrix and Gaye, Rhiannon Cecilia Jaymes, a nobody from nowhere, a girl without a story of her name but who always mysteriously felt an inexplicable pull to '70s music, pieced her answer together.

"That song is—for me," she said.

Keith narrowed his eyes.

"Where's that man?" she asked with a quiver in her voice. That parent was not a loony-tune. He was hers. She'd never heard the call from her biological parents, but she'd heard the call from that era of music. Why had she chosen the Atlanta festival, anyway? She shivered. It was like something deeper had led her there...here. "He's telling the truth. Cal Leonard is my father!"

"Holy one-hit wonder." He handed her a cup of water, which she shotgunned. The medic checked her blood pressure again as her friends sprinted to the cops.

"This is crazy." She spent seventeen years feeling different, invalidated without a birth certificate and birthplace and family tree, unaware of family medical history, background, nationality, or a simple story of why they chose this name. It was as if she didn't exist, a fluke, an unwanted item discarded because it was too heavy. A *burden.* But now, for the first time, Rhiannon was where she was supposed to be. This musical call on her heart brought her here today.

Of course I'm like a Woodstock baby! The draw to the music all made sense now. She chuckled, and slowly it turned into a laugh. Pure, unadulterated laughter flowed through her body.

She begged the hunky medic to wheel her to the police car. There, the officer stood talking to the man, who was not handcuffed. A platinum blonde talked with security, while Jolene—who'd become the big sister she never had—batted her eyelashes and kindly asked the cop if her "poor, sweet intern" could speak to him before he got hauled off to the clink?

"You want to talk to him?" he asked Rhiannon.

"If this is Cal Leonard, I need to. Please?"

"Name on license says Leonardowski."

"Leonard might be a stage name? And can you, like, um, drop this? It was just an annoyance."

"We'll decide that, but you may speak with him. We'll be right here, miss."

They called him over, and Cal approached her gurney slowly.

She drew a deep breath. The stranger's worn, worried expression seemed...somehow familiar. Maybe Gert was right. Maybe she was struggling to understand the time—or just longing to know her parents—in all those old albums, because her first thought was he had a stature like Harry Chapin's. A smile like John Denver's. A pensive look like Jim Croce's. Deep brown eyes like McCartney's. A way of Billy Joel's. Yet the wrinkles on his forehead revealed a genuine concern for her very life. The way Gert looked at her whenever she left with car keys. She knew it in her gut then. He was her father.

"Glad you're getting checked out," he said. "I'm sorry I was loud and scared you."

"No, it's okay, you were just—" *What exactly?* She studied him, a zillion questions dancing through her mind.

He rested his rough hand on hers. "All the buried stuff tumbled out."

"Your song is beautiful."

"It's your song, to say I'm sorry. The draft letter came, and I was in a bad place and alone, and I panicked and drank and went about everything all wrong. I have shame and guilt for that." He paused. "But the love I had for you was there. The intent was true. You came first. I wanted you to have a better life."

"No." But she meant the moment was too much to take in. She breathed to slow time. He took off his sports coat and pushed up his sleeve. There in the ink of a brilliant, intricate sunrise, shined Rhiannon.

She covered her mouth as tears misted her eyes. "It's... really... you."

"I've missed you forever," he choked out. "Your story about Atlanta... did you know there was a guy there who fell for a beautiful Beatles-tattooed gal, a smitten couple in a faded newspaper picture now, but who found moments of peace and joy in the music of a sunrise together? They loved and lost, but they loved their baby girl for always."

She looked at him with a stunned compassion. She'd always wanted to know, *who* am I? But how silly that was, asking him who she was. She didn't need them to validate her. It was like in "I Am...I Said." Neil Diamond wrote of how you existed, so you mattered, even with no one seeing you. It took a long time for her to get the existential lyrics. Gert would say, "Just because the apple in the family tree that keeps the doctor away falls in the forest with no one hearing it, doesn't mean it didn't fall!" Gert might've mixed metaphors and old wives' tales, but she got it. Rhee was okay, no matter the back story. But now, she knew where she started, a concert of peace, love, and music, and warmth filled her body.

Her father's hand clutched hers. There would be time to understand. But for now, to question was to miss this moment. To dwell in a sad place. To hurt, to keep it inside, guarded in turmoil. Hadn't she done that most of her life?

"I understand if you hate me forever," he said.

She felt his watery eyes deep inside her own heart and shut her eyes and expelled a breath, releasing a lifetime ache. She let go, holding on to the tenderness, freeing herself to accept the love. The lump broke free to full-fledged tears. She lifted her arms to him.

He leaned down, squeezing her with the ferocity of a father who'd missed his only child for nearly two decades.

"I don't hate you. But why didn't you ever—" Feelings caught in her throat, and she swallowed hard. "--come back for me?"

"There's no good answer. I ultimately blame myself. Know I thought of you every day and wanted to find you. My heart was always hurting." He pulled out the new song's handwritten lyrics from his suit coat. "My first song was for you, but I brought you this one to tell you my story. I'm sorry I—"

"Gert was the best. I miss her so much."

"I understand. More than you know."

Clamor rose, and Keith called out, "I want world premiere rights to play that song at WHAP Muse Radio."

Rhiannon cracked a smile as station directors, sporting nametags of WMMS, WMJI, WNCX, and WLTF, interjected requests. The Reporters of Rock chairwoman asked, "Can I interview you all and write this story?"

"You okay, darlin'?" said a blonde woman with a kind smile. "Hi, I'm Heather, your dad's friend and manager. If you'll excuse me while I negotiate the new song and ensuing publicity...hey everyone, you can catch Cal Leonard on an upcoming *Solid Gold* show, date TBA."

"*Solid Gold*? Heard they cancelled that show."

"They might do a spin-off. Oh, quick medical history tip, fainting runs in the family."

"Now you tell me."

"But if I hadn't fainted, I wouldn't have met your mother in the medical tent. You two saved my life."

"The song said...she left? Did she die?"

He shook his head. "Sighting in Missouri in the '80s, though she mentioned LA and Dublin in an old letter from the '70s. But who knows?"

"You'll tell me everything?" But only one question toppled Rhiannon now, like a, well, landslide. *Did she ever look for me?*

"I want to understand too—" His voice trailed off, but there was something in the gleam in his eyes, lost in a long-ago place and time.

"Love is a Battlefield," Rhiannon said.

72

"We Are Family"

Cal, December 27, 1988

Cal stood at his bathroom sink shaving, glancing outside to the SOLD sign, then to the boxes stacked in the hall. "Our empty house is emptier, Mort. And you haven't helped one bit." Mort rolled over and yawned.

"Driver's Seat" played from a new dollar store CD of seventies British one-hit wonders. "Band's called Sniff 'n' the Tears, pal, in case you wondered." He sang the refrain, inhaling the shaving cream's woodsy campfire scent, dabbing the razor in tepid water. The music room reflected in the mirror. When the morning sunlight streamed in like this, it popped the yellow room into a golden hue. His single on the wall even looked like a gold record. Out the new window, a songbird crooned at the fully stocked feeder.

The DC-area real estate market had exploded in the fall, and once he advertised "cozy bungalow inside the Beltway, steps from public transportation," he sold the fixed-up fixer-upper for a windfall. Since Judith had cleaned him out, the real estate agents called it "immaculate and decluttered," and it sold for top dollar. He paid off the mortgage, half of the divorce and medical debts, and banked a chunk for Rhiannon's college.

"Did you know when we move into Gert and Rhee's house, it will be my four-hundredth day of sobriety?"

Mort snored.

The move was at Rhiannon's invitation. They began getting to know each other by comparing '70s album collections. He choked when he learned hers was sprung from his neighbor Steve's garage sale. To think his daughter had been *next door*! He started helping her by caring for the 1940s Cape Cod. First up, the sagging roof. He also maintained Gert's precious artifact, the Pinto, and yard while she filled out college applications. Cal welcomed questions, be it about him, her mother, the Troubles, the war, and she wrote her college essay about her Vietnam War Memorial visit. He warned her of alcohol, too, trying to make amends for making life decisions while inebriated.

But when Rhiannon introduced him to her new boyfriend Nick, Cal asked the divorce lawyer if he needed to file adoption papers for his own child, and he began to move his stuff over with Rhiannon's green light. His paternal role besides teaching about the checkbook and bills and fixing her house, as he saw it? Curfew Enforcer. "There's no way a teen girl should be in an empty house with a teen boy," he said to her rolled eyes. "Or a car."

When Rhiannon leaves for Kent State in Ohio next fall, studying radio broadcasting and interning with a Rock Hall development office, Cal will pay her his rent, commute to his day job, and still play at Quincy's. His plans include renovating Gert's huge attic, building a third bedroom, second bath, and a music den, where he'll write the long-awaited album. Thanks to the new single generating airplay in Cleveland and Asheville, and a booking on the *Solid Gold* spin-off, a small label signed him.

"Mort, be a good dog for Judith. She's driving for two whole days to see you. The lawyer suggested this visitation, and since I know what it's like to miss your baby, I agreed. Huh? Yeah, she's bringing Pauly. Yes, I know his whistling disrupts your twenty-hour nap marathons, but be nice. You're about to become Boo and Ezzy's sibling, so learn how to share the love, pal."

The mailman's truck sounded from down the street. Mort jumped up, his folds and long ears flopping as he skirted to the window and howled.

"Tommy only gives you a treat because you're the master of the sad eyes." Humming, Cal hooked up his leash and they walked out into the frozen air to fetch the mail.

"A package forwarded to me by *Solid Gold*?" he said at the curb, his breath forming a little cloud. Mort gobbled up his treat, sadly watching the truck pull away as Cal tore open the eight by ten padded envelope. Shivering, he emptied a note, a sealed card, and two items into his hands.

Cal's mouth dropped open, and his heart skipped a beat. "You're not going to believe this, Mort..."

There, in his callused hands, lay Mama's sunglasses and her Beatles 8-track tape.

73

"Midnight Train to Georgia"

At the grand opening and housewarming, Nainsi stepped away from the crowd and stood in the foyer, gazing at the full moon. She'd expected it, so her playlist blared Cat Stevens's "Moonshadow," Van Morrison's "Moondance," and Thin Lizzy's "Dancing in the Moonlight." For grins she even invited Dublin's own U2 and Sinead O'Connor tonight to her new place, "Father McKenzie's Poems, Prayers, and Promises," nestled in the foothills of the Wicklow Mountains south of Dublin, high above the River Liffey. She adored this new cottage, where the upstairs loft held her living quarters and the renovated main floor held three rooms for customers and clients.

As the wind gusts swirled against the double-pane window, she squinted as a fog rolled in obscuring the city lights. A twinge of disappointment crept over her that no one could see the view tonight, but maybe another day. Today was about celebrating this place instead. The sign out front cast a soft light, welcoming visitors like a lighthouse. Twinkly lights weaved around pine trees, and luminaries lit the swept sidewalk. A wheelchair ramp led to the freshly painted red door where a cedar balsam wreath hung. The front room held two blue suede chairs near bookshelves of used albums, videotapes, chapbooks, music books, and *"Sultry and Sorrowful '70s One-Hit Wonders"* CDs. She paid no mind to the crazy talk that someday people would load songs and books on computers. No, the future would always hold something to pull from a shelf, grip it close, touch the words, breathe in the smell.

Nainsi turned, looked around, and nodded, grateful the work finally came together. She felt a pride glancing at the decor, pictures from her career on the wall dotted with nostalgic memorabilia too, like a sunny promo poster of the second Atlanta Pop Festival and framed Hendrix, Allman Brothers, and Richie Havens albums. She'd also framed a 45 of what had become her mantra long ago, "All Right Now," from when she and Cal met.

Satisfaction and hope came from the center room. That space held comfy leather couches Cara had found, anchored by a well-loved mahogany table Liam found and Michael refinished, a yellow vase atop that Nainsi had painted with "Our House," a symbol of hope for Rhee. A sign hung above, a counseling philosophy she'd learned from Fr. M: "Meeting you where you are." Here, when she finished her graduate music therapy degree, she'll run music support groups for women—welcoming all backgrounds, nationalities, and faiths, be they Catholics, Protestants, Jewish, Hindu, Buddhist, Muslim, or other beliefs— using music to help them know they're not alone.

Her eyes looked towards the third open room, her office, holding a couch draped with Mrs. H's quilt, a free-standing stove fireplace, and desk, on it a Mary statue, and a framed picture labeled "Surprise Joy." It was of her and Ma, snapped the day of the Beatles' rooftop concert, glowing with beaming smiles. The door sign read, "Nainsi Murphy, FMPPP owner & music therapist."

Her breath caught in her throat at the sight of her family standing by the crackling fireplace, bathing them in a soft glow. Liam and cousins

Matthew, Mark, Luke, and John, chatted about "Dublin's Great in '88" birthday and the new busty statue of Molly Malone. Newlyweds Mary Louise and Da doled-out refreshments, Michael and Cara chased toddler Rosie, and her brothers and sisters-in-law poured champagne into Waterford flutes. This night was as festive and full of family as they came.

Almost. Someone was always missing.

She cleared her throat and toasted the crowd. "Thank you all for coming. May peace, love, and music fill your heart and soul and light your days. You'll each hear a song I've picked out for you, for a special memory we share." She paused and whispered, "You too Ma."

"Hear, hear," said the crowd.

The door opened and bells jingled, ushering in a cold December gale.

"Hello!" an eighty-something voice said, shuffling in with a cane.

"Father McKenzie!" Nainsi set down her glass and hugged him and Dana tight. "Thank you both for coming from Scotland!"

"Wouldn't miss it," they chimed in unison, and they both began to chat easily with her family, while Nainsi took their coats and hung them on a corner rack.

That was when the door opened again. Another howling, blustery wind blew in, as a tall, attractive man with short, wavy salt-and-pepper hair entered. The man gave a warm smile and waved her invitation. "Got any Hendrix?"

Their eyes met and she gasped, like he did when he got her card and Mama's things forwarded, and just like Rhiannon did that day in Ohio. Her hands flew to her mouth. "Cal!"

They would each later tell that rock reporter in Cleveland who had asked to write this family's story that time stood still in this moment. Their eyes locked, the old spark flickered, and the years melted away, like they were rocking out in Georgia again, taking a chance on living, two grieving young people escaping for a weekend respite, wandering souls stumbling into joy. They would each say later, too, the anger dissipated at that fast minute, forgotten for now, lifted from shoulders like a swirl of smoke, because they so chose. Seemed Billy Joel's advice to "Leave a Tender Moment Alone" was solid. Besides, it was easy to let go, they said. Cal just drew a breath, saw the Beatles ankle tattoo peeking out over her high heels, heard the genuine warmth in her voice, gazed at the same sparkling woman who seized every moment. In her breath, she saw the same soulful guitarist who gave her the shirt off his back, the guy who just needed a little love and hope too. For a flash, Cal and Nainsi even wondered if they should've held on tighter back then and never let go, yet would they still have found themselves?

A broad smile came to Cal's face, and he opened his arms wide. "Hi Nainsi."

"You got the invite! I can't believe it!" Nainsi's body filled with a fierce warmth as she melted into his muscular arms and wide chest and burrowed into his welcoming embrace. She pulled away to admire his craggy face, as sexy as ever with a few more lines of texture now. Yet in his gaze, she still saw the stargazing eyes of a concertgoer lying on the grass, the deep eyes of a hopeful musician at a noisy, smoky pub, the loving eyes of a dad strumming a tune for his daughter, and the pleading look of a man throwing his mama's ring as love drove away. "You're really here, from across the pond!"

"They have planes now," he teased. Questions would come later. He would ask where the Mustang went first. Absolutely. But then, he would confess the hard stuff. He didn't know how to say what he'd done. But as she'd folded into his arms, he cherished the moment, the comfort of warmth, the call of rest, the glow of reunion. It's all right now. "Someone wants to meet you."

When Cal opened the door and Rhiannon stepped in, Nainsi drew a sharp breath, her hands coming to her mouth. Her daughter's gleaming eyes were exactly the same, holding the tearful sparkle of innocent gentleness and soft trust and remarkable strength. Eyes emblazoned in a mother's heart forever. A primordial love flooded her, and a deep sob swelled up. Her arms flew open, and to her relief, Rhiannon walked straight into them. Nainsi squeezed with an unbreakable clutch, an embrace that held the might of a thousand mothers missing a child, a thousand mothers fearing for a wayward son or daughter, a thousand women lost in an unconditional love that transcended years and circumstances.

Minutes passed before she composed herself. "Baby girl, you're beautiful! This can't be happening! I thought this day would never come! I've missed you so much, so terribly, even if I...I'm so, so sorry...I never should've..." Nainsi's words sped, tumbling over each other as she touched her girl's auburn locks. She searched her daughter's dazzling face, the same precious look she gazed at all those years ago, when they were only pleading to understand each other. She hadn't had a *baldy* notion of how back then. Now she wouldn't waste a beat. She'd daydreamed their meeting whenever she heard Cal's song, JT, "Rhiannon," "Our House," or even "Mother-Child Reunion." But now she had reparations to make. *Was it even possible?*

"It's okay," Rhiannon said, inhaling this cozy room, her eyes scanning each retro poster, and her ears longing to devour every album here. "Like, I'm a senior. Can't imagine having a kid now." Like when she met her father, an unexpected warmth filled her instead of anger. She couldn't love this woman yet—yeah, it'd take a "Lotta Love"— but a tenderness gripped her. To Rhiannon, this moment spelled hope. Now they had the chance to build a bond. Sure, she wanted to talk to her, to understand the whys, but answers to her questions would come. Maybe she wasn't dwelling in bitterness because Gert gave her a humble, stable, loving childhood. How else could she have learned five uses for one teabag, or that Bertram ended every victory mail letter to Gert with "I'll Be Seeing You." Who knows, maybe Gert's prayers to the Infant of Prague, St. Ronan, or St. Cecilia—a "Higher Love"—guided her here today?

What did she feel now for the woman standing before her, crying, wrecked in--what? Guilt, love, or both? Who was this mother whose being she dreamed of, who seemed larger than life, like Whitney or Aretha or Barbra vocals? She was more than a question mark now, more than the red hair of Bonnie Raitt's. Her voice carried the warm tone of Karen Carpenter, the kindness of Olivia Newton-John, the depth of Linda Ronstadt, the power of Donna Summer, the passion of Pat Benatar, and the strength of Tina Turner. And if Nainsi reminded her of the rock icons, Gert offered the generosity and enduring love of legendary Dolly. *I Will Always Love You, Gert!*

Nainsi's tears streamed down her face. "I don't deserve your grace. How can you ever forgive me?"

Rhiannon shrugged, for Carly gave her a mantra long ago: "I Haven't Got Time for the Pain." She wished both parents would ease up on themselves, because when she slipped into their shoes, when she understood their ages, era, and intentions for her, compassion rolled off the tongue. It was easy, really, to forgive. A newfound family was within her reach because of it. "It's okay--"

She stopped. *Mom?* She couldn't make that leap. Gert didn't want to be called that, but she was the woman who mothered her, and she'll always be grateful for that extraordinary gift. Grief caught in her throat, and she swallowed hard. The big, boisterous family clamor pounded in her ears, and she was eager to meet this elusive tree. A lifetime of questions could wait.

Just then, "A Long and Winding Road" played from the speakers. Was it luck? Kismet? Coincidence? Serendipity? Divine providence? *Déjà Vu?* Who knew, but...

Cal thought it a perfect moment.

Nainsi thought it a perfect moment.

Rhiannon thought it a perfect song.

Cal wrapped his arms back around Nainsi, who enveloped Rhiannon. They all closed their eyes for the hug, shutting out the world for a few more tender moments, wrapping themselves in a warm embrace of forgiveness. Just like when two teens soothed a baby on a sweltering summer night, they swayed into a family slow dance. Maybe it was to steady each other, or maybe it was nostalgia. But maybe, just maybe, it was to hold on to peace, love, and music a little longer, just like it was 1971...all over again.

74

"Paperback Writer"

Epilogue, 1990

Dear Mr. Cal Leonardowski, Ms. Nainsi Murphy, and Miss Rhiannon Jaymes:

Here are the first copies of the book. Thank you for your interviews, letters, articles, newspaper photo, handwritten lyrics, rockumentary, transcripts, and music therapy thesis, "Healing Individuals and a Family System with Yesterday's Songs." Enclosed is also the music diary Rhiannon miraculously retrieved from the Vietnam War Memorial warehouse. Wishing you peace, love, and music ahead!

Chairwoman, Reporters of Rock

About the author

K. Meldrum Denholm is an award-winning writer whose work has appeared in *USA Today, Washington Post, Northern Virginia Magazine, Chicken Soup* books, and dozens more. She earned a BA in journalism magna cum laude from Duquesne University, wrote for a federal press office in DC for ten years, and as a mom of three in Virginia, worked as a freelance journalist writing magazine and newspaper articles. With her children now grown, she writes and edits from the shores of Lake Erie, where she's hopelessly devoted to working on her next novel, blasting '70s and '80s music, visiting the Rock and Roll Hall of Fame, and rooting for the Cleveland Browns. Sometimes, one of those makes her cry.

One link: https://my.linkpod.site/KMeldrumDenholm

Author website and newsletter: https://www.kmeldrumdenh olm.com

Yesterday's Song blog: https://www.kmeldrumdenholm.com/ blog

FB page: Kristine Meldrum Denholm, Writer; FB group: "A Song from the '70s" for 1970s music talk; IG: @writerkmd

If you enjoyed the novel, please leave a review at the site of your retailer, tell your friends, or ask your library or favorite bookstore to order it. Thank you for supporting books and authors!

The Chorus: "Shower the People"

Since I wrote the first full draft five years ago, and rewrote, revised, and edited this work constantly for the years since, it's been a true labor of love, blood, sweat, and tears. As Ringo sang, "It Don't Come Easy." I'm grateful to the following rock stars at different stages of the manuscript: Thank you to editor Francine LaSala (and Jessica Moreland) for the first manuscript evaluation in early 2019 and to the agents and workshops I queried then who shared feedback. Thank you so much to developmental editor Elizabeth Brown for her most helpful critiques of middle drafts in 2022 and 2023, and to final 2024 copyeditors Lori Whitwam and Kimberly Hunt of Revision Division. Also, Ashley Brown, Kim Urig, and Amy Collins gave feedback on first pages, and thank you to author Hope Clark for her excellent edit suggestions of Part I. Thank you to Damonza for the cover design, Shannon Ahlstrand for author photo, and Mark Schrankel who created amazing artwork that helped me refine my characters. With a journalism background and education, I'm continually working on the creative craft of fiction, so thanks to authors and editors teaching webinars, WFWA, and *Writer's Digest* conferences. Bestselling novelist Camille Pagán has inspired me for years, in her outstanding writing and in individual and group coaching; she asks insightful questions that helped so much. I also highly recommend her podcast and grateful for novelist James Thayer's podcast as well. Thanks to beta readers for bearing with my excited but too-early first draft, giving time, feedback, encouragement in the process, and postage:

Anne, John, Ann D (nod to Porches, Strasburg, B & N), Christine, Kendra, and Stephanie. Thanks to blurb test team: Lisa, Mark, Christie, Maria, Abby, Mary, Selena, and early readers. Thank you to experts who answered my questions: Kelly N. and Michelle K. (medicine), Meagan E. (Atlanta festival), Lou F. (Atlanta festival), David B. (musician; era), Chris L. (musician), Mark S. (musician), Scott W. (Mustangs), Larry G. (Vietnam veteran), Larry T. (Vietnam veteran), Doug K. (firearms), Linda C. (Scotland), Catriona (Ireland), Ward G. (Ireland), Mary K. (Dublin), Brian O. (radio), S (adoption language.) Any mistakes are mine. Also, years ago, I've interviewed for articles: a musical therapist, a teen birth mom, adoptive parents and adoptees, a class of pregnant teens learning about parenthood, and caring social workers, and their stories helped inform me. Research from Ken Burns and Lynn Novick (*The Vietnam War*), and the late Lynda Van Devanter (years ago, I wrote an article about her book *Home Before Morning*, the first memoirs of a Vietnam War nurse, who wrote of veterans getting spit on) helped create and inform Cal. I have submerged myself in '70s music while writing this work, so thanks to all who surrounded me: the great voice of Neil Diamond led the way (as a superfan) as did so many other great singer-songwriters, 70s on 7, The Bridge, Yacht Rock Radio, Cleveland and DC radio, top 40 Casey shows, Midnight Specials, concert clips, trips to Rock and Roll HOF. A shout-out to the music lovers at my "A Song from the '70s" FB group, too. You rock!

The deepest love and thanks to my family, this "Peace Train" who endured my long journey of frustration trying to get a first novel perfect—yet it never will be: Rich for his brilliance, legal counsel, reads, saves, history discussions, music, books, and unwavering support of this manuscript, and to our three kids, I love you to the moon(shadow) and back, thank you for encouragement and pep talks, especially C for the art and promotions advice. To Mom, thanks for your incredible eye for detail in reading everything since childhood, and for instilling Neil and

Barry and Lionel in my early years, and to my late Dad for his mad trumpet skills and "Barbara Ann" and blasting Midnight Train so loud it made the Impala shake. My late grandparents, wonderful "Lib" and Al, a WWII veteran, inspired Gert and Bert, and my grandmother Georgia inspired the first setting of peace being Georgia, and I send love to all of them up there. Finally, a loving thank you to my dearest lifelong friends, strong, caring people who are family to me and have showed support of my work and this novel; I adore you! Posthumous note: I lost two dear friends, a family member, and the greatest assistant ever during the five years work of this novel, and they always gave peace: RIP to Tom Cooperider and Tom Mendyka, who personified peace, love, and music, as did early reader John Crothall, a truly eloquent and gifted writer. John, you are missed, and your literary knowledge, listening, and thoughtful critique were so valued. To the best editorial assistant ever, the late great Buckeye, the most beloved dog who ever trotted happily on this planet, who endured each keystroke, interview, read aloud, song, class, video, and conference, sighing and snoozing at my feet, "Miss You Like Crazy," baby...you were unconditional love and peace. Above all, thank you, God. To all, since "We May Never Pass This Way Again," "Whenever I Call You Friend," know I'm thankful for you all! – @writerkmd

Book club questions: "Heart of the Matter"

- Why was Part I titled, "How Can You Mend a Broken Heart," Part II "Who Are You," and Part III "I've Got a Name?" What themes did you take away?

- Why did Cal and Nainsi sense a kindred spirit in the other? Was that enough? In what ways were all characters affected by losses? How does feeling alone affect life choices?

- What helped each character find their voices and power separately?

- Pop music was key to this story. What song titles did you recognize? Has an old song ever connected you to people? Has music ever made you feel a sense of camaraderie? What songs bring you back to an exact moment in time, in childhood or teen years, weddings, break-ups, celebrations, lullabies, or just everyday life?

- For each of the three main protagonists, who was the antagonist? Are we our own villains at times? In struggles, do we use our voices or acquiesce to others' voices?

- Nainsi considered Judith's warning of stepping back for her child's best interest; Cal agrees with her as well originally. What do you think of that decision?

- What role did internal and external validation play in this story?

- Who were the cheerleaders of each character? How did that help empower each character?

- The author included several near misses and coincidences. Which ones did you find? Do you believe in coincidences or fate? What role do "could've been's" play? Do you have small world stories?

- How did each character inspire others, even unknowingly?

- What role did living in the moment play, i.e. "All Right Now"?

- What role did pets play?

- What did they learn from each other? Do you think they ultimately forgave each other after the story ended?

Cal: In 1970, how was Cal's grief affecting his decisions, including with Nainsi's news? In 1971, Cal chose law and duty to country; what other factors influenced his decision about Rhee?

- Why did Cal choose Vietnam service as a medic? Why didn't many soldiers have a homecoming then? How did his war trauma last for a lifetime?

- How were Cal and Judith matched or mismatched? What did they learn from each other? Was it right when Cal gave up his budding music career and finding Rhiannon for Judith?

- Do you and Cal see "one-hit wonder" as a negative or a positive?

- Cal doesn't talk about pain to avoid feeling it, but how did the pain still materialize? What role did Cal's songwriting--and performing to an accepting audience--play in healing?

- What aided Cal's recovery?

Nainsi: How did Nainsi's background affect her choices? In 1971, Nainsi chose between her secret family of creation, family/country/religion of origin, and a career and a promise to herself and Ma. Could a mother choose *herself* then? Can a woman have it all then...and now? What differences do you see?

- Father McKenzie met Nainsi where she was, literally at the PD, and figuratively, with his name and offer of "Poems, Prayers and Promises" connecting with her music passion. Do you meet people where they are? Has a wise friendship ever helped validate you and evaluate choices?

- Father M., like Gert, did not share the full truth. Are lies by omission okay for one's good?

- How did Nainsi's love of music shape her future?

- Years later, when Nainsi reveals to her family the truth, she's surprised when they accept her secret. Why were they more accepting? Do you think her vulnerability affected them?

Rhiannon: Rhiannon asked herself "what would Carly/Linda/Stevie/Tina do?" Why? Are there artists who inspire you? How did Rhiannon's music journal help her? How did Gert recognize her passion? How did that help her?

- How did questions of origin family affect Rhiannon? When she set out to find her father's voice, she found her own. How did her musical passion help her, and how does she in turn help Keith?

- Gert never reported the baby at church and honored Cal's

wishes to stay anonymous. After Rhiannon "wasn't claimed" after the war, Gert never revealed the full truth about the scene, song, and birthday invitation until her deathbed. Why? Should she have?

- When Rhiannon let go of the expected outcome of finding her father, she left her music journal at the Wall. How does letting go hurt or help you?

- What role does "Let It Be" and Gert's statues play?